THE
HARRAD
EXPERIMENT

NOVELS BY ROBERT H. RIMMER

That Girl from Boston
The Rebellion of Yale Marratt
The Zolotov Affair (also published *as The Gold Lovers*)
Proposition 31
Thursday, My Love
The Premar Experiments
Come Live My Life
Love Me Tomorrow
The Love Explosion
The Byrdwhistle Option
The Immoral Reverend
The Resurrection of Anne Hutchinson

(The last three are available from Prometheus Books)

NONFICTION

The Harrad Letters to Robert H. Rimmer
Adventures in Loving
You and I . . . Searching for Tomorrow
The Love Adventurers
The X-Rated Videotape Guide
The Adult Videotape Guide, Vols. 3 & 4
Raw Talent: The Autobiography of Jerry Butler, Porno Star,
     as told to Bob Rimmer and Catherine Tavel
Whips and Kisses: The Autobiography of Jacqueline,
     Mistress of S/M,* as told to Rimmer and Tavel

THE
HARRAD
EXPERIMENT

**SPECIAL
25TH ANNIVERSARY
EDITION**

ROBERT H. RIMMER
With Exciting New Material

Prometheus Books • Buffalo, New York

ACKNOWLEDGMENTS

The author and publisher are grateful to the following institutions, publishers and individuals for permission to quote from the works described below. These works are copyrighted as indicated.

John W. Gardner and the Carnegie Corporation of New York for extracts from *Renewal in Societies and Men* by John W. Gardner, Copyright © 1962 by the Carnegie Corporation of New York.

Rudolph Von Urban, M.D. and Dial Press, Inc. for permission to quote from *Sex Perfection and Marital Happiness* by Rudolph Von Urban, M.D. Copyright © 1949 by Rudolph Von Urban, M.D.

Archibald Mac Leish and Houghton Mifflin Co. for *The End of the World,* a poem by Archibald Mac Leish, Copyright © 1952 by Archibald Mac Leish.

Pantheon Books and Alan Watts for *Nature, Man and Woman* by Alan Watts, Copyright © 1958 by Alan Watts.

CONTENTS

Introduction   9

The Harrad Experiment   15

The Harrad/Premar Solution   252

Annotated Bibliography   277

Loving, Laughter & Ludamus:
The Autobiography of Robert H. Rimmer   291

INTRODUCTION

Six years ago, my wife Margaret and I wrote a paper for the *North American Journal of Sociology,* outlining a program designed to achieve sexual sanity. Essentially, our method consisted of teaching a new sexual ethic and moral code by conditioning and indoctrination throughout a four-year period to a select group of male and female college students of unusually sound character and high creative ability.

The paper was the result of ten years of work in family and marriage counseling and years spent studying the sexual habits and mores of man throughout recorded history.

My wife and I felt that, in order to survive, Western man must take the long step away from primitive emotions of hate and jealousy and learn the meaning of love and loving as a dynamic process. Such a program would counteract the decadence that is slowly infiltrating our society.

During their four years of college life, our students would live together, not only under the same roof, but (preselected on the basis of careful psychological tests) heterosexual couples would share the same quarters: a study room, a bathroom, and a bedroom with twin beds.

This unconventional living arrangement was the keystone of our proposal. The student body should be small, no more than 200 males and 200 females, and would be, in a sense, a pilot study. This study would provide the blueprint for a new sexually oriented aristocracy of individual men and women who were free of sexual inhibitions, repressions, and hate, and were thoroughly educated into the meaning and the art of love as distinguished from the purely sexual relationship.

This program is in sharp contrast to our present system of segregating boys and girls of seventeen or eighteen, when they are at the first peak of their emotional interest in each other, and forcing them into abnormal living patterns during their college life. Social pressure for prolonged continence often creates fear, anxiety, and actual repulsion between the sexes. The results: too early marriage ending in divorce, unwanted children born out of wedlock, sexual frustration before and continuing into marriage, and a sex-obsessed society with little or no knowledge of what dynamic love is. A society that deeply frustrates human interrelationships creates fear, hate, anxiety, and a feeling of loss of identity which are the keynotes of modern life.

Students living together under the proposed program would attend classes at established colleges or universities. Arrangements would be made for full accreditation. Functioning in this way, our student body would receive their educational requirements in an unusual social and intellectual environment.

One important feature of our proposal was a required four year seminar tentatively titled "Human Values." Every aspect of man's attempt to organize society religiously, sexually, economically, and politically would be examined. We felt our program would relate to the religious background of most of our students but that it would be wise to seek students who had a liberal religious background. We would be striving not to inculcate any predetermined values, religious or otherwise but rather hoped to open the door for each student to evolve his own philosophy and orientation of his own "self" to the world.

Since our program encouraged premarital relations among our student body, we would, very early in the course, make a complete study of contraception. Roommates might live together with or without sexual intercourse, and with the possibility, if desired, of having alternate roommates. Any marriage commitment during this period would be discouraged, but we assumed those students living together in this program would ultimately seek marriage with another student because they would have become so successfully conditioned by the program that they could not easily find an equally mature mate.

With a sincere belief that each individual should be made conscious of his responsibility to society and to any new life resulting from his mating, our proposal included the stipulation that couples who were responsible for the creation of new life would be dropped from the dormitory program and required to marry.

We expected that this program, if it continued in existence for any length of time, could lead to a healthy development in marital patterns for many of our graduates.

According to our predictions, a goodly percentage of our student body would ultimately become involved in monogamous marriage; we believed that there was the possibility that others would become involved in a close and lasting friendship with another couple of the same. background. Because these two couples would have had their college and intellectual training in an atmosphere of controlled sexual freedom, they would be equipped to realize the many advantages of entering into an informal group marriage.

Without fear, jealousy, repression or inhibition they would recognize their need, not only for sexual varietism, but, even more important the stimulus of living together would add depth, meaning, and breadth to the intellectual crosscurrents of life. Possibly, they would move into a common household and pool their financial as well as intellectual and emotional resources.

Keep well in mind that we are not recommending either this premarital program or this later possibility of group marriage for society in general. Obviously it would be too startling a change in sex and marriage behavior for the average person in our present culture. The point we made was that the time to begin is now. A start must be made somewhere. Too much is at stake to permit our basic social and family patterns to drift on the currents of haphazard marriage and distorted sex relations.

Our paper proposing a Premarital Living Program at the college level met with a great deal of unfavorable reaction. Margaret and I did not expect any definite action to result from our proposal, at least in our lifetime.

To our surprise, five years ago, and more than a year after the original article was published, John Carnsworth approached

us with the offer to support such a program with an initial contribution from the Carnsworth Foundation of $10,000,000. In
the past six years we have had the privilege of working closely
with John Carnsworth. Without his guidance and perspicacity,
undoubtedly Margaret and I would have made many unfortunate
fumbles in creating Harrad College on the grounds of the
Carnsworth Estate in Cambridge, Massachusetts.

When Robert H. Rimmer, who has been closely associated
with John Carnsworth, approached us with the suggestion of
telling the story through the journals of actual students at
Harrad, we gave a great deal of thought to the idea. The journals
are kept by the students as a private record of their reactions and
feelings to the Harrad Experiment. There were a great many
advantages in permitting the outside public to see the Harrad
program actually evolving in this way through the minds of the
students. It became immediately apparent, however, that in
making the selection from the wealth of material in these
journals the students have freely turned over to us we could be
accused of selectivity to prove our thesis. Rereading the journals
that we have chosen from the various journals given to us by the
first graduating class, I think we have avoided this pitfall. At
times all Harrad students have had great doubts as to whether
they were being educated in a sound environment. They too
often wondered, especially in their freshman and sophomore
years, whether the microcosmic society we have created at Harrad
would be valid in the outside world. Occasionally, the program
for individual students created its own insecure world, but
largely the individual graduates of this first class discovered the
roots of their insecurity and mastered them in a way that would
be impossible in what we now label a normal premarital environment.

While the Harrad College Experiment will now for the
first time be made public and subject to the winds of controversy,
we are continuing our policy of not exposing our student body to
the public eye. How students at Harrad are living their personal
lives in this new environment, who present Harrad students are
and where their homes are, and the kind of parents that have
permitted their children to attend Harrad will continue to be

closely guarded information. The material from the journals of Harrad students which comprise the body of this book has been carefully disguised both as to the names of the students as well as to any reference to local institutions or other points that might make identity possible.

Harrad College is no more than what we accomplish for the individual. In this book you have the rare privilege of meeting exceptional individuals embarking on a voyage into an unexplored land where the premise is that man is innately good and can lift himself by his bootstraps into an infinitely better world. Margaret and I hope a glimpse of this kind of world will enrich your life; and, while you personally may have not been educated in the manner of this Harrad Experiment, you may give the option of leading a full premarital life to your children.

PHILLIP TENHAUSEN
Harrad College
Cambridge, Massachusetts, 1966

EDITOR'S NOTE

The journals selected for presentation here are only four, culled from seventy-six possibilities. But since these four journals cover the activities of six individuals whose lives become irrevocably intimate and integrated, they are even more significantly indicative of the Harrad College Experiment.

No one journal is presented in its entirety. To do so would involve many volumes, since each student entering Harrad is asked to keep as detailed a record as possible.

As the reader will note, the journals are on an almost day-to-day basis for the first year at Harrad College. This frequently drops as we approach the third and final years, largely because the students have "adjusted" to the Harrad goals and are quite at ease in discussing ideas and reactions with one another, rather than setting them down on paper. Also, as the exchange of intimacy and ideas increases, the individual students tend to be less concerned about the privacy of their innermost feelings.

The only editing given the journals has been to remove complete days and months. But the continuity is accurate, and the journal entries presented here have not been altered in any other way.

THE HARRAD EXPERIMENT

FROM THE JOURNAL OF STANLEY COLE

September, the First Year

So this is Harrad College . . . ye Gods! How did I ever get myself in this place? My friends back in Public School 133 would call it mad. Strictly mad . . . or just plain kooky.

Following instructions from the Tenhausens, all students at Harrad are expected to keep a journal . . . strictly private stuff of their reactions. Phil Tenhausen is a nice guy, a little owlish behind those glasses, and his wife Margaret . . . wow! Since when did Ph.D.'s come in such nice packages?

This morning we got the big indoctrination lecture in the Little Theatre, a new modernistic building located across the quadrangle from the Harrad dormitories.

"You are entering a new phase of you life, quite at variance, not only from your past emotional life, but from what present day society calls the norm." Phil Tenhausen told us. "After this meeting I'd like all of you to pick up spiral bound notebooks at the bookstore, and use these to keep a journal of the emotional and intellectual history of your days at Harrad. Write down who you are, your joys, your fears, your reactions to your roommate, your reactions to the Harrad Experiment. These journals do not have to be works of art. They are your private place to blow off steam. As time goes by we think they will be particularly helpful to you in assessing your growth, and the meanings and purposes of your life. While we don't make it compulsory, we do hope that someday before graduation, or after your graduate, you will turn your journals over to Harrad to be used, not only for improving our program, but also as guideposts as to what we have achieved or failed to achieve for you."

So, okay, Phil and Margaret, I am writing! Hunched over her desk is Sheila Grove, my roommate . . . a girl. A girl . . . with breasts, and a fanny, and a pussy, trapped with me! While I knew it was going to happen, I can't quite believe it. Some of the time Sheila is writing . . . when I look in her direction . . . but mostly she's staring out the window. The sun has almost disappeared, just a few rays catching at the upper branches of the elm trees that tower over all the grounds and seem to hide this building and the Carnsworth gardens. Maybe Sheila and I are lost in some magic forest, and outside the world has stopped.

Back to this morning. I might as well write down what Phil said. Who knows? Someday a thousand years from now if some one discovers this journal I may go down in history as the man who chronicled an upheaval in the male and female relationship. Phil's words!

Phil sat informally on the edge of the stage as he talked to us. "The purpose of this meeting is to get you into the Harrad groove. Many of you, in coming weeks, are going to wonder if the groove is a rut and if we actually know what we are doing, or if we have a definite program at all. Admittedly, some of our approaches in this first year are tenuous. You are in the enviable position of creating a new approach to life with us. If it doesn't work with this group, the project will probably be abandoned. Both as a group and as individuals you have the possibility of making our pipe dream come true or puncturing it rudely. After studying your scholastic aptitude scores and your various achievement tests, I can tell you that Margaret and I are more than a little frightened. I doubt if anywhere in the world there is an equivalent group of a hundred students who have a scholastic ability equal to this group. How this pairs with your emotional development remains to be seen.

"Tonight, without guidance and without preparation, you will begin to live in close proximity to a member of the opposite sex. At the beginning, you'll have to make your own adjustments to this situation. Next week our required course in 'Human

Values' will meet daily five times a week, here in the Little Theatre, directly after dinner, from 7:00–8:00 P.M. We may later shift this to an afternoon schedule, depending on how your courses at the various colleges and universities in this area jibe with an afternoon time slot.

Right after this meeting you will pick up your appointments, which have been arranged with the various colleges that you will attend. For the remainder of the week you are going to be busy with your prime responsibility of developing your own personal program of study. Practically all of you will be taking advanced placement courses, but in no case should you overextend yourself. The course in Human Values which is the only required course at Harrad, is a stiff one. At the same time you will be expected to maintain in your other scholastic studies the same high standards that have permitted you to participate in this unique project. If any of you have the idea that your four years at Harrad will be an indolent sexual picnic, you had better resign now. The thought has actually occurred to us that you will be so busy we are not even sure you'll have time for sex."

Phil waited for the laughter to subside, and then continued. "Now, the problem of transportation. Realizing that we are a commuter based college, we have permitted all students who have automobiles to bring them to Harrad. We have forty-six cars available for one hundred students. Working cooperatively, we should be able to pool transportation and get everyone to classes on time. By Saturday we will announce car-pool arrangements.

"By this time you may have met your roommates. Margaret and I expect yowls of protest from some of you; first, because there have been no formal introductions. Keep in mind that if you were attending a regular college and living in a dormitory you would meet your roommate of the same sex without formality. We feel that this is the easiest way for rapid adjustment. Second, some of your may wonder how and on what basis you were selected for roommates. Let me tell you that Margaret and I, through our intense documentation on each of you, probably know more about you than you know about yourself. In a sense, at least temporarily, the faculty of Harrad is a composite parent choosing one possible mate for you, and doing this with more knowledge of you as a person than you yourself or your parents have. If you question our choice, we ask that you bear with it through the first semester. Many ideas you now have are going to change rapidly. However, we want you to know that there is no rigidity in any aspect of our program. It will be possible for students unable to make an adjustment to form their own splinter groups, and room alone, or if available, live with a member of their own sex. We are betting this won't happen, but we are not overlooking the possibility that it might.

"Because of your overall intellectual capacities, I assume you are all well aware of the hows and wherefores of human conception. But after this conference, you will all please pick up a copy of *The History of Contraception,* by Norman Himes, at the bookstore. This is a very detailed study from the earliest known history of man's attempts to prevent birth. While the book is about six hundred pages long, we expect you will read it within the next week and be ready to discuss it in our first conferences in Human Values.

"Ultimately, we expect you will have normal sexual relations with your roommate, therefore we want to reiterate a basic concept of Harrad. Hexterosexual relations among strangers is a very nonsatisfying relationship. Even though you may be living in close proximity, we actually assume that a love requirement (in a wider sense which will become clearer to you as the year progresses) will occur concomitantly or prior to any actual sexual relationship. Again, this is a personal matter and we simply want to make you aware of the pitfalls. With the present day knowledge of birth control methods available to you, and with the complete knowledge that we will give you of their use, there is no need for any of you to have fear of unwanted children.

"Moreover, we believe that until you finish Harrad College, you are all, without exception, too young to enter a monogamous family relationship. In a sense, you are the vanguard of future generations who, we believe because of the world population growth or explosion, as the press calls it, will be required by law to limit your progeny. The act of sexual intercourse will, if human beings are to survive, be an act largely of pleasure and emotional depth, and not one devoted to irresponsible procreation.

"We are fortunate in having attached to the staff of Harrad, Tom and Sandy Jelson, and Doctor Anson Fanner. Dr. Fanner does not live on the grounds of Harrad. He is an M.D. whose practice is in Cambridge. Dr. Fanner will discuss contraceptive techniques with you as a group and will be available for individual consultation with your roommate for specific methods to fit your own emotional needs and personalities.

"Tom and Sandy Jelson are a nationally famous husband and wife team who are in charge of our Physical Education program. They are also thoroughly familiar with contraceptive techniques.

"One of our responsibilities at Harrad is to maintain a sound mind in a sound body. Because we have accepted you in good health, we plan to keep you that way. One hour of Physical Education is compulsory daily. The hour you choose, or you and your roommate choose together is up to you. In our long experience in dealing with high I.Q. students, we do not believe we can put Phys. Ed. on an honor system. We are fortunate in having on the Harrad grounds a fine gymnasium with a large indoor swimming pool. The pool and the gym will be open from 8 A.M. to 5 P.M daily. Each student will have a time card assigned to him and must punch in and out daily. A minimum of one hour daily five days a week will be expected, and the only excuses will be on the basis of ill health or for female students during the time of their monthly period. Incidentally, Mrs. Jelson will maintain for each female student a complete record of her periods. This record will not only help students avoid obviously fertile periods in their sexual contacts, but will also quickly reveal any female who is overdue. Naturally, we hope this won't happen, but if it should, we have limited arrangements for married students. Of course, if all of you decide that you must immediately have children, then the Harrad Experiment will come to a rapid conclusion. The next four years of your life is not the time to have children. It is the time to prepare yourself for a responsible marriage.

"One other aspect of the Physical Education program will tie in with our seminar in Human Values. All sports, exercise, and swimming in the pool will be done in the nude."

Phil stopped talking, and grinned at the gasp of disapproval from the female students. "My lecture is over. For those who are shocked, I can only say that we are not nudists, *per se*. Nudism as a society or a way of life would be inconvenient. But we must face the fact that man took to clothing to keep warm and for personal adornment. You will find the gym well heated in the winter, and you'll be very comfortable without clothes. From a psychological aspect, we feel that it will prove extremely healthy for you to view each other calmly and objectively as naked human beings."

That was Phil's lecture. Actually there was a lot more, but if I keep going I'll fill this notebook in a couple of days.

I wonder what Sheila is thinking about? I'll bet she's scared to death. All the kids were raving and kidding at dinner, but Sheila didn't have much to say. We've been in the room for over an hour and she hasn't said two words. It's eight o'clock. Within a few hours one of us has got to make the move to go to bed. I'm not going first. I'm going to sweat her out. I'll bet a dollar no man . . . boy? . . . has ever seen Sheila in her birthday suit.

How did such a prim broad ever get herself into such a predicament? Maybe her mother thought this was the only way she'd ever get a man. Well, you're elected, Stanley Kolasukas. Yeah, elected; but you don't have to take office. Nothing in the Harrad rule book says you have to go to bed with your roommate. How the devil did they ever pick us for roommates, anyway? The only thing that I can figure that we have in common is that we are both the silent type.

Well, it's my luck. There're fifty other girls enrolled in this mad paradise. Some of them are really stacked, and I get Miss Prim-Dim for my one and only. Maybe she wouldn't be so bad if she wore a little lipstick. I wonder what's under that droopy sweater? It wouldn't fit tight on an elephant. She has a nice face, though . . . big sad brown eyes. Hells bells, why get myself in a stew over a dame? I'm not really convinced, anyway, that this mad Utopian idea of living with a girl will ever work.

I was in love once, I guess, with Joan Austin. When we did it that night on the couch in her family's playroom it wasn't much fun. Joannie was scared to death. Hurry . . . hurry, she said, and she didn't want to look at me while I fiddled with that damned rubber. Well, I guess a man is no beauty . . . his prick red and kind of ugly looking . . . and then I was inside her, and I guess it hurt her. And then wham I came, and Joannie was crying, and I was telling her that I was sorry, and then we heard her father and mother drive into the garage, I was scrambling into my pants, and holding that sad little balloon filled with a teaspoon of what had been in me, and now was just as much trouble outside as inside, and I finally crumbled it in my handkerchief, and somehow there we were playing a phonograph record and saying hello to Mr. and Mrs. Austin, as if nothing had happened, and I was agreeing that it was late, and Joannie should be in bed. Then I was saying goodnight to Joannie and telling her that I was sorry, and she was saying that it was all right, but we would never do it again . . . would we? . . . until we were married? and I was wondering as I took the bus home, was that all there was to it? You got married just for that? I didn't feel any better . . . or any worse, than if I had jerked myself off. But the damnable thing was that the next day I didn't feel so depressed and was ready and eager to get Joannie's pants off again, if I could . . . which I never did. So what does it all add up to? How did a man get put together that he drives himself nuts to get his prick buried into a girl's snatch and when he succeeds neither of them . . . the man or the girl . . . think the result was worth the effort. I wonder what it is really all about?

Across the room Sheila is probably thinking the same kind of thoughts I am writing. I'll bet, if we could just talk about it and really say what we think and feel we could find the answers . . . or maybe understand. What the heck? In a couple of days classes will start. My schedule for honors work in History and Government is going to go a long way to keep my mind off sex and girls.

One thing I can say is: Phil Tenhausen has made it abundantly clear that he and Margaret will be willing to discuss any problems of sex and love but they are not going to be concerned with any student at Harrad who cannot maintain a top academic standing. Like one of the fellows said at dinner. "It's a conspiracy. Harrad hands you the lollipop on a stick, but if you start to lap it or enjoy it too much they'll snatch it right out of your hand."

I stopped writing last night at this point because right out of the clear blue sky Sheila started to talk. I guess that I might as well try to write down the conversation, because it was a lulu. I wonder if Sheila is doing the same. Be fun someday to read what she is writing. Like two authors given the same plot and out come two different stories.

"Do you think that I am kind of a drip?" Sheila asked.

I guess I blushed. I'm wary of this kind of mind reading.

"How can I say? I only met you this morning," I said. Might as well stall and see where this was going. "You look just like any other girl . . . you know, girl as distinguished from boy."

"That's just it." Sheila sighed. "Nothing special. Now, you take you. You're the dreamboat type. You should be groaning out gooey love songs to all the teen-agers. You'd be a big hit."

"I don't sing . . . only croak," I said cheerfully.

"Well, if I had been doing the matching at Harrad, I'd match up the beautiful and the homely separately . . . seems more logical and less likely to cause problems. I'd have matched you with that blonde girl . . . Beth Hillyer. She's really a knockout."

I really felt like agreeing with Sheila, not because I think I'm any Hollywood type, but rooming with Beth did seem to have its advantages. But being brought up with four older sisters has taught me that you shouldn't always agree with a woman on questions of this kind.

I said: "You look all right to me. You've got a pretty face. Maybe because you wear your hair so tight it makes your cheek bones stand out. Anyway, you know what the song says: "Always marry a woman uglier than you!"

I guess that wasn't very tactful, and it made Sheila kind of mad, because she stopped talking for a while. Finally, to break the silence which was getting a bit thick, I said: "Look this idea of having a girl for a roommate is all right, I guess . . . and probably will be an interesting experience, but it isn't throwing me.

I'm lucky to be here. My family are poor Polish people . . .
couldn't afford to send me to a school for dog catchers. I just
happened to win a Carnsworth scholarship . . . all expenses paid.
The Tenhausens talked me into Harrad. I'm here to learn enough
so that I don't have to go to work sticking nuts and bolts on
automobiles like my father. If my old man knew what the set-up
was at Harrad he'd probably say: "Why in hell do you want to
live with a woman at eighteen? Time enough to suffer when one
hooks you and you get married."

Sheila smiled. "Maybe he's right. Maybe after four years
of living with girls a man might decide its better never to get
married. I don't know how boys can stand girls, anyway. I don't
like girls much. Most of the time I don't even like myself." Sheila
paused. "What do you think of this journal idea anyway? Are
your writing about me? Will you let me read what you have
written someday?"

"Not on your life," I said grimly. "What's more, I think
we'd better make some rules."

"Like what?"

"Anything in my desk is private. Anything in my dresser is
private. Half of that bedroom closet belongs to me, and you
keep your stuff in your half. My bed is the one next to the wall."

"Would you like to draw a chalk line across the room?"
Sheila asked sweetly. "While you're at it, your rules for me apply
to you in spades . . . plus, when I undress and get ready for bed,
you stay out of the bedroom until I'm in bed. In the morning you
can dress first . . . and I can assure you I won't look . . . and that
bathroom is private. When I'm in it, you can stay out. No
visitors."

"Okay, settled," I said, "but what are you going to do about
Physical Education. I won't *have* to peek then!"

"What do you mean?"

"What were you doing? Sleeping this morning? Didn't you
hear Phil Tenhausen? He's read all the Utopias; Plato, More,
Campanella. He's putting their ideas into practice at Harrad.
One hour of Phys.-Ed. is compulsory at Harrad . . . Greek style
. . . everybody bare ass."

"Oh yeah," Sheila said, "Not for this gal! I'm not stripping in front of a lot of men."

I shrugged. "Seems kind of unfair to you, though."

"What do you mean?"

"I'll see Beth Hillyer in her birthday suit."

"Oh . . ." Sheila said. She looked uncomfortable.

FROM THE JOURNAL OF SHEILA GROVE

September, the First Year

Sheila Anne Grove. That's me . . . born eighteen years ago on March 12th. Astrologically, I am a fish swimming upstream and downstream at the same time. In other words, I don't know whether I am coming or going. I guess that's a fair enough statement to sum me up for the first eighteen years.

I know a couple of things. I'm rich . . . well, not a millionairess, although I may well be if Daddy doesn't leave the rest of his loot to his second or third wife. Anyway, on my eighteenth birthday he put five hundred thousand dollars in my name. I guess Daddy figures by the time he dies he may have been through a few more wives, and this might have the effect of dividing up his wealth considerably. Since he earned all his money himself by founding the Grove Oil Corporation, what he does with his money is his business.

The second thing I know is that no one in this whole damned world loves me. According to some of the psychology books I've read, believing this entitles you to a front seat in the nut house. But not me. I don't care.

My life is pretty fouled up. Mother divorced Daddy when I was twelve. She couldn't stand two things about him, his desire to get rich no matter what . . . and the richer he got the more women he thought he could go to bed with. Daddy told Mother that it really was too bad she was divorcing him, because he loved her. But Mother's idea is that you can only love one person

at a time. So, she married a nice homey man who takes her
fishing in a rowboat and builds all kinds of jig-sawy things in his
cellar workshop. Harold Tripp is his name, and he is an ac-
countant of all things in the eastern division of the Grove Oil
Corporation. As Mrs. Tripp, my mother, has presented him with
two boys and a girl in their six years of marriage. Either they
like babies, or Harold has never heard of contraceptives. It is
likely, however, that my Mother is responsible. She likes babies.
She couldn't do much about it married to Daddy, who was too
busy making money to want a family. My guess is, I was strictly
an accident.

I have a room in the Tripp's home when and if I want
to live there. But I feel like a fifth wheel, a living contradiction to the lines framed in the front hall, which read: "Let
me live in a house by the side of the road, and be a friend
to man." Such a poem would irk Daddy, who puts his trust
in money.

To solve the problem of Sheila, I was sent to a very posh
boarding school for a while, and then to Brightwater Academy.
For a couple of summers I tagged along to Europe with Daddy
and the current Mrs. Grove. Somehow or other I must have got
underfoot. The first thing I knew I was enrolled in a very proper
school for French girls and spent my summer in middy blouses
. . . very giggly, girlish, and far removed from male eyes.

This kind of life made me a book worm. Plunging into a
book is for me the worst form of escapism. I guess I live in a
kind of dream world. So what else?

Since I haven't had very much of what you might call an
adjusted home life, I got the idea that if I read all of the Great
Books, I might find why I had been born, anyway. Harold told
me I needed God, and Daddy insists that God helps those who
help themselves. I didn't like either of these ideas. I figured God
needed me . . . but if He does, he hasn't given me any indica-
tion. All my reading accomplished several things. I have been at
various times, in my mind, a Unitarian, a Jew, an existentialist,
a communist, a brilliant teacher, a loving wife, a whore, a dic-
tator, and a sad-apple, which I am at the moment. Sad-apple
Sheila Grove, who graduated last June from Brightwater Acad-

emy with the highest marks in the history of the school. Summa
Cum Laude . . . ugh! Three boys were Magna, and two girls and
eight boys . . . Cum Laude. My boy friends, as you can see, were
limited.

I guess I am a phenomenon . . . a spook of some kind. When
Daddy informed me (by telephone) that I was half a million-
aire, I told him that's nice. I'm half a virgin, too. That got him.
Especially when I told him the unvirgin half was mental
only, and how I was worried that even with a half million dollars
I would probably end up a full time mental unvirgin.

I guess Daddy got the message because a few days later
Margaret Tenhausen asked me to lunch. Daddy, who knows practically everybody with money, knows John Carnsworth, who was
spending his life giving away to mad-cap projects all the millions *his* father and grandfather had begged, borrowed and
cheated out of sober citizens for nearly a century.

Margaret is nice. I tried to tell her I'm rather shy and certainly introspective, and the idea of going to a college where I
roomed with a boy was terrifying and scary. Margaret implied
that I'd better get associated with other brainy types if I ever
expected to lead a full life . . . that I would be an anathema to
any solid, middle class citizen who wanted a fluffy, non-argumen-
tative bed-mate. So I agreed and for two solid days I took every
test the half-witted psychologists ever devised to find what makes
another human being tick.

I must have met whatever standards Harrad is looking for,
because here I am. Daddy knows. He laughed when he called me
from Dallas.

"Relax and enjoy it, Sheila," he said. "I think the Tenhausens have a splendid idea. Maybe if I had got it as a balanced
arrangement when I was a kid, I might have got it out of my
system, and still be happily married to your Mother."

Knowing Daddy, I doubt it. He could never settle with one
woman for life. Whatever kind of cake he is looking for, women
are only the frosting on it, and he eats that first!

If Mommy knew, she'd die of shame. Those are her words.
But all her life she has regularly died of shame, so I guess it
isn't fatal. Mommy is happy to believe I am going to a nice col-

lege in Cambridge, Massachusetts. Mommy doesn't know too
much about colleges . . . "Harrad College is a nice name, Sheila,"
she said. "It sounds better than those places called universities."

I drove up to Harrad yesterday from White Plains in my
Buick convertible. I arrived in Cambridge about two-thirty. Using the mimeographed map the Tenhausens had sent to new
students, I finally located the grounds. I would guess that few
people in Cambridge know that Harrad College or even the old
Carnsworth estate actually exists. The estate, which must be fifty
acres over all, is completely surrounded by a stone wall about
eight feet high. Set into the wall and rising another two feet
above are sharp iron pickets. Ivy has obliterated most of the wall
and conceals the pickets. Whoever built this wall was not interested in being stared at.

I finally located the entrance, a one lane tarvia road between
two stone pillars that supported an iron picket gate. The gate
was open. On one of the pillars a new brass plaque was engraved
with one name: Harrad.

Feeling a little shaky, I drove slowly along a tree-lined drive.
I had entered a nineteenth century world of ancient greenhouses,
manicured gardens, tall trees, and carefully mowed lawns. Here
and there a water sprinkler indicated that human beings did
exist somewhere. About a quarter of a mile further in, I turned
into a circular drive and stopped in front of a home that looked
as if it might have been built by one of the nineteenth century
robber barons. It was a huge imitation of an English hunting
lodge. In sharp contrast at the rear of the lodge, was a modern
three story stone and glass building about five hundred feet long.
I saw some kids walking in front of it and a couple of girls
sunning themselves in beach chairs. This was evidently Harrad.

Having got this far last night in my journal, I finally
couldn't stand the silence on the other side of the room any
longer. I don't really know how to write this . . . it is so crazy
and impossible. Here am I, Sheila Anne Grove, sitting in a
strange dormitory room with a boy I never saw until this morning. A boy whose name is Stanley Kolasukas . . . now Stanley
Cole, because, as he told me, it was simple and he liked things
simple.

Stanley and I ate dinner with a bunch of other kids in a very pleasant wood-paneled dining room with round tables big enough to seat eight people around them. We picked up our meal cafeteria style. All I remember (I was so jittery) was taking some roast beef and other stuff that was shoved on my tray. I guess I ate it, but I wasn't actually conscious of doing so. I wondered how I was ever going back to my (our) room with this smirking character Stanley Cole. He has wavy brown hair and his sideburns—at least an inch too long—are strictly Greenwich Village (my room-mate, God help me). I tried to keep abreast of a conversation with Harry Schacht and his roommate Beth Hill-yer, who sat on one side of me. Across the table; Dorothy Staple-ton and Valerie something-or-other belong (yucks, is that the right word?) to Herbert Snyder and Peter Longini. I felt like a blushing, tongue-tied simpleton. Especially so because Beth Hill-yer is enough to scare any plain jane like me half to death. She has blonde hair—natural—blue eyes, a turned up nose, and every-thing else to go with it. I'll bet a dollar she would be asked to pose for one of those pull-out pages in *Playboy*, the kind where the girl, naked, is lying half on her hips so that in one glance you can see her breasts (big) and shapely behind, with a smile on her face that says to all boys with their tongue hanging out: "Wouldn't you like to cuddle me?" Beth has this and in-telligence, too. During most of the dinner, she and Stanley car-ried on a long discussion about our foreign policy and the bad image the United States has created in African countries. Why the heck didn't the Tenhausens pick them for roommates?

Everybody was aware that I had a bad case of aphasia, and politely avoided directing any questions at me. Finally, we fin-ished eating. Some of the kids went into a huge recreation room just off the dining room and played ping pong, others turned on a stereo phonograph and listened to Mozart, and still others went downstairs to a basement "nightclub" called the Cellar Club, where they danced to a juke box. I tried the Mozart group a while. Here, conversation was frowned upon. Stanley disappeared.

About an hour later Stanley walked in, said he had taken a walk. He then relapsed into silence, occasionally staring at me as if I were some kind of ogre. Finally, he decided to walk back to our room with me, where the silence continued until finally I couldn't stand it any longer. I asked him if he thought I was some kind of drip.

Stanley didn't agree or disagree. He tried to give me the impression that girls were girls and that I wasn't so bad. And then he, with his smart haircut, tries to tell me that maybe my hair is too tight. Of course, all the time I know that he is thinking about Beth Hillyer. Then he pulls the old chestnut that handsome men should marry homely women. I felt like hurling this journal right at his smug face. So what if he looks like Hollywood's answer to a teen-ager's prayer?

I wonder what he is writing? I'd give ten dollars to read what he has to say about me. When I suggested the idea . . . real nicely . . . to him, what does he do but start a lot of guff about his privacy. He can have his nasty little privacy, but if I ever catch him leaving his journal around, all bets are off. Harold Tripp has some old World War II posters in his cellar with Hirohito on them looking very hideous, and underneath them in big red letters: KNOW YOUR ENEMY! Good tactics, I'd say.

Since we were making rules, I decided to get this going to bed bit straightened out. I had wanted to ask some of the other girls what they were going to do, but between the fact that I was too embarrassed to initiate the conversation with just any girl I didn't know, and the way the Tenhausens kept us hopping from one thing to another all day (I made appointments to talk with the deans of "A" College, and "B" University),* I never did solve the problem.

The funny thing is that by myself I'm not really modest. I have often lain on my bed naked and read, or looked at myself in a mirror. I have even touched myself once in a while and made believe that I was both me and some nice boy who liked me, and once I must have even masturbated. I guess I did, anyway, because while it was happening it was just impossible to

* All references to the actual names of colleges and universities in the New England area have been eliminated from these journals. Students in these colleges who have become acquainted with Harrad students assume that they are "day" students, or "townies". This is in keeping with our purpose not to encourage overt publicity.

stop, and then afterwards I felt awful. But no one has ever seen me naked since I was old enough to wash myself, and Stanley Dreamboat Cole isn't going to break that record . . . at least, not easily.

So, after we got these points settled, it was about eleven-thirty. I told Stanley that I was going to bed. I locked the bathroom door, did my business, brushed my teeth, and scrambled into some new pajamas I had bought. Then I turned out the bedroom lights and burrowed into my bed. I gave Stanley the all clear, but remained very rigid. Let Mr. Cole try something and he'd regret it, by gosh.

What did Stanley do? He sauntered into the bedroom, turned on his dresser lamp, looked at me with my eyes squeezed tight, and then calmly undressed right down to his bare skin. Okay, so I watched him through my eyelashes. Didn't I say "Know your Enemy?" Besides, I had never seen a boy naked. Stanley looked very nice. A little round-shouldered, a little hair on his chest, a very small behind, and nestled in a soft growth of hair, a fragile looking penis that wobbled when he walked to the bathroom. Somehow, he seemed much younger naked . . . as if he might be a scared little kid, too.

He finally got into his bed, still naked.

"Good-night, She," he said softly.

"Good-night," I whispered, and felt like crying. How did he know Mother and Daddy called me She . . . once, a long time ago when they lived together?

FROM THE JOURNAL OF BETH HILLYER

October, the First Year

Three weeks at Harrad and by this time I don't know whether I'm afoot or on horseback. Funny thing, its not the environment of Harrad that's got me bugged. It's trying to find time to get all the work done.

Pops told me last summer, "Keep in mind, Beth, just because you come from a medical family you don't have to be a M.D. Your grandfather is still practicing. You've got one brother interning and one in Ohio determined to make a living as a General Practitioner . . . and there's me. Four Hillyers determined to help mankind is probably enough. Maybe a very pretty girl like you should take a nice easy college course at some girl's college, then get married and have children. After all, that's what your mother did."

Pops knows how to goad me. I love Mommy and all that, but I want to do more with my life 'than have babies. If you're a girl and you're pretty, everyone thinks you should be a dumb bunny who lives and breathes just because some man (your husband) lives and breathes. Reminds me of a story by Chekov, *The Darling*. The poor girl in the story had no personality or individuality of her own. Just a big cipher. When her husband died she had to get another in a hurry . . . with each new husband she acquired a new identity.

"Listen, Pops," I told him. "It can be done. I love medicine. I've lived, breathed, and slept with Hippocrates since I was hatched. I'm going to do it. I'm going to be a doctor . . . I'm going to marry a doctor . . . I'm going to have babies . . . and my own husband will deliver me. And when your female patients see me hang my shingle out next door to yours . . . you're going to lose them all . . . especially the ones with big bellies, because I'll know more of what's happening in their head and in their womb than you and Gramp do if you live a million years."

So Pops, you can chuckle, but even this load of courses which includes: Advanced Chemistry, Sophomore Biology, German, English, and American History, not to mention the Tenhausen's course in Human Values, in which they assign books as if there is no tomorrow, doesn't frighten me. It's fun. Everyday is new and exciting, with a million-billion things to learn.

What's more, I've got a roommate who is a brain . . . and he looks it, too! Harry Schacht. He wears big Hollywood-style tortoise shell glasses. Since he is nearly a six-foot string bean, the thing that impresses you most is that Harry looks like someone's day dream of a science-fiction superman. But Harry is only nearsighted. When it comes to fine print and reading just about everything that has been written, Harry terrifies me because he knows so much more than I do. But there're compensations. In the ways of women, Harry is just a frightened boy.

Last night when I was undressing, Harry was lying on his bed, watching me.

"I can't get over it," he mused. "You're the most beautiful girl I've ever seen. The Tenhausens certainly wanted to keep the tea-kettle boiling. The only possible reason we could have been picked to room together is that we're both planning to go to medical school. You know what the kids have nicknamed us, don't you?"

Naked, I jumped on his bed and landed flat on him. He was wearing clothes, which I guess was lucky. "They call us Beauty and the Beast." I kissed him, a quick peck, and scrambled under the covers into my own bed.

"Don't you think that excites me?" Harry leaned on his elbow and looked at me.

"Sure, I guess so. Maybe I'd better not do it again. I just thought it would be nice to be friendly."

"Oh, gosh, don't stop being you. I look forward to it. I never dreamed I'd go to college and have a room-mate who kissed me good-night." Harry sighed and started to undress. "I really like you Beth . . . you're so sunshiny, and I'm so gloomy." Still wearing his shorts, he turned down his bed.

"Why do you wear shorts to bed?" I asked.

"I don't know. I'm embarrassed to have you see me."

"I see you naked practically every damned day in the gym."

"That's different. There's a lot of other kids around."

I laughed. "Your shorts don't conceal a thing. I can see your jamoke, and it's sticking in the air."

That made Harry laugh. He took his shorts off and stared at himself. Still laughing, he stared at it. "That's a pretty good name for it. How did you ever get the way you are, Beth?"

"What do you mean?"

"I don't know . . . so easy . . . so spontaneous . . . so un-embarrassed."

"I guess it's being brought up in a family of doctors. In my family we call a spade a spade, and devil take the hindmost. Most doctors don't pussyfoot around about the facts and functions of life."

Harry got into his bed, turned out his bed light, and we talked about an exam that was coming up tomorrow in Chemistry. By the time we finished questioning each other for more than an hour, I knew we had it licked. I think we were practically ready to take mid-years instead of a lowly lab test. "Gosh," I said finally, "I've got to go to sleep. I'm not a night owl like you."

"Beth, can I ask you one thing?"

"Shoot."

"Do you think you and I will ever actually have intercourse."

"I'm ready when you are," I said, grinning.

"You make it sound so casual."

"It isn't going to be casual with me. It's going to be nice and snuggly, and lots of fun."

"How can it be fun with a Beast."

"Harry, you are not a beast. You're a nice warm skinny boy who is scared to death because he's living with a girl. Aren't you learning anything in the H.V. course? Love is in your head, and I am sure proud of what's in that head of yours."

"You mean you love me, Beth?"

"I like you a lot . . . that's a darned good beginning."

"Beth, have you ever made love with a boy?"

"Yes."

"Oh?"

"Harry, you sound gloomy again. I did twice. With a very nice boy. He was scared and I was scared. I was sixteen. He was nineteen. I kept wondering what if I had to marry him. He was very handsome. He sang all the popular songs, and knew the words by heart. In fact, the only words he knew to make love with, he parroted right out of songs. Did you ever hear that song, "Too Young" . . . he sang it all the time, and threatened to commit suicide if I didn't marry him."

"Did he commit suicide?" Harry asked hopefully.

"In a way. He got married last year. His wife is pregnant for the second time."

"You must have liked him. You kept track of him."

"Harry," I said, "Go to sleep. He called me last summer, and wanted to have a date. He was bored with his wife, and told me we could make beautiful music together. I told him that I loved music but was only interested in music for unaccompanied violin. You didn't know that I can play a violin, did you, Harry?"

"I can play the piano," Harry chuckled. "We should try it sometime. They sound good together."

FROM THE JOURNAL OF HARRY SCHACHT

October, the First Year

I'm in love . . . not just with Beth Hillyer who is utterly, completely wonderfully feminine, but I'm in love with Sheila Grove and Dorothy Stapleton . . . in fact, I'm in love with fifty girls. "Bless them all, the long and the short and the tall. . . ." That's a World War II song my father used to sing . . . and there's another. "Thank Heaven for little girls." Only these aren't little girls . . . they are fully developed women with breasts and swaying behinds and soft round stomachs.

Every day when I go to Physical Education, there they are . . . girls . . . naked, swimming in the pool, playing volleyball, doing calisthenics . . . yelling, screaming, soprano-joyous. If I stand by the pool, one of them is likely to shove me in. When I come up spluttering in the middle of other girls, they splash me, or challenge me to a race, or toss a beach ball at me . . . and the hour goes by so fast that I can't really believe it is over . . . and then back to the room and I yell for Beth, only she hasn't come back from her classes . . . so I lie down on my bed and think awhile before dinner.

Mostly, I think I am a very lucky Beast. What good fortune saw to it that a homely guy like me should be so lucky? Four weeks ago I had never been nearer to a girl than ten feet. Even when that happened, I used to get perspiry and so wound up inside that I couldn't even talk to one if she ever happened to speak to me . . . which was seldom. Now, it's easy to banter

with them or talk seriously, and they talk back to me . . . easily
. . . unashamed.

Like, yesterday . . . I was sitting at the edge of the pool just
watching about ten fellows and girls playing water volleyball
when Sheila Grove dropped out of the game and scrambled up
beside me. She was puffing from the exertion. She pulled off her
bathing cap, and with her hands swished the droplets of water
off her face and breasts.

"Woo! I'm pooped." She grinned at me. "You know just two
weeks ago when I first came here and had to walk out in front
of everybody naked, I thought I'd die of embarrassment. Now it
seems the only way to be . . . naked. Stanley isn't such a big
shot, either. He told me that he was really scared to death he'd
have an erection . . . right in front of everybody. He still gets a
little worried about it."

"It's mind over matter," I said, grinning at her. "Like if I
thought how nice it would be to kiss your breasts . . . wingo, I'd
be in trouble."

Sheila looked at me with a teasing expression in her brown
eyes. "Maybe I should keep you thinking about it. Males are so
funny," she chuckled. "Roger Wilnor had it happen to him yesterday. Jane Atterman challenged him to a wrestling match. She
said she could wrestle better than any of the boys. I guess Roger
was thinking about something beside wrestling because suddenly
he was really pointing in the air. Everyone who saw him laughed
and kidded him."

"You see why a boy can't wrestle with a girl," Roger said,
blushing.

"Don't you worry," Jane told him laughing. "Once I got
you in a hammerlock, you'd forget all about that!"

"He might relax and enjoy being suffocated," I suggested.

"Seriously, Harry," Sheila said, "what do you think of this
whole idea of boys and girls living together this way? If what's
happening at Harrad ever leaked out, an awful lot of people
would be shocked. How do we know this kind of life won't make
us all promiscuous? Maybe after males and females have been so
casual with each other they never can really fall in love or will
never want to settle into a monogamous marriage."

"I guess what the Tenhausens are trying to prove with us is that you can love," I said, "I mean, really love many people in your lifetime. How we will react when we get to the point of settling down with one person is a question that I'll bet even the Tenhausens don't know the answer to. We are sociological guinea pigs. Anyway, at the moment I'm quite happy."

"Have you gone to bed with Beth yet?" Sheila asked and then looked uncomfortable. "Maybe I shouldn't ask?"

"Why not? The answer is no. How about you and Stanley?"

"No . . . but it's bound to happen sooner or later."

"Would you go to bed with me?"

"You mean now . . . today?"

"I don't know really when. Sometime . . ."

"I don't really know, Harry. I think the Tenhausens expect it to happen."

"Did you ever stop to think that one bad little girl with nymphomania or something could wreck the place?"

Sheila smiled. "I doubt if that will happen. Remember, one of the cardinal rules is that a Harrad girl will sleep only with one man between her monthly periods. Any girl here will be pretty strict about that. After all, if there is a slip-up, she'll want to know who the father is. So, if some girl here develops nymphomania, she isn't going to be able to play the field. At the rate of one man a month, it would take her the whole four years, including summer vacations, to accommodate all the men in the freshman class. Anyway, Harry, most girls aren't like that. The feminine pysche is pretty exclusive. I'll bet you that ninety-nine percent of the girls here within four years will not have had sexual experience with more than three men . . . four at the most, and maybe lots of them with just one. Harrad provides the female an exposure to many potential husbands and gives her an opportunity to indulge her natural sexual desire and curiosity without fear and furtiveness."

"You sound like Margaret Tenhausen," I said. "But what about jealousy? Supposing some month you decided to sleep with me. Suppose Stanley was in love with you, but you weren't exactly in love with him."

"That could be messy," Sheila chuckled. "But you overlook

the way the Tenhausens are very carefully attempting to reorient our values. Everyday we are being shown, and I think convinced, that the individual human being is ultimately good. Jealousy is within our own control. It's strictly a man-made emotion. Love and sex are two different concepts, interrelated but impossible of satisfactory existence alone. You *can* love man in general . . . but to really enjoy the peak experience of the contact of genital organs with one specific person, you must know that individual deeply . . . emotionally, in . . . a thorough empathetic contact based on a desire to rationally understand the other person and care for him. The mucous will flow in my vagina and your penis will become erect without this understanding, but the result is simple rutting. Animals do that. Man persists in saying that beneath the cultural veneer he remains an animal . . . but it simply doesn't have to be true any longer. If individual men can be taught to make the effort, they can learn to love other human beings in a brand new way that gives the male and female security and value in each other's eyes . . ."

"You mean," I said, "if I were in love with you and valued you, that you wouldn't be jealous of some other person I might think I was in love with?"

"Harry, I don't know." She playfully flipped water on my penis with her toe. "I'm Sheila, spouting Tenhausen gospel. I'm not Beth. If you slept with Beth, I don't think I could ever understand why you'd want to sleep with me. Would it be because you wanted variety? And if you wanted variety wouldn't you devalue me, and yourself?"

I laughed. "It's fun to try and find the answers. I think my own answer would be that I am studying to be a doctor because I find human beings endlessly fascinating. The awe-inspiring mystery of what makes you Sheila, and not Beth, could still make sexual intercourse with either one of you . . . without devaluing either of you . . . a wonderful exploration. Come on, I'll race you to the shower, and I'll scrub your back because it's Sheila's back and very nice and fragile and freckly . . . and I'm glad you exist in my world."

FROM THE JOURNAL OF STANLEY COLE

November, the First Year

Last Saturday I went to "E" College for a football weekend. Sheila arranged it. Tom Brierly, a fellow she met in her Pre-Elizabethan drama course at "R" College has a brother at "E" who is a sophomore. Sheila was Tom's date and I had Tom's sister, Ruth, for a date. Sound screwy? Well . . . more to come. I went along as Sheila's brother . . . Stanley Grove!

Of course, one thing we have all been cautioned about from the very beginning is that Harrad College doesn't exist. If students at other colleges ask us where we live, we pretend we live somewhere in the Greater Boston area and commute to classes. This is probably good sense. If the outside world were aware of Phil Tenhausen and the Mad Hatter world he has created, we would be all living in a fishbowl with a million sober citizens up in arms screaming that the Tenhausens were destroying the morals of the country . . . those are Phil's words and we all agree that he could double them in brass.

While this secrecy has its complications, it gives Harrad a sense of unity, and most Harrad students seem to think it's a ball to be the "villains" in the drama. Sheila is no exception.

"I think we should see how the other half lives," she said. "Please . . . please it will be fun to pretend you're my brother."

"Other than picking up your bra and panties, and trying to find my way into the bathroom through a forest of nylons, I might just as well be your brother," I said, teasing her.

"At least, you've seen me in my birthday suit," Sheila grinned. "I can assure you Tom Brierly isn't going to have that privilege."

"Big deal . . . I've seen the entire freshman class of females at Harrad in their birthday suits at one time or another."

"Has it given you a let down?" Sheila asked. "No more feminine mystery . . . just girls, big, skinny, plump. Do they drive you crazy? . . . Do you think about sex all the time? I think you should let me read that monstrous journal of yours so I would know better what you are thinking."

"Stay out of my journal," I warned her. "And don't get yourself in a tizzy. I've been studying so hard these past three weeks that I scarcely know you exist."

"Then why do you watch me when I dress and undress?"

"To tell you the truth, I can't believe that you'd ever get so relaxed."

"Neither did I," Sheila said, grinning. "For eleven days I analyzed myself and wrote at least thirty pages in my journal . . . all of which sounds silly. Now I take it for granted. You're just like some girl I could be living with."

"That statement, my full-breasted friend, is, to use the current vernacular, the living end!"

"Well, I admit I like your anatomy better than a female roommate's. It's more interesting, and there's no competition . . . please, Stanley . . . will you go as my brother?"

So we went, and I guess it was a good idea, because it gave Sheila and me some sharp contrasts between life at Harrad and life at a small New England all male college.

Contrast # 1: SEX. Sex is number one topic of discussion both at Harrad and at "E" College. But the difference in approach is night and day. At Harrad if you get into a male discussion of sex . . . the question is when . . . not IF. I know, for example, that I will eventually make love to Sheila. We talk about it often, and have long discussions about man and woman. But we aren't really intense about it. I think we'll know almost simultaneously when we want to make love. Things are considerably different at "E" College.

We left Boston about nine-thirty and arrived at "E" about

noon. When we finally located Bill Brierly's fraternity, we found it jammed from attic to basement with fellows and girls. The men were drinking beer and the girls had weak Tom Collins.

Bill Brierly, full of at least two quarts of beer, grabbed Susan like a starving man. "Gotta hug my bug," he said, enthusiastically kissing her. "Don't worry if we get separated," he told his brother. "We'll be around."

I could see where this was going to become complicated. Sheila had one Tom Collins. Dubiously, she watched Tom attacking bourbon with beer chasers. I kept Tom company in his drinking, and we reached a happy state of euphoria.

Bill introduced us to a mountain of nondescript *hors d'oeuvres,* telling us how he and his fraternity brothers had worked on them until midnight. We ate politely, showed more enthusiasm at some boiled hotdogs, then began the trek across campus to the stadium.

Walking through the pine woods toward the football game, Bill joyously began feeling Susan's behind. Tom walked closely with Sheila, talking to her intimately. I was polite and circumspect with Ruth, who seemed none too pleased with me.

I was obviously not behaving according to "E" College patterns, since I had made no offensive based on the simple fact that Ruth was a girl and I was a boy. Ruth is pretty enough. She is a freshman at "L" College just outside of Boston. As she made quite clear on the ride up to "E" she isn't going to college to learn anything in particular. She had just read Betty Friedan's *Feminine Mystique,* and in Ruth's opinion the author was plainly a kook.

"Sure," she said, "there are girls at "L" who are planning to be scientists or what not . . . but they're creeps. I feel sorry for them. They have no choice. If a girl has anything at all, she'd darned soon rather get married and live in suburbia. The hell with how dull it was. Anyway, darned few men want to marry a brainy woman. They want somebody to tell them they are wonderful, and be ready to cuddle with them or baby them."

"Maybe a girl can be intelligent and cuddly, too," I suggested.

"Sure, intelligent," she replied. "She can read the best sellers and take on little civic problems in her women's club . . . but let her really get her own interests . . . let her not be completely children and house oriented . . . then watch out, she's in for trouble. Take you, Stan. You're going to major in History and Government. I don't really give a damn about history or who runs what. Now, just supposing that I married you and I was a career woman, a doctor, or make it simpler, a dress designer, or worse, for the hell of it, a lawyer. Do you think we'd stay married long? Heck no! Most men want three things out of a woman . . . a nice social hostess for their friends, a good mother to their kids . . . and a sex pot in bed."

"Supposing we were married, and you *were* like that?" I could see Sheila, sitting in the front seat of the car, straining to hear our conversation. "What would we talk about?"

"Gossip, kids, sickness . . . your job . . . what's in *Time Magazine* . . . what's the sexiest best seller, who some movie star is shacking up with . . . what some neighbor is doing to some other neighbor's wife . . . and television when we ran out of higher thoughts." She looked at me archly, "That's what my father and mother say and do. What do you want in a wife . . . in a marriage anyway?"

Since I wasn't so sure I knew, I dropped the subject. I also had the feeling that if I weren't careful, Sheila wouldn't be able to stand eavesdropping any longer, and both Sheila and I would end up expounding marriage a la Tenhausen to her.

By the time we stumbled over more sober spectators and finally located our seats, the first quarter of the game was nearly over. This was the football game of the year pitting "E" College against their arch enemy "G" College. In sixty years, according to the program, "E" was only one game up on "G." I sat with Sheila on one side of me and Ruth on the other. Tom had a flask of straight bourbon which he passed around. "E" College was aggressively murdering "G" College. By the half the score was 21 to 0, and three men had been carried out of the game on stretchers while the cheerleaders paid special tribute to them with frenzied cheering. Everytime "E" College made a small yardage gain, or it looked as if "G" College might recover the initiative, Tom, Bill, Susan, and Ruth would jump up and scream wildly and cheer in voices cracked and shrill from previous cheerings.

It was nothing new. I had done it myself at football games. The last year at high school, when I was captain of the football team, three colleges had offered me football scholarships . . . but I had suddenly got fed up with it. Get yourself murdered . . . for what? A lot of screaming maniacs . . . a crowd that is only interested in you for the moment. Only two guys came to see me in the hospital after that last game I played. So I was a limping hero for a couple of weeks. Big deal.

From the quick glance Sheila tossed in my direction, I could tell she was reacting to this spectacle of mayhem much the same way I was. In the second half, "G" College, evidently goosed to activity by the coach and old-grads, came to life. After wreaking their share of vengeance on "E" College, they were only a field goal behind.

I guessed that Sheila and I both felt like anthropologists studying the tribal rites of some vanished, primitive civilization. After two months of exposure to the Tenhausen's Human Values course, I was beginning to sense the eventuality of all of us at Harrad, for good or bad, evolving into a new form of man and woman. Not that I was disgusted at the game or even aloof. It was interesting enough. But I knew I was observing and not reacting like a typical college student. It was an odd experience.

This, then, is CONTRAST # 2. Group spectator sports seem atavistic to Harrad students. If they arrived at Harrad with this as a feeling, Harrad will eventually make it articulate. Not that Harrad students aren't aggressive. I think they are considerably more aggressive than most students, but they are not competing against each other. They are unified against a common enemy . . . man's own lack of knowledge, and the immensity of things there are to know in the world.

This leads to CONTRAST # 3 which is a by-product. The entire Harrad environment has been created for and revolves around individual competition. It isn't a competition of man against man, rather it is man, like the Greek heroes, against Nature (meaning all that man doesn't know). Result: Harrad students don't rebel against studying. A good example is the course in Human Values. Sometimes, I think the Tenhausen's feel we shouldn't sleep. In addition to the six courses I'm carrying, (all practically at the sophomore college level) we are required to read an average of a book and a half a week in the Human Values course. In eight weeks we have read *The History of Contraceptives*, by Norman Himes, *The Meaning of Love*, by Ashley Montagu, *Motivation and Personality* and *The Psychology of Being* by Abraham Maslow, *Becoming* by Gordon Allport, the *Art of Love*, by Erich Fromm, and three books on how-to-do it sex, by R. Street, Van de Velde, and Albert Ellis.

This reading course and the level of discussion in the daily group meeting produces a rapid and fundamental change in everyone at Harrad. Thus, the story of what happened at "E" College as recorded by me, Stanley Cole, self-appointed Harrad historian and observer, seems to reveal to me that the Tenhausens are obviously succeeding in reconditioning most of the Harrad students. Anyway, one advantage of being a *human* guinea pig is you can always ask the question, Even if they succeed . . . then what? Harrad students may end up wiser, and, superior citizens, but they will be the smallest minority in the world, and democracy somehow or other has a neat way of trampling over minorities who deviate.

After the football game, which "E" finally won, 27 to 21, we brought the girls back to the Weatherly Inn, about a half mile from the campus, where Bill Brierly had rented a room for Sheila, Ruth, and Susan. We left them for two hours to get cleaned up for dinner at the frat house.

Back in the frat house, Bill and Tom and a dozen other brothers swarmed into Bill's room. Stripped to shorts and T shirts because the weather was god-awful hot for a November twelfth week-end, we drank endless cans of beer and discussed the game and women and sex.

I learned that Bill had met Susan last summer. Susan had just finished her freshman year at "L" College. They had pursued their summer love at beaches, on her father's Chris Craft, and in drive-in movies.

"She's as sexy as the devil, but she doesn't put out," Bill said morosely. "Some nights I could get her bra off . . . some nights her panties. Never both at once. One night I said, 'Listen, Sue, we've been French kissing, hugging, and touching for two hours. You're whimpering and I'm bursting. How about doing it the way men and women are supposed to do it . . . just for a change.' She says, 'Oh, Bill! I want to . . . I want to! . . . but, I can't . . . I can't.' "

"Why not?" one of the brothers asked.

"She can't until she's engaged," Bill said, laughing.

"That's the big hint, brother," Tom said. "Why didn't you pin her and get it over with?"

"Hell, it wouldn't be honest. A lot of guys in this house do that, but not me. I've got principles. I'm not using my pin to seduce virgins. If I ever got that hard up, I'd just go downtown. There're plenty of girls working at the mill who'd just as soon screw as piss."

"All the college broads are the same," one of the brothers said, philosophically sucking on his pipe. "They'll neck like hell with you, let you play with their boobs. After you get to know them awhile they'll even relieve you of your misery . . . by hand, and they'll let you return the favor . . . but they are scared to death to go all the way . . . and, brother, if they do . . . kiss yourself good-bye . . . you're hooked! Remember Joe Tingsley. The poor slob is a runner down in Wall Street. He couldn't finish his junior year. He knocked up that little doll he had up to house parties. Her old man got him a job as prat boy in his brokerage firm to help support his darling daughter. So that's the sum total of it. If they let you go all the way, it's like playing Russian Roulette. Not for me, buster. I'm playing it cool . . . play it their way. Let them play with your pokey . . . but be darn careful where they put it!"

"You fellows don't know what love is," one of the older brothers, evidently a senior, said. "When you meet the right girl . . . you'll forget all about your little animal self. You'll go around starry-eyed, and virginal!"

"Sure, and when you meet this one and only, and you're up here in the woods at this male monastery, writing her bloopy, soulful letters, the chances are that she'll be out necking her ass off with some other guy."

"The gals have to get experience," Bill Brierly said. "The more they know, the better they are. Speaking of experience, what's the strategy for tonight? I got the key to Sam Tobey's shack. It's a huntir.g lodge, Stan," he explained for my benefit.

"There're a couple of sacks and a fireplace with a bear-rug. We'll toss for who gets the bearskin . . . very conducive to romance. One thing is for damned sure, I don't want to hang around here and spend the night arguing with Susan, and trying to persuade her that every other creep in this house without a date isn't watching us . . . which they will be. The Fertility Room, that's the cellar, Stan . . . will be jam packed. Down there you could be kissing your best girl while your dearest brother, who wasn't making out, was feeling her rear end."

Tom shook his head. "I don't know, Bill. Tobey's place is going to be kind of awkward and confusing. Remember . . . you got relatives mixed up in this. Ruth is our sister . . . and Stan is Sheila's brother. Are you going to throw our sister to a wolf like Stan?"

"Are you a wolf, Stan?" Bill asked, grinning at me. "No . . . you look more like a dirty dog."

"I don't mind some hugging," I said. "But if you are really protecting your sister's virtue, I'll be careful."

"Don't worry about Ruth . . . she knows the score. If your old man has got any dough, and/or your prospects look good, she'll add you to her waiting list, and tease you just enough to keep you dangling and sighing for her. Ruth is using her four years at college to line up a sufficient selection of males so that the day after graduation she can get married in the chapel . . . and, if possible, arrive in her marriage bed *virgo intacta*."

"What about Sheila?" Tom asked me.

Poor Sheila, I thought. You asked for this. "To tell you the truth, Sheila is really my stepsister. I haven't seen too much of her in the past year. She's been travelling in Europe with her father."

Tom brightened. "Everything being equal, I think perhaps we should run out to Sam Tobey's shack after all. Maybe we can stay for breakfast."

At dinner, when I alerted Sheila to our new relationship she looked at me angrily. "You think that you're a wise guy, don't you," she hissed. "You'll be sorry . . . tossing your roommate to the wolves. From now on when you feel like discussing Mediaeval History with me, I'll refuse to listen."

"Okay," I told her, "Beth Hillyer has a sympathetic ear."

"You dog," Sheila scowled at me. "I hope you fall madly in love with Ruth Brierly and live with her in suburbia with ten pimply children while your matronly wife reads all the best sellers and eats chocolates until she weighs two hundred pounds, at which point she will finally achieve her life long ambition and be elected President of the Women's Clubs of America, and drag you around with her to meet all of her chubby friends."

. . . I stopped writing at this point, yesterday, because Sheila finally persuaded me to let her read my journal. She decided it would be more interesting if, in the future, we used our journals as a place to write back and forth to each other. This way we could say things to one another we might not actually want to discuss aloud. She got so enthusiastic about the idea that she wanted to suggest it to the Tenhausens. While I agreed, as a temporary idea, I think some problems may arise.

"Even in a marriage," I told her, "a person has to maintain some private area of his own. Once I know and you know that we are reading each other's journal, neither of us will really say what we think. We will write what we think the other person wants to hear."

"I don't agree," Sheila said. "The most important thing in a marriage is that two people be very close . . . so close that their intimate thoughts are revealed to each other."

Since you are now reading this, Sheila . . . I say to you as your roommate, as your lover . . . as your husband (if that should happen) I'm not too sure you'd like my most intimate thoughts if I revealed them to you. I'll give you an example. In addition to thinking of going to bed with you, I also think of making love to Beth Hillyer. How do you like that? Bet you a dollar that thought makes you see red!

FROM THE JOURNAL OF SHEILA GROVE

November, the First Year

I'm floating on a soft dreamy cloud, Stanley. I love you. I love you. Yesterday, you let me read all the wonderful, crazy things you've written in your journal, and I let you read mine. When you got to the point where I hoped you would have a long, dull placid life with Ruth Brierly, you stopped writing about our week-end at "E" College.

"Stanley," I protested. "You haven't finished it! Just when it was going to get interesting."

We were lying in your bed. Outside, the temperature had dropped more than forty degrees, and even Indian summer had given up the ghost. A slushy New England rain was splashing against our window.

You kissed me and said, "I've got to get back to the cruel world, and study. I've got an exam in European Government tomorrow. Anyhow, since you have convinced me that we should in the future read each other's journals . . . there's no sense in duplicating. You haven't written a thing about yesterday. All you have done most of the day is sleep with an angelic smile on your face. When are you going to study?"

"For your information," I said, "when I knew that we were going to "E" College, I did all my work in advance. I'm really covered through Tuesday except for Vatsayana's *Kama Sutra*, which we are supposed to have finished by Tuesday for Human Values. I'm in good shape."

"You can say that again," you said dreamily. You snuggled against my breasts, sucking first one nipple then the other. I could see you were ready to start all over again, and I wasn't going to need much more encouraging.

"Not now," I said practically. "You might wear it out . . . and I wouldn't want that to happen. What bothers me, if I finish the story in my journal it won't be the same . . . your reactions would be different from mine."

"See, I told you," you said. "Like all females, you want your cake and eat it, too. Anyway, in the infamous history of our weekend at "E" College, I don't think our reactions would be too dissimilar."

"You may be right," I said. "I'd rather be me in bed with you than be Ruth or Susan . . . but I can't believe the boys in the fraternity are so bad. They are just frustrated and confused."

"I didn't say they were so bad," you said. "I just feel sorry for them. They're not only frustrated now, they *will* be for years. Anyway, remember what I said. From now on, since you are determined that we read what each other writes, even if I disagree with you, I'll write it down."

"You already have," I said. "And it nearly made me choke! But now . . . after this wonderful morning and afternoon . . . do you feel the same? . . . or are you more selective?"

So okay . . . Stanley Cole . . . don't answer . . . but what could you do with Beth Hillyer that we haven't done in the past six hours . . . that's what I'd like to know, by golly! Anyhow, here's the rest of the story of "E" College seen through the eyes of the late, *but not mourned*, virgin . . . Sheila Grove.

As you know, after dinner at the frat house, we all went downstairs to the Fertility Room. I finally got you alone at the bar for a few minutes.

"Don't be a complete rat," I begged you. "I've figured out Tom Brierly's tactics. He's trying to get me loaded . . . and when I'm good and tipsy he thinks I'll relax and enjoy 'it'."

"What's 'it'," you asked.

" 'It' . . . is . . . according to the best tradition in dating circles . . . Four Finger Feelies. With his right hand and arm

Tom keeps me in a suffering position. FFF logically proceeds to simultaneous P.O."

"What the heck is P.O.?" you asked.

"I can see that you are not well acquainted with defensive action that is the female stock in trade. P.O. is Peripatetic Osculation usually attempted from head to toes."

"Not a bad idea," you said.

"Maybe . . . but for me . . . not with just anybody."

"Okay, where do I come in?" you asked.

"Well," I said, "I understand we're going to some place called Tobey's. It sounds to me like a S. D. . . . Seduction Den. My gosh, Stanley, you are nineteenth century. Anyway, I figured the only way to get out of a really serious clinch with Tom Brierly and do it gracefully is to pretend that he has succeeded beyond his wildest expectations."

"I don't follow your torturous thinking," you said hurriedly. "But you better get it off your chest fast, because Tom is arriving with a Mephisophelean smile on his manly face."

"Listen," I told you hastily, "If I pretend I'm really whooshed . . . believe me, I'll only be pretending. I'll just be hoping that the "E" College ethics dominates Tom's morals, and he wouldn't be interested in making love to an inebriated girl. If I guess wrong, then I'm counting on you to save me."

I know this plan seemed cock-eyed to you but I think you'll agree that it should have made for harmonious relations and a more pleasant evening than if I pursued the untouchable virgin formula. By this time, I was back in Tom's clutches, so I couldn't discuss it further with you. Tom told me that Bill, Susan and Ruth were all raring to go to Tobey's. Bill had run downtown for food to make breakfast, and in no time at all the car was loaded with liquor and we were on our way.

You can say that a more logical approach to the evening was to freeze Tom in his tracks every time he made a pass at me . . . or make it abundantly clear to him that I was a nice girl; but you must remember that most of my (adult?) life has been *sans* boys, and I was quite frankly curious to see in practice what I had only heard secondhand. I honestly agree with you that Harrad is changing our liv s, but at the moment even you are not entirely sure where all of us are going . . . and whether the results will be better than the tried and true way of female defensive countering male offensive until they end up in marriage and live unhappily ever after.

So, if I acted like a prude, I was obviously going to put a damper on the whole evening so . . . well, darn you anyway . . . why explain my motives until you explain your bombshell daydream of enjoying Beth as well as me?

We drove to Tobey's, and I admit that even with you sitting in the front seat beside me while Tom drove, that maybe, after all, I was really playing with fire. Because while I was only playing a game, maybe you were playing for real.

Oh, Stanley . . . this morning and afternoon have been so nice. I never guessed that having you touch me and being so big inside me could be so warm . . . hungry . . . gentle . . . tender. Are there any words in the world to describe how I feel?

"I love you," you said, and you told me you weren't really interested in Ruth. But before I "passed out," I did see you entwined with her on the bear-skin rug in front of Tobey's fireplace. Well, I'm not jealous. After all, we don't own each other, do we? Would you want to own me? I kind of agree with the Tenhausens that if our love survives Harrad and continues throughout our life, it will be because we have inextricably interwoven the threads of what really is the real you and me. Here and there, threads might unravel, or we might drop a stitch and have to go back and unravel it, but the total pattern would be constantly emerging and assuming a "Gestalt" that was the unity of us. Ye gods . . . I'm becoming a philosopher. But any other way would be dull, stagnant, and boring. Wouldn't it?

Enough of Sheila pontificating.

After driving through miles of woods and dirt roads full of pot holes that jounced you and Ruth even closer together, we arrived at Tobey's, which turned out to be a log cabin on the edge of a moonlit lake that extended black and silver-rippled into the night. I was correct. This was a place where a maiden screaming for help would only get her own echo for reply. Inside were knotty pine walls, open ceilings, two bedrooms to the right and left of a huge fieldstone fireplace, and outside plumbing. Tobey is a former Chi Psi, or Deke, or something, who used the place in the summer for fishing (Ho! Ho!). He'd loaned the key to some brother or other from whom Bill had conveniently borrowed it. Bill and Tom had obviously been there before. (With whom?) Big dark mystery, but obviously dames . . . chicks . . . broads—such interesting names men have for us!

We danced. That is *you* danced with Ruth to a hi-fi phonograph. Almost immediately Bill and Susan disappeared into one of the bedrooms. Slowly, inexorably, Tom Brierly plied your heroine with Tom Collins' first and martinis next (faster?). He didn't grab or try to touch; just talked in soft endearing whispers until I began to wonder if I would "pass-out" in reality and not have to pretend at all. Such a conversation. Here's a small extract:

"You are really quite a fascinating girl, Sheila."

"Really quite ordinary," I said.

"No . . . you have a unique charm. A *savoir-faire* aloofness that is captivating."

"Oh?"

"I find myself vibrating to you. Even your hands-off manner is a kind of invitation."

"Invitation to what?"

"Call it reciprocal response. Beneath your cool exterior lies a full-grown, fiery woman. Do you ever let your hair down?"

"You mean literally?"

Tom grinned, and before I could stop him he had unpinned my up-do and my hair was on my shoulders.

"You're quite experienced in handling women's hair," I said.

"Sheila, with your hair down you're breath-taking! May I kiss you?"

"I'm afraid to get too close," I said. "I'm a little dizzy. I'm afraid I'd see you double." There was some truth in this.

"You don't have to look," Tom said agreeably. "You're supposed to close your eyes."

"And sigh passionately?"

"Sheila, I'm a little crocked, too. It's warm enough. What do you say for a little swim in the lake?"

"It would be too cold for me. Besides, I have no bathing suit."

"It's amazingly warm for this time of year. Come on. We can skinny dip."

"No thanks."

"Take off your shoes and stockings. We can walk in the water along the edge."

"No thanks."

"Sheila," Tom said, passing his hand over his face. "I'm really crocked. Would you mind if I lay down in the bedroom for awhile?"

"Of course not. Go ahead!"

"Well, you can't hang around out here watching Stanley and Ruth. Will you come and sit beside me?"

You can see, Stanley, that I was finally trapped. I followed Tom cautiously into the bedroom, and he actually did lie down. He looked as if he were not long for this world. I went out in the kitchen, and pumped some water, and put a damp rag on his head. Then when I was being a really good and tender nurse . . . he grabbed me. "Oh, Sheila," he moaned, imprisoning me in his arms and kissing me enthusiastically. "Forgive me. You're so lovely, I can't help myself!" With a swift movement he unzipped the back of my dress and released the snaps on my bra. I fought him desperately while he held me in a bear-hug, whispering: "Sheila, Sheila . . . I won't hurt you . . . just relax. You knew when you came in here what the score was. Bill and Susan are in the sack right now. You don't hear her struggling. You can't go back in the living room, Stanley and Ruth are bound to be in a clinch. Honestly, I promise. I won't try anything funny."

"What you are doing right now is funny enough!" I hissed at him, trying to first unclasp his hand from my breast, and when I succeeded, I discovered that his other hand was prying at my middle. "Take your hand away this instant!"

"All right," he said, "But let me take your bra off."

At first I refused, and there we lay. Me silently wriggling and trying to escape, and Tom inching his fingers inside my panties. It was time for the *coup d'etat* . . . MINE . . . not his!"

"Tom," I said, "I'm awfully dizzy. I think I'm going to be sick . . . or just pass out." So saying . . . I "passed out" and lay absolutely limp across the bed. I crossed my fingers. Would he be a gentleman? Tom let go of me, jumped out of bed and lighted

a lamp. I made believe trying to rise, but instead slipped gracefully to the floor in a heap, breathing as if I were about to toss
my cookies. Obviously aghast, Tom lifted me off the floor and
dumped me back on the bed.

"Oh, I'm so dizzy!" I moaned.

He took the damp cloth I had gotten for him and put it on
my face, telling me that I'd be all right. And then what does he
do but proceed to *thoroughly undress* me, telling me all the time
that I'll be just fine . . . that I need to unloosen my clothes, and
there's really no need to get my dress wrinkled. In two seconds I
was lying like a naked corpse on the bed, not knowing what to
do. If I jumped up and revealed I was really quite sober, it would
go over like a lead balloon. If I yelled for you to save me, things
would be even worse. While I was trying to find a course of action,
Tom stripped and jumped in bed beside me whispering that his
lovely Sheila would be fine . . . just fine. He took my limp hand
and folded it around his penis. I was shocked. You can laugh . . .
Stanley . . . but never in my life had I ever touched a man . . .
not even you, until this morning. After two months at Harrad, a
certain naivety in my previous character has vanished. Even so,
I never imagined what sizes a man can grow to, and I never
really believed that this long heavy apparatus would fit com-
fortably inside a woman. I snatched my hand away. Murmuring
passionately at me, Tom placed my hand back on his weapon.
We went through this routine at least five times. All the time
Tom moaned lugubriously, telling me to just move it for him.

Suddenly . . . I don't know why . . . I felt very sorry for him.
He was obviously quite distraught with emotion. So I held him
hard and felt him move against my fingers. After ten seconds and
a groan of sheer desperation, it was over.

I pretended not to know what had happened, I lay there
with my eyes closed while he wiped my hand and himself. And
then, I got a terrible emotional let-down and started to cry . . .
sobbing hysterically. I knew I was a little drunk, and I know
you were shocked when you burst in to the room and found me
lying there naked, and Tom struggling into his pants, in dismay,
at the havoc he had created. But what you didn't know was that
I was crying my heart out for the world, and the way it was and
the sheer, animal drive that made Tom seek something he so

desperately needed . . . love . . . affection, only to end up with
such a hollow triumph. And I wondered if this was what the
Tenhausens were trying to achieve at Harrad; a world where
men and women can and must relate their sexual drives and
needs for one another into a unified whole so that the act of sex
is a perfectly wonderful consummation of a much larger ecstasy
and pride and joy and respect for the amazing fact that each of
us, man and woman, are human beings, and we loved because
we liked each other. Overflowingly liked each other as human
beings. Didn't Phil say one day that each individual should live
as if he personally were the God who created other individuals?
From such a perspective a man or woman could not judge; they
could only love. For each person in the world would be each
other's own creation, and be the best creation that he, acting as
God could accomplish at the moment. Maybe if there is a God,
he has created men imperfect to give them this potential . . . and
as they realize it they become God themselves.

But, of course, Tom standing there . . . disgusted at me . . .
at himself . . . didn't know what I was thinking. To him Sheila
was a mechanical hand that had done what he had been com-
pelled to do by drives momentarily beyond his control.

So . . . we didn't breakfast at Tobey's. There was no way
back. The whole thing had taken on a nasty aura. Ruth, Susan,
Bill thought I was a typical virgin bitch, and you, as my brother,
volunteered to take me back to Boston by bus. Bill drove us
glumly to the bus station. I had ruined their week-end.

But somehow, on that lonely two A.M. bus ride home, walking the empty streets of Cambridge back to our room at Harrad,
and the long wonderful night that we held each other, naked, in
your bed . . . not making love, but just feeling the warmth of each
other . . . without words, somehow we had swept away the gap
that exists between people. Ten weeks ago we were strangers,
Stanley. I'm glad that the Tenhausens found us for each other.
Can I say I love you? I don't like to use the word lightly . . . it's
beyond love. I just *like* you immensely. I even like your sideburns, and I'm sorry I teased you so much that you shaved them
higher. Only . . . only, you really wouldn't want to sleep with
Beth? Could you . . . after today?

FROM THE JOURNAL OF HARRY SCHACHT

November, the First Year

A long week-end that went by too fast. Tomorrow, classes. But my mind is not on Chemistry or Physics tonight. I have an uneasy mixed-up feeling I can't quite pin down.

For more that an hour, pretending that I have been writing in this journal, I have been watching Beth studying. Her hair is twisted with curlers. "So that you can see how disillusioning living with a girl can be," she told me grinning. She is wearing a white terry-cloth bathrobe with nothing under it. I can't help thinking how her body looks. Seeing right through the bathrobe . . . seeing her spine, curved as she hunches over her desk . . . seeing her full breasts, one unconcernedly crushed against the edge of the desk as she leans her head on her elbow and ponders the book she is studying . . . seeing the curve of her belly which is so flat when she stands up and now must be a warm ripple of flesh merging into curly pubic hairs . . . seeing her calves, soft, the muscles relaxed into two graceful mounds firm on her chair and ending in her bare knees, flexed as she impatiently jiggles her legs and digs her toes into the rug in the pursuit of answers to the problem she is working on.

In a little while she will ask me to talk with her about Chemistry or Biology, and her eyes will flash with pleasure if she has arrived at equivalent solutions, or if she hasn't we may end up in a long discussion, and I will be listening and carrying on with perfectly sensible answers with one facet of my mind, and

at the same time I'll be thinking . . . Beth, Beth, I love you . . .
the way you are . . . your flashing enthusiasm, your breathless
intensity, the warm flesh of you . . . and I am more than a little
frightened that a homely, ordinary man like me has permitted
himself such delight . . . such an overwhelming feeling of tenderness toward another person. I am very vulnerable, and that
vulnerability is predisposed toward . . . toward what?

Stanley and Sheila with Peter Longini and Valerie Latrobe
were here a little while ago, and we talked about the English
Literature course we're all taking.

Something has happened this weekend. I could sense it
with them, and earlier at dinner. Not just because it finally happened to me, but something intangible almost . . . a deeper sense
of affection. Stanley and Sheila seemed wrapped in a little cloud,
and they seemed unable to stop a sort of hand touching game
between them. While we all talked generally I got the feeling
we were all wondering on a subliminal level if we shared this
wonderful sense of involvement with each other. How hard it is
for people to communicate the feelings that make them what they
are. This has been a mating week-end. If Phil and Margaret took
a survey tomorrow, and everybody was truthful, I would bet
that there are few virgins left at Harrad.

Not that anyone said anything openly. Love is a private
experience . . . incommunicable despite the desire . . . often
the need to communicate it. But you could sense it in the various
roommates' reaction to each other. Most of the sexual flippancy
and embarrassment of the past weeks was gone . . . the bantering
. . . the teasing, suddenly seemed superfluous. They have had
coitus. They know they will again. No girl or boy (man or
woman) at Harrad can ever respond to one another quite so inde-
pendently again. As if we all had been a brand new litter of
kittens, fumbling around for weeks with our eyes closed, we
suddenly now see each other for the first time, and for some of
us, at least, the other person seems to be wearing a unique halo.

At dinner those at our table got into a discussion of premarital petting. Some sexologists in the books the Tenhausens
have assigned us to read, evidently feel that the gradual, fumbling
approaches a boy makes toward a girl, and vice versa . . . weeks

. . . months . . . years of sexual touching . . . withdrawal . . . exploration . . . even finally mutual masturbation when a relationship has proceeded to this point, is a very necessary and important prelude to marriage and that without it the male in particular, might never achieve the necessary practice to create a responsive and happy wife.

"Maybe," Dorothy Stapleton said, "but the environment of doing it . . . in a car . . . on a living room couch . . . in a motel . . . catch as catch can probably makes the average boy and girl feel guilty. Guilt, because what they are doing is against all religious codes; guilt, because society in general says one should wait . . . and mostly fear, because, no matter what the sex books say, it isn't healthy for a boy and girl to fumble at each other for years and build up repressions against doing what is natural."

"Yes, but take our situation at Harrad," Valerie Latrobe said. "Does the very nature of this environment automatically exclude romance?"

Everyone at the table smiled in gentle disagreement.

"Okay, laugh," Valerie said. "Right at this moment I get the impression that a lot of us are floating in a wonderful multicolored bubble. But how do we know that ultimately, before we are finished with Harrad, that a male and female won't just jump into bed . . . no preliminaries . . . no petting, what an ugly word! . . . and then just wham bang, with the boy maybe polite enough to wait for the girl; but that's about all. What I mean to say is: won't making sex so easy finally devalue the whole experience? Everything you read about marriage indicates that finally in the average marriage sex gets boring . . . a sort of 'oh, hell I've done this so many times attitude,' that the whole business no longer has any meaning."

"Do you feel that way now, Val?" Peter asked.

"No," Valerie murmured, and I was surprised to see her, so usually composed, blush a little.

"There is one considerable difference at Harrad," Beth said laughing. "Namely . . . we aren't married! Hence the area of possessiveness that engulfs and swamps a lot of marriage doesn't exists here. In a marriage, somebody *owns* somebody because the magic, legal, and sacred words have been said. Here, unmarried, with no claims except a genuine liking for each other, we must automatically work at retaining that *like* or love. Mostly, married people don't bother. The woman says: 'I've got a wedding ring.' The man says: 'Without me, you'd starve . . . and anyway, who'd want our kids except me?' They call marriage a tender trap; more likely it's a barbed-wire, booby trapped, No Man's Land."

"You overlook one thing, Beth," I said. "The roommate system right here is a trap. How do you get out of it? It is completely unlikely that any given set of roommates are going to arrive mutually and instantaneously at an agreement that they are unhappy or not fully adjusted to each other."

"You may be right," Beth said seriously. "The Tenhausens may ultimately find themselves acting as divorce lawyers for the student body."

I suppose it is silly, but the way Beth responded sounded like a complete refutation of the complete amazing surrender of ourselves yesterday.

"Oh, Beth . . . I am really writing this to you. So far I haven't been a very faithful "journal keeper" . . . but what happened I must write down as best I can. You may never read it. Or maybe someday years and years from now I would read it to you somewhere in another world and you would remember and smile happily as we recalled our wonderful craziness. Do you feel the same way as I do? I keep looking at you, and I want to say, "I wasn't dreaming . . . was I, Beth. Yesterday actually did happen, didn't it?"

They call a day like yesterday Indian Summer. A blue-sky placid day, soft and balmy, with the temperature climbing almost to eighty degrees. Harrad was deserted. Most of the kids had gone to football games. A gang of them were going over to "A" College stadium. They had invited Beth and me to go along. When I asked Beth why she hadn't gone with them, she said: "You didn't invite me. I didn't want to go alone."

"I'm sorry," I said. "See, I told you that I was an odd-ball. I guess I don't really like football. But I would have gone if you wanted to."

"Harry," Beth said, "I'm the cheerleader type . . . didn't you

know? Rah . . . rah . . . har . . . rah . . . Harrad! Go, Team! Go!
Dopey, if I had wanted to see a football game, I would have
twisted you around my little finger. But don't think I haven't got
ulterior motives. You and I, Harry, are going exploring!" Beth's
smile was mischievous, a blonde pixie. "See this box. In it are
two ham and cheese sandwiches . . . by tomorrow you may be
dead mixing *milchik* and *fleischik*. In this thermos bottle is some
dago red wine that cost me one dollar. See, I have all the in-
gredients and I'm proposing: 'A loaf of bread, a jug of wine' " . . .

"I'm thou," I said fervently.

"No, I am Thou," Beth said "You're Omar, the Tentmaker."

So we went exploring. Beth held my hand, and I carrried
the sandwiches and the wine. She brought a book of Dylan
Thomas' poems which she promised to read to me with my head
in her lap.

"That's the way it's done in all the romantic movies," she
said, smiling happily. "I'll bet you don't know it, but I found
a book about the first John Carnsworth. It tells of the days he
lived here in Cambridge. Somewhere in the middle of these
grounds, running right through them, is a brook. Years ago they
had a fish hatchery, Carnsworth kept it stocked for his millionaire
friends. The Tenhausens have been so busy teaching us about
love and life, they've overlooked the pastoral things."

Beth, dressed in a green skirt and white V-necked blouse,
skipped along like a six-year old, her blonde hair flying, her face
flushed with excitement. She, hastening me along a wooded path,
was a reincarnation of Rima, transplanted from a South American jungle . . . but now quite real and tangible. I measured
my ordinary pedestrian steps to her rhythm and soon I, too, was
buoyant as the leaves floating unhurriedly as they glided down
from the nearly naked maples and elms.

"Isn't this our day, Harry?" she asked me. "For a moment
we are the only two humans in the world."

And it was our day. It held us in its sunny hands and filled
our nostrils with the dry musty odor of millions of leaves, earthy
and crumbling beneath our feet. And then we found the brook,
about twenty feet across, studded with alluvial rocks and running

rapidly with clear bubbly water flowing over a mulch of soft black muck and slippery leaves.

Near the brook on a dirt road two gardeners who took care of the Harrad grounds were unloading a Ford pick-up truck piled high with leaves. They waved at us good-naturedly.

"We've found other humans," I suggested to Beth.

"Not really humans." Beth took off her shoes and paddled in the water. "Just a picturesque back-drop to the stage we are acting on."

We sat on a rock near the edge of the brook and dangled our feet in the water. The gardeners drove away in their truck and then came back with more leaves. We watched them while we ate our sandwiches and took swigs of wine from the thermos bottle.

"They must be collecting leaves from all over the grounds," I said. "Should we go somewhere else? . . . Rude practicality has invaded our dream world."

Beth shook her head. "It's Saturday afternoon. They won't work much longer." We watched several of the piles grow to more than ten feet high. "What are you going to do with them?" Beth asked one of the gardeners.

"Too dry to burn them . . . We'll compost them next week," one of them replied, wiping his brow and looking longingly at the water. "Cripes, if I were a kid I'd strip bollicky and go swimming in this little puddle," He scooped up some water and splashed it across his face.

"Come on," the other gardener said. "It's twelve-thirty. We're knocking off. You kids go to Harrad?"

We nodded.

"What kind of monkeyshines are goin' on here? I heard a rumor you kids sleep together. Is that true?" he demanded.

"Does it sound likely? " Beth asked, her eyebrows raised.

"Hells bells, with the younger generation anything is likely. I tell my son, I know you won't be good . . . but for godsake be careful."

They drove away chuckling, leaving us with the blippety sound of the water and the skeletons of the trees. I stretched out on the ground beside Beth and I looked up at the few remaining leaves wispy and brown against the clear blue sky. Beth read, in a deep throaty imitation of a Welsh voice, Thomas' *Fern Hill*, *Do not go gentle into that Good Night, Poem in October* and *In my Craft or Sullen Art* while I listened dreamily, charmed as much by her seriousness as the words of the poems.

We finished the wine, and for a long time, her back against a tree, her eyes closed, Beth said nothing. Then softly:

"Harry, I think sometimes I am a very erotic person."

"Why?" I asked.

"I get very sensuous ideas. Once in the middle of winter, I took off all my clothes and ran out in our back yard. It was snowing and blustery. Drifts four and five feet high swirled into small knife-edge mountains. The snow was soft and powdery. For a moment, though I knew I was half frozen, I felt that I wasn't me. I was snow itself, and I was whirling in a mad snow dance. Then you know what I did? I jumped and rolled in the biggest drift and rubbed the snow all over me."

"Did you catch cold?"

"My, you are practical, aren't you, Harry?"

"I would have liked to have been there," I said.

"Would you have jumped in the snow with me . . . or would you have watched?"

"I guess I am practical."

"Well, jiminy I could have used you, anyway . . . to snuggle against. Afterwards, I got into bed and shivered all night. Why did I do that, Harry?"

"I don't know. Maybe you were all tense, and it relaxed you. You seem to have a wonderful ability to just let go. Everybody has to find some form of release."

"No, I don't think so, Harry. I think it was a throwback."

"Throwback?"

"Did you ever see a dog or cat roll on the ground . . . right in the dirt?"

"Or a pig or rhinoceros in the zoo just wallow in the mud?"

"Sure. My guess is that it is a sexual response of some kind."

"Maybe masochistic?"

"Ugh . . . no! Just plain sensual. After all, man is linked to the earth. One's body crying for the earth from which it came, and an ecstasy at being re-united."

"If you'd like to roll in the mud," I said laughing, "go ahead. I'll roll with you."

"Let's play in the leaves instead. Did you ever play in the leaves when you were a kid, Harry?"

"Sure. We had leaf houses, and burrowed in them, and had leaf fights and itched for days afterwards. But they weren't our leaves. They belonged to the city. Maybe that's why I never got the urge to roll in the snow. We have no back yard, and when it snows the city cleans it off the streets within a day."

"Come on, Harry," Beth said. "Stop mourning your youth. Take off your clothes and follow me!" In seconds she stripped off her blouse, skirt, bra, and panties. Yelling with sheer joy, she plunged naked into huge piles of leaves. Tossing them about her in mad abandon, she sank deep into them and disappeared from view.

Naked myself, I followed, burrowed in after her, and grabbed her. Laughing hilariously, we tumbled and leaped and jumped, and worked our way deep into the pile, tossing leaves at each other, and in the air . . . and then we rolled together and Beth hugged me as we sank deep into the crackly pyramid. Sunlight filtered down through the leaves covering us. Beth kissed me fiercely.

"What is love?" she whispered.

"A girl, a boy, their hearts beating . . . happy with simple things like leaves and each other," I said.

"You look like Pan . . . or maybe like Bacchus. At least you're full of wine," she said. "Harry, you said a boy and girl. Not a man and woman? Love is youth? When you are fifty, and a staid old Doctor, you wouldn't roll in the leaves naked, would you? I guess not. Daddy and Mommy wouldn't . . . but I will, Harry, because I believe love is laughter, too."

I couldn't answer her. I could only see her through a film of tears that came in my eyes. Oh, Beth . . .

"Rub the leaves on my body, Harry," she sighed.

And she lay there, luxuriating, sensuous, while the leaves

crumbled in my hands and turned her white breasts and shoulders and stomach dusty brown.

"We're going to need a bath," she chuckled, rubbing leaves over me until I was as dusty as she.

"Harry," she whispered, lying back in the leaves, her legs wide apart. "I am a very devious person. I practiced with that diaphragm this morning. It's kind of god-awful . . . but . . ."

"But what?"

"I left it in."

"I never did it before, Beth," I said.

"According to everything I have read in the books, you are ready enough." She grinned at me and carefully picked the leaves off my penis. "Please, Harry. We've waited long enough."

She shuddered and raked my back with her fingernails. "Harry . . . Harry . . . hold me . . . I'm afraid . . . I'm afraid . . ." she whimpered, and then with a banshee wail she clasped her legs around me, rocked me fiercely, kissing me and sobbing while I kissed her dusty face and breasts and held her so hard that her poor body must ache even now. We lay together for a long time in our leafy womb, and I could feel the soft undulating movement of her vagina keeping me happily within her.

"Was that love, Harry?" she asked.

"Yes . . . and this whole day, and yesterday and tomorrow is love, too."

She gave me one million two hundred and thirty-nine thousand little kisses, and then, laughing and screaming at the cold chill of the brook water, we washed the dirt and powdered leaves off each other, and dried ourselves as best we could with my shorts and her panties.

And then last night she slept in her own bed; and today she has been very serious and subdued. When I said: "I love you, Beth," she smiled affectionately, but she didn't say: "I love you, too, Harry."

Oh, Beth . . . why am I afraid to just ask you what you are thinking?

FROM THE JOURNAL OF BETH HILLYER

November and December, the First Year

Suddenly it's no longer simple. Because I had intercourse with Harry, am I supposed to love him? I like him, in fact I like him very much, but I don't have an overwhelming feeling of love.

Making love in that mountain of leaves was more than just playful fun. I think I almost lost consciousness. I was no longer me. My brain lost control and I surged . . . profoundly . . . esctatically . . . much like surf gathering on an ocean shelf, cresting unbelievably high, and then pounding helplessly on the shore, cresting again and again as if the mass of water rising toward the sky would never tumble back to earth . . . and when it finally did I was swirling in a vortex, and a flood of tears unaccountably poured from my eyes. Nice. Not one orgasm, but a recurring series of orgasms . . . for a moment, two Beths . . . one helpless, a creature of emotions . . . and the other a dimly perceiving and appreciating brain.

But. Must there always be a but? I couldn't relate it to Harry. He was the instrument . . . the leaves . . . the musky day . . . the sunlight, were the exotic setting, but all the time I was really only interested in me, Beth Hillyer, whoever she is. Not once during that wild culmination did I care about Harry or what was happening to him. I was completely centered in my own emotions. It frightens me. Given the moment, the setting, the mood couldn't any man have produced the same response? I am afraid that may be true.

With Harry it was different. His awareness, even during his violent ejaculation, was mostly for me. He was afraid he might be hurting me. He was almost nauseating in his tenderness toward me, worried about the scratches the dried leaves were making on my body, later over-solicitous as he tenderly dabbed away the dirt and mud. How could I respond to tenderness when I would have welcomed a fury of passion equal to my own?

And, now, in the last few days Harry has assumed a terribly proprietary manner toward me, not in a masterful way but anxiously, worriedly. I know he expects we should sleep together practically every night.

"I love you Beth," he said last night. He got into bed beside me. I lay on my back, and he snuggled against my breast like a child, kissing it and sucking it. When I didn't respond he was unhappy. "What's the matter?" he asked, still kissing, "Are you sorry it happened?"

"No, I'm not sorry," I said. "We'll probably do it again."

"It was three days ago, Beth. I could make love to you every day."

"We aren't married," I told him. "If we do it every day it would probably get boring.

"I guess I don't understand you," Harry sighed.

"There's nothing to understand." But there was, and I knew what it was. Harry as a friend, as a room-mate, was fun . . . someone to kid with. Harry as a lover, demanding, fawning on me, expecting me to hold his head against my breast and be a baby sucking a teat again, just didn't inspire me to return his emotion. Oh, damn! I'm too confused to keep writing. What is the matter with me, anyway?

I haven't written in this journal for four weeks. The study pace at Harrad is so fast and so demanding that while we all live in a presumably titillating environment, most of us forget the sexual aspects much of the time. Harry finally stopped trying to probe into what was the matter with me. Do I know myself? We resumed our earlier friendly, bantering relationship. I like studying in our room at night with him. Harry has a wonderfully keen mind. We act as a catalyst on each other. I know that we will both finish the term with straight A's. The kids in our chemistry course have labelled us Monsieur and Madame Curie. Several students at the university have tried to date me, and look at me incredulously when I tell them I am going steady with Harry. Wouldn't they be surprised (shocked?) if they really knew!

"You mean that you are going to marry him someday?" Jon Wainstrom, who sits beside me in Honors English, asked. "Good God, your children will be swinging from trees!"

I got kind of angry at him. "Harry is just as nice looking as you, and, what's more, he doesn't have a face full of pimples."

Jon chuckled good-naturedly. "But Harry will always have an eagle's proboscis."

Another boy in Chemistry laboratory, when I refused to go out with him, said. "But Harry's a Jew. You won't marry him. Jews only marry Jews."

I wonder if that's true. Of course, I *know* it isn't true. Anyway, I don't plan to marry Harry. Why is it that every time I start to write in this damned journal I get all tangled up with my emotional reactions to Harry? I guess it is because I know that I am going to have to make a decision. Most of the roommates, so far as I can determine, are enjoying sex with each other on a more or less regular basis. I have avoided Harry ever since that day in the leaves. What should I do? What can I do?

Oh, dear . . . oh, dear God! I guess I feel more like crying than writing. I couldn't get it off my mind. After the Human Values course today I decided to talk with Margaret Tenhausen. I tried to tell her how I was reacting to Harry.

"The truth is that I don't really love him." I said. "I don't know why. I just don't."

Margaret sat behind her desk and listened while I told her about this morning.

"I was awake before Harry! I was half dozing, looking over at him in his bed and watching him sleep. Suddenly, I noticed his eyes were squeezed together tighter. His body had stiffened beneath the blankets. He jerked spasmodically, and then in a few seconds he opened his eyes and looked at me . . . unseeing at first, and then bewildered. He blushed, 'You know, I guess I've been thinking about you too much!' he said. 'I just dreamed I was making love to you, and it happened.' He got out of bed and looked at himself ruefully. His stomach and his hand were wet.

"'Oh Harry, I'm so sorry!' I couldn't hold back the tears in my eyes.

"'No need to be sorry, Beth. It happens in the best of families. Besides, it was a nice dream.' He took a shower, and at breakfast I asked him why it happened.

"'I don't know,' he shrugged. 'Man knows very little of the whys and wherefores of the human body. Maybe if we ever become doctors, the interaction of the brain on the body would be worth studying.'"

Margaret made no comment on my tearful recital. "Do you think maybe Harrad is a bad idea, Margaret? A boy and a girl living so close together and not doing anything?"

She smiled. "Harry would have seminal emissions whether you were rooming with him or not, Beth. It is a natural bodily adjustment for the male. Nature protests, perhaps, but provides the solution."

"I guess I should sleep with Harry whether I love him or not?"

"What is love, Beth?" Margaret asked. "From what you have told me and the way you have reacted I think in many ways you actually do love Harry."

"I like him." I corrected her. "Love is something else."

"What else?"

"I don't know. Something more dynamic, all-consuming. Something that makes you want to kneel down before somebody, humble yourself to him. Give yourself irrevocably."

"In other words, the way Harry feels about you?"

I looked at her puzzled. "Yes . . . but woman to man . . . not man to woman."

"I hope this happens to you, Beth," Margaret said. "I think you may react differently if you ever experience this overpowering loss of identity to another person. If it happens to you at Harrad, I hope you will tell me your feeling then."

During the two weeks before Christmas vacations, I slept with Harry five different nights. Harry was delighted. Wonderfully gentle, deeply possessive, hungrily oral as he fell asleep on

my breast. And all I learned is that I am a terribly passionate
woman. I scare myself. Each night was a repetition of the fury
of our introduction in our mountain of leaves. But while I was
an explosive, sexually wracked body enjoying the demon Beth's
violent coupling, a part of my brain stood aside and watched. I
was, unhappily, not in love. My God . . . what is love?

Sometimes I wonder whether I am fully responsible for
what happened or whether Sheila Grove was purposely testing
Stanley. A week before Christmas vacation she offered Stanley
her Buick for the Holidays. He could drive it to his home in
Detroit if he wished. Sheila wasn't going to use the car since her
father had invited her to fly down to Palm Beach for Christmas
and New Year's. To Stanley, who comes from a poor family, this
was a king sized gift. He immediately planned a junket which
included driving me to Columbus, and then proceeding on to
Detroit.

As Stanley's plan grew in magnitude it finally embraced an
idea contributed by Jack Dawes, who lives across the river in
New Jersey, that as many as possible of us, meet in New York
City for a New Year's Eve blast. Harry was enthusiastic, and soon
Jack had organized twenty of us with a contribution of fifteen
dollars apiece to hire a hotel suite and provide food, liquor, and
entertainment.

We were all due back at Harrad January 5th. As many as
wished could squeeze into Sheila's car for the return trip. Those
left over could fly or take a bus. Jack made reservations at the
Hotel Astor because of its proximity to Times Square.

By this time I think Sheila was sorry that she was involved
with her father. While she couldn't promise she was determined
to try and fly back from Florida and spend New Year's Eve with
all of us. Some details of this junket would have to be glossed
over with my family, who would much prefer that Beth spend
a less merry time in Columbus, but I figured I could convince
Pops.

On a freezing cold afternoon of December 20th, after our
final classes, Stanley and I, alone, in Sheila's car, drove to the
Mass Turnpike. We were on our way to Columbus. Neither
of us had mentioned the obvious. Columbus was more than
seven hundred miles away. We were either going to drive all

night or stay overnight in a motel somewhere enroute. Stanley was singing as he drove and seemed unusually happy and gay.

"Do you think Sheila approves of this?" I asked, snuggling into a corner of the seat near the window.

"Why not?" Stanley asked. "She wanted me to use her car."

"But she didn't expect that you were going to drive me home, and then pick me up a few days after Christmas and drive back to New York City."

"You aren't saying what you really mean," Stanley grinned.

"Oh, you think not?"

"I know not. You really mean: will Sheila approve of us sleeping together?"

"What makes you think that we are going to sleep together?"

"Beth, don't be devious. You could have taken a train or flown home in half the time. Why were you so eager to drive with me?"

I was silent. It is disconcerting to have the truth served up ungarnished.

"Besides," Stanley continued, "even if we don't sleep together in the same bed, we will sleep together under the same roof, because we aren't going to drive all night. And, furthermore, to the contrary, not withstanding, and all that gleek . . . no matter what, the die is cast. Sheila will believe we slept together."

"Stanley, do you love Sheila?" I asked.

"Yes, I do." Stanley smiled at my reflection in the car mirror. "The Tenhausen theories have captured me. I love you, too, Beth. I loved you from the first night we got into that argument about American foreign policy. I thought what a wonderful thing it is that Beth is a girl . . . that her eyes flash, and for this moment we are two interacting, thinking human beings."

"You mean you like me . . . not love me."

"I love you. I couldn't love you if I didn't like you."

"You can't love two women."

"I think you can love every woman . . . every man, if you really try. I honestly believe that the Tenhausens are right. Both you and Sheila evoke a responsive chord in me. As females you make me feel male . . . protective."

"Ha . . . you have vanquished your own argument!"

"How?"

"You couldn't love a girl like Valerie Latrobe, who is quite blustery and dominant."

"I do love her." Stanley chuckled. "Aren't you confusing love with going to bed with someone?"

"I don't think you can love everybody, even the way you term it, what ever that may be. It sounds kind of lucky to me. Like the Salvation Army or Candide. Anyway, so far as going to bed goes, I don't really enjoy going to bed with Harry. I like him . . . but I don't love him. He doesn't make me feel feminine . . . only motherly. The sad fact is, I have no mother instincts. At the moment, anyway."

"Have you told Harry how you feel?"

"No. Harry and I can talk endlessly about our studies . . . but when it comes to our intimate feelings, we can't seem to communicate."

"God," Stanley sighed. "The Tenhausens are right. Man is at a low level in the art of expressing himself."

"How is it that we talk together so easily? I don't really know you the way I do Harry."

"Because I love you as a person. I'm not afraid of you so I can accept you as Beth for whatever you are or may be. Such an attitude creates a magnetic field of compulsive attraction." Stanley smiled at my look of disbelief.

"Stanley . . . you're not for real," I said. "You're too good to be true."

We arrived at Niagara Falls at eight o'clock. It was Stanley's idea of an appropriate place to spend the night together. At a Holiday Inn Stanley registered us as Mr. and Mrs. Cole, and with great enthusiasm insisted in carrying me across the threshold of our room.

"This is nutty," I giggled as he tumbled me on one of the beds. "We're not married."

"We might be," he grinned, and tossed a pillow at me.

I flung it back, and for ten minutes we engaged in a free-for-all pillow fight which left the room in shambles and me stretched out on the bed, weak with laughter and lack of breath.

"Come on," Stanley said, puffing while he undressed. "We'll take a shower together and then eat. I saw a candle-lighted dining room as we drove in."

In the bathroom he horsed around in the shower. Dripping wet, we covered each other with soap from head to foot, then walked around the room admiring ourselves in the mirrors. Stanley took great delight in soaping my breasts and pubic hairs and behind. I responded by thoroughly soaping his penis until he pleaded "uncle." Then we let the needle spray shower restore our equilibrium.

Rubbing my back with a towel, Stanley kissed me between the shoulders and whispered, "You are very beautiful Beth . . . and fun."

At dinner, while slowly drinking a bottle of red wine we ate veal parmesan. I asked Stanley how he resisted making love to me before we ate. "I was ready," I said softly. "So were you."

"I'm making love to you now, "Stanley said happily. "Just talking with you, feeling that glow that emanates from you is an exhilarating experience."

"It is for me, too," I said. "I know what you're trying to say. How can we sustain this moment? If we lose it, how can we make it come again?"

"Did you read Maslow's book, *Motivation and Personality?* Remember when he talks about *peak experiences.* The last hour with you, Beth, has been like that . . . an experience of sheer wonder at the loveliness of you as Beth a physical person, and you as an ineffable mystery . . . a mystery that even now makes your eyes glow and trembles on your lips. I think I could recapture this feeling with you thousands of times . . . even though I knew you a lifetime."

"Have you had the same feeling with Sheila?"

"Yes." Stanley noticed that I seemed more subdued. "Beth, it doesn't lessen the moment with you, it heightens it. I'm becoming gradually aware that such a feeling as Maslow describes is not wholly mystical. I think it can be recaptured at will. It means simply developing a willingness to respond to all the infinite mystery of life and do it from a perspective of joyous humility at just being alive and able to participate."

"To see the world in a grain of sand, and heaven in a wild flower," I said, grinning. "William Blake said it . . . the Tenhausens are saying it. Will the world itself ever listen?"

"Are you?"

"Yes, I think so, Stanley. Anyway, right or wrong it is a positive philosophy. It is better than the apathy that seems to have most of our generation in its grip. I read an article yesterday that said dissent has largely vanished from America . . . that the average American is in an emotional vacuum with an overwhelming feeling of uselessness engulfing everybody. Everyone is demanding something worthwhile from the world and can't seem to discover it. Maybe Harrad College will succeed in ushering in the Age of Positive Dissent."

"It's dissent, all right," Stanley said, "but it is going to take some awfully good minds to encompass it . . . believe in it . . . and make it work in a general way. For example, would you be able to explain Harrad up until now . . . or tonight, to your father and mother?"

"No. Would you?"

"Absolutely not!"

Back in the room as I was undressing, I told Stanley I was expecting my period. "I've got twinges already . . . so I may be an uncomfortable mess by tomorrow."

"Should we make love?"

"It's not that," I said. "You know the Harrad rule . . . no more than one boy a month. I've been with Harry this month."

Stanley smiled. "I guess Phil overlooked the fact that proper timing would make it possible for a girl to negotiate two men in a month without risk of pregnancy."

"I doubt that most of the girls would be interested. Anyway, in most cases events wouldn't coincide to make it possible."

We lay on the bed, naked, and watched television for awhile. I held Stanley's hand and nibbled his finger-tips; and then we didn't hear the television, though it continued to play; and the light it made danced on the ceiling, and when our ecstacy was over Stanley laid himself half across me, his face against my breast. I suddenly felt very tender toward him, and caressed his back softly while he dozed. For awhile I wasn't sure whether I held Stanley or Harry. Did it really matter? I guess that somehow or other I loved them both . . . and I . . . me . . . whoever Beth was, was destined to be the archetypal mother to her men.

FROM THE JOURNAL OF STANLEY COLE

January, the First Year

Recapitulation is in order. I haven't written in this journal
for more than a month . . . and small wonder. Events have moved
faster than Stanley Cole, the historian, could record them.
Historian. That's me all right. Historian of my own demise . . .
the man who wrote his own obituary.

As the moment, according to Phil, I simply lack perspective.
Someday, through the soft mists of time, I will be able to look
back and laugh at Stanley Cole's miseries. Maybe. But I doubt it.

I'm writing this as though I am bursting with laughter . . .
the truth is that I am punctured, deflated, with the last hiss of
despair emerging from the balloon that was Stanley Cole. In
the chessboard that is Harrad I have been put in check not by one
queen but by two. Check and mate! All my queens have vanished.
I have a new roommate . . . Harry Schacht! Some difference! Beth
has moved in with Jack Dawes, and Sheila is living alone. In
fact, right after the Holidays I would guess that about twenty-five
percent of the Tenhausen's house of cards went through an internal reshuffle. This probably taxed the Tenhausen's patience
to the breaking point, and must have made them think the
whole structure was in danger of collapse.

How did it all happen? I'm not sure I know, myself. I suppose it stems back to me, blithely accepting Sheila's car for the
Holidays. But that's only the surface factor. Eventually I would
have slept with Beth, somehow. Anyway, I am firmly of the

opinion that Sheila was guilty of testing me. Did she really expect me to act like some kind of mediaeval hero and sleep beside Beth encased in steel armor? The simple truth of the matter is that Sheila is jealous. Unnecessarily, of course.

"Not particularly of you," she told me very coolly. "I just can't adjust to the idea of sharing *any* man I might love with another woman. I might have loved you very much, Stanley . . . but my love is possessive. I discussed it with Margaret and Phil, and they finally suggested that I live alone, for awhile, at least."

"Why don't you let Harry Schacht move in here?" I suggested. "He needs solace from his wounds."

"I'm not going to make a career of mending hearts that Beth Hillyer has broken," Sheila said stiffly. "Thank you just the same."

"My heart is not broken," I grinned at her. "I love you, too, Sheila."

"Ugh!" she said.

So . . . I'm not sorry. I slept with Beth twice. Once in Niagara Falls, my own very good idea (and of course Beth *had* to tell Sheila), and once in New York City, in the Astor Hotel, which was undeniable, anyway, because Sheila found us in bed together.

Just in case I ever become your roommate again, Sheila Grove, and you get the idea that you should read my journal, I'll tell you right here and now that I am not mad at Beth, and I love her. Beth is confused. She is determined to find the ideal man, and then, very practically when that has been "taken care of," get on with equally valuable parts of her life . . . such as being a doctor. Beth is very practical . . . except in bed, and there her body takes over and Beth is a feverish, passionate woman; and not all subdued like you, Sheila. Where you surrender, Beth wants to be conquered. My own male reaction is that you both need a little of each other. But why am I bothering to write you words you will probably never read? If you do, they'll no doubt make you even more angry. But I would do it all over again. Even if it were a foregone conclusion that I would end up living with Harry Schacht!

Christmas was sticky. Arriving home with Sheila's car convinced Ma that I wasn't really going to college in Cambridge, that I must have fallen in with cheap gangsters. When she occasionally dropped the subject, it gave my old man (who has a vague idea of what is going on at Harrad) an opportunity to try to discover if I really had a female roommate and if I had slept with her. I told him the whole business was strictly chaperoned and I really wasn't nearer to going to bed with a girl than I had been with Joan Austin.

This pleased him. He admitted that a young man couldn't avoid chasing "skirts." God made him that way, and all that, but that I should keep in mind that the chase was more fun than the capture.

My sisters invited me to a Polish Christmas dance with their husbands, and I spent one god-awful night dancing polkas with a big-breasted, high school senior who was overly impressed at dancing with a boy who went to college. Breathlessly, she introduced me to her father and mother, and I could see a picture of me marching down the aisle in all their eyes.

On December 29th I drove back to Columbus and stayed overnight at Beth's house. Beth's family is very nice, but her mother and father are in complete disagreement over Harrad. I was subjected to a third degree and was glad that I wasn't Beth's roommate. I think I would have been embarrassed to discuss the fact that I was sleeping with their daughter, which from their standpoint I wasn't, but, of course, I actually had and was planning to do again.

Beth's mother believes the entire Harrad program is quite impossible . . . that her daughter is certain to regret it . . . that they have a family understanding that no one in Columbus nor anyone outside the family will ever know about it . . . that Beth is a headstrong girl, too much indoctrinated with modern ideas of feminine achievement . . . that Beth's father is much too easy with her . . . that all modern parents are letting their children dominate the family, which is decidedly wrong, etc., etc., and what did I think about it? Beth's father listened quietly to all the discussion, a little smile on his face. I have the feeling that he really isn't so much dominated by Beth, but he has a great deal of confidence in her. Anyway a lot of things were left unmentioned in detail such as the fact that Beth's roommate is Jewish. To them, insulated Mid-Westerners that they are, this was somewhat surprising. Oh well, they would be even more surprised if they read the details that follow.

After much hugging, and various admonitions and restatements of the fact that they loved her very much, and to please be careful driving, Beth and I finally left Columbus about three o'clock in the afternoon on December 30th. I suggested to Beth that we could stay overnight again in Niagara Falls and get to New York by noon on the 31st.

"Never go back to a place where you had fun," she advised. "You can't recapture it. Let's drive straight through to New York City and sleep in the suite at the Astor. We should be able to get there by nine or ten o'clock tomorrow, and sleep until three or four. We'll have it all to ourselves. None of the Harrad kids will show up until seven-thirty or so at night. Jack Dawes said the Astor was right in the middle of Time's Square."

It seemed like a logical idea. We split the assignment and drove right through the night and finally arrived in New York City, got the car parked, and were in the Astor, looking red-eyed and somewhat beat, by ten-thirty in the morning. A bellboy brought us to the suite and started opening connecting doors. Jack had reserved two connecting suites. Despite the fact that there were three bedrooms, two baths, and two living rooms, it was going to be a good question where ten couples were going to sleep. Beth's reaction was, "Who wants to sleep on New Year's?"

"You must be expecting a gang," the bellboy commented.

I nodded, feeling somewhat glum. I pictured a noisy all night blast . . . a lot of drinking, and tons of drunken conversation. At the moment at least, a big feather-bed with Beth, snowed in somewhere in the North Woods for several days seemed a lot more interesting.

By the time I tipped the bellboy, I had to search through the bedrooms to relocate Beth. She had pulled down the shades and was undressing.

"I'm too pooped even to shower," she sighed. "All I can see before my eyes is miles of super highway . . . like a bad dream of hell where you might enter a purgatory condemned to drive an automobile forever and ever." She plopped into bed naked. I joined her.

"I can't keep my eyes open," she said, "and I'm probably somewhat smelly."

"But you wouldn't mind being kissed," I said, kissing her belly and then her breasts. "It's been torture sitting beside you for twelve hours and not being able to touch you for fear we'd both end up highway statistics." I slowly sniffed her from head to toe. "You smell surprisingly nice to me."

"On second thought," she said sighing happily, "if we didn't waste too much time, it might calm our nerves." She rolled on top of me. "Let me be the man."

"I thought you were exhausted?"

"Don't worry, Stanley," she whispered, kissing me enthusiastically. "It will only take a minute."

Well, maybe it took three. Joyously satiated, she collapsed on top of me, pretended to snore; and then she really was asleep.

I awoke slowly . . . certain that I was dreaming. Suspended over our heads was a giant balloon. I stared at it through slit-open eyes, trying to make up my mind what strange dream I was immersed in. Beth was sprawled on her stomach, one arm across my chest. Her face was half turned on the pillow. She was softly breathing in my ear. I closed my eyes tight, convinced it was a dream, and then the balloon broke. Several tons of water cascaded down on our heads. Sputtering and yelling angrily I knew it was no dream. Almost simultaneously the room was filled with an explosion of laughter, and Beth and I, dripping wet, were surrounded by Jack Dawes, Peter Longini, Herb Snyder, Valerie Latrobe, Dottie Stapleton, Jane Atterman, Roger Wilnor, and at least a dozen others, all screaming and choking with laughter. As I wiped the water that was dripping from my hair into my eyes, I recognized Harry Schacht and Sheila Grove in the background. Valerie was doubled over with laughter.

"Look at them! They look like two half-drowned cats."

"We thought that damned condom would never break," Peter Longini said, gasping with delight. "We've been tip-toeing around this room for more than twenty minutes filling it, trying to find a good way to hang that safe full of water over your heads. If you two hadn't been sleeping under it like there's no tomorrow, you would have heard us."

"Of all the god-damned fool kid tricks," Beth yelled at him. She sat up in the bed, clutching the soaking wet blanket around her. Her wet hair was plastered against her head. Her blue eyes were wide with murderous rage. "What crazy, bastardly son-of-a-bitch thought this one up?"

"Me," Jack Dawes said, smirking. "I just wanted to prove a properly made contraceptive could hold the semen of a Gargantua. Not to change the subject, Beth, but you look as if you've been had by Stanley-the-Giant-Killer. How long have you kids been at it . . . since Christmas?"

"Five days in bed!" Roger Wilnor groaned. "Obviously a world's record. Stan . . . what will your roommate think?"

I didn't have to answer . . . Sheila standing at the foot of the bed . . . speechless. The tears in her eyes, living testimony to what Sheila thought. I saw Harry Schacht standing near the door. His face quivered a little. Then he walked out of the room. Sheila followed him.

Jack, obviously feeling the effects of several drinks, tried to yank the blanket off the bed. Beth struggled to hold it, and then gave up. We were both sitting in bed naked.

Beth jumped out of bed. "Now that you've had your nasty little fun," she snarled, "please have the decency to get the hell out of here while Stanley and I take a shower and get dressed."

Beth had more aplomb than I. Still sitting on the bed I watched all of them leave, listening to their giggling and crazy laughter. Slightly stunned, I tried to figure out what to say to Sheila . . . or Harry. We had been caught . . . how do they say it in law courts? . . . "in flagrante delicto."

Leaning dejectedly against the washstand in the bathroom, I watched Beth calmly take a shower.

"What is the matter, Stanley? Are you sorry for your sins?"

"No, I'm only sorry that Sheila thinks they are sins . . . and so, obviously, does Harry."

"I know," she said. "Three months at Harrad hasn't reversed tried and true morality . . . for them, at least."

"Has it for you?"

"Heavens, Stanley," Beth said, stepping out of the tub. "Dry my back and stop being mournful. It's New Year's Eve. We are the cynosure of Harrad's eyes. Everybody in the other room is probably clucking about it . . . We are the first promiscuous ones."

"I can still see the expression on Sheila's and Harry's face. They were shocked."

"I know," Beth said, and shrugged. "But I'm simply not worried about it. We made love. We like each other . . . quite a lot, I think. Isn't that what the Tenhausens expected would happen?"

"Will you room with Harry again?"

"No," Beth said, fastening her bra. "He wouldn't be happy with me."

"Would you room with me?"

"No, because I'm only partially amoral. You said you love Sheila. Sheila would have to love me . . ."

"It's too complicated," I said . . .

"Too impractical, you mean," she said and slapped me on the behind, "Come on, Stanley-the-Giant Killer . . . get ready. A New Year is coming up!"

FROM THE JOURNAL OF SHEILA GROVE

December, January, February and March, the First Year

Well, I did it! I made it possible for Stanley and Beth to be together. If you love a man, do you consciously test his love? Could I love Stanley so much that I wouldn't be jealous of him if he went to bed with Beth? Could he love me and even consider such a thing? Could I love Stanley and permit myself to have intercourse with Harry? No! . . . No! . . . No! . . . unless I loved Harry. Could I love both Stanley and Harry? According to the Tenhausens this is possible. But loving and having sex with two men . . . that's decidedly different. I couldn't do it . . . I don't think. Anyway, that's not really the point of my problem. It just comes down to this . . . I do love Stanley. In a hundred ways we think and feel alike about so many things. Stanley is gentle, affectionate, and a wonderfully passionate lover. I would marry him. What is love? What is marriage? A person with whom to share your loneliness? Isn't this what every human being must have . . . someone who lets the little tiny thing that is really and truly "you" out of the shadowy hiding place in your brain, and accepts this strange "you" and loves whatever this something is that makes you what you are . . . loves the mercurial "you" that maybe even sometimes you don't understand yourself? And you love him in return in the same way, though there are no words for it and it "passes understanding." Is that kind of love possible except between one man and one woman? And if you could love two men, wouldn't something be subtracted out of each relationship?

God, it's confusing. Tonight, while I was eating at the most exclusive country club in Palm Beach, dressed in a three hundred dollar evening gown, trying to smile at Gregory Caldwell, and respond to him, Beejee Grove, my third mother, by adoption (insisting in a whiskey tenor that Gregory was a good catch and his family owned just piles of Humble Oil Stock), . . . tonight, while I drank two martinis, four glasses of champagne, refused oysters and wasted a huge lobster . . . the leftovers from all our meals would have fed a family of four (and who was really happy?) . . . tonight, Stanley Kolasukas (whose family probably couldn't even afford a Christmas turkey) and Beth Hillyer are somewhere between Boston, Massachusetts and Columbus, Ohio, in my car. I wonder what they ate for dinner. I wonder what they . . . No, Damn it, Sheila, stop it . . . stop it!

Why did I come to Palm Beach, anyway? I had two choices. Mother's house, with a Christmas tree and all the kids, and Sheila feeling like a maiden aunt while she helped her step-brothers and step-sisters play with their dolls and games. Or Daddy's current winter-time house, where my newest mother, Beejee, is entertaining an endless procession of sleek friends; confiding in any male who cared to listen that sex with Daddy was hellza-poppin, and who said a man of fifty wasn't any good? Where Sam Grove got the energy she would never know . . . saying all this with a piercing look, hoping (I bet) that the listener might challenge her husband's bed prowess. During the holidays I noticed several men who seemed eager to enter this kind of Olympics, and perhaps did. Beejee is a remarkably good-looking woman, and being only thirty-seven probably has a stamina for combat that would surprise Daddy, if he knew.

"You know, Sheila," Beejee told me, "your father is a very energetic man. Unfortunately, sex for him is only a necessary incident to sandwich in between other occupations. See what I mean." She waved at Daddy, who was in the library making a long-distance phone call. "You know what he is doing? He is calling Iran. He wants to check the political situation and see whether the student uprising will spread to the Grove Oil prop-

erties. You know what he was doing twenty minutes ago? He was
in bed with me. Ten minutes before that he was on the telephone
to San Jose. Some fun!"

So, Beejee plays the field. And during the incessant round
of parties and continual drinking, I began to wonder if any sane
person would be really shocked by Harrad College. A good
portion of the (adult?) world was obviously on a sexual merry-go-
round, with everyone who was married trying to catch a new
brass ring as it whirled by. But the laughter and high spirits
seemed to have a hollow sound. It reminded me of Archibald
MacLeish's poem "Sonnet to the End of the World." I learned it
by heart at Brightwater.

> "Quite unexpectedly as Vasserot
> The armless ambidextrian was lighting
> A match between his great and second toe
> And Ralph, the lion, was engaged in biting
> The neck of Madame Sossman, while the drum
> Pointed; and Teeny was about to cough
> In, waltz-time, swinging Jocko by the thumb
> Quite unexpectedly the top blew off.
> And there, there overhead, there, there hung over
> Those thousands of white faces, those dazed faces
> There in the starless dark, the poise, the hover
> There with vast wings across the cancelled skies
> There in the sudden blackness, the black pall
> Of nothing, nothing, nothing—nothing at all!

Oh damn, damn to hell with such morbid stuff. I know . . . I
really know the answer. It was all so clean and good . . . those
weeks in November with Stanley. For him, too, I'm sure. Can we
recapture it? Can I recapture it . . . or will I build a cross out of
Beth and nail Stanley to it?

The day after Christmas I couldn't stand it any more. I
begged off a very special party aboard the Caldwell's fifty-foot
Chris Craft. I was sure Greg would find me a "good miss," anyway. I mooned around the swimming pool, thinking it would
be fun to have it all to ourselves and swim naked in it with
Stanley, and then make love lying on that rough Florida grass,
and watch the stars and the black sky through the palm fronds.

Finally I decided that wishing wasn't going to make it so, and I went to bed in the big guest room that Beejee had given me for the holidays.

To keep my mind off Stanley and Beth and sex and God knows what wormy thoughts were slightering through my brain, I turned on the late show on television. Propped up in bed I watched an old movie called *Wings of the Eagle*. Now this *was* a mistake! Here's John Wayne, portraying a man who actually lived, Frank "Spig" some-thing-or-other, who was a naval hero. John is married to a very nice woman, played by Maureen O'Hara, and they have a baby boy. Are they happy? Well, John is. He spends his time crashing up airplanes (for fun), or establishing new flying records, or mostly brawling around with the "boys." He hasn't much time for Maureen or any sissy-like stuff that a man and woman might do together. Then their baby dies. Does John put his arm around Maureen and want to be close together in their tragedy? Hell, no! He sits in the living room; holds his head in his hands and smokes a pack of cigarettes. Big strong men don't cry . . . see? Anyway John doesn't get drunk. He just tries to get cancer in one night. Next scene. Why worry? There's more babies where that one came from. Here come John and Maureen, *each* pushing a baby carriage. Each with a daughter. Obviously a few years have snuck away. But John is still itchy . . . not for Maureen. Hell, no . . . for the Navy! He is now flying around the world and hasn't been home for years. Maureen has to take her daughters to the neighborhood movie theater to see their Daddy in the newsreels. Mummy, is that man with the goggles really my Daddy? (No . . . no . . . that not my Daddy. My daddy not ugly so!) Then lo and behold! Daddy John comes home. The children don't recognize him, but Mommy does! She's sex-starved, I bet you. After years and years they finally go to bed in *twin* beds. Daddy John wakes up in the night (his first night home), Maureen is snoring in the other sack. Does he hear his darling children crying in the night? He does. Rushing out of the bedroom (the jerk has been away so long he's forgotten he's sleeping on the second floor), he tumbles down two flights of stairs and breaks his neck. Literally, no kidding!

Does this make him a better man? Do Maureen and John

come closer together? No, sir! John knows he's been a bastard. So now he'll be the big strong hero and not tie Maureen down to a poor crumb who has to stay on his stomach for ever and ever. How does he evacuate, I begin to wonder . . . stretched out like that? This bothered me so much that I lost the thread of the plot for awhile. Anyway, Maureen loves John, broken neck or broken thing-a-ma-jig. But John is adamant. She must get out of his life! She should have skipped out singing! Not Maureen. She slinks bravely down the hospital corridor, struggling to contain her tears.

After months and months on his stomach (unable to evacuate, I guess, and hence pretty constipated) John, with the help of a Navy buddy who loves him, manages to wiggle his big toe, proving that whatever brain he had was finally equal to this effort, anyway. After this singular accomplishment, John becomes a famous writer (I was getting pretty sorry I had turned on the knob that started this whole mess). John makes a fortune writing stories, movies and plays about the wonderful boys in the Navy. Does he miss Maureen, who lives alone in another city? Misty eyed and slightly bald, he occasionally looks at photographs she has sent him of herself with her daughters. Time has passed— the kids are wearing baccalaureate hats. Finally, the guy who has taught him to wiggle his big toe convinces him that he might need a wife to take care of him in his old age.

Unannounced, after what must be ten years or more, Big Daddy John calls on Maureen his hat in his hand, a bumbling, sheepish boy. He finally persuades her that "home is the sailor" or some such gush, and she figuring perhaps that since the old boy is on crutches, maybe he will stay put while she fetches his pipe and slippers. They turn on the radio. Wham! It's December 7th, 1941 . . . Pearl Harbor. Goodbye, Maureen . . . my country needs me! Our hero hobbles to Washington, offers his services, invents an ingenious plan to beat the Japs, wangles his way onto an aircraft carrier, practically wins the Pacific War and then has a heart attack. Is he dead? Sweat through the deodorant and cigarette commercial. Nope . . . Big John has three months, six months to live, who can tell? Get out your handkerchiefs, wipe your sniffly nose. Here comes John hobbling across the aircraft carrier while all the men stand at attention and the bugles play. With tears in his eyes, he salutes his "boys" and he is escalated off the carrier to a waiting destroyer . . . homeward bound. While it isn't shown in the picture, you know that Maureen will get the pleasure of burying him.

By the time this movie was over I was really depressed. Was this supposed to be the story of a good man? Obviously. The big wonderful lovable brute could destroy the lives of his wife and daughters, but he was really and truly a man . . . a hero, and isn't love a secondary pursuit, after all?

I sometimes wonder if the Tenhausens seriously believe what they are doing. Man, so amazingly ingenious at mastering his environment, creating such incredible things as automobiles, airplanes, television, computers, controlling life and even death; man dreaming of the stars and the universe, has so little interest or feeling or desire to really know and love another person. All you have to do is read the morning newspaper to know that it must be easier to invent a hydrogen bomb than to put your hand out to someone and say, "I understand . . . I sympathize . . . I love you because I am you."

My life so far has been a tryst with loneliness, an overwhelming longing to find someone to run to, to hold myself against, to find someone in the world I could surrender to, to blend myself with; not essentially in a physical sense, but in a mutual involvement that was so strong that we would come to each other willingly as naked, defenseless human beings.

Does man ever achieve this with man, or are we all so fearful with one another that even after years of living together most men and women are afraid to surrender to each other completely? I guess surrender of one's self is against all concepts of the Western World which demand self-mastery; virility beyond any man or woman's real capacity for virility. I would think people in love, in marriage, could do this with one another and yet for the most part I guess they can't. We are all little, fearing souls . . . afraid . . . afraid of what? . . . Of being scorned . . . of being laughed at. This must be the reason that there are priests, psychiatrists, and social workers in the world. Someone a person can go to and attempt to be what he really is. But for me neither

the priest nor psychiatrist nor social worker would be able to
release the springs of my being. They would be unable to be involved with me, try as they might. Unless they, too, lived and
responded to me in a defenseless way, I would know they were not
really participating but inevitably would be judges. So most
people never really have anywhere to turn.

Today and yesterday, alone here at Harrad, I have been reading *Toward a Psychology of Being*. Maslow sums it up: "Expressing one's nature . . . refers to effortless spontaneity which permits
the deepest, innermost nature to be seen in behavior. Since spontaneity is difficult, most people can be called 'human imper-
sonators,' i.e., they are trying to be what they think is human,
rather than just being what they are."

What I'm really trying to ask is why couldn't I have *really
been Sheila* New Year's Eve? I arrived in at La Guardia Airport
buoyant, happy. I was going to see Stanley again. I would be
with all the kids at Harrad, and the uneasiness of my Palm
Beach "vacation" would dissipate.

About four-thirty, I walked into the Harrad Suite. A bunch
of the kids were sitting in the living room. Bottles were stacked
on the coffee tables. Although everyone was drinking, they were
talking in whispers and their eyes were bright with excitement.
They hushed my noisy greeting. Jack Dawes, followed by Peter
Longini, Roger Wilnor, and Harry Schacht emerged from one
of the other rooms. I thought Harry had a strange, flushed expression on his face. Jack Dawes broke the embarrassed silence.

"Sheila," he whispered, "I hope you are in a good mood and
still have a sense of humor." I took off my coat and looked at
him, puzzled, "What the heck is going on . . . it looks like a
meeting of the Communist International."

"Beth and Stanley are in one of the bedrooms . . . sound
asleep. We've rigged up a surprise for them." Peter chuckled.

"It's awful," Dorothy Stapleton said, but she obviously didn't
think so. "We all got here an hour ago, and Jack discovered
them. They haven't even heard us. Jack and the boys filled a
'safe' with water and hung it over their heads. It's hanging there
like a huge bloop ready to burst any minute. It must have a
gallon of water in it."

"You mean they slept through all of this," I asked, feeling as if the pit of my stomach had sunk through the floor to the lobby.

I followed them through the connecting suite and into the bedroom. It is a wonder that I didn't burst into tears. Beth was sleeping with her arm across Stanley's chest. Stanley looked as peacefully happy as a male angel.

I didn't have time to even gasp in disgust (was it disgust? or hate? or more a feeling of terrible submission before the lash of a whip?), because the safe collapsed, and deluged the sleeping cherubs. Jack yanked the blanket off the bed, and Stanley and Beth, naked and dripping wet, awoke from their sweet dreams to a world of yelling and screaming maniacs.

I ran out of the room, followed by Harry Schacht, and finally the rest of the kinds. Was that a mistake? Maybe. Harry and I could have stayed in the bedroom with Beth and Stanley. For the rest, it was none of their business. Maybe somehow I could have spoken the rush of emotions I really felt. Stanley, I love you, I'm not really shocked. Only a little frightened to know that I have shared you . . . that maybe while you were making love with Beth you were laughing at me.

Later, back in the living room, with Harry silently drinking and Beth much too convivial with the rest of the Harrad kids, Stanley said to me: "I'm sorry if I hurt you, She."

"Why don't you just sock me in the jaw?" I asked sarcastically. "You might just as well finish the job."

Stanley looked at me sadly. "Loving isn't a game of subtraction. I love you no less."

"It isn't a game of multiplication, either. Let's not talk about it."

And we didn't . . . nor could I, no matter how much I wanted to, talk with Stanley the rest of the evening. Like Faust I let my soul go to the Devil (not for knowledge) but for pride. All I really had to do was try to talk with Stanley . . . or listen. I could tell by the expression on his face that if we were alone for a minute he would have kissed me or touched my hand and maybe somehow have made me believe that what had physically taken place between him and Beth did not automatically undermine the joy we had and still might have with each other. Although I dimly perceived that in some utopian world it might be possible for several men and women to interweave their lives so their sexual acts with several mates not only did not diminish them individually, or for each other, but actually might become a cornerstone on which an even greater arch of love and life might be erected, it was only a dim perception. So I grabbed Mephistopheles' tail and plunged into New Year's Eve. Or was it really a Walpurgis Night that began with a condom swaying from the ceiling over two lovers and ended on Hartz Mountain with Sheila nearly raped by horrible demons?

The second meeting with the Witches began when Valerie Latrobe, instead of letting the whole episode sink into oblivion, insisted (in the true Harrad tradition) on cleansing the wound in public.

Harry Schacht tried to shut her up, but her persistent probing and laughing re-hash of what had happened in the bedroom finally commanded the attention of the entire group.

"I really don't see why you are so darned shocked, Harry," she said imperturbably. "So . . . if Stanley and Beth slept together? Isn't that what you expected would happen at Harrad?"

Harry shrugged. "Drop it, Val. I don't feel like discussing it."

"It's better to discuss it than drink yourself to death. Do you think that's sensible? We are supposed to be a superior group. You are acting like television's idea of a spurned lover."

"What am I supposed to do? Jump for joy?"

"No . . . if Beth likes Stanley, find some other girl. There's Sheila. Why don't you two switch roommates?"

"Valerie," I said, "you better get off the subject. I like Harry, but I'm not providing a haven for Beth Hillyer's wounded lovers."

"What's so wrong with loving Harry and providing a haven just because he is Harry, and he's wounded?"

"You cuddle him on your breasts and pat his head," I said nastily. "If you're so concerned, why don't you invite him to room with you and Peter. You can love them both. You're big enough."

Valerie just laughed. "Boy, that's a grouping the Tenhausens haven't considered. Maybe we should try it Peter? Would you be agreeable?"

Peter looked at her sourly. "Val, you've had too much to drink."

"Damn it, Peter, I asked you a question. I am not drunk. I would never drink to excess. I like to have a clear mind. Now, I can see clearly that we don't really have a fluid situation at Harrad at all. We are stuck just as firmly as if we were going steady at some regular co-ed college. Maybe worse. We have an irrevocable commitment to the roommate we started with."

"That's the truth," Jack Dawes said enthusiastically, "I agree with you, Val. Only you are really missing the point. The Tenhausens are pussyfooting around. I think we should get this sex business right down to essentials. All this romantic stuff is just a cover-up. I don't know how the girls feel, but I'll bet there isn't a boy here wouldn't like to swive . . ." Jack paused, chuckling. "Hey, that's a good word . . . Swive every girl in this room."

"Jack, you are crude," Roger Wilnor said.

"So, I didn't say fuck! Anyway, euphemisms aside, I'll bet, despite the fact that the Tenhausens picked you as a soul-mate for June Atterman, that if Beth Hillyer took of her clothes and shook herself at you, you'd point right in the air and be ready to take her on."

"Would you, Roger?" Jane asked. I could see Beth grinning. Roger was out on a limb.

"I've seen Beth naked a hundred times in the Harrad gym," Roger said weakly.

"Sure, in the Harrad gym. But here in New York with a drink in your hand the moral climate is different. Frankly, the way I feel about it, there is only one solution, males being what they are, and maybe females for all I know, we should all just communally fornicate when-ever we feel like it. If we did that Harrad would make sense. We would get rid of sin and itchiness and be able to concentrate on learning as much as we can to survive in this unpleasant world."

"Wham! Bang! Thank you, mam!" Beth Hillyer laughed. "I don't think Jack really believes it. He's just bitter. In case you

don't know, Eleanor Rupp quit Harrad. Jack is our first
'bachelor'."

"There you are, Sheila," Valerie said triumphantly. "You
don't have to room with either Stanley or Harry. You can move
in with Jack."

"You're a nice kid," Jack put his arm around me. "But, I'm
not your type, Sheila. A few minutes ago I asked Beth if she
would room with me. She's thinking it over. Who wants to punch
me in the nose first? You, Harry? Or, you, Stanley?"

I looked at Stanley. He shook his head with a weak grin, but
he was obviously shocked. Harry, propped against a chair,
stared at the ceiling. "Beats jumping in the snow or rolling in the
mud," he said.

Beth looked at him queerly. She poured herself a drink
from one of the bottles of Scotch perched in the middle of the
floor along with an ice bucket and a wastebasket filled with ice
and cans of beer. "I'm sorry, Harry. I partially agree with Jack.
We've got four years at Harrad. Maybe we are taking it too
seriously. I know it sounds really crazy, but I love you all. It
just makes me feel warm and good that we are all here . . . talking, thinking; discussing things most people are afraid to discuss.
I can't help it if I don't feel possessive . . . and yet I do. As long
as I live, I hope I feel this way . . . just as if I could run around
this room and kiss you all, or if my arms were big enough, give
you all a big hug, I'm glad you're alive in my world." Beth looked
at me, "You don't feel that way do you, Sheila?"

I wonder what would have happened if I'd said I did . . .
or that I was so confused that I didn't know how I really felt.
Would I have saved myself a Faustian trip through New York?
Instead of trying to put my muddle of thoughts into words, I said
"No, I don't feel that way. Some things in this world are between
two people . . . and two people only."

"You sound like Eleanor Rupp." Jack Dawes fished a letter
from his pocket. "Here's some extracts from what she wrote me:
'I was brought up differently from you and the others at Harrad.
My mother and father have always let me do what I wanted to do,
but even when they agreed to let me go to Harrad they didn't
like the idea. Now I know that they were right. I guess I never

believed that a boy and girl who weren't married would actually sleep together. I know that you wanted to sleep with me, Jack. You kept telling me how all of your friends had slept with their roommates. I guess I am a puritan, but I think it is terrible. It may be all right for a girl to room with a boy and get to know him as a friend, but just to hop into bed and casually do 'it'. That's bad. If the Tenhausens believe, as they say, that marriage can come later they are wrong. What's going to happen to a Harrad girl who sleeps with her roommate or several different roommates, but who never marries any of them? What happens when she goes back home and tries to find a husband? Supposing a man who never went to Harrad finds out about her? She'd be no better than a whore in his eyes!' "

Jack crumbled the letter. "Ellie is a good kid. But the way I feel about it the Tenhausens are overdoing the love aspects, even more than Ellie. Sure, a guy wants a woman . . . but Christ almighty, he can't make a woman and all her petty little daisy plucking his whole life. Sure, a man and woman have to get married eventually. She thinks they vibrate together, maybe he does, too. Maybe, they want to have kids . . . ego glorification or something, but the girl is always pulling the petal that says "he loves me not" . . . and the guy isn't giving it a thought one way or the other because he knows that it isn't really basic. Somehow, he's got to keep them and their brood from starving. Finally, what really is the biggest force in his life is not the woman and not his children but his own big desire to be somebody . . . to succeed in the world. The Tenhausens are overlooking that we are all cogs in an economic machine, and we either find the place we mesh with the other cogs or we will strip the gears of the whole cotton picking mess and grind ourselves to pieces."

"You mean you never made love to Ellie?" Herb Snyder asked.

"Hell, no!" Jack said. "The only time I ever saw her naked was in the gym. Isn't that a laugh? I knew a dozen girls in New York who would hump just for the exercise . . . so I spend four months at Harrad, the sex college, living like a male monk."

"What's all this conversation adding up to?" Stanley asked. "So far as I can see, Harry, you and I are going to move in together and commiserate with each other. Unless some guy has quit Harrad, or unless some nice girl will welcome us for room-mates, you and I are going to live a celibate existence."

"There's only one solution," Jack said. "Once a week we should all have an orgy. Come on girls what do you say? When we arrive back here tonight we all will take off our clothes and have a New Year's Saturnalia. After a night of good clean fun, all these little worries about sex and who sleeps with whom will as-sume their normal perspective."

Jack kept returning to his idea of a rip-roaring orgy. He pictured all nineteen of us naked, running from room to room, playing swapsies all night long until we collapsed from ex-haustion.

I think you're ugly and repulsive, Jack," Dorothy shuddered. "Is that all men think of . . . just sex, and nothing else?"

"Jack is obviously suffering from frustration," Herb said. "His rutting instincts are dominating his otherwise clear mind."

"You're right," Jack said, laughing. "Seeing all the Harrad girls naked for four months, walking around with a perpetual erection, has driven me off my rocker. Won't some girl here, please take pity on me?"

"Why don't you do a hundred push-ups and sublimate your-self," Beth suggested. "Then maybe we can go out. It's New Year's Eve. What are we going to do?"

Jack flopped on his belly, pushing himself rigidly up and down, while he explained to us, puffing, that we were all invited to a private party at a night club in Greenwich Village called The Last Gurgle.

"A friend of mine, Bad Max, owns it," he gasped. "It's a tourist trap. Bad Max wears an uncombed beard, uncombed hair, and tight dungarees. Admission is ordinarily three dollars and fifty cents a head. For this you get folk singing, beat poetry, from-hunger ballets that Bad Max conceives on Sundays and Mondays when The Gurgle is closed. Ordinarily he uses his time more profitably investing his ill-gotten wealth in the stock mar-ket. Weekdays, Bad Max sneers at the tourists and tells them they are dirty capitalists."

Jack collapsed on the floor, perspiring. "You're right, Beth.

I've purged my sinful self. To hell with women." Standing up, Jack undressed down to his skin, calmly flinging his clothes around the room. "After a hot and cold shower I'll never think of pussy again!"

All nineteen of us, yelling and offering inane advice, crowded into the bathroom and watched him take a shower. To get rid of us, he turned the place into a steaming inferno. After we got him dressed, all of us noisily invaded the lobby of the hotel, until finally the manager and several bellboys escorted us into Times Square. Not knowing what to do, or how to adjust to the fact that Beth had calmly shucked off both Stanley and Harry, and with an it-serves-you-right feeling toward Stanley, I ignored his protestations and bundled into a taxi with Harry, Roger and Jane. Harry sat in the front seat, uncommunicative, while I, in back (a fifth wheel), watched Roger and Jane snuggling together, holding hands, and ignoring me.

In the small lobby of what had been a former off-Broadway playhouse, Bad Max greeted us and explained that tonight The Last Gurgle was closed to the public. Instead of muddy coffee, he was serving Gurgle punch made from one hundred-and-ninety proof alcohol. All of his Village friends had been invited. Entertainment was to be spontaneous, self inspired, and anyone who wanted the stage could have it.

Proudly, Bad Max showed us the club trademark: A bathtub drain with the final water in the tub disappearing into the sewerage with an unrestrained bloop of despair. "I'm having it revised," he said, "so that a hairy hand emerging out of the drain is clasping a naked ankle about to drag the body down, too. It's symbolic of the state of the world."

Seeing me standing alone and obviously unescorted (I had repulsed Stanley so thoroughly that he made no further overtures), Bad Max took me by the arm and forced me to reveal that I was Sheila Grove.

"You can be my girl tonight," Bad Max said, leering at me. "I'm at least twice your age, so you are safe with me. My own true love, Frankie, a very unpleasant trollop, caught me making love to Captain Bligh . . . or was it Nellie? . . . She has temporarily deserted me. Truthfully, last night she got so steamed

up at me that I took a pitcher of water off the table, and to the
delight of the tourists, heaved it at her. Several ice cubes struck
her in the face, and she entertained, unrehearsed, for ten minutes
with the most fascinating and far-out cussing I've heard since I
was Captain of a four-master rounding the Cape of Good Hope.
That was in my youth, of course. Tonight, Frankie is in bed
with pneumonia, a black eye, and pre-menstrual tension. As her
husband wearily takes her temperature she is no doubt telling
him in a wheezy voice (I'm psychic, by the way) that it all happened when she fell down skating at Rockefeller Center with two
girl friends."

By this time we were inside the club. While he talked Bad
Max had managed to feel my behind, approved the fact that I
wasn't wearing a girdle, and suggested that if I felt like doing a
strip act that he had invented a new one. "You just come on . . .
see, in a special gold evening gown. You walk upstage, light a
cigarette, and then very coolly walk back and forth smoking it.
As you walk, the music is growling. The audience is licking its
lips. You stare at the audience. Then you crush the cigarette out.
Blackout. Get it?" he asked, patting my rump. I shook my head.
He sighed. "Hell, it's symbolic. The audience stripped you while
you smoked. The dream beats the reality."

As we worked our way past the tables, greeting friends of
Max, I discovered that fresh air had disappeared forever. The
Club was lighted mostly by candles dripping into wax-covered
bottles. The cigarette smoke was thick and the whole place
seemed to be in motion, with silhouetted people weaving between
the tables or rubbing against each other on a tiny dance floor.

We finally located several empty tables in a far corner. Bad
Max led us to a huge iron-strapped barrel and invited us to join
the crowd around the spigot. He filled a coffee mug for me. It
tasted like plain grapefruit juice, but I was soon aware that it
could make me seriously dizzy in a very few minutes. In the dim
light I had lost track of most of the Harrad kids, but noted that
Beth and Jack, chaperoned by Stanley and Harry (who looked
somewhat glum), were at a table next to us.

Bad Max, proprietarily taking over, encouraged me to have
another Gurgle. Waggling his beard in my face, he demanded to

know if I believed his story of Frankie. "Of course, it isn't true," he explained. "I'm really ambi-sexual, delighting in sexual congress with both men and women. My wife, an elderly lady of sixty-four, supports me and puts up with my heinous behaviour so long as I service her regularly on Tuesday and Thursday mornings at half-past ten. Don't laugh," he said, "This schedule leaves me in shape for my own preference in belly bumping on Fridays and Saturdays.

"I'm not laughing; I'm crying." I said.

"We are all crying," murmured a hollow voice from the opposite side of the table.

In the flickering candlelight I discovered that our table companion was a sunken-eyed skeleton. A curved emaciated nose protruded over the skeleton's neatly trimmed black beard. The skeleton's face, staring at me mournfully, sucked a cigarette which grew out of the corner of its mouth. Occasionally the skeleton emitted a stream of smoke from its nostrils.

"Meet Warner Bondieu," Bad Max said. "We call him Good God for short. Good God, this is Sheila Grove."

"Grove? Grove?" Good God asked. "An interesting name. Used in the Authorized Version of the Bible as a camouflage."

"Good God is a poet," Bad Max explained. "He wears a tomb of useless knowledge between his ears."

"Max is correct," Good God said, grinning. "Let me demonstrate. Grove is the translation that was given to the Hebrew word *Asherah,* which actually means *yoni* or the female sex organ, viz: *First Kings, Chapter Fourteen, Verse Twenty Three.* I quote: "For they also built them high places and images, and groves, on every hill and under every green tree." It seems that our early forebears were happy worshippers of the sex organs. As time went by this was not considered a very elevating idea, so the translators of the Bible substituted grove for *yoni.* As you can see, re-writing history was discovered long before the Communists."

"Very enlightening," Bad Max said morosely. Cautiously, he sipped some of his own punch. "The way I feel about it, we should reinstitute this useful custom. If Miss Grove has no objection, we will begin by worshipping her pussy. Salaam!"

"In that event," Good God chuckled, "we should go the

entire way. Let me turn your companion into a sex symbol. Take *Sheilah* . . . a name of Irish origin . . . related no doubt to the *Shelah-na-gig:* a curious carving of a female exposing her genitals, found in the keystone arch of ancient Irish places of worship. An emasculating snatch obviously put there to scare the crap out of the devil."

"My middle name is Anne," I said, fascinated in spite of myself.

"From the Hebrew, *Hannah,* meaning Grace. A nice contradiction which, of course, is typical of life. Max, my brain is stimulated. I will now offer this curious assemblage of the thinking rabble a personal reading of my latest poetry."

Bad Max stood up and yelled to someone in the balcony. "Turn the green spot on the stage. We are about to be blessed by a rendition from Good God."

I can't hope to write down Good God's poem, or remember half of what it was about. It lasted at least a half hour and seemed to be a wordy diatribe against poets, artists, businessmen, politicians, sex, marriage, children and the world in general. During the last fifteen minutes, as Good God recited, a girl with long black hair hanging down below her behind, sat on the edge of the stage and emphasized his snarling words with dissonant chords struck on her guitar. Toward the end of the poem, Good God took off his shoes, then his stockings, then his T-shirt, and finally, in a gesture of despair, unbuttoned his dungarees, and continued to recite as they slipped around his ankles, leaving him a naked, swaying, green skeleton, bowing happily to the cheering spectators.

Still naked, carrying his clothes, he and his guitar-playing companion rejoined us at the table. She was introduced as Petey Love.

"Another symbolic name," Bad Max said. "She adores diminutive peters. Put your pants on, Good God, before she demonstrates."

Struggling into his tight dungarees, Good God demanded to know if anyone had written down his poem. "It's lost forever," he said, brushing the tears out of his eyes. "All my greatest work is extemporaneous. I shall never achieve such heights again!"

"It was derivative," Petey said. "You have been influenced by Allen Ginsberg's *Howl*. But never mind. You took off your clothes with more *éclat* than Allen ever did."

"Thank you, thank you, for that accolade," Good God sighed happily.

I excused myself to find the ladies room, and was followed by Petey. The only vacant stall had no doors, and worse had one of those damned female stand-up toilets. Petey watched me hoist my skirt and fumble with my panties, while I silently cursed the man who thought a woman could urinate standing better than sitting. To make matters worse, Petey watched the whole procedure with interest.

"You'll burst your bladder holding that long," she remarked.

I tried to ignore her invasion of my privacy.

"Women make the best lovers, don't you think so?" she asked.

"For men?"

"No, silly . . . for women."

I didn't wait to watch Petey. I scrambled back to the table wondering if she meant it, and feeling slightly sick. Some of the Harrad kids waved at me. Stanley and Harry had disappeared. I noticed that Beth and Jack were talking intimately. A new "act" had started on the stage. I told Bad Max I was leaving.

"Leaving? Where to? It will be midnight in two hours. Then the place will really start jumping. Besides, you don't want to leave The Last Gurgle without seeing Bad Max's bedroom. I'm going to show it to you personally at midnight." He pushed me back into my chair and pointed at the stage. "Just watch this. This is the sexiest strip act ever put on in New York City."

Reluctantly, I watched the stage while Bad Max gave me a play by play description.

"This is a modern interpretation of the story of Prometheus. I whipped it together one weekend. Tonight you'll see the uncut version. On weekdays, for the tourists, we clean it up."

Accompanied by the high squeal of a cornet and thundering bongos, two male dancers leaped into the center of the stage and were followed by lightning flashes of purple and yellow spot lights. One dancer tugged against chains that looped his body, the other, brandishing a dagger, forced him to the rear of the stage. While the bongos beat furiously, the dancer with the dagger fastened the other dancer to a red brick wall, where he weaved and struggled hopelessly against his chains.

"The one with the dagger is Hephaestus," Bad Max explained. "He is sad at being forced by Zeus to bind Prometheus to the Rock. But Zeus is adamant. Watch."

His face distorted with despair, his hands aloft, Hephaestus offered his dagger to Zeus. Evidently refused, he turned suddenly in a grand *jeté*, landing in front of Prometheus and slashing his clothes, until the writhing and twisting Prometheus was naked against the wall.

"How was that?" Bad Max breathed in my ears. "It took some doing to devise Prometheus' robes so that Hephaestus could slash them off without cutting him to pieces. The first performance, Prometheus was wiggling so damned much that Hephaestus nearly de-balled him."

In spite of myself I couldn't help staring at Prometheus. His tall, naked, muscular body, hairless except for the pubic area, fought against its chains in an agonized movement that was obviously meant to portray frustrated sexuality.

"He's a handsome brute," Bad Max sighed. "All the women want to take him to bed. But he's a man's man . . . as was Prometheus. Does the idea shock you?"

I shook my head. I wasn't shocked. I just wanted to cry.

Five girls, naked except for diaphanous skirts wound lightly around their hips and unshaved pubes, appeared *sur les pointes*, and danced mincingly around Prometheus.

"They are the daughters of Oceanus," Bad Max explained. "They are angry with Zeus, and in despair because they know that Prometheus will never be forgiven."

As they danced by him, the daughters of Oceanus lightly caressed Prometheus, who arched his pelvis in suitable reaction to their touch.

"Good thing he prefers men." Bad Max grinned at me. "How do you like the way I've sexed up Aeschylus?"

Another naked girl, wearing horns on her head and a tail suspended from behind, danced onto the stage and did a *pas de poisson* into the arms of Hephaestus. She was pursued by another male dancer, who snapped a whip at her.

"That girl is a damned good dancer," Bad Max said, clapping. "She is Io who was turned into a heifer by Hera. Hermes is pursuing her. Do you know the story?"

I nodded. "Io was loved by Zeus. Hera punished Zeus by turning Io into a heifer and forcing her to wander the world endlessly."

Hermes was now dancing menacingly around Prometheus.

"I am the originator of the nude ballet." Bad Max grinned at me. "You can readily see that the movements of the body are expressed in the entrechats, the lifts, the *pas de bourree,* are much more entrancing when seen naked—a beautiful flow of controlled flesh in motion. Now, watch! Prometheus has refused to tell Hermes the name of the person who will eventually usurp Zeus' power. Hermes indicates that for his defiance of Zeus, Prometheus must suffer interminably. Here is the *tour de force.* I have made the eagle, who will gnaw endlessly on Prometheus' liver, a woman!"

For a second all the stage lights went out. While a cornet snarled and the bongos thumped in an increasing intensity, the floodlights slowly turned the stage a misty green. A woman, naked except for black wings strapped to her arms, literally flew on stage. Floating down from above and inside the curtain, she glided toward Prometheus, her face made up like a vulture, her body held incredibly straight and rigid with only her arms moving slowly up and down. It was impossible to see how she was suspended. When she alighted on the stage, she hurled herself, naked, against the naked Prometheus. The stage slowly darkened, the bongos thundered, and the cornet wailed until the sound became supersonic.

Good God broke the trance. "You should have made the eagle a man. The end would be more Grecian and not nearly so nasty."

"Why didn't you make them both women?" Petey asked.

"Christ Almighty," Bad Max exploded. "How do you please everybody?"

I finally escaped Bad Max by telling him I wanted to talk

with some of my friends. Locating my leopard coat under a heap of fur coats in the unmonitored cloak room, and without daring to look behind me, I dashed to the street and freedom.

Signalling wildly at taxis that ignored me, I discovered Harry Schacht, quite drunk, leaning against a street light on the corner of MacDougal Street.

"Hi," he said, peering at me without recognition.

"I'm Sheila," I said. "Come on, we are going back to the Astor."

"I'm sick," Harry said. "Don't feel good."

"Well . . . not good."

"Well . . . Well . . . Down in the Well," he sang as I moved him into a taxi that finally heeded my frantic signalling.

Inside he collapsed against me, murmuring: "Beth . . . Beth. . . . I spun the *dreidl* and lost . . . lost all my candy down the well."

"Your boy friend?" the taxi driver asked.

"I guess so."

Harry slumped against me. I took off his glasses and put my arm around him. By the time we got back to the hotel he was snoring. Somehow, I piloted him through the lobby and up the elevator to our rooms. Harry ran for the bathroom, and I could hear him vomiting. I held his head over the toilet fearful that his wracking spasms would shake his frail body apart.

"Oh, Sheila . . . I'm very sorry," he moaned. "I never really drank anything in my life before except beer."

"Why did you drink tonight?"

"Because I lost the only girl in the world that was ever nice to me."

"I'm being nice to you."

"But you don't care about me."

I kissed the back of his head. "I care for you, Harry. Come on, I'll help you get into bed."

He sat on the toilet, and I washed his face and unbuttoned his shirt. Guiding him into one of the bedrooms, I pushed him into a twin bed, took off his trousers, shorts, and shoes, and after a great deal of tugging, finally got him under the covers. Then I couldn't help it. I sat beside him on the bed and sobbed.

"You crying, too?" Harry opened his eyes and stared at me.
"No. Go to sleep."

I knew I couldn't say in the motel and wait for the Harrad kids to come back. I couldn't face Stanley or Beth or any of their New Years' gaiety. I had to go. Go where? Anywhere. I wrote a note on the hotel stationery. "Stanley, I've gone to LaGuardia to take a plane back to Harrad. You can drive my car back. Take care of Harry. You owe it to him." I pinned the note to Harry's trousers, grabbed my suitcase, and ran for the hotel lobby.

It's March. It's snowing. Harry just went back to his room. "Aren't you lonesome?" he asked just before he left.

"Yes," I said, "But I'm not ready for a roommate."

I haven't been able to write in this journal since the week after New Years. Harry is the only one who knows the frightening conclusion to my New Year's Eve. Even now when I remember how terrified I was . . . so sickeningly afraid that I actually wet my pants . . . I don't like to think about it. But I know I have to write it down. If only to try and stop it from endlessly unreeling in my brain like a slow motion horror movie . . . if only to ask as I have a thousand times since; why? why? God . . . why does love escape us?

When I dashed out of the Astor, I was ruthlessly sucked into a maelstrom of screaming, yelling, laughing, cursing, drunken, whirling, twisting, world-gone-mad people, all hovering on the brink of midnight. Thousands and thousands of them, drinking from bottles, throwing streamers and confetti, cracking noisemakers, hugging, grabbing, goosing, kissing, slobbering against me as I tried to find my way to 42nd Street, and a possible taxi. It was hopeless. I was shoved deeper and deeper into the crowd in the opposite direction.

"In five minutes it will be New Year's Eve," someone screamed in my ear. A man swung me around and kissed me with wet slippery lips. Trying desperately to hold my suitcase, I couldn't fend him off. He kept kissing me, his breath heavy with whiskey and cigar smoke. I screamed, and he was dragged away with the crowd.

"Dearie, it's awful," a woman muttered. "A lot of people are going to get trampled to death before this is over."

Someone whirled me around and blew a noisemaker in my face. I stumbled back . . . was pushed forward . . . and then I tripped and fell to my knees. I could feel my nylons split under the sharp impact. Someone grabbed my suitcase. A hand clutched my armpit. Strong fingers bit through my fur coat and jerked me to my feet. Numbly, my knees aching and bleeding, I stared into the faces of three boys who had formed a wedge against the crowd.

"Hey, we found ourselves a doll," one of them yelled.

Another, brandishing a fifth of whiskey, shoved it in my face.

"You're slopping it all over her, man," the one holding my arm said. I could smell the cheap liquor on his breath. "Where's your boyfriend?"

"Would you help me get a taxi?" I begged him. His hand was still a vise on my arm. Hundreds of faces, laughing, angry, contorted, flowed by us like water pouring over a dam, never ceasing, an endless stream of grinning eyes, and mouths shouting Happy New Year.

The boys stood their ground, viciously punching at anyone who tried to push them into the swirling, undulating mass.

"I dub thee Sir Galahad." The boy holding the whiskey sprinkled some on the one who held me. "I dub thee Sir Launce-lot." He splashed some on the other boy, who angrily jabbed him in the ribs.

"Cut the crap and stop wasting that stuff."

"Don't talk to me like that. I'm King Arthur. Get on your god-damned white horses. Break a path through this stinking pile of humanity. We will rescue Lady Tit-Quim from the mad dragon-bagons."

King Arthur, who had long black sideburns, pulled me away from Sir Galahad and shoved him and Sir Launcelot into the crowd. I noticed that the back of their jackets were lettered with the word "Chasers."

"We're tit-and-pussy chasers," King Arthur said, laughing raucously as he propelled me forward.

Pushing, shoving, flaying their arms, Sir Galahad and Sir Launcelot flung themselves against the tide of people who were moving in the opposite direction. They stamped on feet, straight-armed, jammed people in the middle, and cursed them. When one man angrily refused to give ground, they lifted him by the armpits and tossed him bodily into the crowd. Ignoring the cries of hoodlums and punks that were screamed at them they finally reached the corner of 47th Street. At last we were free of the helpless revellers. I tried to thank them and asked for my suitcase.

"You won't get a cab here until the crowds thin out," King Arthur said. "We'll walk you through to 9th Avenue."

I tried to assure them that I was all right.

"We haven't finished saving you, Lady Tit-Quim," Sir Galahad said.

"Have a drink and calm down," Sir Launcelot said. "We are jolly knights of the round table." He grabbed my other arm. With Sir Galahad leading, they pushed me along 47th Street.

"Please, Please! Let me go!" I screamed.

"She's looking for a place to have a leak," Sir Launcelot explained to the curious passersby.

King Arthur held me menacingly. While Sir Launcelot and Sir Galahad stood in front of us, preventing anyone from seeing what was happening, King Arthur snapped open a long switch knife and pushed it deep into my fur coat. "If you yell like that again, I'll slit you in two from your skinny neck right down to your hairy crotch. Get the message?"

We were now quite a distance from Times Square. The few people hurrying by ignored us completely. The noise and bright lights had disappeared. Our footsteps echoed on the empty street.

"Please," I begged, paralyzed with fear as they forced me to walk faster and faster. "If you want money, take my pocket book."

"What are we going to do with her?" Sir Galahad asked.

"This looks like a rich quiff," King Arthur said. "I think we'll look into her suitcase."

"There's nothing in it, please, please . . ." I said, unable to hold back my tears, "Let me go!"

"Take her damned pocket book," Sir Launcelot said. "Let's get the hell out of here. I don't want to get tangled with the fuzz."

"There's an open-air garage across the street; we can take her there. Check it out, Chaser."

Sir Galahad ran across the street and disappeared. We waited on the corner. Helplessly I watched the automobiles speeding by us, praying they might see the terror on my face. A taxi slowed down, but Sir Launcelot waved the driver on.

In a few minutes Sir Galahad returned, puffing. "There's a stairway to the roof floor. Nobody up there. A couple of trucks is all."

When we reached the garage, Sir Galahad yanked open a metal door leading upstairs. I screamed. King Arthur shoved me inside and slapped me twice across the face. "Try that again, sister, any you've had it."

They dragged me up the stairs to the roof. I was sobbing hysterically, only dimly aware that it was freezing cold. In the background the tall buildings of Manhattan and the shimmering lights looked frigidly down on us . . . disinterested stone and glass.

Sir Galahad jumped up on the tailgate of one of the trucks. "This crate is empty. Toss her up here. Let's get out of the wind before we freeze to death."

They pushed me into the truck. Sir Galahad explored my face with a pocket flashlight. "Stop blubbering. We aren't going to kill you."

King Arthur pushed me to the back of the truck and forced me to sit on the metal floor. Slumping down beside me, he took a swallow of whiskey from the bottle Sir Launcelot handed him, and then grabbed me by the back of the neck. "Open your mouth," he hissed. Digging his fingers into my neck he pulled my head back. I finally opened my mouth. He poured the whiskey slopping it in my face, forcing me to swallow. I finally gagged.

"For Christ sake, leave her alone," Sir Launcelot said. "Let's grab her dough and get the hell out of here before we all freeze to death."

"I thought we were going to shag her," Sir Galahad said. "This looks like good stuff."

"Shut up, you fag," Sir Launcelot opened my suitcase and dumped it on the floor of the truck. Using pocket flashlights they pawed through the mess. King Arthur held up my brassieres and panties and sniffed at them. "There's nothing in the suitcase. Dump out her pocketbook."

Whistling with amazement, they counted the money. "Two hundred and thirty-two smackers. We've hit it rich."

"What kind of coat is this?" King Arthur demanded, rubbing the fur.

"It's leopard. Please, for God's sake, let me go."

He grabbed me by the arm. "How much is it worth?"

"Fifteen hundred dollars."

King Arthur started to pull my coat off.

"Let her go. We're not snatching her coat." Sir Launcelot said, pulling him away from me.

"This is a rich bitch," King Arthur snarled. "Listen, you crumb, when did you ever get so near a babe who wore a thousand buck coat?"

"Her snatch must be made of gold. "I want to stick my shaft in her little gold mine," Sir Galahad pinned my arms with one hand and tore open the top of my dress with the other. "You first, King Arthur. I'll hold her.

I kicked my legs wildly but King Arthur managed to push my dress up. He ripped at my panties. "Jesus, she's pissing herself, he said, drawing his hand away. And I was. So terrified that I no longer had control. I locked my legs together, but it was hopeless. King Arthur stuck the point of his knife against my navel. "Open your legs up wide, sister or I'll stick you." He drew the knife across my belly, increasing the pressure until I was certain that I was bleeding. Moaning, trying to writhe away from Sir Galahad who held my breast I finally opened my legs. King Arthur examined me with a flash light.

"Looks like any other tail . . . only damper," he said. "Maybe it feels different." He unzipped his pants.

"Okay," Sir Launcelot snarled. "You've had your fun. Let the kid go!" I heard the snap of a switch knife.

"You're off your rocker," King Arthur said, ignoring him. "Take a drink and watch a man knock off a piece." His penis in his hand he started to lower himself on me.

Sir Launcelot shoved him with his foot. King Arthur fell forward on me yelling angrily. He jumped up. I heard a knife swish through the air. Sir Galahad let go of me and tried to stand between them.

"Cut it out, you two! What the hell are you fighting about?"

"I told him to leave her alone," Sir Launcelot said. "Get the hell out of my way."

"You crazy bastard, I'll kill you" King Arthur snarled. He pushed Sir Galahad away and lunged at Sir Launcelot. Then he fell back, screaming in agony, clutching himself.

"You slashed me," King Arthur sobbed. "Jesus, I'm bleeding. I'm going to bleed to death."

"Why in hell did you do that?" Sir Galhad demanded. He examined King Arthur with a flashlight. "He's bleeding like a pig."

"He's a pig, all right." Sir Launcelot said grimly. "It's only a slit on his belly. He's lucky I didn't slice his prick off." Sir Launcelot grabbed me by the arm and pushed me out of the truck. "Come on, get the hell out of here before things get rough." He rushed me down the garage stairs. At the bottom of the stairwell he pushed me against the wall. I was shivering so hard that I could scarcely stand.

"Are you going to run to the cops?" he demanded.

"No! No!" I shuddered. "Just let me go. Please!"

He still held the open knife in his hand. "Aren't you going to thank me for saving you"

I really looked at him for the first time. He had a sunken, pock-marked face. Except for his eyes, which seemed sad, he was frighteningly ugly. He couldn't have been more than nineteen. Trying to stop sobbing, I shrank against the wall. An open light bulb glowed dully on the staircase landing. Frantic with fear, I was certain I was going to faint.

"Maybe you didn't care. Maybe you wanted him to do it."

"Please. I thank you. Please. Let me go."

"Are you afraid of me?"

I nodded dumbly.

"Don't you want to know why I saved you?"

To rape me yourself, I thought, but said nothing.

"I would have liked to screw you," he said. "I never had a girl. Girls wouldn't have anything to do with me. I can't help my face. But I wouldn't ever want a girl that didn't want me. Do you think a girl like you would ever make love with me?"

"Yes," I said, and my teeth were chattering. "If you were nice to her, and protected her, a girl would want to make love with you."

He stared at me for a minute, trying to determine if I meant it. "Okay, you can go. I'm sorry about your money and your clothes."

I'll never know why, but I kissed him.

"Thank you, thank you," I said, and I ran. Afraid that he might be following me, I looked back. He was just standing there. Sir Launcelot.

Somehow, I got through the lobby of the Astor without attracting attention. I looked at the clock unbelievingly. It was only twelve-thirty. Less than forty-five minutes ago I was holding Harry's head while he spewed out his stomach in the toilet. None of the Harrad kids had returned from The Last Gurgle. Harry was sleeping where I had left him.

I stared at myself in the full length door mirror. Tears were pouring down the face of the girl who looked back at me. Her hair was disheveled, her lipstick smeared, the top of her dress was ripped open, and her stockings were ravelling around her ankles. As I looked at the stranger in the mirror, the full horror and shock of what had happened struck me. I ran into the bathroom and threw up.

As I leaned over the sink, I felt a hand on my back. I screamed, and then recognized Harry's face in the mirror. He was naked . . . skinny; looking at me worriedly. I rushed into his arms and he held me while I sobbed uncontrollably.

"I'm so lost, Harry . . . so very lost. I just can't face anyone else tonight."

"We'll lock ourselves in the bedroom," Harry said softly. And we did. Harry washed my face and helped me take my dress off. Tenderly, he washed the caked blood from the scratches King Arthur's knife had left on my stomach. Shivering in his arms, crying my heart out; I told him what had happened.

"I just can't believe it, Harry. Those boys must feel some love toward *some* girl. Maybe they've even held a girl close to them, protecting her, soothing her fears, caring for her. If they've loved someone in their lives, cared for someone once, how could they deliberately hurt a stranger?"

"You haven't been reading your history lately," Harry said. "Has man made any progress in the last twenty years? Really? The Nazi and Commissar mentality is still rampant. Man's an emotional infant. When it comes to love, we are all strangers."

"I don't feel strange lying here naked with you."

Harry held me close to him. We didn't talk. Though his penis felt big against my belly, he didn't try to make love. I wondered if we would be lovers one day, and I was glad we could be quiet with each other and still be happy and secure. When the rest of the Harrad kids came back to the room and banged on the door, Harry refused to open it. "Go away," he yelled, "I feel anti-social. There's plenty of room to sleep on the floor."

No one asked where Sheila was. Perhaps no one cared.

FROM THE JOURNAL OF HARRY SCHACHT

February, March, the First Year

Four weeks ago I was determined to quit Harrad. I told Phil
Tenhausen it was the only sane thing to do. I would take a room
in Cambridge or Boston, finish out the year, and then in the fall
transfer to a regular college . . . preferably male.

"You are giving up at your first crisis," Phil said. "Somehow,
it doesn't sound like you, Harry. I thought you were a pretty
clear thinking young man."

"Not when it comes to love, Phil," I told him. "I've thought
a lot about it. I have two counts against me. I'm homely . . .
maybe ugly, and I'm Jewish. That not being sufficient, I lowered
my guard, and let myself fall in love with a WASP (White-
Anglo-Saxon-Protestant). It's not your fault there are no Jewish
girls at Harrad. I'd bet there will never be any . . . nor any
Catholic girls. The whole idea is too much in conflict with tra-
ditional beliefs and theology. Really, in a way, it's a good thing
for me that Beth didn't play me along. When I went home for
vacations I suddenly saw my family through Beth's eyes. My
mother and father are not really orthodox, but they respect our
customs. I could imagine Beth's home with a Christmas tree,
holly, a big turkey dinner, Christmas carolling . . . all the excitement that goes with Christmas, and I contrasted it with
Chanukah, and my mother lighting the candles in the menorah
for eight nights, our token gifts, and our endless procession of
relatives joining us for *latkes*. As I listened to all the excited

conversation, interspersed with Yiddish slang, and Yiddish jokes I knew that if Beth had been there she would have felt foreign . . . a *shicksa,* and while my mother and father would have tried to make her welcome, Beth would never feel a part of this life . . . anymore than I could ever be honest with myself singing *Hark the Herald Angels Sing* . . . or what have you? What I would like to know, Phil, is why? Why did you ever put Beth and I together as room-mates?"

Phil smiled. "We chose you as two potentially intelligent people who have a great deal to offer each other. We expected and hoped a switching of roommates would occur. In all probability, even the current shifts will not be final. All Harrad students are in a unique position. They have the opportunity to know and understand more than one person of the opposite sex intimately and develop emotional relationships with them that are far more mature than any similar relationships occurring in what we term a normal premarital environment. While we have suggested that the best approach to each other would be for roommates not to particularize their love; we guessed that inevitably, having been raised in a culture which believes that love between male and female must be specific excluding all others, that many of you would repeat the same role at Harrad; demanding exclusive love in return for exclusive love.

"I was never demanding of Beth," I said, angrily.

Phil chuckled. "You expected because you loved her . . . that she would love you in an identical way, didn't you? That's an extremely demanding idea. It can lead to the following conclusions. You either blame yourself, telling yourself that Beth didn't love you because you are ugly or you are Jewish or any of a host of masochistic ideas that you may dream up to whip yourself with; or you take a more positive approach and tell yourself that Beth is really not a good person because she didn't respond to your good love. The first approach will destroy your identity and probably lead to insanity, the second approach which is more typical, will ultimately bring you to the following: 'I really dislike Beth. She is promiscuous and will never love any one except herself.'

"Depending on how strongly you react, it is a simple step to move from her apparent rejection of you to your rejection of her. This makes life simple. You reduce your problems to black and white. In this case: 'I hate Beth.' All of this is extremely unrealistic thinking. You are planning to be a doctor, aren't you Harry? In our opinion many of the illnesses that you will encounter will have been triggered by this type of thinking. Hating is a self-indulgence that eventually leads to self-destruction. Where are you at the moment, Harry?"

"I guess I've already arrived at the second phase. Yesterday, Beth had the cool nerve to ask me if we could study some Chemistry problems together. Jack is planning to major in economics and he is only taking a bare minimum in sciences. So you need me after all, I thought. I may not be a smooth operator like Jack Dawes, but you are glad to pick my brains. I almost told her no; then, I agreed. We studied in her room. Jack had gone to an evening lecture at "D" University. After dinner, when I went to their room, Beth greeted me dressed in her terry cloth bathrobe. She knew that I knew she never wore anything under it.

"She was shy and formal. 'I appreciate your coming, Harry. I'm glad you aren't angry with me.'

"I tried not to look directly at her. We reviewed several chapters and solved two of the problems that were bothering her. I started to leave.

" 'Can't we just talk, Harry?" she asked.

"You must be crazy," I said angrily. "What do you think I am? Nothing but a Great Stone Face? In a few hours Jack will be here, and you'll take that damned bathrobe off. I'll be back with Stanley, imagining you making passionate love with Jack. What are you trying to do . . . drive me insane?

"Then do you know what she did? She took off the bathrobe and sat in my lap, naked, and kissed me. 'I like you, Harry,' she said, 'I always will. Take me in the bedroom and make love with me.'

"Why don't you screw a red light over your door and go into business?" I asked. "How many men do you want, anyway?"

"Beth stood up and put her bathrobe back on. 'I finished my period yesterday. If I had made love with you tonight, I

would have told Jack,' she grinned at me. 'See, I'm a good
Harrad girl. If you should get me pregnant, I wouldn't want
Jack to think he was the father. Honestly, Harry. You have no
sense of humor. Look at how grim you are. You think I'm
promiscuous. I have had sexual intercourse with three men at
Harrad, and you are one of them. From each person I've made
love with, I learned something . . . mostly that the act of sexual
congress is simply not so damned death-defying, all encompassing
serious. It is not the alpha and omega of love or marriage. It's
fun. The really wonderful thing about it is, if you come to the
act of love defenseless, willing to give yourself to another person,
and the other person shares this feeling, then for a few moments
in your life it's possible to be wholly and completely the real
you. If two people make love this way, and stop playing roles
with each other, and can enjoy and accept each other for the
frightened little people they really are . . . then sexual intercourse
becomes a way of saying 'I am for a moment no longer me. I
am you!' "

"I like that," Phil said thoughtfully. "What did you say?"

"Nothing," I went back to my room. Truthfully, for the moment I hated Beth. If I had made love with her it wouldn't have
been nice, I just wanted to conquer her. I wanted her to admit
that she was wrong . . . that she couldn't love me and Jack
and Stanley. Why did I ever fall in love with her, Phil?"

"Supposing you could have perfection?" Phil asked. "Supposing Beth reacted just exactly as you wished."

"I would love her forever."

"Wouldn't you really be loving your own reflection. Narcis-
sus gazing in the pool, enamoured with himself. You are too
smart for that Harry. You would get bored. I'm sure that if you
stay at Harrad you will find another girl. When you do . . . love
her for her uniqueness as an individual. Love her as a particular
female with all the wonderful attributes and mystery of the generalized female and human being. Stop worrying about whether
she loves you. One thing is fundamental; if you give love instead
of asking for it, if you love openly, defenselessly discarding forever
the proposition 'I'll love you if you'll love me,' which most
people live by, then you will discover a wonderful serenity in

your life. Give love, tenderness, affection, warmth, interest, be unafraid to share your fears and worries, show people that you need them, too, and you will have love in abundance."

"Sounds Christian to me," I said. "Turn the other cheek."

"It was a Jew who said it."

When I told Stanley, he said: "Harry, I think Beth has you bugged. Why didn't you make love with her? I would have. You enjoy your suffering. You're so convinced you've failed with a woman that the failure is more real to you than Beth. Yet it hasn't thrown you entirely. I've watched you studying. If Beth is affecting you so much, how can you concentrate and prepare your courses so thoroughly? Not to mention the fact that every night you go across the hall and visit with Sheila for at least an hour. On the other hand, take the sad case of Stanley Cole. Sheila doesn't find me an exciting conversationalist the way she used to. Beth will argue with me on any subject *at dinner*. Yesterday, I went skating with her. She gave me a great big hug when I laced up her skates, but she didn't invite me to study with her."

"Maybe it's deprivation," I said. "If we were going to a regular college we probably would never have made out on a regular basis with any girl. But here at Harrad we have both experienced the delights of the bed. After a wonderful idyll, it's hard to go back to the reality."

"What is reality?" Stanley asked. "If someone from some other college or university around here had been listening at the keyhole to our discussion, I wager he wouldn't consider it reality. It would sound like a pipe dream. Anyway, since both Beth and Sheila seem to have lost interest in Stanley Cole, Valerie Latrobe has decided that she might like to room with me for a month or two. Next week Peter Longini is going to move in with you."

I looked at him, astonished. "This sounds like a kid game of musical chairs. You mean to say that Peter isn't angry?"

"He suggested it. He wants to see what will happen when an irresistible force meets an immovable object. Meaning that Valerie needs a mental spanking, and I've been elected to give it to her."

"This place is getting pretty damned casual about the whole business," I said. "I wonder where it's all going to end up. It looks to me as if we are all building our future on sand. After four years at Harrad no one will really love anyone very much, and none of us will have a secure love relationship."

"I think you're wrong, Harry. I agree with the Tenhausens that a rapid shifting of sexual partners in the outside world would certainly devalue the sexual and interpersonal relationships, but here at Harrad we are very much a contained community. All of us are developing on a high intellectual plane and simultaneously being indoctrinated into a much saner view of the male and female relationship. I am much more than the Stanley Cole who arrived at Harrad seven months ago. I am me plus Beth and plus Sheila and plus all the other influences that I have absorbed as well as the courses I am studying. Not one minute that I have spent with Beth or Shelia has been casual. When we made love it was not sex for the sake of sex. It was because we liked each other and wanted to share the depth of that like in a natural release of our affections. The real joy in the act of love is when the normal human defenses are down, when role playing and posturing are gone. This is the key to everything I've learned at Harrad. Most people go through their whole lives and never learn that in the act of love the great catharsis is not the orgasm. That's too short-lived. It's the simple, blinding revelation that you and this female you care for are both small fumbling creatures needing to be loved. The world, man in aggregate and the blind forces of nature which man will never understand, are not hostile; they're rather disinterested. So the only peaceful harbor is the warm, bubbling laughter of individual man's love for each other and for his wonderful, ridiculous humanity."

"Everybody at Harrad spouts the Tenhausen gospel," I said. "I'm still provincial. How could you make love to Beth now . . . knowing she made love with me as well as Jack Dawes? That's all I would think about."

"Why not? Is she less a person? If she still retains the delight of love and doesn't become bored and casual, which she won't if she has any real intelligence, then she may actually have become more rather than less. You know, Harry, there's one amazingly beautiful thing about the act of love freely given between a man and woman who trust each other. If they understand what is happening, they're no longer just existing; each one is becoming. You are *you*, extended in the delight and confidence of the other person. It would be a wonderful world if what the male and female could learn in this interaction could be extended to embrace every human interrelationship. As Phil Tenhausen says, 'We are living in a world that sneers at idealism, or sentimentalizes it. The mission of Harrad is to make all of us practical idealists!' "

As I try to write down this conversation between me and Stanley, I suddenly realize that many of the words I put into the mouth of Stanley are really my own words, but if I read them back to Stanley, he'd accept them as his. It's interesting and somewhat frightening. Since most of us come to Harrad without any real philosophy of life, after four years most of us probably will have absorbed the Harrad philosophy. God help us if the Tenhausens are wrong and the tried (and true?) ways of society are right.

Last night after supper I walked with Sheila to her room. She seemed unusually quiet, remote and withdrawn into her own world. I noticed she'd bought a painter's easel. On it stood a strange painting of shadowy, blue-black houses with window shades drawn nearly to the bottom, revealing pale yellow lights behind them, and in the sky a moon, mostly obscured by black-edged clouds.

"I didn't know that you were an artist."

"I'm not," Sheila said. "I've been taking a course in art. We learn to appreciate by attempting to paint. It's far more enlightening than just looking at a picture. You learn how difficult it is to handle oils, or water colors, and express yourself at the same rate."

"This looks pretty good to me."

"It's neither good nor pretty. It's symbolic."

"Symbolic of what?"

"I don't know . . . loneliness."

"Well, symbolic things irk me! Why does everything in art have to be symbolic, or have hidden meanings, or be written on two planes? Why does man want to be so damned subtle and put a shroud around the world? Life itself has so much mystery that man should spend his life trying to uncover it rather than muddying it up with symbols. Why don't you and I say what we think with each other?"

Sheila smiled. "All right. Here's what I've really been thinking in the past few minutes. I have cramps. I got my period this morning. Why do I flow so much? Will Harry leave soon . . . or will I tell him I have a headache? I really have to go to the bathroom. I'm sure that the tampon isn't working. I think I better use sanitary pads for the first two days. Do I have an odor? I know I do. I really have a headache. I think I'll lie down. I feel like crying. I think I'll put a heating pad on my belly. I'd like to snuggle against Harry. Maybe his hand would feel good on my stomach."

"Hey," I said, delighted. "That's much more fun. Now that I really know what you are thinking, the way you've been acting makes more sense."

Sheila shrugged. "What I told you is only a part of what I've been thinking. No human being dares lay himself completely open to another person. You'd better go, Harry, I really feel quite messy and unconversational tonight."

"What about wanting me to snuggle against you? I'd be happy to warm your stomach."

Sheila looked at me with tears in her eyes. "When I told you that I was thinking, Harry . . . I was really thinking Stanley."

"Oh," I mumbled. "Well, I'll see you tomorrow."

A few hours later I told Stanley what Sheila said. "She's miserable. Why don't you go see her? She really wants you."

Stanley shook his head. "Harry, you have absolutely no confidence. You should have put your arm around her instead of bumbling off like a ninny."

"Oh, for God's sake, Stan. Why should I comfort her when she is thinking about you?"

Stanley laughed. "You know what would happen if I went to her? She wouldn't be happy at all. She'd start a long discussion on how I would rather be with Beth than with her. In ten minutes she'd make herself more miserable than she is."

"Brother," I said. "I just decided to hell with women. They're too complicated for me."

"What Sheila and you both need is some laughter." Stanley looked at his watch. "It's twelve-fifteen. Sheila has gone to bed. She never stays up beyond eleven-thirty. Come on. We'll both jump in bed with her stark naked. We'll tell her we've come to warm her belly. It's high time Sheila stopped being so damned exclusive."

Sheila's door was locked, but Stanley was not to be deterred from his idea. We ploughed through the snow to the maintenance shop, got a ladder, and propped it against Sheila's study window. Stanley went up first. Shushing and shirring each other, we finally eased the window open and squeezed through, into the study. Hastily undressing, we tried to orient ourselves without turning on the light. I tiptoed silently behind Stanley toward the bedroom door, and then he bumped into the easel, tripped and fell against it with an ear-shattering crash.

Sheila, in a shorty night-gown, opened the door, snapped on the lights, and stared at us unbelievingly.

"Oh, my good lord," she gasped, unable to stop laughing. "Look at the two of you! Naked as jaybirds."

"We came to warm your belly." Stanley said, trying to look dignified as he ruefully rubbed his knee.

"See," I said. "No subtlety. No symbols. No secrets."

Stanley grabbed her and pushed her into the bedroom. "Since you really can't make up your mind, get in bed. We're both going to sleep with you."

And we did! Wedged between us, Sheila finally stopped laughing and solemnly kissed us each good-night.

"Thank you, Harry. Thank you, Stanley." she said.

"For what?"

"For caring."

April, May and June, the First Year

Last night when Jack came back from the lecture at "D" University, I told him I had made love with Harry Schacht.

That's nice," was all he said. "I hope Harry is smiling again for a change."

"Aren't you jealous?" I demanded.

"Nope," Jack said. "I know you like Harry."

"It means I can't make love with you for a month."

"That's nonsense," Jack kissed my ear and then took a little bite on my neck. "You've been taking those pills religiously. How could you get pregnant? Anyway, you know the only reason that the Tenhausens set that once a month rule with one boy was really just to slow everyone down a little until they could brainwash us."

"Supposing somehow I did get pregnant?"

"I'd marry you. What else? You'd be a doctor and I'd be an economist and we'd live happily ever after."

"Supposing it were Harry's baby?"

"If you buy a cat or a dog, is it your cat or dog?"

"Sure, I guess so."

"Why?"

"Because you love it and feed it and take care of it and it loves you back."

"*Quod erat demonstrum,*" Jack laughed. "It's a wise father

that knoweth his own child, anyway. Harry and I both have brown eyes, and brown eyes are dominant."

"Do you really believe all this Tenhausen stuff?" I asked him. "Everyone here spouts it, but when the chips are down, then what? Don't you really think I'm immoral? In less than a year, I've made love with three different Harrad boys. You've only made love with me."

"I'm happy. Besides, we've got three years to go."

"Would you want to marry me even if you didn't have to?"

"Do I have to?"

"No! Damn you!"

While this conversation was going on, Jack undressed. I followed him into the bedroom and watched him get into bed. "Open the window, like a good kid," he sighed, and closed his eyes.

"I'm not a good kid," I said. "I really *didn't* make love with Harry Schacht."

Jack looked at me amused. "I could have guessed that. If you had, you wouldn't be so discursive. Really, Beth, your basic nature is that of a big, hungry, affectionate mother. You want all your boys to love you. Harry, Stanley, Jack. You want to hold us fiercely against those lovely tits of yours, pat us on the po-pos, pin on our mittens, and send us to school with tears of sheer joy in your eyes. You go around with the notion that you want a man to dominate you. You think you could be a slave to some willful man, but the few times I have tried the masterful approach on you, you act as if I'm some kind of nut. The plain and simple truth is that you need at least three men and a dozen children to absorb your overflowing affectionate nature."

I snuggled beside him in bed. "I'm really bad, aren't I?"

"No," he said, burying his face in my breasts, "I find you comforting."

The nice thing about Jack is that he doesn't take me seriously. I told him I would only be serious about studying. I was going to medical school come hell or high water, just to prove to Pops that I could do it. But I wasn't going to take anything else seriously. If I live to seventy, I have fifty years to be serious, so I'm not starting until I get at least half way.

Jack pointed out that I was serious about love. I admit it. I'm in love with Jack, Harry, and Stanley, and that's nothing to laugh about. Still, it makes me bubble with laughter. Lately, I've been falling in love with Sheila, too.

Somehow, since early in March, we all seem to have crossed the troubled waters and landed on a quiet island. It started when Harry and Sheila decided to room together. Then Valerie moved in with Stanley. That lasted four weeks. The other night at dinner Stanley told all of us at our table that he and Valerie had decided to give up the Experiment.

"We like each other better," Valerie said, grinning at him. "But we have both discovered that not everybody can room together, even if they get along in bed."

She wouldn't tell us any more, but that night Sheila, Harry, and Stanley visited with Jack and me, and we gradually pumped the story out of Stanley.

Jack and I bought a hot plate, and though it is against dormitory rules, he was making coffee, and warming up some pizzas Sheila brought from her refrigerator. Because all of our rooms are at the end of the corridor, and because we'd become more sexually involved with each other than with the rest of the Harrad kids, the six of us had got into the habit of meeting around ten o'clock to discuss the world in general and us in particular. For the past four weeks Valerie had arrived with· Stanley and joined in the discussion. Now, since Valerie had decided to room with Peter again, Stanley was alone. Dressed in a sweat suit he'd used for cross country running, and ignoring my coments that he definitely had a gymnasium odor, Stanley sprawled on the floor doing a bicycle exercise with his feet.

"My last night with this group," he said puffing.

"Just because Valerie has left you?" Jack asked.

"Sure . . . no room for a Onesie among you Twosies."

"That's silly," Sheila said. "After all, we do know each other quite well."

"Yeah," Stanley grunted as Jack handed him a wedge of pizza. "The last time I slept with you, Harry was on your other side, staring at me all night. Not conducive to romance in my book."

"What are we going to do about you?" I asked Stanley. "Ob-

viously, the Tenhausens overlooked this in their calculations . . .
one person of the opposite sex too many."

"They can even it out with the freshman class in the fall,"
Stanley chuckled. "I'm patient."

Jack suggested that Sheila and I share the problem of Stanley. He proposed Sheila and I work our way around a circle, week
by week, composed of the three of them.

"That would give Sheila the dubious pleasure of sleeping
with me every third week," Jack said, grinning at Sheila, who
looked quite shocked. "Well, you did say a minute ago that we
were all well acquainted, Sheila. I seem to be the only male who
hasn't experienced nuptial delights with all the females present."

"Why do men think that every female is different in bed?"
Sheila demanded.

"I pass," Jack said. "I am a Harrad neophyte. Ask Stanley or
Harry."

"Don't answer," Harry laughed. "Next thing, she'll want to
know qualitative differences."

Stanley chewed a second piece of pizza philosophically. "My
own opinion is that the variation in experience in bed is only
limited by the number of women in the world and the male's willingness to appreciate the infinite and subtle differences which
are not truly sexual but mental . . . hence while the physical characteristics and the physical movements may be similar, like the
notes in a scale, you can compose anything from concertos and
symphonies to low down Basin Street . . . but usually not with the
same woman."

I shrugged. "Most women seek security in love. How did the
world ever get created so that women are perfectly content all
their lives with one good man, while most men would crawl in
the sack with as many different women as possible? The best solution is for Sheila and I to room together. Then these three
males will all be equally deprived."

Though I was jesting, Sheila immediately agreed with me.
"I think that's a very good idea. Sometimes, this whole business
gets me worried. When I stop to think what I have done and
what is going on here, I can't believe it. I never thought I'd actually make love with two boys and not be married to either of

them. The idea of rotating among three men isn't nice at all. It would make me feel cheap . . . like a sexual object rather than a person."

I wondered if Sheila were right. Here were two girls and three boys, all unmarried, sitting around a room in their night clothes, drinking coffee and eating pizza. Sheila's breasts were clearly visible through her nightgown. My legs and the lord knows what else were exposed under my bathrobe. Jack was in jockey shorts. Harry wore pants but no shirt. And Stanley had calmly decided his exercise had made him so warm that he had removed the bottom of his sweat suit. Any stranger to Harrad seeing us would condemn our semi-nudity as extremely immoral. But is it immoral? After eight months of seeing boys and girls naked in the gym and in the communal showers of the dormitory, I not only don't usually give it a second thought, I simply can't conceive being naked as anything but an interesting fact of life.

Are there really any absolute standards of morality? Maybe there is one. Sheila skirted the fringe of it when she said she didn't want to be a sexual object. Once any of us in this room ceased to care deeply for each other, we would move into the category of object, not person. The moment that occurred, we would be behaving immorally. I tried to evoke this idea.

Harry agreed. "But none of us knows whether a human being is capable of maintaining a sexual relationship with several persons without having the whole business become casual and devalued."

Jack flopped on the floor beside Stanley. "Most of the early writers on love, from Ovid to Balzac to Stendhal, feel that all human love proceeds inevitably to the phase of boredom and casualness, and that even great lovers like Romeo and Juliet, or Paul and Virginia, or Heloise and Abelard, if they had entered into any long relationship, or, God forbid, marriage, the charm they would have had for each other would soon have vanished." He shook Stanley who was, lying on his back, staring at the ceiling. "Now here we have an authority who can throw some light on the subject. How come you and Valerie petered out so fast?"

"You know," Stanley said, "it's amazing. Even the students at Harrad get the surface idea that everyone here is doing nothing but climbing in the sack night and day. Yet, I'll wager that the actual amount of sexual intercourse to a climax is relatively small. Before I answer your question, Jack, tell me how many times you have had intercourse with Beth in the last two weeks?"

Jack grinned at me. I blushed. Conversations at Harrad between males and females and even nonroommates have become very matter-of-fact and blunt. But I'm still devious enough to think everybody shouldn't know everything.

"All right," I said finally. "Twice."

"How many nights did you sleep with each other?"

"Six or seven."

"There you are." Stanley said triumphantly. "In case you don't know it, here in a free sexual environment we are all functioning on a much lower quantitative sexual level than the Kinsey statistics for newly-weds." He looked at Sheila. "What about you?"

"Once," she said shyly.

"Now how in hell do you figure it?" Stanley demanded. "I roomed with Valerie two weeks and we had intercourse twice. If any of us had functioned as normal married men, we would have considered it our moral duty to 'knock it off' every other night, at the very least. Why is Harrad different?"

"We aren't married!" Sheila and I chorused.

"It's not only that," I continued. "Without realizing it most of the girls want to be very sure of love, and the security I mentioned, before they are psychologically able to surrender themselves. I think the continual hammering by the Tenhausens that our love motivations evolve on a rational basis . . . that I love Jack because he has a pimple on his behind and I know it hurts him, or that I love Stanley because he, or his gym suit, or both, need to take a shower, that I love Sheila because she is timid, that I love Harry because he looks so absent-minded and can't find his money to pay a restaurant check . . . all these new evaluations we are learning about ourselves in relation to people make everything about the sexual relationship at Harrad more mature. We are learning, early in life, to evoke what people long married may know but can't even put into words."

"It's the difference between the thrill of a roller coaster

ride," Sheila said, "and the pure joy that exists between two people when they are simultaneously reacting to experiences outside themselves in an identical way. Not that I don't enjoy the roller coaster ride, too." Sheila laughed.

"The reason that Valerie and I decided not to room together," Stanley said, "was because there never was any capitulation. Basically Valerie believes in complete equality between a man and a woman, I don't. I need a woman to protect. Valerie is completely self-sufficient. Peter is able to coexist with her. I desire interpenetration of my personality with a woman. Anyway, while we decided we could love each other as surface friends, we knew we could never work out our lives together."

"Have you found any girl who meets your qualifications?" Sheila asked.

"Yes . . . you and Beth."

"Good God," I said, "where does that leave us?"

We couldn't arrive at any solution either for Stanley or for our composite futures, but I think there is one thing we could all agree on: The five of us were developing an inter-dependency and need for each other. I have noticed, many similar groupings of friends have occurred at Harrad. We've discovered that the roommate system is greatly enhanced by multiplying our relationships on a discussion level. In this way, we share the thinking of several minds. In the process of pooling our reactions to the world, to our experiences, to our fears and hopes, we expand the horizon of our own life on a level not usually achieved by ordinary friendships.

I wonder where this is all leading us? After four years at Harrad, will the five of us, or six of us (we've obviously got to find another girl) . . . or any Harrad student who has shared this communal approach to life for four of their most formative years . . . (communal love, ugh . . . somehow I hate that expression. It's inadequate somehow) . . . will any of us be able to settle down into a strictly monogamous relationship? Could I, right now, marry Jack, move into suburbia, have children and exist as a housewife? If I finally manage to get through medical school . . . then what? Could I live life where I practiced medicine and lived like Pops in a world of Doctors who know little else but their specialities and the patients they practiced them on? No. I'd want somebody around me like Sheila or Stanley, who'd enrich my world with their very different worlds. If I married Jack, I'm not sure I wouldn't want to go to bed with Stanley or Harry. Where does *that* leave us, Phillip Tenhausen?

I haven't really led a sane life since I moved in with Jack Dawes. He plays the guitar and sings his Economics homework in crazy rhyming songs I listen to in spite of myself. Jack believes he has been endlessly reincarnated and occasionally slips into complete historical and cultural dissertations on the world circa 500 B.C., or during the Middle Ages, when he claims he was reborn again, as well the specific year, 1778, when he claims that he was eighteen years old and a soldier in the Revolutionary War. He dates his next rebirth sometime in the twenty-fourth century; and if I'm around, he promises to say hello to me. He is a faddist, plunging into the study of things, like Astronomy, Religion, Witchcraft and Alchemy, and then after littering the room with books and talking incessantly on the ideas these pursuits have generated, he drops the whole subject and moves on to something else.

One thing about Jack: he is never dull. The moments when I'm not trying to reform him and make him come down to earth, I suddenly realize he is making me wonder who I am. Which of the Beths I show the world is the real Beth? Is it possible for anyone to be completely whole and honest with any one single person in the world?

I, Beth, certainly am not really me so far as my mother and father are concerned. I am their daughter. I look like a composite them. In many ways I can share my overt thoughts with them. I want to be a doctor. So when I talk about medicine I can talk with Pops. I suppose that I will be a wife and mother one day. So I can talk homemaking, children, and cooking with Mother. I can also talk about music with Mother because she is responsible for my taking violin lessons. Mother plays the viola well and belongs to a group that meet once a mouth and play chamber music all night. Pops not only finds chamber music exceedingly boring, he refuses to make any attempt to understand it. Any discussion

of his musical deficiencies ends up with him proudly explaining
that he has a "tin ear".

To Pops, I am Beth who loves medicine. To Mother I am
Beth who loves music. To neither of them am I Beth who likes
to go to bed with a boy. Beth who likes to have a man's hands
and lips touch and kiss her breasts and her genitals.

One night a few weeks ago when Jack was gently kissing me
between my legs and I was kissing his penis, I started to laugh
and couldn't stop until I almost had hiccoughs. When I asked
Jack what his mother would think that after almost twenty years
he had his head between another woman's legs he began to laugh,
too. We nearly forgot to make love.

So, to neither Mother or Pops is Beth a sexy woman. Nor can
she ever tell them she is. From Pop's standpoint, if Beth ever has
a child, I am sure, despite all his familiarity with the necessary
methods of impregnation, Pops will consider one more immacu-
late conception has occurred.

Will Harry Schacht ever know the complete Beth? Yes, on
the score of interest in medicine and music. Never, of course, the
multiple Beth that could make love with him as well as Stanley
Cole and Jack Dawes. Each man I have known releases a different
Beth. I have never really been able to be my giddy, zany self with
Harry. I just couldn't be silly or pout or tease him, because Harry
would be bewildered. If we were in the act of intercourse and he
was having a wonderful metaphysical rapport with me, and I,
too, should have been having other-worldly thoughts, and then if
he would ask me what I was thinking, instead of replying some
heavenly nonsense such as: "I am ecstatically floating on a cloud
of love" . . . if I dared reply: "I was wondering if I should put
my hair in curlers," or, "I really love you, Harry . . . but right
now you are crushing my left breast beyond recognition" . . .
Would Harry have laughed, or thought it kind of funny? No.
Harry has a very tender ego. It can't stand laughter. When it is
laughed at, it runs away and weeks are needed to coax it out of
hiding.

What about Stanley? Stanley would soon know Beth, the sex-
pot, inside out. In fact Stanley, as a lover, would leave no nook or
cranny of Beth unexplored. Stanley's ego is tougher than Harry's,

so he can laugh at himself a little, too. Not so much as Jack Dawes, because Stanley is essentially the poor boy who has licked his environment but always feels the danger of the past reaching out and clutching him back. He is a man who, even if he becomes wealthy, will always live his life as if one foot is caught in the quicksand of poverty. Would Stanley ever know the Beth who loves medicine? Would either of us ever thoroughly understand the other's drives? We might live together fifty years, make love regularly, have children, and still neither of us be able to reveal fully the deep-down inside person of ourselves that makes us really tick. So while Stanley would know the Beth who was a hungry sexual animal, he would never know many aspects of the Beth that could really unite us; two separate people.

What about Jack? Jack is a year older than me, but that doesn't give him any right to treat me like a wayward child. Yet, I always have the feeling with Jack that I am a little girl. Sometimes I am a bad little girl and I yell and scream at him, but he doesn't yell back. Jack works on the principle that you simply can't get mad at bad little girls. You just scoop them up in your arms, open their bathrobes, or pull up their dresses, and kiss them very thoroughly from head to foot. If they beat you with their hands and legs, and nearly scratch you to bits while this is going on, well, this is just one of the hazards of dealing with naughty little girls; you just chuckle or sing little songs, such as "Sing halle-lujah, hallelujah, put a nickle in the pail, get another piece of tail," or "Ball of yarn, ball of yarn, it was then I spun her little ball of yarn," or "ay, ay, yi ay, in China they do it for Chili" . . . and pretty soon the bad little girl is a laughing, co-operating little girl.

Does it all mean everyone in life is doomed to be one-dimensional to everybody else? Margaret Tenhausen told me this wasn't really the problem. The important goal and what most people failed to achieve is understanding *ourselves* in three-dimensions.

I asked her what she meant.

She said: "When the spiritual, mental, and physical Beth is unified and you are cognitively aware of your real self, all the many Beths you now perceive will vanish, and you won't be one-dimensional, to yourself at least."

Since April, Harry, Sheila, Stanley, Jack, and I have spent Saturday nights together. We usually go to Boston and eat in Chinatown, or poke around Hanover Street and eat in some Italian restaurant. Last Saturday we had tickets for *Who's Afraid of Virginia Woolf?* which was being rerun at the Charles Playhouse. We ate in Omonoia, a small Greek restaurant, which Jack had discovered in a very dreary part of Boston. Upstairs we were in another world, enjoying the resin-flavored Greek wine, shish kebab, bakalava, and Greek coffee, all served to a background accompaniment of Greek folk music. We drank two bottles of Pendelli, and to me everybody seemed bathed in a soft halo. I was in my usual I-love-everybody mood when Stanley spoiled it by announcing he wasn't going to sweat through Albee's play. He'd read it and listened to it on the original cast recording. To him it was sickening.

"It presents a very good case for never getting married," he said. "Two very stupid people who are presumably representative of the typical college faculty, and by definition middle class America, hate each other out loud for about two and a half hours, and then have a drunken catharsis as a result of shock because they nearly slept with each other's spouses." Stanley grinned. "Phil Tenhausen should use it as a good example of the moral bankruptcy of Western society. A sick country that exalts a sick playwright. Anyhow, tonight I feel like going exploring."

"Exploring?" Jack asked. "Where . . . for what?"

"For a woman," Stanley said coolly. "What else? I've been celibate for nearly eight weeks. Do you think I'm made of stone?"

"You mean you'd just go to bed with anyone?" Sheila asked.

This started a discussion in which Stanley demanded to know why should he be so angelic and other worldly as to not want sexual relations. He asked Sheila if she would sleep with him, and when she didn't answer, he asked Harry if he would loan Sheila to him.

"I don't think you are very nice," Sheila said stiffly.

Stanley just shrugged. "There's any number of people who wouldn't think you or anybody at Harrad was very nice but wouldn't give a second thought about a college boy on a fling about town. What I propose to do is the accepted morality. What you and everybody at Harrad is doing is downright illegal and immoral."

We knew Stanley was trying to aggravate us, and since we couldn't dissuade him, we finally persuaded him to meet us in the lobby of the Hotel Bradford around eleven-thirty, after the play.

I like the Charles Playhouse and its three-quarter stage. Jack bought another bottle of Greek wine, which we drank between the acts in paper cups. Maybe it was because I was in a pleasant state of alcoholic euphoria, but I enjoyed the play. If you don't take Albee literally, but simply respond to the laughter of an unhappy man and woman excoriating each other, and then watch the surface hatred get out of control and move toward tragedy, it is an interesting experience. Judged from the Harrad viewpoint the whole play is unnecessary. But one thing even the Tenhausens fail to emphasize enough is: Harrad isn't the world . . . yet. We must live our lives with one foot in Utopia and one foot in reality.

We waited in the Bradford until a quarter of twelve, me defending Albee against Jack, Sheila, and Harry, while we waited for Stanley. We were about to give up. Jack had us convinced that Stanley was probably in bed with some whore, when Stanley walked in looking slightly wan and uncommunicative.

Jack grinned at him. "As my old man used to say, did you get your ashes hauled?"

"Let's not be crude," Stanley said. He refused to discuss what had happened to him. "I drank five bourbon and sodas and I'm as drunk as a Kentucky Colonel."

Back at Harrad, I asked Jack if he'd mind if I went to Stanley's room and talked with him.

"Mother Beth is worried about her little boy," he said, smiling at me.

"Stanley was kind of moody on the way home," I said as I undressed and put on my bathrobe. "I think he needs a good listener, someone to talk with."

"You mean to sleep with, don't you?"

"Are you jealous?"

"No. I don't own you."

"Do you want to own me?"

"In a sense, I believe I do own you, Beth. I'm beginning to believe the die is cast, and somehow, you, Stanley, Sheila, Harry and I will always be involved with each other. In that sense, I think we have made a commitment deeper than ownership."

"You *are* serious tonight, aren't you?"

He kissed my cheek. "Go see what's eating Stanley. If you don't come back tonight, I won't be angry."

I found Stanley sitting at his desk, naked, writing in his journal.

"Maybe I should have locked my door," he said disagreeably. "Good God, nobody has any privacy here. Suppose you walked in without knocking and found me masturbating . . . or something?"

"Are you trying to shock me?"

"Sure . . . why not? I have masturbated on occasion."

"If I had found you so occupied, I would have helped you."

"Happy days! You can start now!"

"Not until I find out what happened to you."

Stanley closed his journal. "I was going to write it down, but knowing you I might just as well give up and tell you. Only, there's a catch. If you want to find out what happened, you'll have to sleep with me." He stood up and grinned at me.

"My . . . you are quite excited for a man who only an hour ago . . . what did Jack say . . . 'had his ashes hauled'."

"Would you make love with me anyway?" Stanley asked.

"Not until you had scalded your jamoke. Do you think I want to get diseased?"

"Let's stop kidding," Stanley said. "After a year at Harrad I have discovered that I make love with my brain, not my penis. I spent an impotent evening. The title of the play I saw was: *Who's Afraid of Vapid Vulvas?* . . . and the answer is me: Stanley Cole."

"All right," I said, taking off my bathrobe. "Let's get into your bed while we talk."

I waited while he kissed my eyes, and lips, and nose, and breasts. I kissed him back gently.

Finally, he said, "You know, Beth, it's a God-awful sad and futile world. I found this joint I had heard about. It was filled with men lined up against a long bar, or sitting at tables around it. Behind the bar a continuous procession of girls were going through the motions of stripping . . . ending up with their breasts in nets and their mounds covered with triangles of rhinestones. They shook and gyrated dispassionately for a while, and eventually were followed by another girl who went through the same routine. Those poor sad men, drinking and staring, have no other way of seeing a girl naked. They probably have to make love to their wives in the dark. If they are married, their wives are the only women, from their wedding day on, they are supposed to get close to, or touch. Each one of these strip "acts" had three phases of teasing, and lasted at least a half hour before this boring denouement was achieved. During the acts and between them, the girls, fully dressed, sold cigarettes and propositioned the men. The price: twenty-dollars for one hour."

"Finally, after four bourbons, I decided that I, Stanley Cole the sociologist, would invest twenty dollars to discover the whys, whats, and wherefores. I picked a pretty brown-eyed woman about thirty years old. She had just finished her act. She was quite well-shaped.

"You were thinking a lot more than the whys and wherefores, Stanley Cole," I said, interrupting him. "You mean you would have actually resisted a pretty woman who offered herself to you? I don't believe it."

Stanley shook his head. "No girl offers herself without conditions to a stranger, so the question answers itself. The conditions make it possible to resist. Anyway, I followed her around the back of the bar into a kitchen of the joint, and then down a flight of stairs and through a passageway that led into the next building. In the basement, next to the garbage and trash cans, was a service elevator that she explained would take us to her room in the hotel which was next door to the barroom. We got off at the eighth floor. I followed her down a hall that smelled of centuries of sweat and dirty underwear to a room which she unlocked and carefully relocked when we were inside.

" 'Okay,' she said. 'Twenty-dollars . . . in advance.'

" I paid her and sat on the edge of the bed, which had been

stripped to a mattress and a sheet. In about two movements she
was stripped naked and tried to shove her bush in my face.

" 'No tit squeezing or sucking,' she said, making the rules. 'I
don't trust you college kids. You think they're made of rubber.
Here's a safe. Put it on.' She lay on the bed with her legs open.

" 'I want to talk awhile,' I said.

" 'Oh, Jesus,' she said disgustedly. 'Not that routine. Come
on get it over with, then you won't feel so conversational.'

" 'Why do you do this?' I asked her. 'You are pretty enough
to have a husband who would support you.'

" 'Kid,' she sighed, 'I am married. My husband makes a hundred bucks a week. Some weeks I make six hundred. We have a
Cadillac and spend the winter in Miami. Why don't you can the
Freud approach and do what you paid for?' She started to rub
my pants."

Stanley chuckled. "I could see I was playing out of my league.
I told her I wasn't really interested in sex. Quick as a wink she
got dressed.

" 'Okay, let's go,' she said.

" 'I paid for an hour,' I told her. 'I've got forty minutes
coming.'

" 'I could have you tossed out of here on your ass,' she said
nastily.

" 'Go ahead.'

"She sat on the bed and stared at me despondently.

" 'There's no love in the world,' she said. 'Woman is to
man a good fuck or a bad fuck. My old man worked in a foundry.
He seared his eyeballs. When he was fifty he started to go blind.
Every fuck my mother ever had was one more kid until she was
finally bedridden. She had fifteen fucks in her life, three of which
ended in miscarriages. All I ever wanted for the first fifteen years
in my life was something to eat besides potatoes. I found a way.
This is a good living while it lasts. If I manage to save up a million dollars from fucking and moved to Newton or Wellesley,
society would accept me with open arms. How could anyone com-
plain even if they knew how I earned it? Most of the rich people
in the world, or at least their grandparents, fucked somebody one
way or the other to get their money.' "

Stanley sighed. "I certainly had gotten in deeper than I had anticipated. You know what she did then? She cried. For the next half hour she sobbed. I stroked her face and tried to soothe her."

" 'Thanks, kid,' she said finally. She wiped her eyes and stared sadly at me.

" 'I'm sorry,' I told her.

" 'Forget it.' She took me out of the hotel through the lobby, and I found her a taxi. As she was getting in the cab she gave me a kiss on my cheek. 'You know, something,' she said. 'I'm not married, and I was never poor. I read all that crap I told you in some damned book written by an ex-prostitute. I tell it to all the college kids. It will make good reading in your term paper.'

" 'Why did you cry?' I asked her.

" 'For you and me and the god-damned world,' she said."

Stanley shook his head. "Thus ends the saga of Stanley Cole." He kissed me. "What's life all about, Beth? Where are we all going?"

I couldn't answer. I kept thinking about that girl. Stanley held me close . . . as if I might somehow vanish. We made love with a deep need for each other. Finally, I said, "I think she was really looking for something beside potatoes. She needs someone, somewhere, in her life who needs her."

"I guess that's what life is really about," Stanley said.

FROM THE JOURNAL OF STANLEY COLE

September, the Second Year

People who faithfully keep a journal or a diary, like Samuel Pepys or James Boswell or Arnold Bennett, do so out of a need to communicate as well as evaluate what is happening to them on a daily basis. Casanova, on the other hand, wrote his Memoirs in his lonely old age largely as an escape from the bitter present and as an attempt to relive his youth spent joyously jumping in and out of the beds of lovely ladies.

Phil Tenhausen assigned all six volumes of the Memoirs as summer reading in Human Values. The other day Sheila informed us in the seminar that she had counted the women Casanova had made love with. She arrived at the total of one hundred and twenty-two. But I am wandering. The real point is I have had no need to keep a journal either out of loneliness or the need to communicate. Harrad and the way we live here almost eliminates these feelings . . . at least as problems. For me the value of this journal is for recapitulation. Since June, events happened to me so fast that for the most part my reactions have been objective and not subjective.

Not without cause, either, because this past summer has been "My Sam Grove Summer". Since June fifteenth until I landed back in Boston on the twenty-fifth of August, I was dominated by Sam Grove, and Sam Grove qualifies in my book for the most objective and completely self-oriented man I have ever met.

Sam met me in June at the airport in Houston. "I don't usually go to such trouble for a young squirt," he said. "But since you are a potential son-in-law, you merit special attention."

"You may have a doctor for a son-in-law," I told him as we drove to the headquarters of the Grove Oil Corporation. "Sheila and Harry Schacht have moved into an apartment on Beacon Hill for the summer. Sheila is studying piano at the Conservatory of Music and Harry has attached himself to the Mass. General Hospital as a bed-pan orderly."

Sam stared at me, "So, my virgin daughter has at last become a woman. Did you sleep with her?"

I told Sam I had. "I like Sheila. Not because she conned you into giving me a summer job, and not because she is rich. I like her because I never believed a girl with so much money could be so honestly straightforward and undevious. Money means nothing to her."

"Depite what you might have heard to the contrary, money is not the motivating factor in my life," Sam grinned. "Sheila intimated to me that you screwed around with some other broad . . . but I gather she still likes you. I don't give a damn who Sheila marries, just so long as she is happy. Beejee, Sheila's stepmother, is always trying to arrange a merger with some other oil money, but Sheila ignores her. She is a lonesome kid . . . had a fouled up life, largely because of me, I suppose. That's the way the ball bounces. Some men can sacrifice themselves to the ideals and goals of a particular woman. I couldn't.

"Sheila's mother is a happy peasant. The salt of the earth type but really dull, boring, and fixated on her little problems of survival. In love with everything that is certain and stable and routine. It is a characteristic of modern man, though most of them will deny it vehemently. Each generation must produce a few Sam Groves or the world would sink into the mud of contented lethargy. If I had been born in another generation, I would have been with Alexander or Caesar, trying to unify the world, or with Ericson or Columbus or Magellan, trying to find a new world. I only click with people trying to achieve the unattainable. Grove Oil has millions of dollars sunk into space research. My only regret in this life is that I may not personally get to the planets. I have an intense curiosity about everything. I violently disagree with Phillip Tenhausen. He is most certainly cracked, but I find him challenging. He appeals to me because he is flinging himself against the impossible. Human nature will always remain the way it is, and whatever is good in it will easily be swayed and dominated by the crass, the vulgar, the ordinary." Sam chuckled. "I look at the newspapers every morning, expecting to find the biggest scandal since the Boston Tea Party . . . the story of Harrad College."

Sam was still talking when we arrived at his Penthouse on the thirtieth floor of the Grove Building. He took off his shoes, stockings, and shirt, and strode around his office, a barrel-chested, slim-hipped man, stripped to the waist. "The rest of this building is air-conditioned," he said. "Nobody tough left in the world. All most people want is their little creature comforts. Give them that, and they'll trade you their souls. The trouble with people today, they're all scared to death of a little sweat. I get in bed with Beejee, and she smells as if she had been sleeping with some Paris coutourier. I tell her I like the smell of her skin, to wash off that crap. She tells me I stink. What kind of man are you, Kolusakas? You changed your name. What's the matter? Are you afraid of your origins? That's one count against you. You couldn't hold my daughter because you screwed another woman. That's two counts against you."

By this time I was getting pretty fed up with Sheila's egotistic father. "You haven't managed to hold your women, either," I said angrily. "Sheila says you've been married three times. I'm not asking any big favors from you. Just give me a job in one of your oil fields. I'm not afraid of sweating, and I'll earn my keep."

Sam chuckled. "I can hold my women, son. The only reason I have been married three times is that I get bored with the scenery . . . not the physical scenery of pussy, tits, hips, ass and legs, but the mental scenery that puts the physical scenery in motion. Women, by and large, are mentally dull. Most of them never find one damn thing to occupy their minds creatively. Rich females subsist on the latest fashions, doing what is socially 'in', seeking admiration from men for their sexual appurtenances, and daydreaming of ideal love. Middle class females imitate the rich ones. The poor female simply propagates endlessly because that is her duty to her husband, who arrives with a stiff cock in his hand, ready to discharge like a helpless salmon swimming upstream against the current, because his seminal vessels tell him he must spawn before he dies."

"What are you doing for the world?" I asked him. "What makes you so much more valuable?"

Sam looked at me thoughtfully."

"I created a business that employs some twenty-three thousand people . . . most of whom are intent on over-populating the world and making their grandchildren's existence here considerably less tenable than their own. I don't believe in philosophizing. I am forty-eight years old. I can live twenty more years or drop dead tomorrow. . . . My major problem at the moment is that my only heirs are a daughter, two ex-wives, and one current one. My personal estate is in excess of thirty-six million dollars, and this does not include my holdings in the Grove Oil which will be transferred to the Grove Foundation when I die. I'd like to transfer control of this product of my imagination into the hands of my non-existent grandsons."

"Are you afraid of dying?" I asked.

"Hell, no! What's that got to do with it."

"Then why do you care what happens to Grove Oil. What's really bothering you is that you're not immortal. In lieu of that, at the very least, you'd like to look down from heaven at this tower and your oil producing properties, rub your hands together, and say to God, 'Look what I did . . . and there's my grandson, Samuel Grove III still running it.' Why don't you impregnate your current wife? That's the only way you're going to get a male Grove in the picture." I had taken off my shoes and stockings and propped my feet on Sam's magnificent blond mahogany desk. "If I married Sheila and she inherited this empire, her first official act would be to elect me President, after which I would immediately change the name to the Kolasukas Oil Corporation."

Sam looked at me gloomily. I later learned he'd had an operation on his seminal tubes and couldn't have children. "Stanley, you are a nervy bastard," he said. "Don't they teach you to mince words at Harrad? All I have to do is push a button and have you

chucked out of here. You are still wet behind the ears. No one in
the Grove Oil Corporation dares to talk back to me. Get the hell
out of here. Tomorrow report to the personnel department on the
eighth floor. I'll find something unpleasant for you to do this
summer."

Sam was good at his word. Three days later I was on a jet
plane to Iran. At the Abadan airport I was picked up by a grinning Iranian who was driving a Grove Oil jeep. He drove me to
Agha Jari where the Grove Oil operates producing wells under
licenses from the National Iranian Oil Company. Grove is a member of the Consortium that plans Iranian Oil production. A new
well had just come in. Molloy, a taciturn Irishman in charge, explained that this baby would produce 25,000 barrels a day. He
told me to report to Gach Saran, where a gravity pipeline was being built to Khark, a small island in the Persian Gulf about a
hundred miles south.

All summer I sweated continuously, ate sand and slop from
a field kitchen, slept in the open, inhaled the odor of camel dung
and urine until I was certain it was my own odor. With a team of
Iranians, we inched our way across grubby country, working
from sun up to sun down, and laying a quarter of mile of pipe a
day; welding it, wrapping it, and burying it, until one day it
would become a continuous tube of slow moving oil, flowing to
storage tanks on the island of Khark. With the *Memoirs of Casanova* to read (the only books I could carry on the plane and stay
within the weight limit), and for companionship Neville and Sin-
cher (Britishers, in charge of the construction, whose idea of
recreation was endless games of pinochle accompanied by oceans
of gin and orange squash), by August I had convinced myself that
Sam Grove's plan was to turn me into a screaming idiot. I was
ten pounds lighter and deeply tanned, but I had received no pay.
When I questioned Neville on the subject, his opinion was that I
must be on the headquarters payroll, since no provision had been
made for me on the field payroll. Since there was no place to
spend money, anyway, Neville's feeling was "why worry about it
... think of the experience you are having."

On the second Saturday in August, two official Grove cars
from Abadan led by Sam Grove in a jeep, which he was driving

himself, screeched into our current location and stopped in a cloud of dust.

"I see you survived," Sam said, grinning at me. "Get your stuff together; you're coming back with me."

An hour later, hanging onto the edge of the seat for fear I would be catapulted out of the jeep, Sam drove us at top speed over dirt roads toward Khark.

"Sheila is mad as hell at me." Sam clutched the steering wheel with both hands to steel himself against the bumps and road shocks. "She got your postcard in June from Abadan, and hasn't heard from you since. I told her I'd come out here and either escort you home or give you a military funeral."

"You can pay me, too," I said. "I've worked for Grove Oil for ten weeks. I figure that you owe me at least six hundred bucks, tax free, as depletion allowance on human flesh."

Sam handed me his billfold. "Take ten one hundreds. I wouldn't want to underpay a possible future son-in-law."

His bulging billfold must have had at least one hundred hundred dollar bills in it. "It's only money, son." He said, noticing me staring at it. "I always carry five to ten thousand. Never know what might turn up where you can use a fast buck."

I took the thousand and asked him how Sheila was. He told me she was living alone in Boston. Harry Schacht had gone out to Columbus to visit with Beth Hillyer until school opened. Some interesting wheels had been turning, but Sheila hadn't given Sam any detailed information on Harrad developments.

In his hotel room in Abadan, as we drank gimlets together, Sam became expansive. "I operated out of a suitcase for years," he told me. "I was worth five million dollars and I didn't even have a desk. It's easy to make money, son. Just think of it as a commodity. Borrow it as cheaply as you can and make it work for you. I made my money using other people's money. If I needed a hundred million tomorrow, I could raise it in twenty-four hours. Do you want to be rich, Stan?"

I grinned. "Anyone who is poor wants to be rich. But I don't want to be so rich that I don't have love."

"That's Hollywood and television crap, son. I can have any kind of love you can think of. Love . . . screwing . . . that's not a man's whole life. A man lives for what he can personally create in this world. Not children. Children are simply one product of his creative energy . . . but the recreation of his world, his environment; a man's ability to design the tallest building and then have it constructed, dig the longest canal, conquer the ice and snow of Antartica, literally project himself into the stars . . . that's man's purpose, and if there is a God, that is why he created man . . . to emulate Himself. Man is closest to God when he is determined to achieve the impossible, seek the unattainable."

The next morning on a jet plane to Calcutta, where Sam had a conference with the officials of an Indian refinery controlled by Grove Oil, we continued the discussion.

"The Hindu is closest to God," I told him, "and achieves the Brahmin state when he no longer seeks the material wealth, possessions, and attainments of this world. He achieves the Unattainable with a direct merger of his own being. All else is *maya* or illusion. When he has pierced through the veil of materialism he returns to Nirvana and reunites himself with the unending consciousness of the Universe."

Sam laughed. "All the mystics and the logicians in the world ever offer man are rationalizations for poverty. Jesus Christ preached to forsake all others and follow him. If the Christians had taken him seriously, the way the Hindus and Chinese have taken Ramakrishna and Buddha, the Western World would be wallowing in dung. If all men lived their lives for the next world, man would never have invented the flush toilet. He'd be up to his ass in his own shit. Wait until you have seen the dregs of Calcutta, son. You'll see what living for the next world can do to man in this one."

At dinner in the Great Eastern Hotel in Calcutta, we were still at it.

"From what you told me about Harrad and the Tenhausens," Sam said, "I'm convinced the whole idea is unrealistic. Their theories of educating a man in such a close contact with women will ultimately feminize the male. The average male today has already gone too far. He seeks the female ultimate . . . security."

"If virility is hydrogen bombs," I grinned, "it may not be such a bad idea."

"Do you expect you and Sheila will achieve this perfect love and maintain it for a lifetime? It sounds a little sloppy to me."

"I don't know, Sam. I do know that if Sheila and I, or some other woman, develop and grow together, it won't end up in the vast wasteland of modern suburban marriage. The marriages the Tenhausens envision would have constantly evolving strength and drives, not for money or power but to project for all men a higher image of themselves. The idea behind Harrad is infinitely larger than pre-marital sexual adjustment. Ultimately it is a belief that man can take one more step up the evolutionary ladder . . . lift himself by his own bootstraps, and develop a society and culture that is emotionally and mentally in control of itself. What we would be seeking may be just as unattainable as the goals you set for yourself. The difference is that the values that drive us are not so ego centered as yours."

The next day Sam took me on a tour of Calcutta. "I want you to see a small portion of this best of all possible worlds, Kandy Kolasukas." He was delighted with his own joke. "Get it, son? Candide? . . . Kandy? Okay, Kandy Kid, look around you."

Adamantly, Sam expounded his philosophy of hopelessness. In a taxi driven by a Sikh we drove through miles of poverty-stricken shambles overflowing with Indians living little more than an animal existence. We pushed our way through markets crawling with flies, plunged into alleys reeking with slop and sewage, forced our way into mud and bamboo houses that gave shelter to families of ten or more plus chickens and cows all living in one or two rooms that completely eliminated privacy. In the sweltering heat, on the edge of a muddy tributary of the Hoogly River, we watched men and women bathe, washing themselves while they still wore their shabby saris and dhotis, in water thick with silt.

For a few rupees Sam convinced one Indian family to share their meal of grimy rice and fish, and grimly insisted that we both eat the tasteless concoction, while they watched us with grinning approval. We finished the day at the burning ghats, a funeral practice of which Sam heartily approved. "Millions of them die before their time. Very sensibly, they realize that any man's life on this earth is not much more than a few puffs of smoke."

The next night Sam had to go to a formal dinner at a British

Polo Club, but he continued his campaign to unnerve me, hoping, evidently, that I would renounce my "Pollyanna" philosophy. He had reserved separate rooms for us. In case, as he put it, something turned up. I think he was disappointed when I told him that I was going to bed early.

Around nine o'clock, just as I had flopped on the bed with a sigh of relief, I heard a knock on my door. I scrambled into my shorts, opened the door an inch, and was staring into the saucer brown eyes of a very pretty Indian girl. She was wearing a red sari, a simple necklace, a tinkling profusion of bangles on her arms, and tiny bells on her ankles. She smiled timidly at me, revealing very white teeth that contrasted with her mocha skin. She handed me a piece of paper. It was a note from Sam: "Less than an hour ago this girl was given a thorough medical inspection. She's clean, healthy. No V.D. She knows at least ninety positions and will demonstrate them with no thought of love on her mind. She isn't even a good business woman. She's yours for the night. Fifteen rupees. Pay her when you finish. Compliments of Sam Grove. She didn't ask to be born a whore. It just happened that way in this best of all possible worlds."

"I'm sorry," I said to the girl. "I wouldn't enjoy it."

She just stared at me, refusing to understand. If possible, her eyes grew even larger as they overflowed with tears.

"Do you understand English?" I asked her.

"Please, sahib," she whispered. "I have no one. I need money."

"Didn't Sam Grove give you any money? Where did he get you, anyway?"

She looked at me puzzled. "The other American. They call Sam. He not want me tonight. Not give rupees. Too many of us. Say all his money not give every Indian even one rupee. So why start?" She grinned at me as if this made good sense. Sam was handing me the world's problems in a microcosm. Still, it was difficult to restrain my anger. If most men were as thick-skinned as Sam, the world probably was hopeless.

I invited the girl in the room, wondering what I was going to do with her. She sat dumbly on the edge of the bed, waiting for me. I touched her breast through her sari. She suffered my explorations in silence. I suddenly realized my penis was erect. My body and some uncontrolled part of my mind were telling me to have dispassionate intercourse with this girl, pay for the (pleasure?) and send her on her way. Sam was betting that after ten weeks in the Iranian desert that my sexual desires would overwhelm the Harrad philosophy I had been spouting. I told the girl to take off her sari, and when she did, and stood naked in front of me, not more than five feet three inches tall but beautifully formed, I felt a terrible sadness. She was a fragile, defenseless child, offering the only thing she had of value in the world.

"What's your name?"

"Asoka Devi," she said eagerly. "I part Indian. My father American soldier."

"Does he know about you?"

"Long time ago. He not know. Not care. My mother very sick. She die. Small village in Assam. No one want me. I go to government school."

"How old are you?"

"Fifteen, I think. Maybe fourteen."

"Will you marry?"

Asoka shrugged. "Indian man marry Indian girl. Not me. No dowry. Very bad."

"How many men have you been with?"

She didn't understand me. I don't know why I pursued it. I felt as if someone had punched me in the stomach. Finally, she said, "First man . . . twelve. Hurt bad." She smiled. "Many men."

"You have baby some day?" I found that I was matching my English to hers. It made conversation easier.

She shrugged. "I not want."

When I tried to discover what she was doing to make sure that fate didn't have other plans, she didn't understand me. "Indian women have many babies," she said.

I pushed her down on the bed. She lay there passively, staring at me, wondering, probably, why I didn't climb on her and get it over with. I turned up the airconditioner, turned off the lights, got in bed beside Asoka, pulled a sheet over us, took her in my arms, kissed her cheek, and told her to go to sleep. When she finally realized I wasn't going to make love to her she sighed, curled up against me, and snuggled her face against my chest. In the morning I awoke first and found her curled in a little ball, sleeping like a child still in the womb, two fingers in her mouth.

It was eight-thirty. I telephoned Sam's room and could tell from the sound of his voice that I had awakened him. "Your Indian girl friend is here in my bed," I said.

"For God's sake get rid of her," Sam chuckled. "We're leaving for Bangkok on a six o'clock plane. Tonight you can try some Thai shmooie. Quite a different flavor than the Indian stuff. I hope you have some strength left."

"Do you know this girl is only fifteen years old?"

Sam laughed. "They start young in the Orient. I hope you aren't getting sentimental Kandy."

"What if she were your daughter?"

"She isn't. You can't cry for the world, Stanley. Forget it. See you at breakfast in a half hour."

I tried to convince Sam that since Asoka was half-American he could adopt her, or endow her, or do something for her. "What would it mean to you, Sam?"

"Oh, for Christ's sake, grow up!" Sam hung up the phone.

I called him back. "Sam, if you don't do something for her, I'll tell Sheila." I slammed the phone down before he could hang up again.

I found Asoka squatting on the toilet. I waited until she finished, and then ignoring her protests pulled her into the shower with me and soaped her from head to foot. A vague thought was slowly blossoming in my mind. I made her unknot her hair which was tied in a bun. While she gasped in indignation, I washed her hair clean of the rancid-smelling oil. When I finished, it was obvious that, among other things Asoka would need a haircut.

I finally got her to breakfast in the hotel dining room, where we were greeted with some shock and surprise by the Indian maitre d' and the Indian bearers who waited on us with great distaste.

Not knowing what mad thing I'd do next, Asoka scarcely touched the food. "Not good," she said. "Not belong here."

Sam finally joined us in the dining room. "All right," he

said. "I decided to humor you. I telephoned a friend and got her a job as a maid with a British family. They are sending their driver for her." He stared at Asoka, noticing her hair hanging down her back. "A good looking doll. I see you couldn't stand the smell of chicken fat in her hair."

"I'd like to put some money in the bank for her."

"You must be kidding."

"No, I'm not. What's more, I want to meet the British family where she will live."

Sam stared at me, dismayed. "You don't trust me."

"No."

"Okay. There's no British family. The driver will bring her back to Dum Dum where she lives. It's about twenty miles from here. Now, let's get to reality. Life isn't moral or immoral. It just is, and you can't change it." He handed Asoka twenty rupees. "There you are. My treat. You can tell Sheila anything you want. I couldn't care less. She knows by now that her father is no paragon of virtue."

I decided the only way to deal with Sam was by not letting him know the low bastard I was convinced that he was. I told him that since Asoka was paid up I might just as well enjoy the rest of the day with her. I would meet him at the airport in time for the flight. After Sam had thoroughly applauded my conversion to reality, I took Asoka back to the room. It took me nearly an hour to convince her Sam really loved her and wanted her to come to the United States. By ten-thirty I located a department store, commandeered a British manager, and explained that I wanted to buy Asoka a complete Western style wardrobe. Leaving Asoka in his charge, I asked for the loan of a typewriter, and using some Grove Oil stationery I had borrowed from Sam on the plane, I wrote a to-whom-it-may-concern letter explaining that Asoka Devi was an employee of the Grove Oil Corporation and was being transferred to the United States for one year to work at the Company headquarters at Houston, Texas.

By noontime Asoka, wobbling a little on her high heels, ecstatic over her new clothes, and still dubious over her amazing good fortune, greeted me with tears in her eyes. There was still something missing. She needed a fast haircut. I found a hairdresser, pawed through a book of hair styles, and watched while Asoka was being shorn, and transformed into a sexy looking waif with an elfin style, windblown Italian hair-do. When they finished I had no doubt she would pass for eighteen or nineteen years old. With her large brown eyes and coffee cream complexion she was strikingly beautiful.

By two o'clock I had her in the American Embassy and within an hour convinced an undersecretary to arrange a passport. While Asoka watched, I filled out the forms. No one questioned why Grove Oil was hiring an Indian employee who couldn't write English. By three-thirty Asoka had been photographed and was holding her passport and airline tickets on a flight to Houston. I arranged with the airline officials to take care of her on any stop-overs or transfers. As the coup d'etat, I put in an overseas phone call to Beejee Grove. It took until four-thirty to connect. By this time I was really sweating. I had no doubt that Sam would leave without me if I failed to show up at the airport. The telephone connection was erratic, but Beejee finally grasped who I was. I told her Sam had asked me to call her. I told her she was to meet Asoka at the Houston airport in approximately two days; to take care of Asoka until Sam arrived; that Sam would explain it all to her when we got back.

After paying for Asoka's clothes and the airline fare, I had seventy-five dollars left, which I put in Asoka's pocketbook. I hugged her and told her that she was going to have a wonderful new life. Two days from now she would be in Houston, Texas. The airline hostesses would take care of her all the way.

"I not know your name," she whispered in my ear.

"Mud." I grinned at her. "My name is mud from now on."

When our plane took off for Bangkok, I asked Sam when he planned to be back in Houston. "No hurry," he said, "I need a little vacation. Tonight we shall *both* enjoy the ultimate pleasures of sex with some lovely Thai girls. I promise you an experience without which you have not lived. Then when we get bored, we will take off to Los Angeles. Maybe we will run down to Tijuana. A few days in that quaint little town will give you a new perspective on Harrad College. Sex is simply a commodity on the periphery of life. Now that you have learned this in Calcutta you have taken the first step. The Tenhausens are attempting to give sex a sacredness that neither the act nor the aftermath is equal to."

I was beginning to wonder if I was going to have the courage to tell Sam about Asoka Devi. "Sam," I said, "I think you are wrong. The Tenhausens are not only trying to teach that there is no ultimate pleasure in the orgasm unless a particular man and woman are deeply involved with each other as individuals. They go further and envision a society where all men and women care so much for each other that the basic dishonesty or inability to communicate in most human relationships is completely eliminated. Imagine a world where I could say: "Sam, that Anglo-Indian girl is a human being whose heart beats, who can eat food, digest it, and defecate, who has a vagina and a womb to bear children and breasts to feed them, and above all, a brain that remembers and correlates her memories. She is a blinding miracle. How could I treat her simply as a warm sheath into which I ejaculated? Imagine a world instead where every human being was trained from birth that every other human being was the most amazing, wondrous beautiful fact of existence."

Sam stared at me. "Jesus Christ," he muttered.

"No," I grinned. "Even Jesus failed to understand. He insisted on something beyond to explain the miracle, and then the theologians gave man something to lean on. A God who exacted retribution, or answered prayers. If there is a God, why should He expect more from man than to appreciate the miracle of his own existence?"

"You don't believe it," Sam said. "You are spouting words. Man is not good. He has the capacity for evil. He is selfish, hedonistic. In business for himself. Your ideas won't work in this world. Kandy Kolasukas. You'll grow up one of these days and discover it for yourself."

I looked at my watch. It was seven-thirty. We would be landing in Bangkok soon. By now Asoka was on a jet to Honolulu. I decided now was the time to tell Sam. He listened to me in complete disbelief. He told me I was trying to get his ass. He told me I could never have accomplished it in eight hours. It was impossible to convince the officials and get a passport so quickly.

All the time he talked, he was both cursing me and trying to laugh me into a confession that it was all a hoax."

"Sam," I said chuckling, "I thought I'd better tell you now. Just in case, tonight, I got feeling the same way about some Thai girl. I haven't any more money, but the first thing you know I'd be asking you for a loan, and you would end up with a harem in Houston.

"I suppose you told Beejee this girl was a whore I had slept with," he said sourly.

"No. I simply told her Asoka was fifteen, an orphan, and you had decided to take care of her education."

"If it's true," Sam said, grimly fastening his seat belt, "I'll put your ass in a sling. No one ever pulls a fast one on me and gets away with it." He grinned at me nastily. "Keep in mind, Kandy, I haven't had your Harrad education. I don't believe in this namby-pamby crap. For Christ sake, there's four hundred million Indians and just as many Chinese. What would it prove if I saved one miserable human being?"

"You aren't going to save her, Sam. You are going to save yourself. There's a lot more important things in this world than discovering oil or flying to the moon."

Sam's only response was "Bullshit!"

When we landed in Bangkok and were in our room at the Ratanakosin Hotel, he put in a long distance phone call to Beejee. "Don't get in an uproar," he said when he finally was connected. "I was just confirming Stanley's call. I know it sounds a little unusual, Beejee. Just meet the kid at the airport. I'll explain it to you later." He hung up and stared at me. "You miserable son of a bitch," was all he said, but I detected a note of admiration in his voice.

We didn't go in search of Siamese whores, nor did Sam show any further interest in Tijuana. By the time we landed in Houston, three days later, conversation between us had deteriorated to such a point that I was able to finish volume Four and Five of Casanova's Memoirs. Beejee met us with Asoka, who had arrived the day before.

"Sam," she cried, bussing him enthusiastically, "She's a darling child. Are we going to adopt her?"

"She's no child," Sam said angrily. "She's a whore."

"Sam, don't tell me you slept with her?"

"No, damn it! I didn't sleep with her," Sam exploded. He looked at me warningly.

"Where did you get her?"

"Never mind. It's all a joke. We're sending her back."

"There's no back," I explained to Beejee. "Asoka has no father or mother." I told Beejee Asoka was the daughter of an unknown American G.I., that neither Sam nor I had slept with her, and that Sam was really only perturbed because I was so tender-hearted, that Sam really wanted to give the kid a chance in life but felt that she, Beejee, would think he had gone soft.

"Oh, Sam," Beejee said, crying and hugging him to his great embarrassment, right in the middle of the crowds in the airline terminal. "It's the nicest thing you have ever done." Tears were running down Beejee's cheeks. "I never would have believed it. We ought to adopt hundreds of kids and help them. It would make our lives worthwhile, somehow."

The next morning Sam took me back to the airport to catch a plane for Boston. He handed me a thousand dollars. "Are you going to tell Sheila the truth?" he demanded.

"There's worse things than caring for the woman you slept with," I said, grinning at him. "If you adopted them all, you'd have quite a harem. I'm sure Sheila would be proud of you."

Sam chuckled. "If you want a job next summer, Kandy, please apply to Saint Peter. Grove Oil can't afford you."

When I arrived back in Boston at Logan Airport, I took a taxi to a little street on the north side of Beacon Hill. Trudging up five flights of stairs in an old brick apartment house that had probably been built before the Civil War, I arrived at the top, puffing. I heard someone playing a piano. I knocked, but there was no answer. Finally, I opened the door, and there was Sheila, her back to me, engrossed in Bach's Goldberg Variations. I tiptoed behind her, grabbed her and she fell screaming into my arms.

"Oh my God, Stanley," she sobbed happily. "It's you. I've been so darned lonesome." She kissed my lips, my eyes, my cheeks, enthusiastically. "I was about to kill Daddy when I heard what he did to you. Oh, Stanley. I've missed you . . . missed you."

"What became of Harry?"

"He and Beth corresponded. Then she telephoned and insisted he spend a few weeks in Columbus before school opened. Harry tried to tell her that it wasn't a good idea. He was afraid of her father and mother's reaction. Oh, Stanley, Harry really is so very gentle and such a good person. We've had a lot of fun this summer."

"But you finally decided that you loved me most," I said, messing up her hair and kissing her quite thoroughly.

"How did you know?"

By this time I had unbuttoned the boy's shirt she was wearing and unzipped her plaid skirt. "Sheila," I groaned as I pulled her slip over her head, and discovered a bra, panties, garter belt and stockings. I'll never get through all the layers and find you."

"It's only three in the afternoon," she sighed lying in my arms. "This is a crazy time to make love. How many girls have you slept with this summer?"

"A couple of dozen."

"I don't believe it," she chuckled, "You act starved."

"Are you going to room with me this year at Harrad?"

"I'm going to marry you, Stanley, and have babies with you! But I may still want to be with Harry or Jack once in a while. Will you be jealous?"

"Ho . . . a new Sheila speaks!"

"Yes," she said. "And here's some news for you. Peter Longini decided to quit Harrad. His father has been transferred to Switzerland and he's going to the University of Zurich. Jack is going to room with Valerie Latrobe. Beth and I decided we might just as well simplify things and all of us live more or less communally for the next two years."

"That's simple?" I asked, nibbling her ear.

"Well, it's simpler than being jealous."

"You said two years. What about our senior year?"

Sheila snuggled hard against me. "About November of our last year I'm going to get pregnant by you, and Beth is going to get pregnant by Harry."

"Ye Gods . . . what about Jack and Valerie?"

"Silly . . . we don't know about them yet. Maybe they won't want to get married and have children."

"But you and Beth do?"

"Yes!"

"And who supports all this brood?"

"Well," Sheila said seriously, "Beth and I figured it this way. She and Harry are planning to go to medical school. If you and I apply to do graduate work in the same university, we all ought to be able to get scholarships. Next summer and the following summer we will have a fund of nearly five thousand dollars. Then, when we graduate from Harrad we can take an apartment together or rent a house, and all of us can move in with the children. We can hire a woman to take care of the children when we aren't there. But, anyway our classes will probably work out so that one of the four of us will be there most of the time."

"Sheila," I chuckled and pulled her behind against me so that I was deep inside her. "Do you mind if I change your name?"

"To what?" she asked.

"To Kandy . . . Kandy Grove. And when you write your father be sure and tell him!"

November, December, January, the Second Year

All of the second year class at Harrad are experimenting with a method of sexual intercourse which Margaret and Phil call sexual communion. I can see now that Phil has been preparing us for it gradually. Since September in the Human Values seminar, he has assigned John Woodroffe's *S'akti and S'akta*, John Noyes' *Male Continence, Diana*, by Henry Parkhurst, *Karezza* by Alice Stockham, *Art of Love*, by W. F. Robie, *Sex Perfection* by Rudoph von Urban, finishing with *Nature, Man and Woman* by Alan Watts.

This is by no means all the books we have had scheduled. Phil feels the only sound basis of education is exposure to thousands of ideas. By forcing us into continuous evaluation, he expects our own frames of reference will be eventually enlarged into a workable philosophy of life.

When we groaned that we didn't need to read any more books on how-to-do-it-sex, Phil asked us to be patient. "I would never assign these books to the freshman class. As freshmen you weren't mature enough. Even now with most of you in your twentieth year it may be questionable, whether you can fully grasp these concepts. In the next few weeks we are going to explore the psychological, the metaphysical, and the religious quality of sexual intercourse. Whether you profit by it now, or in later life, the door has been opened. I predict that eventually you will embody these ideas in your love experiences. To our knowledge, outside occasional references to these ideas in various sex manuals, the books we have assigned, are the only writings available on the subject. Yet we will be dealing with a very ancient idea. In practical married life, perhaps many people have learned these ideas by trial and error without ever becoming aware of their tremendous potential in developing communication in its deepest sense between the male and female.

"The original concept stems from the Hindu Tantric literature and is based on the worship of Sakti, or the all pervading life principle in the Universe. As John Woodroffe points out: 'the whole of life, without any single exception, may be an act of worship if man makes it so.' Thus, the Hindu Pancattattva offer five ways for man to unite himself with the fountainhead of the universe. One of these ways "Maithuna" is sexual intercourse of a very special kind. The Tantric philosophy conceives the physical union of man and woman as part of the Divine Nature in action. Thus the body is Sakti. Pursued to its ultimate, man himself is God. When the Divine Mother is seen in all things, man achieves true liberation. In seeking these truths, many means are available. Sexual intercourse, properly understood, is one of the important ways for man and woman to eliminate the polarization of their bodies. In the act of coitus, a man and woman can unite their consciousness into a single pole with the unceasing Consciousness of the Universe. In the sexual act, bodies are left behind and the minds of the participants can merge into a state called by the Hindu Samadhi."

"You can see," Phil said later, during one of his lectures to us in Harrad Little Theatre, "that sexual intercourse taking place in this mental environment is actually an act of worship. By definition it becomes elevated, pure without lust. We are not suggesting that the act of coitus need always be endowed with such high spirituality, but we do have in this yoga discipline a definite and obvious requirement that the male participant be able to delay his ejaculation not for a typical half-hour, but perhaps for a whole evening."

There was a lot of laughter, groans, and comments that it might be possible if the girl would cooperate and not move a muscle. But what fun would that be, anyway?

Phil chuckled. "We are neither prescribers, or enforcers . . . just exploring with you an idea which we believe can enhance and enlarge your own values. So far as we can determine, the Tantric idea which is extremely repugnant to orthodox Christianity and Judiasm because it idealizes sex, and uses sex as a form of worship, has lain dormant in the West for centuries. Whatever knowledge of the basic concepts that have filtered through to the West were ultimately identified with a sexual orgiastic behaviour, and little has been written about them.

"The possibility of delaying the male ejaculation was rediscovered in 1846 by John Humphrey Noyes who described it in a book called *Male Continence*. Noyes' discovery came about through his great love for his wife who had suffered through five pregnancies, with all but one child prematurely born. Noyes persuaded his wife to experiment with prolonged intercourse without ejaculation or orgasm. Keep in mind this was little more than a hundred years ago. Contraceptive techniques were largely unknown. In Noyes' words: 'But what if a man knowing his own power and limits should not even approach the crisis, and yet be able to enjoy motion *ad libitum*. If you say that is impossible, I answer that I know it is possible . . . nay it is easy.' "

"He's crazy," Harry Schacht said when a group of us continued the discussion with Phil after his lecture. "First, a man who had intercourse without ever ejaculating would have aching testicles, and second, I doubt its efficacy as a method of birth control. Some semen would escape into the vagina whether there was ejaculation or not."

Dr. Anson Fanner, who had been attending this series of lectures, shook his head. "I won't agree that male continence is a healthy approach to sex, but it is a method that probably would be effective for birth control. Basically in prolonged intercourse some semen is released into the urethra. This slight release probably saves the male from what you refer to as aching testicles. Since there are no violent muscular contractions in the man who accomplishes this feat, the pressure of the vagina on the penis may tend to crowd any liquid from escaping from the seminal ducts into the urethra back toward the bladder, rather than forward to the meatus."

"You mean a man doesn't have to wear anything until he ejaculates?" Valerie demanded.

Dr. Fanner smiled. "If you are depending on sheaths for birth control, you can probably blame the failure of the sheath at the point of ejaculation rather than the simple insertion of a penis into your vagina for an hour or two. Since you have birth control pills available to you, the problem is academic."

"We want you to realize," Phil Tenhausen told us a few days later, "that we are simply tracing an idea. Noyes' theory of male continence was adopted for a time by the Oneida Community who, at the time, depended upon it as a means of birth control. This community shared wives communally. Male continence probably permitted them to determine with some accuracy a particular father, as well as limit the combined progeny of the group. The real value of the theory is the awareness that the male can control his ejaculation and develop such a yoga like control that it is possible for the female to have several orgasms over a period of several hours without the male losing control."

"This may be well and good in theory," Jack Dawes protested, "but I fail to see the advantage of such lengthy intercourse."

"Only personal experimentation can prove the value of this approach to sex," Phil said, "In the various books we've read, a common body of unique experience indicates that individuals attempting prolonged intercourse may make some interesting discoveries. We, of course, believe that ultimate orgasm for both participants is desirable. As you read these various books, I suggest you collect a series of impressions from them that may point up for you the psychological and mystic experiences that others have obtained from sexual communion."

Stanley hasn't been keeping a journal for the past few months. "I'm too happy to write in a journal," he grinned at me. "I have no problems. *You* underline all the ideas that impress you. When you're finished, we'll give sexual communion a real whirl. We'll climb in the sack and you can read them to me while I'm inside you. Be sure you have enough material to last all night, because I am really a strong yoga."

I challenged Stanley there and then, and he had to eat his

words. But Saturday night he demanded a return match, "to prove the power of mind over matter." By nine o'clock I was in bed with Robie's book, *The Art of Love,* von Urban's, *Sex Perfection,* Alan Watt's, *Nature, Man and Woman,* and *Summerhill* by A. S. Neill. I told Stanley I was ready.

"What has *Summerhill* got to do with this," Stanley demanded, trying to ignore naked me, and looking over the books I'd piled on the night stand near the bed.

"Just in case we ran out of material," I grinned. "In point of fact, you don't look as if you'd last ten minutes, let alone several hours."

Stanley snuggled against my breasts for a moment, kissing them softly. It's probably going to be quite a project," he whispered. "I'm losing confidence already."

"Come inside me," I said, "Then we'll turn on our sides, and we'll lie very quietly while I read to you."

For a minute or two Stanley seemed to have other ideas. He found his way into me with great conviction. Feeling him moving slowly inside me, I was quite certain we weren't going to prove anything. "All right," he said giving me a final kiss and rolling me on my side, "I can see that it's up to me to restrain you . . . you demon! Go ahead and read to me."

"This really is a nice way to read," I murmured into his ear. I was reluctant to open the book, enjoying the pressure of his hand on my behind as he held me close to him.

"You'd better start reading," Stanley chuckled. "I don't dare breathe. I need to think of something beyond how enjoyable this is."

I perched Dr. Robie's book on the pillow just over his head. "This is fun," I said feeling quite bubbly. "Seriously, Stan, I think one of the most interesting things about this book is that it was written more than forty years ago. Dr. Robie was away ahead of his time in understanding sex and love. Here's some of the things I've underlined: " 'Men now find that it is a delight to prolong the love union, and soon discover that mutual delight is given and received under complete control . . . During a lengthy period of lengthy control the whole being of each is submerged in the other, and exquisite exaltation is experienced . . . Perfect control comes by patience and determination and the reward is happy, united lives and each attain to their higher selves . . . To be able to continue the reciprocal movements of communion for an indefinite time without arriving at the orgasm is a matter of education, and will only come after continued endeavor.' "

"He can say that again," Stanley said tasting my nipples. "When I kiss you like that, I feel your vagina contract on me."

"It will do more than contract, if you don't stop. Cooperate and listen," I said, continuing to read. " 'I seem to sublimate my partner into a paradise of tender peace and romantic reverie and thrill her to a sort of soul intoxication of magnetic bliss. The orgasm would seem quite the antipodes of this and a crude shock by contrast . . . All my aim is to establish this wonderful magnetic rapport and this romantic, Poetic ecstacy . . . Words fail . . . We are literally angels in heaven in our innocence and conscious purity an untellable mutual love. Who would care for an orgasm in such an emotional state of divine realization. It would bring all to an abrupt end. Do not even think of it or mention it.' "

"Stanley," I shivered, "stop running your fingers over my belly before I explode. Listen to this. A female doctor wrote this to Dr. Robie more than forty years ago: 'You ask how long the desire for emission should be inhibited . . . You seem to consider reservatus (extended sexual intercourse) as *re*pression while I think of it as *ex*pression of the highest order. As all progress in civilization has been by means of the volitional part of the brain gradually taking over more and more of the processes that were formerly reflexive or instinctive, so the sexual nature is the last to be taken over. Evolution demands that this be done. Fame waits at the door of him to whom is given the task of so educating humanity that it may come to see sexual intercourse in this light.' "

"Are you going to last, Stanley?" I asked.

"No trouble at all," he grinned. "You look so sweetly serious while you are reading, your breasts feel so nice and warm, and your heart is beating so quietly that I really am magically floating on your words."

"Let me finish Robie . . . then you can read from von Urban.

Here, this is interesting! It's from the *Handbook of the Oneida Community*, written nearly a hundred years ago: 'Oneida Communists have a special theory in regard to the act of sexual intercourse . . . two distinctive kinds of sexual intercourse ought to be recognized; one simply social, the other propagative, and that the propagative should only be exercised when impregnation is intended and mutually agreed upon. Sexual intercourse *without the propagative act* (except when propagation is intended) is all that we tolerate in Free Love; . . . So far as this matter is concerned, Free Love, in the Oneida sense of the term, is much less free in the gross, sensual way than marriage . . . We have left the simple form of marriage and advanced to the complex stage of it. We have no quarrel with those who believe in exclusive dual marriage and faithfully observe it, but, for us, we have concluded there is a better way. The honor and faithfulness that constitute an ideal marriage may exist between two hundred as well as two; while the guarantees for women and children are much greater in the Community than they can be in any private family. The results of the complex system we may sum up by saying, that men are rendered more courteous, women more winning, children are better born, and both sexes are personally free.'

"I wonder why other groups haven't tried to form communities like Oneida?" I asked.

Stanley smiled. "There's a lot more than sex in the Oneida concepts. They pooled the results of all their labor. The very thought is abhorent to the average American. We are too individualistic. There were a dozen or more of those communistic societies in the United States in the 1800's. Most of them were based on very stern religious codes, and dominated by one or two leaders." Stanley wiggled away from me and took von Urban's book.

"Hurry back," I sighed. "I feel better when you are inside me."

Joined again, Stanley turned the pages to my underlinings. "This is from a letter to Dr. von Urban: 'Dr. A. B., a former patient of my sanitorium, told the following story: (A week ago I married a beautiful young Arabian girl. We were both very much in love. The strange happenings between us were so remarkable and exciting, that I felt impelled to tell them to an expert. My wife and I lay for an hour, naked on a couch in close bodily contact, caressing each other, but without sex union. The room was in total darkness, entirely blacked out. You could not distinguish anything. Then we separated from each other and stood up; thereupon my wife became visible. She was outlined with a nimbus of greenish-blue mystic light which radiated from her. It was like a halo, except for the fact, that it encircled not only her head but her whole body, showing its configuration in a hazy way. As she stood there, I moved my hand slowly toward her. When my palm came within an inch of her breast an electric spark sprang from her to me, visible, audible, and painful. We both shrank back) . . . Experience has convinced the author that there is a difference in the bio-electrical potential in the bodies of male and female which can be exchanged in proper intercourse, leaving both partners relaxed, happy and satisfied . . . During the following weeks this young couple made further experiments on my behalf . . . During the course of these experiments it was ascertained that if the couple did not lie naked for half hour or longer, in close physical contact, kissing and caressing, but instead started intercourse immediately, the strange radiation did not emanate from the body of the girl, nor did the sparks fly between the two lovers when they stood near each other afterwards, even though the sex union lasted less than twenty-seven minutes. Further the lovers found that every intercourse lasting less than twenty-seven minutes induced an urgent desire, in both, for a repetition of the sex act. But, if this desire was fulfilled by another too brief act, both became nervous and irritated, and sometimes they suffered physical ailments afterwards (headache, heart-palpitation, asthma, etc.) This seemed to show that the tension in the sex organs was reduced, but not the tension of the entire body . . . Intercourse for less than twenty-seven minutes increased the distance at which the sparks would jump to more than one inch, indicating that the tension in their bodies became stronger with each intercourse of brief duration . . . On the other hand intercourse lasting half an hour or more was followed by entire relaxation from nervous tension.' "

"My God . . . what does that prove?" I asked pressing myself even closer against Stanley.

"It's simple. If people like you and me rush into intercourse, and whack it off, the coroner may find only the charred remains. We would have electrocuted each other!"

Stanley stopped for a minute to kiss away my laughter and then he read: " 'The natives of the Trobriand Islands, in British New Guinea, ridicule the sex life of civilized people, caricaturing before mixed audiences, the sketchy, limp and clumsy technique of Western lovers. The audience is amused by this burlesque of a lower state of erotic culture; but they believe that they exaggerate because, in their experience, no people could enjoy a sex act so lacking in preparation, and so hurried in consummation. The explanation they offer is this: " 'After one hour the souls of the ancestors awaken and bless our union.' " For these Island Lovers, the long duration of the sex act is obligatory, a duty to their ancestors. Too brief a sex union would torture them with feelings of guilt and remorse . . . The man does not lie over his mate; to do so would imprison her . . . During a long sex act this would become unbearable . . . Sometimes they lie together with their heads at opposite ends of the sleeping mat, the two open pair of legs fitted together like two pincers in such a way that the sex organs come into the closest possible contact without penetration of the vagina. In this position they sleep together at times when no sex intercourse is intended.' "

"I think we ought to try that for a minute," Stanley said grinning. And we did! . . . But pretty soon Stanley had edged his way back from my toes and was kissing me between the legs. "This is better, and more interesting," he said. "You taste quite nice."

"I can't get over the feeling that it's not a nice thing to do," I said.

"You don't like it?"

"I didn't say that. But the books give it such horrible Latin names."

"All the books say it's quite normal marital behavior. Hey! You bit me!"

"Only nibbled," I chuckled. "But what I want to know is

why? Why do you have the compulsion to kiss me that way? Nothing I've ever read explains why."

"You don't feel the compulsion?"

"A little," I admitted. "But not so much as you."

"But you do like it when I kiss you?"

"Stanley," I shivered. "You don't need an answer to that . . . and if you don't stop, this experiment is going to have a rapid conclusion. You still haven't answered why?"

"Aren't most animals attracted into propagation by the male and female odor?"

"Stanley . . . please, stop. I'm afraid I may have an odor."

"You do. You smell like warm hay drying in a barn. Very aphrodisiacal!"

"Okay . . . that does it! I'm going to read to you from Watt's book."

Once again joined, I started to read but Stanley interrupted me. "The last chapter called *Consummation* is the best thing I have ever read on the male–female relationship."

"I agree," I said fervently. "Listen to some of the things I have underlined: 'This makes it the more strange that conventional spirtuality rejects the bodily union of man and woman as the most fleshy animal and degrading phase of human activity— a rejection showing the extent of its faulty perception and its misinterpretation of the natural world. It rejects the most concrete and creative form of man's relationship to the world outside his organism, because it is through the love of a woman that he can say not only of her but what is other, "This is my body." . . . All this is peculiarly true of love and sexual communion between man and woman. This is why it has such a strong spiritual and mystical character when spontaneous and why it is so degrading and frustrating when forced . . . Sex is therefore the virtual religion of very many people, the end to which they accord more devotion than any other. To the conventionally religious minded this worship of sex is a dangerous and positively sinful substitute for the worship of God. But this is because sex, or any pleasure, as ordinarily pursued is never a true fullfillment. For this very reason it is *not* God, but not at all because it is "merely physical" . . . Sexuality is not a separate compartment of human life; it is

a radiance pervading every human relationship . . . A relationship of this kind cannot adequately be discussed in manuals of
sexual hygiene . . . Their use is consequence rather than the
cause of a certain inner attitude, since they suggest themselves
almost naturally to partners who take their love as it comes,
contemplatively, and are in no hurry to grasp anything from it
. . . and to see that pleasure grasped is no pleasure . . . According
to Tantric symbolism, the energy of the *Kundalini* is aroused but
simply dissipated in ordinary sexual activity. It can, however, be
transmuted in a prolonged embrace in which the male orgasm is
reserved and the sexual energy diverted into contemplation of the
divine as incarnate in the woman . . . Long before the male
orgasm begins, the sexual impulse manifests itself as what can
only be described, psychologically, as a melting warmth between
the partners so that they seem veritably to flow into each other.
To put it in another way, "physical lust" transforms itself into
the most considerate and tender form of love imaginable . . .
Sexual love in the contemplative spirit simply provides the
conditions in which we can be aware of our mutual interde-
pendence and "oneness" . . .

"Stanley . . ." I stopped reading and kissed him. "I think
this man, Alan Watts, has given, in this book, the most important
insights on sex and love I've ever read. It gives me goose-pimples
to read it . . . a sense of identity with another person who thinks
and feels the way I feel."

"There's only one trouble," Stanley said. "To achieve the
heights that Watts says are possible requires a tremendous
ability to surrender yourself to another individual. The key
then is a high degree of education not only in sex as practiced this
way, but also along the lines of philosophy, psychology in fact
every aspect of education. What I mean is that two neurotic
people could not make love this way. They simply wouldn't know
how to escape from themselves . . . into the other person."

"Let me read a little more," I said trying to ignore his happy
kisses on my breast. "Listen: 'One finds out what it means to
simply look at the other person, to touch hands or listen to the
voice. If these contacts are not regarded as leading to something
else, but rather allowed to become one's consciousness, as if the
source of activity lay in them and not the will, they become sensa-

tions of immense subtlety and richness . . . The point is to discover the wonder of simple contacts . . .The psychic counterpart of this bodily and sensuous intimacy is a similar openness of attention to each other's thoughts—a form of communion which can be as sexually "charged" as physical contact. This is the feeling that one can express one's thoughts to the other just as they are since there is not the slightest compulsion to assume a pretended character. This is perhaps the rarest and most difficult aspect of any human relationship, since in ordinary social converse the spontaneous arising of thought is more carefully hidden than anything else. Between unconscious and humorless people who do not know and accept their own limitations it is almost impossible . . . To unveil the flow of thought can therefore be an even greater sexual intimacy than physical nakedness . . . If no attempt is made to induce the orgasm by bodily motion, the interpenetration of the sexual centers becomes a channel of the most vivid psychic interchange . . . The marvellously overwhelming urge to turn themselves inside out for each other . . . Rare as gaiety may be in cultures where there is a tie between sex and guilt, the release from self brings laughter in love-making . . . The height of sexual love, coming upon us of itself, is one of the most total experiences of relationship to the other of which we are capable . . . For what lovers feel for each other in this moment is no other than adoration in the full religious sense, and its climax is almost literally the pouring of their lives into each other. Such adoration which is due God, would indeed be idolatrous were it not that, in that moment, love takes away the illusion and shows the beloved for what he or she in truth is . . . not the socially pretended person but the naturally divine.' "

"Stanley . . . Stanley . . ." I whispered undulating in response to him. "We've done remarkable well for our first attempt. Don't you agree?"

Watt's book thudded on the floor beside the bed.

"Unquestionably, Sheila." Stanley grinned at me.

"Do you want to fall asleep this way?"

"I'm afraid I've passed the point of no return."

I kissed him wildly. "Oh, God! Darling . . . darling . . . so have I. So have I!"

FROM THE JOURNAL OF HARRY SCHACHT

August, after the Second Year

So I am writing this in jail. A few miles west of Province-town. In this first half day of incarceration the philosopher, latent in me, bubbles through to the surface. I can now prove something or other. Possibly, that males and females even after some years of familiarity with the pros and cons of each other need not necessarily lead dull and unimaginative lives. Or perhaps, like some other famous personages in history, Thoreau and Gandhi for example, I have discovered that the confines of a narrow cell are conducive to reflection.

The truth is that in the past year the Tenhausen's journal keeping project simply hadn't dovetailed into the pace of the fast life I have been leading. Admittedly, calm appraisal in the jug and via the pen is somewhat difficult. I have two argumenta-tive cellmates, Jack and Stanley, who feel that I should par-ticipate in their heated discussion about the vagaries of destiny and fate, versus the general perversity of the human animal. Forsaking me, a scribbling idiot, they are now carrying on a long-distance discussion with Beth, Sheila and Valerie. Yes, our female compatriots are likewise imprisoned in this red jail house. They are out of sight, for propriety's sake, in another row of cells at the rear of the building. But definitely, shrilly . . . they are not out of hearing.

The six of us, quietly baking, as a hot August Saturday after-noon sun beats on the flat roof of this dreary penitentiary, seem to be the only occupants of this steaming Cape Cod oven. Stanley, Jack and I have stripped to our shorts. In what state of undress our female mentors are is impossible to determine since we can't see them.

Tearful, rescue-us telegrams have been dispatched to my father and Phillip Tenhausen . . . but as the sun sinks slowly in the west it seems quite obvious that no one is going to arrive to bail out the impenitent six before Monday. Beth, Valerie and Sheila have either been excoriating the plumbing or giggling and laughing hysterically as they recall the events that led up to our capture by the town constable, Ebeneezer Schnook. It really should be his last name! Now the girls are harmonizing . . . "Write me a letter. Send it by Smokey . . . care of this little ol' Cape Cod pokey."

All of which brings me back to the facts of life. If my father arrives before Phillip Tenhausen, I am obviously going to listen to the longest lecture in the history of long lectures on the subject of Harrad College. The rest of my cellmates are indeed fortunate. Their parents live a considerable distance from this stronghold of Puritanism. I can only pray that Rachel and Jake are in the Catskills on vacation. If they receive their telegram before Phil Tenhausen, and after a mad dash to the Cape, they discover their only son's pecadillo first hand; well, they may be able to laugh at the subject of *yentizing* around when a Jewish comedian on the borscht circuit makes a "funny" but as a practical family matter it quite obviously won't be admitted as a fit subject for laughter.

So please, Phil . . . discover us before Jake (my father's name is actually Saul but he tolerates Jake) arrives with his moustache bristling, and behind him my mother wailing; "Es passt nit! I told you Saul, Harry's not too old for a *potch* before he becomes a *paskudnick*."

Before InSix (as we are now known) started out on this mad junket, I had worked the summer at Mass. General Hospital and then spent a week at home. Jake was pleased, and Mother with tears of joy displayed her future Doctor to all the ladies of Hadassah. She was careful to mention only Cambridge, Massachusetts as the locale of my endeavors, hoping, obviously, that by association her friends would assume her son's pedagogical training was being acquired at a more venerable institution in the same area.

Several times Jake corralled me for a man-to-man discussion. "Harry," he said, "I'm worried about you. Why don't you quit this Harrad College monkey shines and switch over to a regular college?"

"Why?" I demanded. "Phil Tenhausen tells me that reports he has on me from "A" University are absolutely tops. All I have to do is keep in the same groove and I can walk into any medical school in the country."

'Oy, such a groove," Jake sighed. "How can you keep it up, Harry? My God, a little piece of. . . ." Jake smiled apologetically. "Well, sex is all right. A growing boy has to learn . . . but everyday you are living with that little blonde *meidele*. Day in, day out. You'll wear yourself out!"

"Jake," I grinned. "It's like any muscle. It grows stronger with exercise!"

"Ha . . . you make jokes. But I still say it isn't healthy. I was reading yesterday about morals on the campus. All this sex so young. You'll grow bored. I was never with a woman until I was twenty-two. Now . . . everywhere you read, boys and girls in college going to bed in their college rooms, yet. And brassy enough to insist this is their right without having even earned it. *Mach a leben* and *then* you have the right. The world has gone to hell. Now a man can only "get himself security," I read it! . . . In bed with a girl. Some security."

I knew it was hopeless but once again I tried to explain Harrad to Jake. "You are wrong about the boredom and security bit," I told him. "You see, the stuff you have been reading is not Harrad.

"It's the way most colleges and universities are right now. Harrad accepts the male-female relationship as completely normal for men and women in their late teens and accepts sexual relations without the requirement of marriage. Harrad has simply leapt forward fifty or one hundred years. The colleges you are reading about and their sex problems are simply not equivalent to Harrad. At the typical college today, the kids are fighting for sexual freedom without social meaning. Sure they will become bored. By the time they are juniors in college many of them have settled into a kind of early monogamy without marriage. They seek love in a moral climate that says if pre-marital sex must exist, then it must ape monogamous marriage; that way it is still guilt ridden but it is permissible. I feel sorry for them. In this environment these students are in effect pretending marriage; playing at being husband and wife. They are discovering that neither the boy nor the girl can give the security or identity that they are demanding from each other. A broken engagement becomes a divorce.

"Harrad students don't do that. One of the common denominators the Tenhausens use in accepting students at Harrad is based on an early analysis made by Abraham Maslow; what Maslow labeled "a dominance feeling syndrome." People of this type are "self confident, socially poised, relaxed, extroverted, have high self-esteem, are self assured, have a feeling of general capability, are unconventional, have less respect for rules, have a tendency to 'use' people, have freer personality expression, are somewhat more secure, have an autonomous code of ethics, are more independent, less religious, more masculine, less polite, and have a love of adventure, novelty and new experience."

I grinned at Jake who was listening to me in a state of semi-shock. "Not all the Harrad kids have these attributes, but they have some. After a year or two, they acquire more. As a result they don't seek "security" from each other. In fact they don't expect or demand anything from one another but a willingness to accept the other person as an amazing human being. It is an interesting side-light on Maslow's study that people of this type when they are married, do not as a rule end up in divorce courts. They make the most successful marriages particularly when they mate with a person with similar attributes. Now place this Harrad student in an environment where sex is accepted as a quite normal enjoyment, and love is based on admiration and deep liking for another person as a person, you have something entirely different from the Western concepts of romantic love and passion. Because I love Beth and she loves me doesn't exclude Shelia or Stanley, and other kids that may come within our orbit of interests. United, we stand to have more interesting and vital lives

than we would performing independent love duets. With only
two of us seeing our own reflections in each other's eyes for a lifetime, a certain glazing would set in caused simply by over-
exposure . . . not lack of love.

"Oh, my God," Jake exploded. "All you college kids do is
spout words. Do you honestly know what the hell you are talking
about?"

"Sure," I said, "but I can see that you don't."

"Look, son . . . it's an insane idea . . . and now if I understand
you, you are trying to tell that every one in your school is going
to bed with everyone else."

"The males with the females, not the males with the males,
or the females with the females," I chuckled.

"I should hope not," Jake said sourly. "But you can't do that
all your life."

"Why not? A great many married people in this country are
doing just that right now . . . and it all ends up in divorce courts,
or gets pretty messy."

"You are going to be a doctor. Who could trust a doctor who
lived like you do at Harrad. You'd have no patients."

"You trust Doctor Neisner. I heard Mother telling a friend
of hers that Doctor Neisner has a girl friend. His wife knows it
and couldn't care less. Old Jewish custom, really. Have you read
the Old Testament lately?"

Jake scowled at me and changed the subject. "So someday
you are going to marry this blonde girl."

"Her name is Beth."

"Will she change her religion?"

"Who cares?"

"I do. Your mother does. You will. If your wife does not
change for you, you can never become a member of the congrega-
tion. A good Jew's wife is an extension of himself."

"Not Beth. She will be herself."

"What kind of Jew will you be?"

"A happy man first, and a Jew second."

"You would give up your faith?"

"No. I have endless faith . . . in man."

Jake looked at me puzzled. "So this is the kind of education I am paying for?"

I hugged him. "This is what happens when you love . . . as any good Jew knows."

If Jake was bewildered then, he's going to be more bewildered when he finds his son arrested for indecent exposure, and on a morals charge involving orgiastic sex behavior. Ebeneezer Schnook just returned with our supper. Baked beans, of course, donated by the Women's Auxiliary who are having their Saturday night supper and bingo game in the cellar of the church across the street. With Ebeneezer were two reporters from the local newspaper.

"This will make the wire servies, Eb," one of them said, gleefully. "You'll be famous. You can run for selectman this fall."

The other character tried to persuade us to grasp the bars of our cell and shout angrily while he aimed his Graflex at us. Failing to get our cooperation he edged his way to the cell, in the rear, where Beth, Shelia and Valerie were imprisoned. He was back in a second blushing. "Jumping Jesus," he yelled. "Those dames are standing there stark naked!" Is that the way you found them, Eb?"

Ebeneezer, snorting, ran to see. "Put on your clothes," we heard him shout angrily.

"You didn't give us time to bring our nightgowns." Valerie answered indignantly. Beth and Shelia were choking with laughter. "It's your fault you dirty old man. Do you expect us to sleep in our clothes?" The least thing you could do is turn on the air conditioning."

On reflection, the reporter with the Graflex stared back to the girl's cell, but Eb held him back. "Who are they Eb? Where did you arrest them? Let me snap a couple of pictures."

"Nope. No dirty pictures in my jail! I don't know who they are. Can't get a damned thing out of them. A bunch of wild college kids is my guess. They moved into Bill Sykes's place up at Nob Point. Been up there nearly a week . . . running all over the place bare-ass . . . taking movies of each other, singing, dancing and drinking all night long. Don't know what in hell this generation is coming to. Couple of them live in New York, I think.

Probably beatniks or bums from Greenwich Village. A damned shame. Stuff like this gives the Cape a bad name."

"If it's bad for business," Stanley asked "why do you want to put it in the newspapers, Eb old boy? I'd hush the whole matter up if I were you."

"Keep your fresh mouth shut!" Ebeneezer snarled.

"Where do you kids go to school?" the reporter asked.

"On a little known planet in outer space." Jack said, a very serious tone in his voice. "We are emissaries from the planet Sub Rosa. We arrived two days ago in our space ship which is carefully concealed in one of the lonely sand dunes nearby. These are not our normal bodies. In actual fact on Sub Rosa we had no bodies but are simply emanations of spirit. To bring our message to your leaders we have temporarily assumed the terrestrial bodies of six nice earth children."

"See what television has done." Eb looked at us sadly.

"It's true," Jack said solemnly. "Within the next few hours you will discover that certain earthlings have disappeared. Contact the parents . . . send them to view us. They will recognize the bodies of their loved ones . . but will tremble at the dark spirits inhabiting them."

I suppose from the viewpoint of more practical and moral earth creatures our Cape vacation and final incarceration does have an other-wordly quality about it. It really all started last March. InSix wasn't planned. It just grew spontaneously as a result of our nightly get-to-gethers at Harrad. Looking back, I would guess that Jack Dawes was really the germinating factor. The night that he accompanied himself on his guitar and sang us a screwball, satirical rhyming version of the news of the day, we kept testing him to see if he could do it extemporaneously. Jack, never at a loss for words, was able to sing off-the-cuff, jazzed-up calypso interpretations that had us all gasping with laughter. A few nights later, Valerie, who can mimic almost any gesture or voice, joined Jack with a skit satirizing the first flight of a man with a woman (she had a slight case of nymphomania) as they orbited out of earth into space together. For the fun of it we worked out several other skits. Sheila, who had mastered the accordion, joined with Jack on the guitar. Stanley provided a beat by banging on any available pan or bottle. He finally got so enthusiastic, he bought a set of bongo drums. Jack taught Beth how to play chords on the guitar, and before long I had mastered it well enough to punk along with them.

By April we had a repertoire of eight musical sketches. Shelia refused to do any acting. She couldn't let herself go like Beth and Valerie. Somehow, Beth always seemed to get cast as the dumb blonde sex-pot, and Valerie as the sophisticated hep-cat. Stanley's enthusiasm held us together with his pipe dream that we were good enough to "go professional." The money we could make would help put us through graduate school. None of us took Stanley seriously until the night he and Jack told us we were "booked" the following Saturday at Joe Gonzi's coffee house in Cambridge. Even then we didn't believe him.

"We're not that good," Sheila objected. "It would take too much rehearsing."

"I'd be scared silly with an audience," Beth said.

"It's only the 'Grinning Eye' Jack said. "Gonzi isn't going to pay us. It's just for experience."

Three weeks later Gonzi offered us one hundred fifty dollars a week for our Friday and Saturday night appearances. Our skits on the parietal rules at "B" College, with Beth and Val paralyzing the audience as the virgin co-ed on their visit to a senior's room, and Jack and Stanley playing the role of the Mephisthophelean seducers of young womanhood; our outer space skit, and a skit with Beth as the naive blonde who comes to college to be a drum majorette and is either constantly dropping her baton or is nearly exposing her breasts as she whirls it in the air, created standing room only at the Grinning Eye. Gonzi upped his admission price. A local recording company told us that if we could "clean up" all eight skits, they would make a long playing record of us.

Still none of us took it very seriously. "It's a lark," Beth said when we all got back to Harrad after one Saturday show, "But it could take too much time. I think we should play it for what it's worth within limits. None of this business of racing around the country or signing a contract the way that agent wants, we are a local fad. We're 'in' for the moment. I wouldn't want to live my life in a sweat of wondering how to stay 'in.' The whole racket is too fickle."

All of us agreed. But Beth had named us. We were temporarily, at least, InSix. Jack and Stanley decided we should be incorporated with the purpose of our corporation to put all the stockholders through graduate school. We finally made the recording and exhausted our repertoire. Much to the relief of Marget and Phil Tenhausen, by June we had forgotten the whole business.

But unwanted success is sometimes hard to dispose of. We had a money bull by the horns. As President of InSix, Inc. Jack kept in touch with us through the summer. Our lack of desire for publicity created interest, mystery and intrigue. Our record began selling beyond all expectation. The recording company wanted to make another one. By mail and telephone, Jack badgered us until we finally all agreed to spend the week before Labor Day on the Cape. Object, to write and rehearse a half dozen more skits.

Shelia and Stanley agreed to meet us in Boston with Shelia's new station wagon, purchased so that InSix could travel together. To our amazement, Jack and Valerie arrived at the South Station followed by porters carrying enough movie equipment to fill a small truck without any passengers. After much hugging and bussing one another (while the local citizenry watched us with their mouths open) Jack finally explained. "I borrowed the stuff from Bad Max. All summer he has been making experimental movies. Ten or fifteen minute jobs that are supposed to give the cinema a new artistic depth and meaning. One of Bad Max's friends won a twenty thousand dollar award from the Ford Foundation. Seems the foundation is encouraging new types of cinematic expression. The joke is that some of the awards were given for 'pornies.' "

"What the devil are pornies?" Beth demanded.

Jack grinned. "Flickers a little on the pornographic side. The public loves them. Makes them feel they can be esthetically interested and still not bored to death. Kook stuff. Nudes with skulls where their breasts should be; a girl sitting like Whistler's mother but dressed only in her garter belt; a girl carrying her tits on a tray; naked witches riding broomsticks, etc., all mixed up with political crap and God knows what, supposedly created by artists and poets who have some mystical message to convey. I decided InSix can do better!"

We finally wrestled all the movie stuff, together with Jack and Valerie's trunks and bags, into Sheila's station wagon. With the six of us squeezed between tripods, floodlights, guitars, accordions and what not there was scarcely room to turn and look at each other. Stanley edged the car slowly through the Boston traffic.

"Get us to the Cape before the transmission is scraping on the highway," I groaned.

On the expressway, Shelia managed to pry a few more details out of Jack and Valerie. "Aren't we going to work on a new record?" she demanded. "Where is making screwball movies going to get us? Where the heck are we going to stay on the Cape with all this junk?"

"Typical female," Jack said hugging her. "Three questions at once. You bet we are going to make another record. InSix is famous. If we want to go on a national television hook-up it's all arranged."

"Nothing doing," Beth said. "I promised Mother and Pops and Margaret and Phil that we wouldn't go any further from Harrad than the Grinning Eye. The last straw would be their nubile daughter barnstorming around the country . . . and believe me Harrad College is next to the last straw, as far as they are concerned."

"I agree," Valerie said. "Let the world come to us."

"The world won't have to come to us," Jack chuckled. "We are going to the world with a movie. When it is finished it will be the rage of the Village. Bad Max promises to run it twice a week at the Last Gurgle. Behold you knaves! Sitting next to you is Jack Dawes, producer and director of the new epic, a twenty minute satire on the women's fashion industry. InSix is going to change women's fashions and clothing styles singlehanded. We'll be famous and infamous. Tell'em Val."

Val groaned. "Jack has lost his marbles. I refuse to comment. Whatever mad project he has afoot we are going to come to grips

with it at Nob Point. Bill Sykes, a kind of uncle-ish friend of my
father (unbeknown to that good man) loaned me the key to his
cottage, a slight token of his affection and appreciation of behind
patting privileges I have rendered him since I was a little tot. It's
a nice lonely spot on a sand dune overlooking the Atlantic, conducive to lovemaking and reverie."

A few miles from Eastham we turned off the highway, bumping and careening along a lonely dirt road that led to the ocean,
we finally located the Syke's cottage. It seemed isolated enough.
The Atlantic a hundred feet below us was a red glaze in the
afternoon sun. A few other cottages were nestled in dunes at a
respectable distance. After we had lugged all the stuff inside and
surveyed the living room, single bedroom and kitchen, it became
apparent that we were going to have to rearrange the sleeping
facilities. Hilariously we tossed the mattresses from the two single
beds on the floor. Sideways with our feet hanging over the edge
all six of us lay down. We were as neatly packed as sardines.

"Those with sex on their minds will have to find a lonely
sand dune," Beth yelled from the bottom of the pig pile we all
made on top of her.

"Who wants sex and with whom?" Val said hugging Stanley.

We all looked at each other embarrassed for a moment. Beth
broke the tension. "Remember me? I love you all!"

"So do we," Shelia and Val chorused. The girls merrily proceeded to kiss Stanley, Jack and me.

Deciding that food was more important than kissing and
hugging, at least for the moment, we drove back to the highway,
found a supermarket, and bought enough groceries for a week,
and Jack bought two cases of aged-in-the-bottle champagne, telling us we earned it for devotion to InSix, besides we had to celebrate our re-union.

An hour later, wearing sweat-shirts that the girls had embroidered with the word InSix lettered inside a heart, and shorts
and panties, we slid down the sand cliff in front of the cottage to
the beach below. Stanley slid a case of champagne down the cliff
and popped the corks at us showering us with geysers of foaming
wine. We cooked hot dogs over an open fire. Wrapped in blankets
as protection against the cold night air (somehow or other I

found Valerie, a sinuous caterpillar, curled up beside me) we chattered incessantly about the world, life and us.

"I guess you've got me for the night," Valerie wiggled closer. "Are you sorry?"

The conversation had become sporadic. I pulled the army blankets partially over our heads and Val and I burrowed into our shelter. The fire of drift wood had turned into a red glow. The sand beneath us was still warm from the sun. Not far away, Beth and Stanley, Shelia and Jack were huddled mounds on the beach. I watched the shadows the firelight made on the planes of Val's face. I held her hand. Silently, we watched the stars in the evening sky.

"Are we bad . . . all of us?" Val asked softly.

"What is bad? That I care for you? That we are just human beings alone . . . and yet somehow wonderfully knit together?"

"Doesn't it frighten you?"

"This moment isn't meaningless. It's wondrous. You know, my guess is that Stanley and Beth and Shelia and Jack are asking each other the same questions. I like the way the six of us surrender ourselves to each other. We have eliminated dishonesty . . . shame . . . pretense."

Val sighed. "I don't know why any of you, Jack, Stanley or you would want me. I'm too tall . . . too awkward. An ugly duckling compared to Beth and Shelia."

I leaned on my elbow and looked into her face. "Val, you have a lovely face; strong, clean cut, big saucer eyes that glisten, a nice body. If you are looking for the ugly duckling in the crowd, you are lying beside him."

"Men shouldn't be pretty. You have character. You look like a genius. But me . . . in high heels I'm at least two inches taller than any of you."

"I haven't heard Jack complaining."

"Do you think we should be mixed up like this? Won't some-one get hurt? You probably wish you were with Beth."

I grinned at her. "I'm not giving it a thought. I think we have all discovered that any two of us could get married and live together so, in effect, we are all married to each other. What's more I think that the 'Idea' of us will last. I used to think we might fight and get jealous of each other. In the first year at Harrad most of us did. And then we simply eliminated jealousy by discovering that it was a very boring and selfish preoccupation. In its place we have developed a strong sense of unity and a fast instant communication."

Val kissed me. "Pull up your sweatshirt, Harry. I want to feel your flesh against me." Later she wiggled out of her panties, and we fell asleep enmeshed.

I awoke with the sun a red crescent on the horizon. Night was reluctantly leaving the sky. Val was holding my penis lightly, half asleep herself. Our climax was sleepy-sweet and hungrily joyful. I was asleep again in her arms when Stanley yelled. "Come on all you young lovers. Last one in the ocean is custard the dragon."

A yelling screaming churning mass of gasping naked flesh, we all plunged into the icy morning water. Shivering and half frozen we scrambled out within minutes. Our courtly naked ladies, their nipples erect, hooted and howled at our shrunken, wizened penises and our dismay at discovering they had practically disappeared in pure shock at such an outrage.

After breakfast, Jack and Valerie opened their Pandora trunk. Jack proudly held up what looked like a roll of cloth, about five yards long. While it looked like ordinary cloth held on the vertical axis it was transparent as clear vinyl plastic.

"This," he said mysteriously, "is something new in the world. It is actually plastic but it is perforated with millions of microscopic holes. In the vernacular of Madison Avenue, it breathes, and behaves like any ordinary cloth. It is not on the market yet, and probably won't be for a few years until the manufacturing costs are reduced. A friend of mine pilfered it from the research laboratory of one of the large chemical companies."

"What will anyone use it for?" Beth demanded.

"Beth!" Jack chided her. "You obviously didn't get enough sleep last night. Your clear mind isn't functioning. It will be used for clothes! What else? Show them you handiwork, Val."

"This wasn't my idea," Val grinned as she fished in the trunk. "If I hadn't been working for a very good-natured dress designer this summer, Jack would never have got them made. A fortune of labor went into them." Val handed Beth a dress which looked quite normal to me until Beth held it up to examine it.

"Jack Dawes, you are mad!" Beth yelled: "Completely off your rocker! Look everybody . . . the damned thing has a transparent behind!"

Sure enough, carefully merged into the seat of the dress in the shape of a perfect heart was a piece of Jack's plastic cloth.

Val produced a similar dress for Sheila. Altogether Val had three street dresses and three evening gowns. The evening gowns had the additional feature of transparent breast cups as well as transparent behinds.

While the girls were excitedly putting them on, their behinds undulating and clearly visible as they walked, Stanley and I tried to stop laughing long enough to listen to Jack.

"How do you like them?" he demanded. "Most entrancing style ever developed for females. Something absolutely unique in female fashions. Original creations by Jacque. That's me! When Val first modeled them for me I nearly gave up my dream of being a movie mogul and departed for Paris to set up a fashion house. But that will have to wait. First InSix is going to make a movie. It will be a satire on the fashion industry. Since I will, of necessity, have to be cameraman and director, I think that Harry and Stanley should take the parts of famous French fashion designers. Get the picture? As the movie opens the entire fashion industry is clamoring for the first view of the fall fashions."

Jack delved into his trunk, and chucked two rubber apemasks at Harry and Stanley. He then produced two full dress morning suits with striped pants. "I bought you costumes for two dollars each from the Morgan Memorial," he chuckled. "Probably taken off rich corpses before they interred them" Jack grinned at Stanley and me who were suspiciously sniffing the shabby moth-ball impregnated clothing. "Now my idea is that our famous designers should appear in full dress, wearing ape masks. This will permit Harry and Stanley to take other parts as the movie develops. So, I give you the idea. Take it from there! The basic point is that women will wear anything if the Paris or Italian designers make it sufficiently *outré*. All we have to do now is to put together a zippy script."

"Don't kid yourself," Shelia said. "No woman would ever bare her fanny to the public."

"These styles are kind of intriguing," Stanley mused. Imagine walking along Fifth Avenue judging and comparing women's behinds."

"The wheels of industry would stop turning," I chuckled. "All traffic would stop, the male population would develop permanent priapism, the girdle and brassiere industry would languish. . . . Maybe we should call the movie, *The Day the World Ended*. I waited for applause but no one got the pun.

"I've got a better title," Beth chuckled, flipping her behind. "Since the style would only appeal to men, it is obvious that drama should climax with the women castrating the designers. Why not call it *The Short Saga of the Fat Asses*." Beth bent over to see what else was in Jack's trunk.

"My God, Beth," Val warned her. "In that dress you should stoop *not bend!* We just saw your tonsils!"

"I think the style will catch on," I laughed. "It reveals entirely new areas of the female anatomy."

"How about *Cheeks of Delight* for a title?" Val asked. She was immediately bombarded with pillows.

For two days we swam, sang, wrote a script for the movie and as the mood seized us, hysterically rehearsed our parts. Stanley and I were given the name Apeneé Brothers. I suggested the addition of meshugana. We finally agreed that the title "Meshugana Freres Apeneé" had a nice esthetic sound that should entrance the critics. By the fourth day, Stanley and I, nearly asphixated by the odor of naphthalene, had abandoned the size 40 striped pants. Dressed in tailcoats, ape masks and nothing else. We horsed through the mysterious motions of designing women's clothes.

Exasperated, Jack insisted that our costumes were too pornographic. The production came to a halt until Shelia and Beth got the idea of designing cod-pieces for us with grinning faces stitched onto them. Their masterpieces were a concoction of brassiere cups, padded, embroidered and sewn onto our jockey shorts. They insisted on sewing on the cups while we were still in our shorts and poked their needles at us with scary abandon!

"A much more intriguing style," Val insisted, "than bare female buttocks."

Since this was to be a silent film with eventual appropriate sound track furnished by InSix, we had to act our parts with broad hammy facial expressions. We finally concluded that the Les Freres Apeneé shouldn't wear the ape masks until the last scene! The masks would be the faces the public naturally expected on the first fateful showing of the new fashions.

Jack, amazingly serious, in his role of director kept shooting miles of film, and even filmed all our insane rehearsals. "This movie will finally be the product of my expert editing and cutting," he said pompously. "I visualize it opening with a whirling montage of breasts, behinds, legs and unshaved deltas. These will gradually dissolve into the interior of the famous Apeneé House of Fashion. It will end with Les Freres Apeneé being pursued right out of their salon into the street by slobbering, hysterical, adoring women. To escape the howling mob Les Freres will discover a convenient ladder and climb to the roof of the establishment. Below the women ecstatic, happily swooning are ready to literally eat their heroes."

Jack spent considerable effort and ingenuity to transform Syke's cottage into a passible version of a French fashion salon. Though we were dubious as to the effect, he was undaunted, insisting that the comic elements would sustain the somewhat garbled backgrounds.

Shelia, Val, and Beth played the parts of fashion models wearing wigs that Jack had brought. They swayed their hips and behinds modishly as they modeled the gowns. Wearing rhinestone sun glasses, no wigs, but with suitable admiring and haughty expressions they also played the parts of the female audience.

Although Jack kept insisting that somehow he would end up with a serious experimental movie, and he spent half his time either lying on the floor shooting scenes or hanging from the rafters of the cottage to get interesting camera angles, each rehearsal for a particular scene became more horsed up and insane than the previous one. Most of the time we were helpless with laughter at our own antics. Jack's pained expression of frustration reduced Shelia and Beth to hysterical laughter and finally they got hiccoughs from drinking too much champagne. This morning the whole meshugana project finally came to an abrupt end. Jack set his tripod up outside the cottage. Stanley and I (wearing the ape masks, Henri and Cecil Apeneé) were to run past his camera pursued by Val, Sheila and Beth. Our coat tails flying, wearing our jockey shorts with the grinning cod-pieces, we scrambled up the ladder to the roof. Below us the girls were begging us to come down. They adored our Fanny and Titty Fashions. In a happy inspiration the girls took off their dresses and tossed them up at us. We responded by tossing our jockey shorts back at them. And that's the way our world ended. Not with a whimper but with a literal bang!

Ebeneezer Schnook emerged from the bushes, actually shooting a revolver over our heads. He was followed by his deputy, both screaming hoarsely. We were a disgrace to the human race. Like Doukhiboors, naked but unbowed, Sheila, Val and Beth stared at them contemptuously angry at their invasion of privacy. Stanley and I tried unsuccessfully to make our exit over the opposite side of the roof. Jack, a model of propriety, in his bathing trunks excoriated Ebeneezer and his deputy, who paid no attention to him. Triumphantly they corralled Stanley and me, their guns levelled at us in a very determined, no nonsense manner.

With horror and pure shock on their faces at their discovery of us, our heroes herded us into the cottage, searched the place for loot, impounded all of Jack's exposed film, denounced our lack of morals, and then with their siren blasting drove us hell bent to the pokey.

Sunday, Phil and Margaret rescued us. They arrived with a lawyer who knew somebody who knew Schnook. Mr. Big, (whoever he was) the lawyer's friend, never put in an appearance. Ebeneezer finally tossed in the towel and accepted the one-upmanship with grim reluctance. He even returned the movie equipment and all the exposed film to Jack.

"Just like a gangster movie on television," Beth said admiringly to Phil, "Even the fuzz don't fool around when the Big Man speaks. Sometimes, Phil it is obviously true that power speaks louder than love in this best of all possible worlds."

But Phil didn't feel philosophical. "Damn it," he exploded

when we were out of Ebeneezer's hearing. "I expect more maturity from Harrad students. You've been acting just like typical college brats. An escapade like this could land Harrad and all of us in the newspapers."

I defended us. "There is considerable difference, Phil. Who were we harming? Were we destroying property or making a general nuisance of ourselves? On the contrary, Schnook invaded *our* privacy. On the opposite side of the fence, my father, for example, feels that all of us at Harrad are going to end up a grim, humorless lot, exposed to sex too early, tied down to marriage, and generally sour from having assumed too much responsibility at an immature age. We disagree. We, InSix, are all in love. We have discovered the fun and laughter and sheer joy of each other as mortal, sexual human beings. We all have Phi Beta Kappa level marks and we're far from being dull. You have no right to be angry with us. If you are angry, *you* have lost the key to Harrad."

"What's the key to Harrad?" Phil demanded, interested in spite of himself.

"The ability to slide out of your skin, be your own "doppelganger." At a moment's notice to be able to step aside and laugh happily at your own serious, concerned, frustrated, conforming other-self."

Phil sighed. "Okay, I asked for it. All of you pack up your junk. Any further movie making will be done in the confines of Harrad. It's obvious that the world and Old Cape Cod, aren't quite ready for you!"

FROM THE JOURNAL OF BETH HILLYER

March, the Third Year

Because Mom and Pops decided they had earned a Caribbean vacation, I am spending Spring vacation in New York with Jake and Rachel. Actually, this took some doing. Rather than have their daughter exposed to Passover, they would have gladly planned their Easter vacation to coincide with my Spring vacation. I received several letters from them extolling the merits of Jamaica, and the value of exposure to other influences than Harrad and Harry Schacht. I owed it to myself to compare and examine all the pebbles on the beach. It is patently impossible to explain to them that having already experienced the delights of the bed with three boys, and being able to continue this joy with great regularity, I scarcely need to extend myself by lying down with other pebbles. They finally grew impatient at my malingering and departed for Jamaica without their ungrateful daughter.

I love New York, and I love Harry's big house filled with uncles and aunts and kids and a grandmother all living under one roof. I really believe they're no longer afraid of me. Still, Rachel worries about her boy.

"Saul and I wanted a big family," she told me yesterday when I was helping her make supper. "I had four brothers and three sisters. Saul had two sisters and a brother. Then after Harry was born I had female troubles, and finally, after an operation, there were to be no more children. So maybe we worry too much about Harry. Being an only child is not good."

"You've done very well with Harry," I smiled at her. "I love him, too."

"Are you going to get married soon," Rachel asked. She looked hopefully at me.

"Next year. Harry and I think that is soon enough. Are you afraid of having a Gentile daughter-in-law?"

Rachel sighed and hugged me. I like her quick affectionate nature. "Saul and I are confused. Our friends, the rabbi . . . our religion, you see, Beth we love you, but I guess we wonder why you love Harry. You are so very pretty . . . and so Goyish. Your father and mother . . . they've met Harry. They can't possibly approve. And then there's Harrad. Oi-vey, I'm afraid this can only end in great unhappiness."

I kissed her cheek. "Rachel, I love Harry. When I first knew him I was afraid, too. He was Jewish, the way he thought, the expressions he used, they all seemed foreign and insular to me. When we first made love, I didn't think I liked his deep concern for me. I thought somehow it wasn't virile . . . that a man should dominate a woman. And then suddenly I saw Harry for the person he really is, dynamic, kind, gentle, affectionate . . . I visualized him as the doctor he will be and I knew that somehow he was my real ideal of a man. I actually feel like socking people who say to me; but "Beth you are so pretty!" meaning that Harry is homely. Harry will be lean, craggy and quite impressive when all the pretty boys have gone to seed, and have developed pot-bellies. After three years, Harry and I have learned we're opposite sides of the same coin. Separated we don't function. To-gether we are a perfectly adjusted, reasoning, emoting whole person. We deeply understand each other's foibles, and love each other for them."

Rachel listened to me while she rolled out and thinned her blintz dough. "These are very nice things you say about my son, Beth. I am glad. But I will feel better when you are married. When you come to our house you both sleep alone in a separate room. I hope you understand. I know you room together . . . go to bed together at *that* college . . . but here in my home, un-married . . . well, somehow it doesn't seem right."

I wanted to hug Rachel. She looked so concerned and wor-ried. "Really," I laughed "It's not so much different. If Harry and I were going to a regular college, we'd probably be sleeping together in motels, or what have you. But I do understand. When I come to visit in your house both Harry and I respect your feel-ings." I didn't tell her about late last night, Harry sneaked up to the third floor where the guest room is and we snuggled to-gether until dawn.

Of course, I realize that Rachel's worries have some basis in reality. Altogether over the past two years, Harry has spent a month with my family in Columbus. Mother and Pops have been cordial with him but it still is a distant cordiality. Harry may be the finest boy in the world but, inescapably, to them, he is Jewish first and a man second. There is no overt anti-semitism in anything my family have said to me. It is indirect. They point out that the Jewish doctors stick together. The Jewish families maintain their own solidarity. They have their own functions, their own groups, their own organizations. It is useless to point out to them that the gentiles have similar walls to hide behind.

Mother and Pops belong to a country club that seeks new memberships very carefully. Thus they avoid a "Jewish take-over." "You can't fight it," Pops told me. "It's the basis of their religion. They don't want us either. From early history the Jew has insisted on his uniqueness in relation to God and non-Jews." When I countered that this was the only basis of Jewish survival in a hostile world, Pops insisted that was beside the point. The past couldn't be changed. Now it was too late. The Jews did not want to be assimilated by any nation; not even Israel if it came to that. Their religious indoctrination, in a larger sense, simply placed them in their own minds above the mainstream of any particular culture. "And, you Beth, you will be neither flesh nor fowl." Pops sighed. "The Jews will never fully accept you, and you will be shut off from your own kind."

It is a sad commentary on the world, but Jake and Rachel could agree with Mother and Pops on one thing, if nothing else. Harry and I shouldn't marry. It bewilders me. If you accept their philosophy to its ultimate, the world would be a collection of inbred cultural islands. Possibly there would be an exchange of goods and some superficial contact between the tribes, but deep interchange of cultural values and of course inter-marriage would be avoided. Years ago I discovered a book in Pops library by a man named Wendell Willkie. He ran for president. Several wars ago, Willkie was campaigning for *One World*. Do we make progress ten steps backward to one forward? Poor Mr. Wilkie. There are now twice as many nations in this one world and all of them grind their axes in New York. They must have named it with grim humor . . . United Nations.

Last night, with Harry deep inside me, my face snuggled against his neck and shoulder, I was in a blissful, talkative mood. "It is incredible to me, that I lived nearly twenty years and never tasted Jewish food until I knew you. Life would be very dull without potato latkes, bagels, lox, sweet and sour meat balls, stuffed cabbage, kishke, knishes, kreplach, chopped liver, gefilte fish, all the wonderfully crazy pareve food, all the enchanting desserts without leavening that have been invented for Passover . . . even borscht . . . which took some doing."

Harry interrupted my breathless recital by kissing my breasts and gently probing them with his tongue. "I like the taste of your breasts better than any food. What's more this diet is not fattening!" Harry stopped kissing for a minute. "You know what Jake says, Beth? "Good food killed more Jews than Hitler." When we are married I'm going to have to watch your diet. You may have a tendency to get too plump. I like skinny women."

"Skinny women with big tits," I said offering him one.

"And firm behinds."

"And a warm vagina," I said oscillating slightly.

"Amen," he affirmed rather loudly.

"Talk softly," I whispered. "If your father walked in here right now he would go into a state of shock. Anyway, you interrupted me. Jewish food is only one of the things I have discovered. I have inherited a whole new group of holidays. Rosh Hashanah, Hanukkah, Passover to mention a few, and with them a whole new understanding of the origins of Christianity. And, I'm learning a whole new Yiddish vocabulary. Hundreds and hundreds of useful onomatopoeic words. *Schlecht, pisk, metziah, plotz, schemiel, fresser, shicker, shmendrick, bobbe, kvetch . . .*"

"Hocken a cheinik," Harry interrupted me.

I bit him. "I am not banging on a tea kettle, or however you translate it. In fact, I'm so entranced and there are such useful words for cursing, too, that I am compiling a dictionary of them. Your father is helping me. And words are not all I've learned, Harry. I've discovered a new Jewish way of looking at life. A new way to worry humorously. Jews have a way of laughing at themselves that is particularly appealing and psychologically healthy. And I like the intensity of Jews, and their keen desire to learn and study. It strikes a keynote in my own philosophy of living." I kissed Harry. "There's a hundred other things. I'm so happy. Thank you for loving me, too."

Harry hugged me. I kissed the tears in his eyes. "Did you ever stop to think Beth, that the basic idea of Harrad is ultimately against a world within a world like the Jews have made. These are the cultural differences from one religion, or one race, or one nation that set us all apart. All the things you admire about the Jewish culture would have disappeared long ago if the world had been able to assimilate the Jews. If you want to consider it from the standpoint of national or racial differences the same thing applies to the Italians, Greeks, Scandinavians, Germans, Japanese, Chinese, or any nation or culture you can name. In a few centuries these ethnic differences will have mostly vanished. Maybe it is necessary for peace in the world that the foreign aspects of humanity are eliminated, but when you look at Japan, for example, as a product of American influence, it is a little terrifying. In a few centuries the Japanese will be as minus a cultural heritage . . . and hence a sense of past and identity in the world . . . as are the Americans.

"I don't believe that the Harrad idea is to obliterate cultural differences," I said. "It seems to me we're being taught to be citizens of the world. We're building our own bridges between cultures. That's the whole educative process, if you really analyze it. Everything that makes a particular culture unique should be preserved. But anything in the folklore of a culture or group that denigrates man or destroys the love of man for all men should disappear from the world. In my world I don't need your Scroll of Laws. I don't need your Moses or the prophets who proclaim Jews are the favored children of God. I don't need Christ on the Cross, or the Virgin Mary, but I *do* need the idea of Christmas and Hanukkah. Just as in the larger sense of love and awakening of the world to Spring, and rebirth, I need Easter and Passover." I kissed Harry and he responded eagerly. "You've come out of me." I said a little disappointed. I helped him find his way back.

"I got so interested in listening I forgot about sex," Harry grinned at me. "A man's mind won't always let him do two things at once."

"Are we talking too much," I whispered.

"No," Harry said. "In our lifetime, let's have billions of words probing our world and our lives. I believe it is the cornerstone of love."

I kissed him in fervent agreement. "One thing I didn't mention: I enjoy the strong sense of family unity you, and many Jewish families, seem to have. You have grown up in a family where aunts, uncles, cousins, sisters, brothers, grandmothers and grandfathers are genuinely concerned and involved in each other's lives. Even disparity in age and income doesn't separate you. Your holidays cement what personal disruptions and conflicts the days in between may have wrought. And if Jewish families are small, they identify quickly and deeply with other Jews. Maybe it's self-protection, or a feeling of being a minority. You are all . . . what does your father say? . . . *Landsmen.* Nevertheless, I think even Jewish families are having a hard time holding out against a philosophy of marriage that believes each generation should live their own lives."

Since I was so talkative, Harry decided to listen to me as he kissed my belly. I let my fingers trickle over his penis and kissed it lightly. "I'm glad that you let me rant and rave, Harry. I love you."

"I'm enjoying it. Your fingers feel like feathers tickling me. Very exotic! Harry grinned. "I know what you are driving at, Beth. It's a part of our mass culture. The economic wheels turn

better when the younger generation creates their own little two-
by-four nests. This way twice as many automobiles, television
sets, refrigerators or what have you, can be sold. One night, a few
months ago, I walked through a middle class suburbia, a few
miles from Harrad. The houses are not like this old firetrap with
fifteen rooms plus a huge basement and overflowing attic. These
new suburban houses are all built to the pattern of families with
two or three children. Possibly they have a bedroom for each
child, and generally a family room where most of the leisure
time of the wife and husband is spent viewing television with
their children, when they are not all engaged in dreary little
"do-it-yourself" projects. In the summer the man and wife mani-
cure their little five thousand square feet of crab grass using all
the latest mechanical gadgets from Sears Roebuck so that the job
can be done in a half hour or less thus freeing them at last to
join all the bored people travelling the highways with their
broods where they finally purchase a Dairy Freeze or a Howard
Johnson ice cream cone. A modern family's Sunday adventure in
togetherness. I don't think I could live like that. On the other
hand, I suppose there aren't many families left who live like we
do. My father and his brother Milt started in business together
during the depression. The only way they could afford to get
married was to move their wives in with their father and mother.
My grandfather built this house with three floors and fifteen
rooms because he liked a lot of people around him. Originally,
my *bobbe* and *zaide* had so much room they took in boarders. As
children were born and they needed the space, the boarders were
pre-empted.

"Finally the wheel came full turn. Two of their children
moved back with them and filled the house with their own
families. At times with Jake, Rachel, his brother Milt, his wife
Annie, their three children, me, Grandma, Gramp and a great
aunt who has since died, there have been eleven or twelve people living here at one time. Yet there has been surprisingly little
conflict. Everyone managed to develop their own inviolate retreat
within the house. A place to escape the general confusion when-
ever they desired. We have no grass, but Grandma has a garden
in the back of the house, a space about twelve by fourteen that

isn't occupied by clotheslines and ash barrels. In the summer Grandma has something growing in every inch of it as well as growing up the walls surrounding it. On warm nights we sit on the back porch, and the neighbors next door sit on theirs. We watch Grandma who continues gardening with an extension light. All of us put in our two cents worth of advice on gardening, or we talk and discuss and argue late into the evening. Finally, we can't even see each other's faces. We are simply disembodied voices, and the words we are saying are like friends holding hands on a summer night.

"Your kind of world, and this house is dying," I said. "Man in the mass will have to find a new way to live. What will happen in the next fifty years when men will inevitably be forced by law to limit their offspring? We'll all have to discover new ways to live closer together and search for values as groups not individuals. The human animal needs the constant stimulation of the never quite attainable, and I don't mean things or possessions, I mean the never-ending lure of knowledge and understanding."

While I was talking, Harry had rejoined himself with me. "I think the Tenhausens are pointing the way to the future," he said. With InSix, for example, you and I, Jack and Val, Sheila and Stanley; we've replaced the vanishing family. We can give it an even larger existence and strength. Our personal commitment to keep learning in the fields of our general interests, effectively breaks down specialization and hence lack of communication, and our love for each other both idealistic, sexual and practical creates a constant renewal of wonder and delight in our humanness and our place in the larger world."

I hugged Harry hard against me. "You know, making love this way, extending the delight, heightening our closeness to each other reminds me of when I was a little girl. I loved ice cream cones. I would eat one ever so slowly, making it last and last. I feel the same way now, blissfully ecstatic. Your lips and mouth taste better than any ice cream cone," I grinned at him. "You won't melt will you?"

Harry laughed. "Not so fast as an ice cream cone, anyway."

Last night at supper I thought Jake was rather preoccupied.

He kept looking across the table at me with a strange expression on his face. He answered Rachel's and Annie's conversation in a monotone, and he didn't probe Alan and Sammy (Annie's and Milt's kids) about their school work or parry business conversation with his brother Milt concerning their day at their dress factory.

"So quiet you are, Saul. Is the business failing again?" Grandma demanded sarcastically.

"In the dress business always we are failing." Jake said morosely. "Styles . . . women . . . phooey. Better women should go naked." He looked at me speculatively.

"Sometimes going naked is nice," I said wondering what I had done that was obviously bugging him. "You don't have to worry though. There will always be a woman's clothing business. Women know they are sexier with clothes than without them. How else would women lure men and impress other women?"

"Not naked!" Rachel snorted. "That's for certain sure."

When we finished eating, Jake made a point of inviting me and Harry into his "hideaway," a little room on the third floor that he maintained sacrosanct to escape the family and mess around with his fishing gear and a stamp collection. We sat on a studio couch facing his desk. From under a pile of albums he unearthed a copy of *Cool Boy Magazine*. As he silently flipped the pages to the center gate-fold, I suddenly knew what the trouble was.

"Oh my God, Harry," I yipped. "They must have finally published that picture of me."

Jake grimly held it up as silent testimony. A full length, full color, naked me stared at us with a decided come hither look on her face.

Harry examined it excitedly. "You are the sexiest looking Cool Girl they ever published. I never thought with all the commotion and argument they would ever get one that good."

"They should have, they took enough poses."

Jake listened to our conversation with an incredulous expression on his face. "Harry, you knew about this? The girl you are going to marry . . . naked for everybody to see. Beth, tell me it's not you! When I opened this magazine suddenly my hands were burning. What if Rachel, or Annie, or Grandma saw it. What would your father and mother think, Beth? Their daughter a sex-object!"

I held up my crossed fingers and grinned at Jake. "Let's pray none of them ever see it."

"You don't have to worry about Grandma or Rachel," Harry chuckled, "I can't imagine they would ever spend a dollar to look at naked women. What puzzles me, Jake, is you. I'd never have imagined you spending good money for such a magazine."

Jake looked embarrassed. "I don't buy it," he mumbled. "I look at it down at the drugstore. Since when should a father have to explain to a son? I look to see what a mess the younger generation is in. Maybe I like to look at pretty girls too. But not my future daughter-in-law! Beth, why would you ever do such a thing?"

I hugged Jake. "For a thousand dollars," I said laughing. "And you don't have to worry about my morals. I was well chaperoned. Harry was there, as well as Stanley Cole, Jack Dawes, Sheila Grove and Valerie Latrobe."

"A thousand dollars!" Jake repeated somewhat mollified. "You mean they paid you a thousand dollars. My God! Any girl in my factory would take her clothes off for fifty dollars."

"Most of them have eaten too many latkes." Harry said. "Even for fifty dollars they would get no takers. Beth looks like every man's idea of the woman he should have married."

"Oh shut up, Harry," I said. "Honestly, Jake I think the whole thing is as silly as you do. The only reason that they sell that foolish magazine is that men don't have the opportunity to see women naked, naturally, in their everyday living. If boys and girls grew up swimming together at public beaches, naked, took gym together naked, walked around their houses naked in warm weather, and simply wore clothes to keep warm, then all this voyeur, frustrated desires to see the naked human body of other human beings would vanish in smoke, and Cool Boy would go out of business."

While Jake listened, obviously wondering whether to continue to play the role of the horrified parent, we gave him a

partially expurgated account of how I consented to pose for Cool
Girl of the month.

The whole business was crazy to say the least, but of course
the thousand dollars gave it an air of practicality. One Friday,
last fall when InSix had finished their act at the Grinning Eye,
a hefty character, smoking a cigar invited us to his table and
introduced himself as Otto Ogleby, publisher of *Cool Boy*. "We
are scouting Boston for a prospective Cool Girl," he told us looking at me with X-ray eyes. "Miss Hillyer has the face for it, and
may be the type. Would you be interested?"

"Not much," I said staring back at him. "I wouldn't feel
comfortable hanging on college and barrack walls while sad little
boys played with themselves and pretended that I was their girl
friend."

"My God!" Otto marvelled. "That's a whole new reaction.
Most girls can't wait to jump out of their clothes for the opportunity."

"How much would Beth get paid?" Stanley demanded, being eminently practical.

When Otto mentioned the fee, and added that it would give
InSix records a real publicity push since the average subscriber
to *Cool Boy* was a heavy buyer of way-out records like ours, I
knew from the expressions on all the faces that I was sunk. Immediately, Val, Sheila, Jack, Stanley and even Harry began to
think the idea was worth considering.

"These are my managers," I said grinning at Otto. "If they
vote in favor you've got yourself a new Cool Girl."

"Take it easy," Otto said when Jack and Stanley started to
ply him for further details. "We have to see the merchandise
before we buy."

"You mean that you want to see me naked?"

"Naturally. You have a lovely face Miss Hillyer and you
seem to stock up very well in clothes, but you may be wearing
falsies, have a wooden leg, appendicitis scars, or other ailments
the flesh is heir to. These would naturally eliminate you as a
Cool Girl," Otto guffawed. "Of course, in other respects you may
be quite cool. Incidentally, I assume you are of age and free to
dispose of your person in ways the law sees fit to allow."

"I'm of age," I said. "Where is the auction block that the merchandise is displayed. And what happens if there is no bid."

"Nothing," Otto grinned. "We give you back to your owners, shake hands and say goodbye. When you get old and droopy you can tell your friends and children, who won't believe it anyway, that you were once almost chosen for a Cool Girl."

Otto handed me his business card. "There's an address written on the back. It's an apartment overlooking the Charles that belongs to an improper Bostonian. Ideal for display and photography. If you want to have us take a look and give you our decision, be there tomorrow morning at ten o'clock. If the decision is favorable you can sign the contract and we'll shoot the pix right away."

"Who's us?" I demanded.

"Me and Hy and Sy Fleshman, our Cool Boy photographic team." Otto leered at me. "They guide my thinking and save me from making erratic choices dictated by reasons other than photogenic. By the way I hope you are not having your period. We've got to get back to Los Angeles on the Monday plane."

"What did he mean by that?" I asked the kids. I was still somewhat in a fog, as Otto departed.

Sheila giggled. "He's afraid you'll arrive wearing a sanitary belt and sanitary pad. Hardly a sex symbol, old girl, by Cool Boy standards. The very thought of such things freeze Cool Boys in their tracks."

We argued about Otto's proposition all the way home to Harrad and into the small hours of the morning. "It's great for all of you to be so damned agreeable." I argued. "You are offering your best friend, like a fatted calf, to the wolves. None of you have to bare your blushing body to a lot of panting strangers." Little did I know that in addition I was going to be poked and pushed and bent and curled into extraordinary positions, (to best reveal the exotic me) as well as stared at from every conceivable angle from floor to the ceiling.

"You are going to do it for InSix" Jack grinned. "I can't wait to see professional photographers at work. Just think, Beth, you will be able to contribute a thousand dollars to our education fund. I don't see why you're so scary about showing yourself naked. You're bare-bottom every day in the gym, and right now all you are wearing is Harry's shirt. So what's different?"

I found out the next morning. At the apartment overlooking the Charles, Otto greeted us at the door with a look of dismay. "We only want you, Kid," he said, putting his arm around me.

"These are my chaperones," I said demurely. "They automatically save your reputation in case anything leaks out."

Paying no attention to Otto, Stanley, Sheila, Jack, Val and Harry invaded the apartment, admired the phallic drawings on the walls, tried the low-to-the-floor sofas, gasped over the view of the Charles from the picture window, and finally captured the stools in front of long well-stocked bar. "Cheer up Otto, old boy," Jack said from behind the bar. "We have brought you the Cool Girl to end Cool Girls."

"My enthusiasm is ended." Otto said somewhat disgruntled by this takeover. "Meet Sy and Hy Fleshman." He pointed to two men who were watching us swarm over the place. "This is our pigeon. She brought all her little friends."

Sy smacked his lips. "Let's see if the second and third acts are as good as the first."

"There's a sense of drama in the disrobing," Hy explained unnecessarily.

"Let's play it cool," I said. "There are some ground rules. Harry tell him."

"It's like this," Harry said. "we've been looking over some previous pictures and stories on Cool Girls. In the case of Beth, beyond the fact that she goes to college in the Boston area and is a part of the InSix singing act, nothing must appear in *Cool Boy* concerning her personal life. You'll have to make that a part of the contract."

"We couldn't care less about Miss Hillyer's brains," Otto grinned. "One of our staff writers will explain that our Cool Girl isn't married, that she likes Beethoven and Mozart quartets, revels in modern jazz, reads Immanuel Kant with her breakfast coffee, cooks a mean cheese fondue in the wee hours of the morning for tall dark men who drive X-KE Jaguars, but sleeps alone and without night clothes. This will be cleared with Miss Hillyer before publication. For the fee, we reserve full rights in perpetuity for all the pictures we take of her."

They showed me the bedroom which obviously belonged to a bachelor. If he were married why would he need such a gargantuan bed? I poked around and discovered an extensive wardrobe of men's clothing. The headboard of the bed however, was the cynosure of the room. It contained bookcases, a radio, a drawer with contraceptives, and numerous illustrated books of erotica, a small refrigerator, television controls to the picture tube which was embedded on the ceiling amidst mirrors. Evidently in case you got bored watching NBC, you could turn it off and watch yourself and companion cavorting; the idea had a certain charm. Since I now had my clothes off I lay on the bed and stared at myself, and forgetting the business I had come for I nearly yelled for Harry to join me. My reverie was interrupted by Otto pounding on the door.

Cooly, the Cool-Girl, I walked into the living room, naked. Sy and Hy croaked their approval. Otto nodded his head savagely. The kids all banged on their champagne glasses. And me! Darned if I didn't blush. I could feel the pink heat spread right from my toes. I clutched myself like September Morn and was about to run. I suddenly realized it's one thing to be naked with other naked people, but it was something else again to be naked with six men and two women all staring at you. I felt like a cow hung on a meat hook while the butchers were deciding which slice would make the tastiest steak.

"Perfect," Sy said. "Otto, you've done it again!"

Hy nodded agreement. "A perfect blending of face, breasts, legs and buttocks. She'll have to shave her bush!"

Everyone laughed while it slowly dawned on me what Hy meant. "You're crazy," I snorted forgetting that I was pretending to be a Greek statue, arms shielding her femininity. "This kid only shaves her legs and under her arms."

Otto examined all that I would let him see. "You should thin it once in a while, Miss Hillyer. There's a few blonde strands encroaching on your belly button."

"To hell with that. Do you want me to look like a ten year old? Shaved, I'd feel like an unframed picture."

"Look, sister," Sy said trying the sincere arm-around-you approach, which I fluttered away from, "we don't care what you look like in your private life! Only in nudist magazines do they have a beaver. Did you ever look at a nudist magazine? My God, really naked women aren't sexy! When we pose you, two million Cool Boys are going to stare with their tongues hanging out. We'll show everything the law allows, right down to the edge of your cleft, which from all appearances is considerably below that blonde nest. But hairs! No! Only on your head."

"It's deeper than that," Hy said. "Nobody airbrushes a Fleshman photograph. We don't permit it. So if a few hairs get in the way we lose our best shots. The law says it and we agree; pubic hair isn't artistic."

"You got to see the whole picture," Otto said realizing that I was still adamant. "Cool girls aren't really females in the ordinary sense; they're just wet dreams."

"I haven't got a razor," I said lamely.

"There's one in the bathroom and plenty of shaving cream," Otto said.

"I wouldn't know how to shave myself down there."

"I'll help you," Harry said smiling broadly. Sheila, Val, Stanley and Jack collapsed with laughter.

I glared at Helpful Harry, but, aided by Frozen Daiquiris, he was already too far in the spirit of things.

"Let's sign the contract first," Stanley said practicality suddenly constraining his hysteria.

"I have a better idea," I said grimly. "I'll sign the contract, I'll let Harry desecrate my femininity . . . but first every damn one of you can take off your clothes. I'm not standing around here being stared at like a freak. It makes me feel inferior, as if all of you were born fully dressed and I'm the only one that has skin and sexual organs."

Otto with his paunchy belly, and Sy and Hy, skinny wrecks with too long hair and sideburns, all looked at me in dismay. They shook their heads in vigorous protest. Sheila, Val, Jack and Stanley voted their immediate approval and started to doff their clothes. At least InSix sticks together.

"Suffering Jesus!" Otto moaned. "I've been had by six nuts.

I tell you the younger generation is going to hell, you offer them a sweetheart deal and right off they start to make conditions."

"I won't do it," Hy said emphatically. "How can I concentrate on taking pictures of a naked dame when I'm naked myself?"

Four drinks later, after Otto, Hy and Sy had tried every gambit from being too fat or too skinny, and even genuine tears that they would be too embarrassed to be flopping around without clothes, we finally convinced Otto, who by now was a little bleary, to undress. Propped in a sling chair, a scotch and ice resting on his white hairy belly, Otto was blubbering that he felt like an ass. Sy and Hy, hairy white skeletons with dangling penises, cursed Otto as they set up their lights and cameras and complained that there must be a better way to make a living.

But Harry, as I sprawled on the bathroom floor, and screamed at the indignity of being plastered with shaving cream in such a vulnerable area, scraped my lovely hairs away, and told me he was going to apply for a job as Cool Girl Scalper, First Class.

Jake listened to our slightly revised version of the story and shook his head. "It's too much for me, Harry. My lips are sealed. *Abi gezunt*, pray your mother and *bobbe* never hear about it."

The day before we went back to Harrad, Grandma took me to the attic. "I have something to show you," she said mysteriously. "Promise you will never tell Harry's father." From an old trunk she exhumed a yellowed book and opened it to pictures of a young naked woman entitled "Woman, walking and turning while pouring water from a watering can." "That is Saul's grandmother," she said smiling at me craftily. "A man named Muybridge took them. My mother was a pretty woman in her day."

I nodded, pretty sure of what was coming next.

"Uncle Levi, the junk man found a copy of that magazine in an ash barrel. He showed it to me. Burn it, burn it, you old meshugah, I told him." Grandma sighed. "Men are all the same. He hung it in his junk shop. Seventy-two and he still has ideas. You are a pretty girl, Beth. Pray that Harry's mother never hears about it."

"Does she know about Saul's grandmother?" I grinned.

Grandma winked. "She should worry! A picture! The body is dust."

I looked at Harry's great grandmother pouring water from her watering can. "I'll be darned . . . they didn't make her shave." When I told grandma what I meant she thought it was a great joke. "I'm glad we have a secret, grandma," I told her, and kissed her withered face.

FROM THE JOURNAL OF SHEILA GROVE

October and November, the Fourth Year

Even when I'm the happiest, most joyful and life is bouncing along in C Major . . . simple, uncomplicated, I always seem to have a minor key melody playing softly and unobtrusively in the back of my brain. Sometimes I can't hear this sad requiem playing in my conscious mind, it is still there ready to be triggered alive often by unrelated incidents.

Mostly a lilting song floats on the surface of my mind. It bubbles and effervesces and makes the entire one hundred and four pounds of me a misty gift of love. Tomorrow evening in the Little Theatre, Stanley and I will be married. Now, I truly know that tomorrow night, when I snuggle in Stanley's arms, there can't possibly be a deeper emotional and intellectual involvement than we already have, yet there is something in the commitment that will legalize our relationship and will validate the children we will have that is essential to the human psyche. At Harrad we have learned that society cannot legislate love, but we also know that the very existence of society, and hence man, depends on regulating and defining the boundaries of sexual behaviour.

Last night about eleven o'clock, when Stanley and I were finished studying, he tiptoed behind my desk, picked me up and carried me into the bedroom. From the look in his eyes I knew words were unnecessary. I kissed his face and cheeks and head while he took off my blouse and brassiere. When my skirt and panties had dropped to the floor and I stood before him naked, I felt suddenly shy.

"Why do you look at me like that?" I asked him, seeing the tenderness in his expression and tears in his eyes. "I'm not very beautiful. My breasts are too small. I'm too skinny." I sat on the edge of the bed. Stanley didn't answer. For a moment he knelt before me and kissed my knees, my belly, my breasts. I hugged his face fiercely against me.

"Shelia," he whispered. "Every time I'm with you like this I'm awestruck, amazed at the sheer wonder of you. As you sit there now, fragile, feminine, your heart beating, your eyes liquid and half open, as you hugged me against you I know that every time I make love to you is the first time, and though I have actually had intercourse with you a hundred times, and will make love to you in our lives thousands of times, the physical joining with you is only a small fraction of my need."

"I know," I said smiling. "Your penis in my vagina is only a small attempt. Maybe you feel the way I do. You want to be simultaneously you and me. I want to vanish inside you and look at the world through your eyes."

Joined, we lay silent for a long time. I was happy in a pensive kind of way. I knew that deep in my subconscious I was contrasting our marriage tomorrow, a beginning, and the strange death of my father in September. A grim finality.

In the telepathic accord we have, Stanley's thoughts bisected mine. "I feel like Ozymandias, today," he said softly. Sometimes I wish I would stay away from bookstores. If you are too curious, the forgotten past, all the centuries that man has lived, have a new way of reaching out and grabbing you with their bony fingers, and crying; "Here I am. Don't forget me." Men or women long dead who once tried to evoke in words the meaning of life. Thousands of people who lived and died, and with them all their effort and striving and everything they held valuable or dear. Some of these books are like a pitiful call across the centuries. People pleading, "Listen, listen. I lived once, too. I knew all your problems and tried to solve them! I held in my hands *The Memoirs of the Cardinal de Retz, The Memoirs of Duc de Simon,* plays by playwrights of the seventeenth century, unknown today.

The Yellow Book, source book of the crime that impelled Browning to write *The Ring and the Book* . . . and as I flipped the pages, read here and there, and regretfully put them down, I felt sad for man who dreams such magnificent dreams, has so many things to tell other men that might give them the answers they so desperately need. There is no time for the past. The men who thought they might bridge the centuries or even the decades will ultimately receive little hearing or even recognition of the few fundamental truths they spent a lifetime learning and attempted to communicate."

I kissed Stanley. "Eccelesiastes . . . Vanity . . . vanity . . ."

"No, vanity is too simple," Stanley said. "Chiding men like your father or me for their strong drives doesn't prove anything. Preaching the folly of ambition doesn't answer the question why. It leads only to negativism and hopelessness. Just so long as we are driven to find the answers to what our individual and collective meaning in the world, then we have a purpose for living. Since it is probably insoluble it is a good quest. From the perspective of man, at least."

I hugged Stanley. "I wish somehow I could relate Daddy's death to my own life . . . to our lives. When I first came to Harrad I had a sense of futility as the minor motif to all my thinking. It came down to this. "What does anything matter in this world? In life? Why bother to study, for example! What does it matter whether I am Phi Beta Kappa, or just a bored rich girl! Either way I'll die, and that will be that. And then I found you, and the feeling was no longer autistic, it embraced us. Now I go around praying that somehow a moment like this could be ever frozen for us, not for the world to view like Keat's Greek vase, but just for us . . . both of us, immobile forever, but sentient. You see my selfishness now includes you. But it is better, somehow, because I know I need you more than I need my own life."

"Your father never even achieved that much," Stanley said, kissing my neck and tracing the contours of my ear with his fingers. "When I think about Sam, I can't feel he was really brave, and yet I know he was braver than I would have been. At least, typically and necessarily for Sam, he was the final 'master of his fate.' "

Lying with Stanley deep inside me, his arms around me, neither of us seeking anything but a joyous loss of personal identity as I had numerous times, I reviewed the last weeks in August and the days in Houston and Newport before Daddy took his own life.

When Harrad closed in June, Stanley and I went to Houston. As he had the summer before, Stanley worked on the top floor of the headquarters in an office next to daddy's.

"You could start at the bottom and work up," Daddy told him. "But that doesn't mean a thing today. Horatio Alger heroes would get clobbered in the business world today. Take me, for instance, I don't run an oil business anymore. I play an never-ending chess game that involves national and foreign politics, local wars, labor leaders, foreign affairs, economic cycles, competition and the movement and direction of top executives who have all the fun doing the job that I used to do; the producing of oil and gasoline and selling it. It's a world which operates without love. The grease that keeps the wheels turning is what it will profit you."

While Daddy continued his unremitting campaign to prove that even his own daughter was simply an interesting adjunct to the more vital world of business, I infiltrated the Office of Grove Employee Welfare. This department, a necessary evil that Daddy shrugged off as a damned fool development, cost Grove Oil several hundred thousand dollars annually because people today not only wanted a job and endless fringe benefits, but expected their employer to be a great white father and love them in spite of all their foolish little woes and misfortunes.

Much to Beejee's surprise, Stanley and I slept together in one of the guest rooms, drove Daddy back and forth to work each day, swam in the swimming pool naked, and generally lived as if we were on our own private island. Beejee, dressed, or in a bikini, occasionally watched us from a pool side chair. A drink in her hand, trying not to stare at Stanley's nudity, and quite obviously disapproving of me, she would propose various dinners and social gatherings, or dances with other young people who she was sure would interest us.

"You two will get bored to death with each other," she said

one day unable to control her thoughts any longer. "I'm not your mother, Sheila, but if I were I would never have permitted you to start this sex business so young. Not even married. God! In a couple of years you'll be absolutely fed up, weary to extinction with each other. Waiting to divorce or just die. What have you got to look forward to?"

"What are you looking forward to?" Stanley asked her. "You're only thirty-six."

"More of the same," Beejee said, "And I'm thirty-three. At least all my surprise packages weren't opened at twenty-two."

"Stanley and I have found the secret of everlasting surprise," I said, grinning at her.

"What the hell is it?" Beejee demanded, and looked rather sour when I told her.

"Curiosity, wonder. Maintaining a child's mind in an adult world. Essentially not giving a damn about all the silly little conventional problems of being what people expect you to be, or what you think they expect you to be . . . and being just yourself. Come on, Beejee! Take off your bikini and dive in the pool! Yell at the cook and your maid who are watching us through the venetian blinds. Tell 'em to come on in and swim bare-ass with us."

"You are nuts," Beejee said. "Even your Daddy would grow faint at the idea of two negroes swimming in his white marble pool."

So the summer was a lovely love summer, and Stanley and I were oblivious to the world. The thought of death was for people who die . . . not us. We were immortal. Then, one afternoon in August, Daddy told Stanley he was going to London. Typically, he left on the afternoon plane without saying goodbye. Beejee was more than a little exasperated. Daddy had promised her that the last week in August, all of us, Beejee, Stanley, Asoka and I would fly up to New England, pick up the company yacht, Shebee (named after me and Beejee), which was moored at a marina near Gloucester, and from there cruise along the coast arriving in Newport for the Cup Races in September.

"This is a marriage?" Beejee asked me angrily. "I'm simply one of your father's possessions. Occasionally he remembers that

he owns me. Then he smiles fondly at me. Insists that I tell him
that he is really nice. All the while he is fawning and offering me
blandishments, his mind is a thousand miles away. Just why did
he have to go to London now?"

Stanley didn't know, but Daddy told him he would join us
in Gloucester on Labor Day weekend.

Beejee exploded. "God damn him, anyway! I have to learn
what my husband's plans are through his flunkeys. No aspersions
on you, Stanley. If it hadn't been you, it would have been Miss
Graves, his pursed-lipped efficient Man Friday."

In retaliation for Daddy's treatment, Beejee immediately set
in motion plans for a houseparty. Guests started arriving on
Friday and were still going strong a week later. When all bedrooms were filled new arrivals from all over Texas slept on the
lawn and beside the pool. No one escaped initiation: being tossed
in the pool, clothes and all. The timid ones were issued dry cotton
dresses from Beejee's enormous wardrobe or chinos from Sam's.
The braver ones simply walked around naked until their clothes
dried out.

The rumor spread that a continuous blast was in progress at
the Grove mansion. Departing friends, unable to face another
drink, were replaced by strangers who didn't even know that
Beejee was the mad hostess. Finally, some days later, Tim Shoaty,
our butler, discovered Stanley and I hiding out on the flat L roof
where we were spying on the proceedings like visitors from space.
Tim informed us that thus far two thousand dollars worth of
liquor had been consumed, several sofas had been set on fire by
female inebriates. The front living room was covered with foam
from fire extinguishers that two drunks had aimed at each other
in great good humor, one of Daddy's Etruscan vases etched with
a man and woman copulating had been used as a football and
missed on a forward pass . . . and if Stanley and I were going to
continue to camp out on the roof and ignore the whole mess, he
was quitting.

Over Beejee's protest (it was her house and if she wanted to
reenact the Fall of the Roman Empire, well, it was her own
damned business), Stanley and I closed the bar, kicked out twenty
or so pie-eyed Romans, telephoned Asoka, who was attending

summer school at Harvard, and escorted Beejee (who after three days, suddenly discovered that she had a god-awful hangover and pounding head) to the airport.

The next day, the Saturday before Labor Day, we were all quietly aboard the Shebee. Beejee swore off liquor trying to convince "Snowy" the Captain and any of the crew who would listen, that drinking was absolutely suicidal. She would take the pledge if they would.

Daddy arrived on Labor Day. Within an hour we were underway. He told us he cabled "Snowy" to load up with supplies. We were well enough stocked to stay at sea until the races started at Newport.

"Your father is acting strangely," Stanley told me when we were in our cabin the first night out. "I know Sam pretty well, Sheila. Something has snapped out of place. I wonder if he is having problems with Grove Oil!"

I watched Daddy the next few days. The only change I could notice was that he seemed much too intent on all of us having a good time. He followed Stanley or me or Asoka around the boat telling us he knew we were bored, he knew this hanging around, reading or sunbathing, or just looking at empty ocean could get awfully dull. Did we want to pull into some yacht club? Did we want to anchor and fish? Should we head for Newport right away? He tried to sunbathe with Beejee and drove her crazy, apologizing. "I just felt the need to get away from people," he kept saying. "Not you ... not my family. Just the mad chase."

He didn't even react when Beejee confessed about the party. When she told him his very special, two thousand dollar Greek vase had bit the dust, he just hugged her, called her "old girl," and told her he didn't blame her a bit. He would have done the same thing if he were a woman and had married Sam Grove.

The morning of the fourth day out, neither Daddy nor Beejee appeared for breakfast. Around noon Beejee came out on deck looking quite radiant. "I don't know whether to cry or shout for joy," she told me. "Your father made love to me most of the night. He was wonderfully gentle and affectionate. Then this morning he slept in my arms like a baby. I don't dare ask him what has happened." Beejee sighed. "In our twelve years of marriage, I've never known Sam could be like that. Pray for me, honey. Pray that it lasts."

Poor Beejee. It didn't last. The next night after dinner, even before the dishes were cleared away, Daddy started drinking heavily. Most of his meal had been liquid and he only dabbled with his steak. When all of us refused further drinks, telling him it was too soon after dinner, Daddy grinned and said hollowly, "It's not too soon for me. It's too late." He slumped on one of the sofas and stared at us. "Sometime tonight I'm going to get drunk enough to walk down to the stern of this ship and consign what remains of Sam Grove to his maker."

"Sam, please. I told you to go easy on the liquor," Beejee said. "Let's play gin rummy and stop talking crazy. I'm really quite fed up with drinking and all the stupidities that people say under the influence of alcohol."

"You are right," Daddy said grimly. He hurled the remains of his drink, glass and all, out the door of the lounge, and over the rail of the boat. "If I'm going to do it, and I must, then I'll do it in full control of my senses."

"What's bothering you, Sam?" Stanley asked. "Has something gone wrong with Grove Oil?"

"Not Grove," Daddy said. He was silent for a long time. "Not Grove. Just Sam Grove. The machinery is giving out. In less than three months Sam Grove will stop running. In four or five at the latest, he will be dead. I have incurable cancer in my stomach, and upper bowel. They opened me up in London to make sure. After taking a long look, they told me a colosotomy and wearing a bag of shit would get me nowhere, that I might as well prepare to meet my maker."

Daddy poured himself another Scotch. "It's true enough," he said quietly. "I'm not the type that would make a joke out of death. I'm going to die. I have had two weeks to think about it, and I'm still not adjusted to it. I suppose we are all going to die, but I've been too busy to think about it before this."

Desperate, we all started talking at once. There must be some hope. When did he first know about it? Why had he been so secretive? The doctors could be mistaken.

Beejee tried to tell him about a distant acquaintance who

had had a colostomy. It was more than ten years ago. He was still living. She sat beside him and held his hand. "Sam, you musn't give up."

"It's no use, Beejee," he said. "I've explored every avenue of hope for several months now. I'm dying and I must face it. I've made thousands of decisions in my life. The only difference between all of you and me is that I know roughly, give or take a month or two, when I'm going to die. I also know that the final month or two will be a slow, agonizing process with me wanting to die, and the doctors morally obliged to fill me with morphine and keep me breathing. At that point I won't be Sam Grove any longer but a shell with a heart that refuses to let go; beating feebly in a body that is already dead. I've had friends go that way. All that anyone could say was, "If only God would take him. If only he would die and get it over with." That's not going to happen to me. I am going to die with dignity. All I am asking you, the only people who really care one way or the other, is not to get maudlin about it. A year from now, the month or so longer that I might have lived isn't going to make a damn bit of difference. Please, Beejee," Daddy patted her hand "Stop whimpering and listen to me . . . you, too, Sheila."

Stanley had listened to Sam dry-eyed but fascinated. "Sam, why do you want to be so dramatic about it? Why prey on our emotions? Are you looking for pity? If I were deciding to kill myself, I'd just do it. I wouldn't make a production out of it."

I looked at Stanley horrified, believing that he had at last revealed an unsuspected cruelty in his character. "Do you have to be so cold blodded, Stanley?" I half-sobbed, half-screamed. "Daddy isn't going to do anything crazy. Daddy needs love and sympathy. We're not discussing the weather or politics." Stanley told me later that he couldn't shake off the feeling that Daddy's dispassionate appraisal wasn't real. . . . We all must be dreaming it.

Daddy shrugged. "Please let's look at it calmly. If I killed myself in a conventional way, I could do it a la Hemingway, and blow my brains out. A very virile ending, and rather in character for a man who has lived like I have. But unfortunately it would have a disastrous repercussion on Grove Oil stock. All the stock holders would be looking for financial reasons. After giving it a good deal of thought it seemed to me that scattering my brains around a room and leaving my relatives to pick up the mess is not only pretty dramatic, but down right shocking. I could do it a la Hollywood, a painless exit, caused by an overdose of sleeping pills. But the truth is that I lack the courage for such a slow approach. I might even change my mind at the last minute and start yelling for a stomach pump. Now the way that I have decided has several advantages. First, it gives me the opportunity to discuss it with you as rational human beings. I can give you brief assurances that your financial security will be no problem for any of you. Second, I plan to do it very quickly. I never learned how to swim . . . too busy making money. I have some trousers with lead weights sewn in. . . ."

"Oh, my God, Sam!" Beejee gasped. "This is inhuman!"

Sam ignored her. "I'm not looking for an audience. A man dies better alone. I'm just telling you what I must do. The third point that I want to make is I am hoping that none of this discussion is ever reported to the press. When you all dock in Newport tomorrow, Stanley can call the police. Snowy will back him up. The crew will keep their mouths shut." Sam grinned. "Money is useful sometimes. Here's your story. We were out about thirty miles. Sam was in pretty high spirits . . . pretty well oiled. Gotta keep oil in it somehow." Daddy grinned and patted my shoulder. "Sam Grove must have fallen overboard. That's all there is to it. Sam Grove drowned. Cut off before his time. It will only make enough news to last one edition. There will be no body to worry about. No mourners. No display of the last remains. No ugly burial. Come on have another drink with me. I think it is a damned fine idea. What's your reaction, Asoka? You've been mighty silent."

"I'm a Hindu, Sam," she smiled. "Thanks to you I have learned some of the philosophy behind my religion. I believe there is no death. There is only ceaseless life that assumes many forms. The form called Sam Grove will disappear, but the essence of what creates the form will live forever."

A bitter expression on her face, Beejee scowled at Asoka. "I'm a simple uneducated person," she said dully. "I love you,

Sam. I don't even know why I love you. All I know is that I can't sit here and calmly discuss you, dead. I want you to stay alive just as long as it is humanly possible. God, Sam . . . Can't you hope! There could be a miracle. Maybe you could live a much longer time than you think."

"I've been all through that," Daddy said adamantly. "If I hang on too long I'll lose the power of choice. I'll be kept breathing as long as possible without regard to whether I am suffering. I'm not going to die that way. I could be bitter about the fact that I have to die, but I'm not. That's the way the ball bounces for Sam Grove. I can't really say that another twenty years of doing what I have been doing is anything special to look forward to one way or the other. I've done it all. The rest is repetition. Let's stop talking about it. I want to talk about all of you."

"Is it so bad to suffer?" Beejee demanded. "Maybe God expects that man should suffer. All your life you've tried to play God, Sam. Why can't you die like a man?" Beejee said the words coldly. To me she seemed as shockingly cruel as Stanley had been.

Daddy simply guffawed. "That's better, Beejee. No damned pussy-footing around. You may be right. The truth is, I am probably a coward. For the first time in my life I'm in a jam and I can't buy my way out of it. I only have one answer. I'm afraid to die like a man. To be blunt, I think dying like a man is just plain horseshit. I personally don't like the way a large majority of men have to die; blubbering tunes of glory."

The conversation suddenly stopped. Daddy had closed his business deal, and with one flat statement wrapped it up. Beejee was still crying. Although all of us were obviously shaken, no one seemed to have any words left to say.

"All right, Daddy," I said finally. I tried to keep my voice from trembling. "You said you wanted to talk about us. I want to talk about me. Did you ever really give a damn that most of my life I never really had very much love or affection from you or mother. I suppose I really should be the most shocked one here. I do love you. But not as a father. As a man, yes. A person who has obviously been nice to me. Why was it this way? Can you tell me why? If I really knew, maybe I could feel something more than I feel. More than the shock I would feel about anyone's death. Oh, God," I said unable to stop crying. "Please, Daddy, I don't know what I am saying. Do you know? Do you understand?"

He stared at me a long time, and then he said, "I guess I know what you mean, She. It comes to this. Why in hell can't people give each other the love they need in this world! I don't know what to tell you. I am what I am. Maybe it would have been different if your mother could have gone along with me. We met in high school. Both of us came from poor families. My old man drove an oil truck. I have two brothers. They've come a little further up the income scale. One of them operates a couple of Grove Oil filling stations. The other is a manager of a chain store. They have never liked me. I let them sweat out their own living. I'm leaving them a half million dollars each." Daddy grinned. "It's no favor. The money will rock the boat of their nice middle class lives. They'll gorge themselves with cars and boats and trips around the world, and eventually drink themselves to death. Daddy paused. He looked thoughtfully at all of us. I had the feeling he wasn't even seeing us. "I suppose you think I'm a pretty cold-blooded bastard. I guess I am. The desire to be something more than a truck driver helped me discover the world was for the tough and ruthless. Five years after I married your mother, I was the sole distributor for Standard Oil in the state of Connecticut. You were two years old, She. I had done it. I was a successful man. Not a millionaire, but rich enough. But somehow I had lost your mother along the way. I guess we never really understood each other. She wanted a husband who was a part of the social life of our town. To me the clubs, the bridges, the teas, the cocktail parties, charity balls . . . all the little people trying to prove their superiority with new fifty-thousand dollar homes, trips to Europe, the latest cars, were a collossal bore. I had met some really wealthy men, powerful men. One of them lived in twenty-thousand dollar house and drove a car that was ten years old. He was a millionaire. Money to him was simply a big power game. He spoke my language. This was exciting. The getting was a hell of a lot more interesting than the idle spending. Without telling your mother (she wouldn't have been interested, anyway), I put most of our money into oil leases. Suddenly, I had made my first million dollars. All I wanted in the whole damned world was someone to tell me how good I was. I wanted your mother to grab me and hug me and say: "Sam, you're wonderful. I love you." Of course, I wasn't wonderful. I was a damned surly bastard to live with. I was generally, by most standards, somewhat anti-social. I knew it. But I didn't need daily confirmation of it from your mother." Daddy grinned flittingly. He shrugged. "All I've needed all my life is to have someone love me enough to understand."

"Understand what?" Beejee demanded. "You never gave me the impression you wanted to be understood or be too close to anyone."

"Christ, I could never give a long tearful explanation of my behavior." Daddy said. "All I needed was tacit, sympathetic realization that I was driven, that I couldn't help it . . . that I was my own worst enemy. I was like a hamster in a cage, whirling on the wheel not because he wants to, but because he *has* to. My drives . . . where they came from weren't important . . . maybe if I went to a psychiatrist, he would say that I was sexually frustrated. . . ."

Beejee scowled and shook her head. "Now I've heard everything!"

"I mean it," Daddy said. "I guess it started with your mother, She. In bed we were a couple of people with a job to do. We did it, and that was that. Neither of us could get close to the other. We couldn't break through to the little sacred people that lived inside of us. We simply ignored each other's emotional needs. I don't mean sexual needs. Hell, I don't know what I mean, maybe just the need to say a million words to each other while we both listened and did our best to understand."

"Have you ever managed that with any woman?" Beejee asked.

"Occasionally," Daddy grinned. "Not with you, Beejee. When I was younger sometimes I took the complete plunge. Dropped my defenses. Then I suddenly discovered that no woman I ever met really wanted to know the real Sam Grove. Hell, I don't even know the real Sam Grove anymore. He lived in another time . . . in another world. If I met him today I'd think he was a pretty sad character. It's too late. I've worn the mask so long, there's no face underneath it. I'm sorry, She. There is no answer. Maybe you wouldn't have become a Phi Beta Kappa, if you had the love and affection you missed. Maybe you would only be a richer version of your mother. And the joke is maybe you wouldn't be one whit happier. You could ask me why you were born. I could tell you that a contraceptive failed. Your mother was shocked, but douches and ergot couldn't stop your rush for life. I was glad. I guess eventually so was she. But it didn't give you what you needed . . . love. Who in this world ever really has it, anyway?"

"Everyone has it, Sam," Asoka said. "The trouble is, most of us don't ever learn to give it. We think if we give love and don't get it in return somehow or other our supply dwindles."

Daddy smiled. "That will never change. It's the nature of the beast. For God's sake let's not talk anymore. I just want to sit out on the rear deck and look at the stars."

Beejee grabbed Sam and hugged him. "I love you, Sam. Please . . . Please don't. . . ."

Asoka and I clutched his arms. Neither of us could speak. Daddy looked at us with tears in his eyes. He kissed my forehead and patted Asoka's head. "Look," he muttered. "I talk a hell of a lot braver than I really am. I'm glad I got it off my chest. I might think about it . . . but I really haven't got the nerve. The next few days we'll watch the Cup races. When they're over I'll check into Mass. General Hospital. Maybe they've got some new miracle cure." He hugged Beejee. "Honest, I promise. All I want to do is get some clean salt air in my lungs."

We watched him through the portholes. He waved at us, and then sat down on a canvas deck chair facing the stern.

"God," Beejee sobbed. "What should I do?"

We tried to talk to each other . . . to comfort each other, and at the same time keep a watch on Daddy. Stanley went out on deck and sat down beside him for a while.

"He's all right, I think," Stanley tried to reassure us. "He just wants to be alone."

At midnight he was still there.

Somehow, exhausted, our nerves shattered, we must have stopped watching.

At ten minutes past twelve, Beejee looked out. "Oh, my God. My God! My God!" she screamed. "He's gone!"

When we started searching the boat, Snowy came down from the bridge. "It's no use," he said quietly. "I saw him go overboard."

Stanley held his arms around Beejee and me. "When I went out to talk with him he told me to tell you that he loved you both. No one could stop him, She. He said if you were going to cry . . . to cry for the living."

During the past six weeks the thought keeps recurring to me, how very much alone each person is in the world. Not one of his three wives ever understood Daddy, and I guess he never was close to any of them. Will Stanley and I do better? I pray that we will. And that's funny. Pray to whom? "You don't have to ·pray," Stanley told me. "All our lives we will work at one goal . . . *being each other*. What we achieve between us we can multiply. In many areas we've already multiplied it by six. It's more than being your brother's keeper. It's *being* your brother."

When Beth and I first decided we would be married in our senior year at Harrad, we knew a church wedding couldn't possibly be right for us. Whatever beliefs we individually had in God, a Supreme Power, call it what you will; the beliefs didn't function in the framework of any religious theologies. On the other hand, a civil ceremony performed perfunctorily by a city clerk or a justice of the peace seemed inadequate, quick . . . without meaning. Valerie got into our discussions because she and Jack had decided to get married too. The boys just listened, amused by our desire for some kind of ritualistic marriage ceremony.

Beth tried to explain. "It's not really a ritual we want, I think Sheila, Val, and I feel the way we get married should somehow reveal our deep feelings for each other as individuals. Maybe we're just being feminine. Maybe we want something to remember . . . something that will give the commitment we will make to each other real meaning. Something neither the church, nor the state can provide. The church rituals are meaningless to us. The state ritual is nothing more than a legal contract."

"Why not write our own marriage ceremony?" Stanley suggested. "If we make it interesting enough, we can invite all the classes at Harrad. Maybe Margaret and Phil will let us use the Little Theatre."

We discussed it with the Tenhausens, who were immediately enthusiastic. They had a friend who was a justice of the peace and could legally marry us. Whatever else we wished to add to the conventional state contract was up to us. With typical enthusiasm InSix ploughed into the problem.

Last night, when it was all over and Stanley and I, Beth and Harry and Val and Jack were married, we agreed that our ceremony was a success. The weeks of discussion needed for planning each step paid off, not only for us, the participants; I think everyone at Harrad found it a memorable experience.

At quarter of eight, the Little Theatre, lighted with electric candles that flickered in all the windows, cast a friendly glow and made soft shadows on the faces of the students. The second movement of Beethoven's Ninth Symphony was playing softly. We had taped the music, amplifying it from four speakers and timing it so that the Chorale Movement wouldn't start until everyone was seated. Jack had made a new translation of Schiller's poem *The Ode to Joy,* so that everyone could follow the Chorale which is sung in German. We had multigraphed this onto the programs. The programs also gave the marriage vows we would take. The timing was perfect. As the chorale *Hymn to Joy* began, growing out of the searching music as it does, a hush fell over the audience. The flickering lights of the candles and the rapture of the music created a feeling of time and people encapsulated, as if momentarily, we were all living in a new dimension and every person in the room was interlinked by a mysterious unity.

As the Chorale Movement concluded, the electric candles were dimmed and the stage was bathed in a blue light that gave the floating quality of swirling mist and fog. Valerie, Beth, and I, in white linen dresses, walked on stage left of center facing Harry, Jack and Stanley who appeared right of center wearing black trousers and white short-sleeved shirts, open at the neck.

In measured steps, as the quiet opening of Gliere's *Concerto for Voice and Orchestra* filled the theatre, we walked toward each other, and then turned to face the audience. Three separate groups, our fingers interlaced, we listened, facing the guests, while the exquisite voice of a coloratura soprano, wordless, but using her voice as the ultimate orchestral instrument in soaring flights of pure sound led the orchestra and probed love, life, God and beauty. After about fifteen minutes of sheer emotion and feeling, when the final measures of the concerto were reached, the students were watching us in hushed silence. We waited silently for a few seconds, and then we spoke in unison.

"I Stanley, I Sheila, I Harry, I Beth, I Jack, I Valerie, having experienced deep love and warm affection with the person whose hand is laced in mine, having joined our bodies many times in a small attempt to convey to each other our love, having experienced the ineffable wonder of surrender of ourselves into the unity of something beyond our comprehension, having the desire to express this feeling in the culmination of the creative act available to all human beings; our children, who will link us with the future of all men and women and perpetuate us in time, as man knows it; having full confidence that our abiding faith in each other as human beings will last our lifetime; seek permission, petition and enjoin the State of Massachusetts to recognize us and bind us in responsible marriage, asking not that our love for each other be circumscribed for a lifetime of single devotion, but recognizing that as our love and understanding grows it may encompass others without harm or deprivation to the one with whom we are legally joined."

We had learned the words perfectly. Spoken together by the six of us, they carried the simple majesty of a Greek chorus. Then through amplifiers, our unseen Justice of the Peace responded in a warm, friendly feminine voice.

"The State of Massachusetts has through me, Sarah Forstner, investigated the physical health of the petitioners and found it good. In full confidence that each of you will approach your lives together in a continuous proud and happy realization of your love and the love of your children, by the laws vested in me, I pronounce you, Sheila Grove and you, Stanley Kolasukas; you, Beth Hillyer and you, Harry Schacht; you, Valerie Latrobe and you Jack Dawes, man and wife. May you treasure this trust and responsibility and live fully happy lives. And now if the respective males have some tangible symbol of their affection they wish to gives their wives they may do so before these friends and witnesses."

The rings the boys placed on our fingers were simple gold bands engraved with our names and the word "Mizpah." We kissed excitedly. And then the six of us, tears running down our checks, hugged each other for a moment, and walked slowly down the center aisle. The voice in Gliere's Concerto filled the theatre in one final trill of ecstasy.

"It was lovely," Beth marvelled before we were joined by the entire Harrad student body milling around us and happily congratulating us. "We wrote it ourselves, rehearsed it, and yet when it actually happened for real, I was so trembly and awestricken I thought I would burst into tears."

Val and I were crying happily. "We are married, Sheila," she grinned through her tears. "I can't really believe it. Somehow, we are all married to each other, too."

And we were married. Not just for better or worse, or richer or poorer, or in sickness and health, but somehow with an even deeper commitment that transcended all of these. We had learned to like each other, and discovered that liking was the leaven of love. Poor Daddy, he loved a lot of women, but he didn't like them much.

FROM THE JOURNAL OF STANLEY COLE

January and February, the Fourth Year

Before graduation, all seniors must turn in a joint thesis to complete their work in the seminar on Human Values. Phil Tenhausen assigned the project in September, with the papers due in May. The subject is "How our present Western Society might evolve, could, or should evolve within the next hundred years into a society where each individual could live lives that realized their full potential as human beings."

The Tenhausens have insisted that we try to keep our projections within the realm of possibility, hence capable of evolving out of the framework of the present economic, social, and religious environment of a reasonably democratic country. We are given two assumptions. One, that with all its deficiencies Western democratic society as we now experience it is probably superior to any form of social, economic or political system now, or previously in existence, in the world. The second condition is that the type of "Psychologic individual," who must ultimately dominate our projected society, has been investigated in a preliminary way by Abraham Maslow in his many analyses of the "self-actualized" healthy human being, and described in some detail in Maslow's book *Motivation and Personality.*

So far as I know, none of the senior roommates have started their papers, but all of us have spent hours of discussion, kicking around various approaches; arguing and disagreeing on the fundamental principles involved in such a society. When we all started to talk about our Utopias, Phil tried to kill this approach. He pointed that Maslow had offered the idea of "Eupsychia," a Utopia where all men were psychologically healthy. From what Maslow claimed he knew of healthy people, he felt he could predict the kind of culture that would evolve if a thousand psychologically healthy families migrated to a desert island where they could work out their destinies as they pleased.

Phil feels the desert island approach is unrealistic, and was evolved to its ultimate stupidity by Irving Wallace in his novel *The Three Sirens.* So Phil is challenging us to a far more demanding solution by insisting that we work within the reality of the Harrad experience and extend the insights we have gained to a larger social environment.

Aside from discussion, Sheila and I had found no logical approach to our thesis. Sam's death and our marriage kept the cross-currents of our thinking from coming into focus. A few days before Christmas, Sheila's mother and her husband drove up to Boston to discuss the details of Sam's will. Reluctantly, Sheila met her at the Charter House Motel in Cambridge. From there they were going to the Boston lawyers who had transcripts of the will and full information for the heirs. Sheila knew in advance that her mother was disgruntled and unhappy at her share in Sam's estate. "I suppose she expects that I'll give her more," Sheila told me grimly, then laughed. "What the hell, maybe I will . . . and then I'll shake hands and say Goodbye Mother for this lifetime. I hope we don't meet the next time around."

I decided that Sam's money was none of my business even though Sheila and I were married. I promised to meet her later in the Harrad gym when she returned. A group of us congregated at the end of the pool and were discussing our thesis in terms of a book called *Images,* by Daniel Boorstin. His analysis of our culture, which depends so much on pseudo-events and pseudo-news, and numerous books in the same vein by Vance Packard and others seemed to show a straight path to an Orwellian future with little hope that reasonable people could halt the roller coaster ride to hell. None of these critics of our society had any real solutions, and were perhaps making their "Reality" even more real by identifying it and then walking away without answers.

Phil and Margaret joined us and our discussion switched to whole-hearted approval of Margaret's well-formed body. Last year she had been pregnant. She and Phil had a daughter aged six and a boy eighteen months. With three children, she still remained as trim as a girl in her twenties. Margaret was trying to convince us it was simply a matter of calories and judicious exercise when Sheila, pattering along the edge of the pool, her breasts bobbling unconcernedly, her face wearing a preoccupied frown, joined us, a little breathless.

"God," she sighed. "It's good to be back after a day among the philistines. I heard what you said Margaret. It's not only calories. It's middle class stuffiness. Millions of Americans are inflated not only by food but by their own pomposity. My mother used to be a fairly simple woman. She claims she left Daddy because she couldn't stand his drive and aggressiveness. She married Harold because he was an uncomplicated person whose hobbies of fishing and home carpentry left plenty of time for clubs, television, and Sunday family togetherness.

"Daddy discovered a very nasty way to prove to her that all men are corruptible. Three years ago, Harold was suddenly promoted from the accounting department of Grove Oil to eastern Vice President and Controller. From eight thousand dollars a year, Harold now earns forty thousand dollars a year. His once simple life has become complicated by a big house in Saybrook, a cabin cruiser, two automobiles, and the kids in private schools. Mother and Harold are enamoured with their prestige and new status in the community. They are owned by their possessions. They spend more than they earn to maintain their new image of success. Mother has passed from girdles to corsets. Harold's favorite occupation is hotel size steaks, which he proudly barbecues with the help of a handy man and maid for his summer guests, while everyone present consumes oceans of liquor and tasty hors d'oeuvres. The men discuss business and tell each other dirty jokes while the women courteously rip apart all their friends."

I interrupted her tirade. "Why did your mother come up to Cambridge?"

"That's the second installment of the sad story," Sheila said grimly. "She's quite upset about Daddy's will. She, and Daddy's second wife, whom they are trying to locate (she married an Iranian prince), received two hundred and fifty thousand dollars each. Beejee got all the property and a million dollars. Asoka got two hundred and fifty thousand. I inherited five million dollars. The balance of the estate is largely the stock of the Grove Oil. It went into the Grove Foundation. I have the entire voting control of the Foundation. Mother is more than exasperated. She feels that I could spare at least a million."

While Sheila had told me the details of Sam's will, the others were surprised and a little shocked by so much money. "Good God," Jack Dawes whistled. "I knew you were rich, but I never thought you were filthy rich. When are you kissing goodbye to Harrad and your proletariat friends?"

"Damn all of you if you feel that way," Sheila flashed. "I'm not interested in money. It can do nasty things to you. Look at my mother. She got a quarter of a million dollars because she slept with Sam Grove a few years and had me. Now she firmly believes that she is entitled to more. And if she had it, what would she use it for? A villa on the Riviera, a house in Palm Beach or Palm Springs, a bigger yacht. A life of sheer waste. As far as I'm concerned, Daddy played her a dirty trick. The two hundred and fifty thousand dollars will give her and Harold sufficient delusions of their own importance to make them completely intolerable."

"What are you going to do with your money?" Beth asked. "Foundations have to disburse all their money. . . . Ye Gods!"

"Sheila is going to underwrite experimental movies," Jack said mischievously. "Now we can finish the *Meshugana Ape*."

Sheila giggled. "I think it would be better, Jack, to set you up as a fashion designer. Such originality as Fanny Fashions should be encouraged. Seriously, I'm going to see that a lot of the Foundation money goes to Harrad. From that point on I'm open to suggestions. With the income from my personal estate plus the Foundation money, the lawyers tell me I'll have about four million dollars a year to get rid of. At the moment, several hundred people are eager to help me figure how to spend it," Sheila grinned. "My only friends are right here at Harrad."

Hilariously, we made Sheila stand up while we all kissed our naked Santa Claus. Phil was last in line. He picked Sheila up, whirled her around joyously, and jumped in the pool with her. We all jumped in after them. Sheila came to the surface gasping, her hair plastered over her head. "Oh gosh," she yelled. "I love you all."

It's strange, the way ideas spring into being. I couldn't offer Sheila any really good suggestions on how to disburse the Foundation money, but the thought of it was in the background of my mind. Maybe the way to have a steady source of new ideas is to treat your mind like an insatiable, giant hopper. Keep tossing everything and anything into the pot. If you don't try to start grinding, eventually when you get enough in the mill, the gears will start turning themselves.

For the past few weeks, in a course in Political Science which I have been taking, we have been studying election returns in the various states. While perhaps I should have been aware of it, I was conscious, for the first time, that the total vote for both candidates for governor of certain states was only a few hundred thousand votes, and the winning margin in many cases was exceptionally small. Theoretically, in those less populous states it was easier to run for governor, both financially and in the area of actual political contact, than in states like California or New York. On the other hand, an exceptional governor of even a small state could very readily create national political interest in himself as well as his state.

I was taking a shower with Sheila, soaping her breasts and belly and pussy, and I suppose my mind should have been preoccupied. She was shampooing her hair and enjoying my playing . . . when somehow *The Idea* snapped into place.

"Eureka, I've got it! I've got it!" I yelled and hugged her soapy body against me getting soap in my eyes and mouth as I kissed her excitedly. "I've got a practical proposal for how a unique society could develop within the framework of United States. Supposing a group like InSix, backed with sufficient money and a complete social program, infiltrated one of the smaller states and gradually developed it as a show-case society for the rest of the country to emulate. That Sheila, my love, is the launching point we can take for our thesis in Human Values."

"Sounds way-out and mad," Sheila said practically as she rubbed me down with a towel. "What state? And how could you change the people within a particular state? After all, for good or bad they're all Americans with much the same perspective, values, and outlook on life. There is no fence around any state."

In no hurry to dress, we lay on my bed and discussed it. "Several states in the Northwest jump into my mind," I told her. "Obviously, the people in these states have some of the pioneering spirit left. Where could we start? Let's visualize a group of six or more men and women with a definite social program designed to help people live to their full potential. Let's assume this Utopian group would take up residence in this State, which they have carefully preselected and studied statistically in every possible way. Our group is thoroughly acquainted with the economics of the state, the racial groups, the political problems, the religious groupings. They would plan the first stage of their program to take a minimum of ten years. The first goal to be accomplished would be a complete rewrite of the state laws. One of the group would have to be a lawyer. Fortunately, most of the laws governing marriage, divorce, censorship, education, wages, and working conditions, all crucial to the new society they have envisioned, are within the province of the state and can be changed, for the most part, without Constitutional conflict. It would even be possible to make changes in the State laws, knowing they conflict with the Constitution, and then wait until these laws have been tested in the Supreme Court. This is where money would come in. Our dedicated group, backed by a foundation with plenty of money available like the Grove Foundation, would carefully plan its long range propaganda and project a complete approach that eventually would give them political control of this State. Once our group is functioning within the State, they would go all out to attract within their orbit all the thinking citizens of the state. Within a few years their plan would be to control the political machinery and elect a sympathetic Governor and legislature.

"My God Stanley," Sheila rolled on top of me, a big grin on

her face. "Are you talking about our thesis . . . or are you pic-
turing yourself as Governor of this mythical State?"

"At the moment, I'm writing our thesis," I laughed. "But
honestly, I believe it is within the realm of possibility."

Sheila must have helped me because I was suddenly aware
that my penis slipped inside her. "I like the idea," she sighed
happily. "So now tell me. What laws do we change?"

"Hey, give me time! Twenty minutes ago I was Stanley washing your pussy. You are making it difficult to make the transition
to His Excellency Governor Stanley Kolasukas!"

I couldn't let the idea alone. Within the next few weeks I
got InSix deeply involved in it. When we approached Phil, he
agreed that if the six of us wanted to attempt it as a joint thesis,
we could do so; but he expected at the very least a paper of one
hundred and fifty pages with detailed analyses of our plans and
proposals. So, with some groans from Harry, Jack, Valerie and
Beth, who complained that even in our final year Phil was still
a slave driver, InSix entered the discussion phase to see what we
could come up with.

Jack decided we couldn't work in a vacuum. We'd have to
pick a definite state in the United States that would be our
theoretical guinea pig. After a week or two of argument and
plenty of statistical research we have chosen the State of X.*

We all agreed that the most important task would be to
change the entire system of education within the State. In this
way, within twenty years, we would have re-oriented most of the
younger generation. Simultaneously we would have to do our
best to re-educate the older generation. We knew that on a wide
scale this would be impossible, but we felt that if we worked
slowly, within a period of two or three years, we could develop
a central committee of sufficient educators, politicians, businessmen and religious leaders who agreed in principle with what we
wished to accomplish. From this group we would gain political
strength, and ultimately be able to sway the average voter. We
knew that we could not reveal our entire program even to this

---

* In a recent letter to Phillip Tenhausen, Stanley mentions that InSix
still retains great interest in the proposal offered in their thesis. For this reason the identity of the State they chose for their proposal has been concealed.

strong central committee. Many of the changes in the basic
social structure of the State that we would ultimately make would
require that a previous change had become firmly entrenched.

Our base premise was: if democracy was to really function
and survive in a situation of exploding populations, it depended
on a citizenry educated in much greater depth than at present.
The present pattern of a generalized high school education, with
a small portion of students taking college courses and the majority receiving a very thin general education, was developing
citizens without historical perspective. Few people had any
understanding of meanings and values in the world either historically or personally. We would aim immediately for a State
supported educational system which would expose all students
in depth to world history, English, languages, social sciences, art,
music etc. Students who showed early promise in the Sciences
and mathematics would be allowed to specialize but even these
students would be required to have thorough grounding in the
humanities. In our State-supported high schools, there would
be *no* trade or practical courses. From the first grade, through a
potential fifteen grades, all education would be directed to
producing the educated, well-rounded man or woman, and developing for each person a complete psychologic understanding
of himself, his abilities, and his relationship to society. For the
exceptional student, capable of doing the work at a rapid pace,
there would be swifter promotions from grade to grade, providing always that the student's emotional adjustments kept pace
with his mental growth.

No student would be permitted to complete his education
in state-supported trade schools or colleges until he was eighteen.
Thus, students capable of moving faster would progress in high
schools to a thirteenth, fourteenth or fifteenth grade. Graduation
to state-supported colleges and trade schools could occur either
from the twelfth grade or the fifteenth grade. The upper third of
all the twelfth and fifteenth high school grades would go directly
to three year colleges, which would be completely reoriented to
the revised high schools, and not waste the freshman year
doubling back on education already acquired at the high school
level. These three year colleges would continue the education in

the humanities, in depth, allowing specialization in the second year only in the area of the sciences and mathematics. All upper-third graduates of these colleges would go on to state-supported graduate work in what-ever area the student wished to pursue.

Students who graduated from the high schools below the upper third of the class would go on to state-supported professional and trade schools and there, in two or three years, complete the training they preferred, acquiring the skills necessary to function as an economic unity in the state.

In the early years of grade school, major emphasis would be placed on developing reading ability. All studies in the first nine grades would be oriented around this objective. The student entering the tenth grade would be able to read rapidly and would receive continuing awards and citations to develop pride in this ability.

From the first grade on, all students would take a required course similar to the Harrad College Human Value course. In the early years, the purpose of all teaching in this course would be to counteract the spurious values in our culture and put the individual's life in perspective in relation to values being destroyed by any advertising and any of the arts which over-emphasized materialistic goals as the basis of success. All the schools would continuously help the students to evaluate the mass communications of our society such as television, radio, newspapers, magazines. All teachers in the Human Value courses would be equipped to tackle and expose the false values being propagated and aimed at particular age levels. These teachers would not hesitate to expose any element of society, whether it was government, business, religion or literature and the arts, which were inculcating values that denied the ultimate goodness and excellence of man.

Since our Utopian planners invading the State of X would be working with a long term master plan, the broad outline of which could not be revealed at the beginning, the relative speed of initial accomplishment would be slow. After some analysis, we selected the City of Y which is the largest city in the state. Here, our Utopian planners would take up residence. Slowly and methodically, several of the group would be groomed to run for the State legislature and ultimately Governor. Our platform of a state supported educational program (which we believe would have wide appeal) would guarantee any citizen, regardless of race, color, creed or financial ability, a complete education in keeping with his intellectual abilities, and would develop his full potentials as an economic citizen as well as a human being. To further implement the educational program, no citizen of the State, after the fifteen year initial program was under way, would be allowed to enter the employment market until he or she was twenty years of age. In addition, these newly educated citizens would be encouraged to leave the employment market at the age of fifty-five. To develop this aspect of our program we envisioned a State Social Security program supplementing Federal Social Security which would guarantee any individual who had been working for thirty years an income equal to the minimum State hourly wage rate.

Citizens of the State leaving the employment market at the age of fifty-five would be guaranteed an additional state-supported educational program of not less than two years, the purpose of which would be to re-orient them into various programs of continuing study and research, both for their personal growth and possible additional contributions to the state in the form of literature, art, science, etc. All persons retiring from the area of economic employment would automatically be required to pursue further optional programs of study at the expense of the State.

In our various discussions, Jack Dawes took over the economic planning of the State, realizing the necessity of adjusting and fitting this into the entire economic scheme of the United States so that the State of X would be financially able to implement the educational and social security proposals. Jack proposed that, eventually, when our candidates for the legislature were firmly entrenched, a complete program of tax and wage and internal price control within the state could be legislated. The first step would be to raise the minimum wage to $2.50 per hour, and concomitantly adopt Statewide price control, freezing all prices at the level of the previous minimum wage. When the wage rate was raised to $2.50 per hour, the work week would be simultaneously relegislated to a nine hour day, five days a week. The new forty-five hour work week would be without time and one half for overtime. All Saturdays and Sundays throughout the state would be State holidays with the only business permitted to operate being those devoted to leisure pursuits.

A flat ten percent of all income after Federal taxes would be collected by the State in taxes, at the source, to underwrite the educational and social security programs. In Jack's opinion, manufacturing industries would be eager to enter the state because while the minimum wage was high the longer work week would increase productivity. Additionally, the total wages paid an employee would not exceed other states working on a thirty-five hour week with time and a half for the additional ten hours. Jack also proposed a state tax on all corporations which would be reduced dollar for dollar on all money spent by a particular corporation for expansion and development of facilities within the state.

Jack also proposed a New Resident Tax to discourage population shifts to this State by individuals who wished to benefit but had not contributed through work and the State income tax. The New Resident Tax would be computed on the amount of taxes paid by a citizen within the state (in the same income bracket as the new resident), and would be payable from the commencement of the program, but could be prorated for a maximum of five years.

All State finances would be put on a pay-as-you-go-basis. Complete income and operating statements of the state, in a detailed breakdown, would be published manditorily in all newspapers of the state on a quarterly basis. The citizens of the state would, by means of all forms of communication within the state, receive through indoctrination (from non-governmental sources) a constant progress report on the state's affairs and achievements.

We assumed that by the third State election, a period of six years, after the original invasion of our Utopian group, that they would have elected a Governor and a dozen or more state representatives who were in over-all agreement on the portions of the program disclosed by the group thus far. It would now be possible to imitate changes in state laws. Radio and non network television stations would have been drawn into the orbit. A non-profit, but commercial radio and television station with a distinct editorial format, subsidized by the Foundation would have been for several years propagandizing for various reforms in the State laws. Within six to ten years, the time would be appropriate for the first proposals for new laws that would diverge sharply from the past social modes of the State.

As soon as the education program had been revamped by changes in the State laws and was now under a State subsidy with a non-political, non-elective education board (to determine all school and college policies, courses and programs of study thus preventing domination by any future non-sympathetic political group) our Utopian planners would demand laws abolishing all censorship of any kind. We estimated that this could occur within ten years, but our group would keep a close pulse on the changing conditions within the state and initiate the proposal sooner if possible.

The moment laws were passed abolishing censorship of any kind, the schools, radio, television, the newspapers and all avenues of communication would be ready to combat the influx of any hard core pornography either published within the state or coming in from the outside. A broad general policy defining hard core pornography would not attempt to censor it, but would subject it to wide examination and reveal its lack of human values, showing in actual examples as they occurred in print, in the arts, or in stage presentations, how the sadistic, and abnormal elements in hard core pornography denied the real warmth and love that one individual was capable of toward another. Without anxiety or fear, the teachers, editorialists, commentators and religious leaders of the state would show on television, quote in print and read aloud examples of devalued sex portrayals and involve citizens of the state in a deep search of the value and worth of any presentation of the sexual impulses, that denigrated man and woman for each other. The weapons would be laughter, ridicule, and a constant revelation and exposé of the stupidity of rutting sex . . . showing its lack of meaning, beauty, esthetic values or love for the participants.

Working with a population conditioned through twelve or fifteen years of the new schooling techniques, (some of us felt that all censorship could be eliminated within six years) our feeling was that hard-core pornography would be laughed out of the State.

With the abolition of censorship, we expect the portrayal of the nude human body would quickly appear in all areas of communications within the State. Graphic depiction, in any form, of heterosexual intercourse would become commonplace. Children would grow up accustomed to the portrayal of the act of sexual intercourse and the birth of children, in all the arts. Judgement of the value of particular portrayals would be on the aesthetic side, and portrayals of the act of intercourse which failed to measure up to the enlarged sense of human values of all citizens of the State would tend to reflect back disparagingly on the person or persons responsible. Our State would "censor" by unanimous disapprobation of its citizens.

As the portrayal of nudity became a commonplace, actual nudity on beaches, in and around the home would become a matter of personal choice and convenience. When the State finally came around to revising the laws regarding nudity, it would be a matter of the law catching up with the actual moral codes and practices within the State.

Beth pointed out a side effect of the complete elimination of censorship: magazines of the *Cool Boy* ilk would simply languish and die for lack of interest. Once nudity was generally acceptable on the beaches, in public performances, and casually around the home, the voyeur aspects of seeing the naked human being would be supplanted by the wonder, delight and amazement of the male and female body. Magazines and movies whose sole purpose was to cater to a natural desire to see the human body of the opposite sex naked would become superfluous.

We came to the conclusion that a complete elimination of censorship within the State, would have emphatic results. Under the aegis of a Statewide program to explore the lack of human values and meaning of hard core pornography, as well as a considerable portion of sexually titillating material now being sold as literature and drama and promoted without regard to human

values, we would finally have the net effect of eliminating most
of these neurotic substitution desires for such material.

To further uproot sexual neuroses, and reorient the individual solidly in society and in the world, our Utopian planners
would gently start propagandizing for a complete revision of the
marriage and divorce laws within the State, with the ultimate
purpose of passing completely new laws. This would be a long-
term project needing twenty years. After the younger generation
had been thoroughly schooled in new concepts of the meaning
of love, and with a new understanding of the taproots of
jealousy, we would be ready for sweeping changes in the concepts
of marriage and the family.

We finally agreed on the following revisions. Pre-marital
living at the State-supported trade and regular colleges, along the
Harrad pattern, would be generally available. Marriage would
become mandatory on the impregnation of the woman. Marriage prior to the birth of a child would be optional. Divorce
would be readily available to childless couples, but probably
not much used, since few would get married until they had a
mutual desire to have children. Divorce where there were children under twenty would be permitted but would be discouraged
and rather difficult to obtain unless *both* parents were willing
to sever all ties with their children and permit them to be
adopted into happier environments. Divorce in families where
all children were over eighteen would be relatively easy to obtain,
but we felt that few couples would avail themselves of the opportunity since the new marriage laws of the State would permit
group marriages to a maximum of six couples. Group marriages,
we felt, would in many cases inject new interests and a revision
of values into marriages dulled by familiarity, as well as providing greater meaning and security for the new group families.
Four or six couples desiring to marry as a unit would be given
rigorous psychological testing to determine their adaptability to
this type of marriage. Group marriage could be dissolved in
whole or in part by petition to the State providing the remaining
couples were willing to assume all responsibility for the children.
Obviously, with the new concepts of marriage and the family,
adultery would have no meaning. The centerpinning of the

family would be children and mutual love and esteem of the partners. Bigamous marriages to a maximum of two men and one woman, or two women and one man would be permitted if all the participants were in complete accord and desirous of such a marriage. Divorce of any of the parties in a bigamous marriage would forfeit all children, under eighteen, to the State.

Since the attitude of the State would be the preservation of the dignity and excellence of the individual human being and the insistence that all children were raised within some form of happy family environment, the entire philosophy of the State through its educational systems would be to encourage a free sexual environment, with love, in its wider sense, and not romance dominating all sexual matings. The keynote would be interwoven individual responsibility.

The other night we discussed these initial proposals with Margaret and Phil. While Phil accepted most of our premises, he insisted on more detailed documentation on showing how we would in actual practice, accomplish our various objectives.

"There are a couple of points that I would like to raise, also," Margaret said. "When you are finished, do you still have a democracy or will the natural conflicting "isms" of democracy defeat your whole program? This leads to the second point. While you have allowed yourself twenty years to accomplish your objectives, your most difficult opponents will be organized religion, and individual religious leaders themselves."

"Of course, we'll have opposition, and plenty of it," I said. "But we would have several advantages. We would be operating with a thoroughly planned program, and would make no attempt to label it or publicize it as a whole. Properly conceived, those who disagree would find themselves boxing with shadows."

"You see, Phil," Beth said, "if the first stages of our State-supported educational program are developed so they have popular appeal, and we believe they can, then subsequent social changes would grow out of this quite logically. Furthermore, we would operate, on the surface, by completely democratic means. But democracy as an instrument of social action never functions without direction. Most citizens of any society are disinterested. The personal processes of existence and making a living in our culture, coupled with inadequate education, produce a mass man who must be directed. Some group of individuals, or a specific individual, democratically elected, decides what they (or he) believes are the goals and purpose of a particular society at a particular time. Then, whether it be a Napoleon, a Hitler, a Roosevelt, or a Kennedy, the leader uses any means society permits to accomplish his or his group's personal beliefs. While democracy is presumably the will of the majority, in recent years, the majority no longer means a substantial majority. When elections (and subsequent policies and changes in social direction) are determined by as small as a one or two percent majority, the democratic processes simply force an almost equally large minority into submission. I don't believe we would be subverting democratic processes with our planned society. Our Utopian Group would simply be deciding what is best for the State, as politicians have done through the centuries, and then force these decisions into reality through the power of money and repetitive mass communications. We believe that the beneficent results of our planning would entrench the social gains that we would make. Which political party, ultimately had State power, would not matter, since, in any event, we would be careful not to identify our program with a particular political party."

Sheila tackled the problem of opposition from organized religion. "We have studied the State of X's religious groupings very carefully. The total Catholic and Jewish faith is a minority. The large majority of the population is Protestant, and hence may be somewhat more receptive. Keep in mind that we would not be challenging any beliefs in God."

Margaret smiled. "But you would be in conflict with most theologies, particularly in relation to sex and marriage."

"That's true," Shelia said. "But we would not be offering a *laissez-faire* society. Once the educational aspects of our program are sold (and keep in mind even today we have a climate of much greater sexual freedom which the churches and religious leaders have already had to adjust to) it will be obvious we're offering the basis of social strength and religious strength based on a strong family-centered system. The approach to marriage and divorce that we're proposing could be easily assimilated into church doctrine. Whether our beliefs in man's ability to raise himself higher on the evolutionary ladder are limited to man's faith in his own ability or man's faith in God, the goal amounts to the same thing."

Phil chuckled, "Margaret, we have done it!" he said enthusiastically. "It really doesn't matter whether you kids make your pipe dream a reality. The important thing is that you can think creatively, and not be afraid to posit a different world. The truth is that Harrad has only begun to solve the problem. Man exists in society. If a few men could find the answers to the sexual confusion of modern times, and make people aware that hate and jealousy are not instinctive behaviour but learned reactions, then they will have at least created an outpost in the vast jungle of human inter-relationships. You'll have to remember constantly that your group would be fighting an unceasing rearguard action. Intelligent men and women who have achieved a greater ability to reason are vastly out-numbered by the normal, the average, the great mass of people who will label them with rubrics and castigate them as deviates, and in the long haul they will wonder whether it is worthwhile to be the innovators in society."

"Phil . . . Phil" Beth interrupted him. "We know the words of your song by heart. It sums up to the fact that mass man, untrained and vastly uneducated, can do little with his hard won liberty except to eventually surrender it. But I'm disappointed in your reaction."

"Why?" Phil asked, puzzled.

"You called our thesis a pipe dream, and inferred that we couldn't make it a reality."

Phil grinned. "Considering the world as a whole, your approach is a little way-out with elements of youthful, wishful thinking."

Jack laughed. "You can say the same thing about Harrad College."

"If we are all nothing but your pipe dream, Phil," Val said, "you better not stop smoking. I couldn't stand the shock."

"You are all safe," Phil said, chuckling. "I promise if I stop pipe dreaming, it won't be until all my actors are one hundred and two years old!"

FROM THE JOURNAL OF HARRY SCHACHT

May, the Fourth Year

Today, Beth and I were cleaning up our rooms chucking out a four-year accumulation of stuff we wouldn't need in Graduate School. I came across my Journal in a bottom drawer. Looking back over the first years and the incredible amount of stuff I wrote, I read parts to Beth and I couldn't help smiling. I haven't written anything in these pages for a year. What happened to all the qualms and fears of Harry the Beast? Would I have ever believed it possible that Beth and I would be married, that she would be calmly walking around the room wearing nothing but my shirt and humming a happy little tune as she surveyed with great pride the new roundness in her belly, or that Stanley and I would watch with joy and laughter as Sheila and Beth, naked, compared their speed of maternal growth? In a few weeks this phase of our life will be over. What can I say that sums it up? In a few words I can only echo Beth: "Oh, Harry . . . I am so happy. I love you. I love everybody!"

It's amazing to me how Beth and I, and InSix as a group, have developed such a fundamental rapport (really, an inadequate word) with each other. Last week is only one example I could multiply a hundred times. So here it is Phil, nothing important really, just a windup to this Journal of mine in case you want it, as you once said you did.

Sheila insisted on treating InSix to tickets for the Metropolitan Operas on their Boston road showing. "If we are all going to live together in Graduate School," she said, "I want to be sure that you are all willing to try to enjoy something outside your own interests. Jack and Stanley have made us experts on folk music, Beth and Harry play symphonies and concertos incessantly. Valerie has dragged us to jazz festivals. I like opera . . . so you will all have to suffer."

Jack groaned that operas had some good music but damned silly plots. None of us really suffered. The girls were ecstatic over *La Traviata*. Jack, Stanley and I watched Anna Moffo through binoculars as she sang *Manon*. Between the acts of *Manon*, Stanley was admiring the blooming bellies of Sheila and Beth.

"I can't help it," he kidded them. "I have fallen in love with Anna Moffo. That's the way it is in opera. Love happens just like that! Manon meets Des Grieux. Five minutes later she runs off to Paris with him. Actually, you know the minute she meets Des Grieux, she can't wait to wiggle out of her knickers for him."

"Opera is opera," Sheila said. "You don't confuse it with life. Tragic opera gives you an emotional catharsis, maybe even deeper because of the addition of music, than any Shakespearean or Greek tragedy."

Jack disagreed. "Most of the popular operas were written nearly one hundred years ago. In these days adultery, spurned love, rabid jealousy and uncontrolled hate were even more than now the modus operandi of life. Today, we are more sophisticated. We can't believe Lucia de Lammermoor would marry someone she didn't love. She'd just tell her brother to go to Hell."

But when Joan Sutherland sang the "Mad Scene" from *Lucia*, all of us stood up. Tears in our eyes, we cheered and clapped. clapped.

"See," Sheila said unabashedly drying her eyes. "For a moment you believed!" For a moment you felt all the longing and terror of Lucia gone mad for love."

Back in our rooms at Harrad we were still arguing about it. "I wasn't crying for Lucia," I said. "I was emotionally involved with Joan Sutherland's voice as she led the orchestra, reaching feelings beyond the power of any man-made instrument. I listened truly spellbound."

"Which proves a point," Jack said. We had all crowded into Sheila's and Stanley's room and were drinking champagne in glasses we'd expropriated and carried off in bulging pockets from the Music Hall's Champagne Bar. "If the Harrad experience is valid, and ever becomes a large factor in the world, a large portion of what we label our cultural heritage in literature and in the dramatic arts such as Shakespeare, opera, classical literature, as well as ninety-five percent of every drama, and novel written in the past fifty years will have absolutely no meaning."

"It's a good point," I agreed. "Given an entire society educated as we have been, the common fare of the dramatic arts or literature, based as they are, on adultery, jealousy, hate, war, murder, sexual sadism, sexual abberations, petty misunderstanding and the simple inability to communicate . . . such material will only have antiquarian interest. It will seem as dull and boring as the medieval astrological writings."

"My God," Beth said. "I don't know as I would envy such a world. The long history of man's arts, his quest for beauty and truth in the world is the only stable thing that we have left. The plot of Lucia, for example, may be silly by today's standards but the idea of love and the heartbreak of Eduardo's *bella inammorata*, in fact all of Donizetti's music represents the tragedy of man caught in his own circumstances, destiny, fate . . . call it what you will. If you wipe out the idea of Laocoön, man struggling to rise above the evil in himself, you have wiped out the essence of man as he knows and understands himself."

Jack smiled. "After four years at Harrad, do you still believe man is of necessity a dualistic creature doomed by his very nature to always have good and evil in conflict within him?"

"No, I don't," Beth said. "But in our future Utopian world with no conflict, with everyone in full accord finally, with no wars, no murders, no hate, no jealousy, what in heaven's name will be the subject matter of the arts? Not to harp on Lucia . . . but it is a good example; what forces in the world will inspire a Donizetti to create his music, or a Sutherland to sing it? I'm sure that man, no matter how good he may be and how much he is in control of his emotions, needs the purge and sudden realization of his insignificance that a great dramatic tragedy can give him."

"There's a thousand subjects," I said. "Imagine a drama and literature built on the principle of Greek drama. Man not against himself but against the gods. For us in the twentieth century the gods are the unknowns. Man against disease. Man against premature death. Man against mass hatred. Man crying for security, or solitude, or love. Man against war or poverty or misunderstanding. Man against greed or corruption. Man against his own desire for achievement. Man trapped on this planet and yearning for the stars. Man against his own ignorance. A new kind of Faust. In this kind of drama and literature the individual good man, the protagonist, the hero, would once again assume his heroic stance. His failure against unknowns, and not the failures of his own petty personal misfortunes, would assume all the grandeur of real tragedy."

"I think you may have something," Valerie said. "A modern Donizetti could write a modern *Lucia*. Lucia could be a southern white girl in love with Eduardo, who could be a negro. Lucia's brother could be a white supremist. With these elements, you could write a new tragic libretto to Donizetti's music."

"Or a new Donizetti could write new music," Stanley chuckled.

"In the new Harrad world of the next hundred years," Jack grinned, "when all of us are coffee colored, and the Negro-White problem has passed into history, that conflict will be just as antiquated as the present Lucia."

"Isn't that a point?" Stanley asked. "Man should use his arts to express the strivings that have meaning for his time. We need new literature and new arts to point the way. Valerie's idea is contemporary . . . but there will always be Harry's universals."

Beth just walked over and sat in my lap. "What are you writing?" she asked. "May I read it?"

When she finished she kissed me. "Feel my belly. I'm so proud of it! Aren't you?"

I admitted that I was.

And that's Harrad, Phil. Millions of things to wonder about and discuss, and new lives eager, if we will help them, to pick up where we leave off. Right now, Beth is waiting to continue this discussion, in a somewhat lower key, with me inside her, and her new belly pressing against me. I'm afraid our conclusions, if any, may never get written down!

A LETTER FROM BETH SCHACHT

December, after the Fourth Year

Dear Margaret and Phil;

We received your letter asking for news of the first class to graduate from Harrad. As we told you last June, we decided somehow that InSix would hang together. Like other couples that grouped together at Harrad, the six of us seem to have developed a built-in unity that seems to sustain us. As secretary of InSix, I have been elected to bring you up to date.

First and most important, Sheila and I gave birth to baby boys, Arnold and Abraham, respectively . . . born within ten days of each other. Valerie is five months pregnant, but (Jack to the contrary) it seems dubious at the moment whether she will agree to suffer through what happened to Sheila and me at delivery time.

But to go back. When Harvey and I were accepted at the University of Pennsylvania Medical School, Sheila decided to do graduate work here in music. After some juggling, Stanley switched from Harvard Law to U. Of P. Law. Valerie gave up Western Reserve and is here working in sociology, while Jack is doing graduate work in economics at Wharton.

It sounds simple when I write it but it took a whole summer of juggling and argument to get us all settled in one spot for another four years. Then it took Sheila, Val and I at least two months of heated disagreement to settle on a house where we could all shack up together. InSix is now the proud owner of an old ten room house in a convenient but run-down section of this City of Brotherly Love. The house cost InSix a down payment of five thousand dollars, and was all hell to work out with the staid Philadelphia bankers who looked down their long noses but finally succumbed to Jack's financial genius. If they knew the whole truth, and not the simple fact that we are poor but deserving students, I fear the sky of Philadelphia would be lighted with the word SIN in red neon; to guide and warn the faltering steps of the good progeny of William Penn and Benjamin Franklin, against a similar immoral course. No, not old Ben! . . . He was a gay dog. I'm sure that if he had thought of it, you and Phil would have been several hundred years too late with Harrad. What a different world it would have been!

I was about to say that Val, who under Harry's tutelage, made an excellent midwife to Sheila and me, is not sure that she wants to be the next "victim".

Safely ensconced in our own beds, Shelia and I had our babies at home. It was no picnic, and it was none of this natural childbirth stuff. It was just plain rugged, but now, as we recall it, neither Sheila nor I can help smiling. We are twentieth century heroines in a world where most births are cut and dried, where mothers labor on a production line, carefully planned for the convenience of doctors who so far as possible keep normal working hours. Our future citizens come into the world in the most modern aseptic conditions. Healthy and antiseptic, I suppose, but definitely lacking something so far as the "poppa" is concerned and maybe even the "mamma". Keep in mind that none of us are advocating a return to primitive child bearing. Sheila and I are still deep admirers of modern hospitals. Only, as Harry pointed out, the modern birth process omits one very vital phase of child bearing . . . the male love, his interest, curiousity and identity with his wife and child at the moment of birth.

Try as he would, Harry could not persuade the doctors, the hospital or the medical school that he and Stanley should have the privilege of witnessing the birth of their children . . . and maybe even hold my and Sheila's respective hands as we labored on our joint productions. It simply would not be possible. No hospital with their crowded labor rooms was set up for such sentimentality. Oooh, did that word make Harry mad. He gave the doctor an extended dissertation on the difference between love and sentimentality.

It didn't take Harry and Stanley long to figure out a simple solution. All Sheila and I had to do was to sweat it out. Inevitably we would give birth. Frankly, about this time Sheila and I were beginning to have doubts. With his usual thoroughness, Harry jumped ahead in his medical studies and stayed up night after night becoming an expert on obstetrics and every facet of childbirth. Then, just to make sure, Harry assured the doctor who was looking after Sheila and me that he would be summoned if the blessed event arrived suddenly and without warning.

When I awoke at four in the morning on October fifteenth, no one had to tell me I was in the first stages of labor. Harry suddenly changed his mind and was going to call the doctor and rush me to the hospital, but I crossed my fingers and told him that I was game if he was. After all, I assured him, I had acquired such a thorough knowledge of what was going on inside me that I really didn't want to be an inert, half-conscious, contracting lump of flesh. My brain wanted to know what was really happening to the rest of me. Little did I know, what I was in for.

The first ten hours seemed to last an eternity, but I wasn't lonesome. Since all parents make a fetish of taking pictures of their offspring Jack decided that Harry and I should do it right and start from scratch. Yes . . . you guessed it! Thanks to Jack, the frustrated movie mogul, and over my howling protests and later Sheila's, we have the nicest movies you ever saw of the birth of our babies. I've watched the film of my stardom, my finest performance, over and over again with awe and pride that I, Beth, accomplished this miracle.

I won't bore you with details. We will bring our movies up to Harrad soon and show them to you. You'll see me with the most amazing grimaces, and Val and Sheila flitting over me like mother hens, wiping my face or rubbing my back while Stanley watches in amazement, and Harry with our good doctor friend (he arrived about nine o'clock with plenty of scowls for all concerned). They finally stopped arguing over recumbent me and counselled each other.

Harry insisted that I would have an easy birth. He should try it! About noon they propped me into a semi-sitting position. Since I had been measured and studied thoroughly day by day for the past four months and also given endless advice by Harry, I was contracting and relaxing on schedule with much happy cheering from the sidelines. Finally it was over. If I was the heroine, Jack deserves the cameraman's Oscar. He condensed the long hours into about forty-five minutes of dramatic deep feeling. He captured my tears and pure joy, and Harry's proud grin when he held Abraham up and slapped him on his fanny. He interspersed this with all the faces of our friends, showing unconstrained, amazed, happy wonder. Of course, Jack doesn't need compliments. He now envisions a new age of home movies, with him as the precursor and founder of a new kind of movie studio devoted to the business. Imagine, newly-marrieds would be able not only to show you movies of their honeymoon (omitting of course the hours of implantation) but would then proudly pass onto the next reel and show junior being hatched.

Now, we are back to normal! I missed two and a half weeks of lectures and classes, but, since we are taking identical courses, Harry kept me up to date. Sheila took three weeks off, but her schedules are more flexible than med school. Sheila and I nursed our babies for a few weeks. We even exchanged the little rascals, who didn't seem to care from which teats they got their sustenance. Before Abraham went on a bottle, Harry tried a taste or two, but wouldn't recommend it for a diet. Now that both babies are on bottles and we have developed an easy schedule, most of Sheila's classes are in the afternoon, so she is morning boss. I take over maternal duties about two-thirty on most days. We have about two hours a day when the boys or Val, or a nice motherly neighbor who lives next door takes the daily watch. Mostly there are no problems since the kids are sleeping.

Do you wonder how our communal life works out in practice? Believe me, it is never dull. First, money. Jack and Valerie, our President and Treasurer, pay the bills. As you know for the past three years we have pooled all our resources into our corporation, InSix. The purpose of InSix is to provide the education and all expenses for the six of us for the next four years. When we started in September, InSix had about twelve thousand dollars from our total summer earnings over the past three years. We also had the income from our record royalties of seventy-six hundred dollars, and one thousand Beth got for posing for the famous Cool Girl picture. After the down payment on our dilapidated mansion, we had about eighteen thousand, so we ought to have enough money to last all of us for at least two years.

We had a stormy family conference here early in October, and the only point of agreement was, that even though Sheila was more than willing and enthusiastic to subsidize all of us, that we would make it on our own. You should have seen us showing the house to Val's, Jack's, Harry's and my father and mother. Such wailing and consternation and fears of perdition for their brood! I can't make up my mind whether Sheila and Stanley were better off; they had no explaining to do. Anyway, Jack made a sporting proposition to the three fathers who were present. If we got into financial difficulty, they would loan InSix a maximum of four thousand dollars each, while Sheila would match with four thousand. So much for finances. We are confident that within four years the world will be blessed with two doctors, one lawyer, and three sundry Ph.d's.

As for day in, day out living, our home is our castle and fortress. Sheila, Val and I do the shopping and plan dinner, the only meal we all manage to eat together. We have one downstairs room strictly for study, with desks, chairs, lamps etc. purchased from various junk shops. Very comfortable. Only one rule in this room, absolutely no conversation. If you don't want to study, but feel unconversational, you can sit and stare and no one would even dare ask what you are thinking. We made one room a music room and here we have a piano (Sheila's donation) and record player. Here we sing, play music, write kooky stuff for records we hope to make and generally horse around. The dining room and living room off it are for eating, discussion and guests. God, do we have guests! Some never want to go home, and on weekends some don't. We find them Sunday morning sleeping on the floor, and the discussions that started Saturday night are still going strong Sunday noon. Naturally, we attract all the screwballs and curiousity seekers from here to New York City. Discussions range from sex to Zen, communism to existentialism. You name it and some one is available for a "pro" and someone for a "con".

Upstairs is the sacrosanct headquarters for InSix. There are five bedrooms but only one damn bathroom. Fortunately this house was built in the days that bathrooms were big. It measures nearly twenty by twenty feet. Since the boys are rather uninhibited about not only their, but our excretory functions, Sheila, Val and I (who are definitely inhibited) made them enclose the toilet with a four wall partition, and that, at least has a door and lock on it! However, anything can happen . . . and since the partition doesn't reach the ceiling, which is at least twelve feet high, I discovered one night that all the giggling on the outside was caused by reflection of Beth sitting on the pot and being stared at in a mirror Jack had ingeniously propped on an appropriate angle.

Bathing, showering etc. is strictly public. None of us, including the boys has any trouble getting his or her back scrubbed . . . or any other part of our anatomy, if we show the slightest interest.

Naturally, sex is somewhat uninhibited. Now that Sheila and I are back in circulation, and after Val has her baby, we've decided not to attempt any more progeny until we've finished our education.

A few weeks ago, on a rainy Saturday afternoon, we were all sprawled across Sheila and Stanley's bed, and Sheila plunged into the discussion of whether we were going to continue monogamous or return to the more or less informal sex life of our Harrad days, and if the latter, how? She suggested that if the mood seized us, we might occasionally want to switch bed mates, but only on the basis of prior non-alcoholic discussion and one hundred percent agreement.

Harry disagreed on the method. "What I can't figure out," he said laughing "is that if I asked you to sleep with me, Sheila, and if you didn't want to, or Stanley didn't want you to, or if Beth didn't want me to, how in the devil would you solve it? All I'd have done is create tension with the three of you. It's really an impossible thing to discuss."

But we did discuss it . . . for nearly three hours. We concluded how impossible it would be to avoid exchanging partners. We were bound to be attracted physically to each other, living as we did. We were married as a matter of direct responsibility to each other, but marriage didn't preclude the feeling of love, and just plain sexual attraction we had for each other. I suggested it would eliminate tension to sleep with our "proper" mates Saturday through Tuesday, and our "improper" mates Wednesday, Thursday and Friday. Stanley protested that this didn't include Val and Jack, and once Val was "back in the lists as a combatant" it would change the sequence. Harry's argument was more fundamental. As much as he enjoyed sex, he wasn't about to make it a "duty" to make love to three different girls in one week. Not that he wouldn't try occasionally, but if he felt sleepy on a particular night he didn't want to arrive on the sacrificial couch with an engraved guarantee.

We finally solved it by agreeing to exchange our spouses for one week at a time with Valerie and Jack included. This is working beautifully. Sheila, Val and I were discussing it last night. If you dig back into the history of marriage, particularly in Briffault's famous study *The Mothers* you'll find that originally most marriages were group marriages. Isn't it possible within the framework of modern society that some of the beneficial aspects of such marriages might be retained? What have we gained in our little society? Whether I am sleeping with Harry, Jack or Stanley, it is not a lustful experience or orgiastic. It is very definitely not casual. We are deeply good friends, and we do not take each other for granted. Each of us brings something a little different to the other, and it "sparks our lives with a real *joie de vivre* and a deep commitment.

Val summed it up. "Every Sunday when my new husband for the week joins me in my room, I feel like a new bride all over again. Sometimes I wake up in the night and for a sleepy moment I may forget whether I am with Stanley, Jack or Harry, and then I feel warm and bubbly. Me . . . Valerie . . . too tall and with big feet and sometimes too bossy . . . three men love me and care for me . . . and I . . . I love us all!"

Really sex with all of us is warm laughter and deep mystery

existing almost simultaneously. What will happen when we finish our education? We talk about it once in a while. We know that inevitably economics and the problem of making a living will separate us and we will pursue our monogamous lives and have our children in a more conventional pattern. But we know, too, that we will plan our holidays and vacations together with the sure knowledge that the pressure of society to conform will never break the bond that we have formed, not only because of sex and the desire for variety within our monogamous lives, but even more because all of us will continue to respond to the challenges of living. And when we meet in the future we will not be dull suburbanites passing an evening of alcoholic boredom, and repressing our sexual feelings. We will be alive, vital, inter-acting, intensely curious and wondering human beings who care deeply for each other.

A couple of things sum us up pretty well. A week ago, we all went up to New York to visit with Bad Max and some of Jack's friends in the Village. Here is a vignette of those who think they are challenging the conservatism and conformity of society. First, we watched a Flashlight Parade and Rally to protest the harrassment of the Arts in New York City. A motley crowd of students, artists, beardos, and what not, all wearing black as a token mourning for the Death of Freedom in the city, were protesting the Licensing of Movie Films, the Censorship of Books, Seizure of Art Works as Obscenity, Harrassment of Coffee Houses by the police etc. Later we watched another group sponsored by the New York League for Sexual Freedom who were picketing the Women's House of Detention carrying placards which read: "Free the Prostitutes". "If it weren't for Sex you wouldn't be here". "32-69 come and join our Picket Line". "Whoop-de-doo, I want to screw, how about you?" "Ballin is good for the Soul" etc. etc. . . .

I'm afraid the six of us felt like visitors from another planet. What these people thought was rebellious and provocative seemed to us pitiful and foolish. For if men and women want to change society, the effective way is the Harrad way. Not sticking your tongue out, or spending your time wailing at the superficial manifestations of man's stupidities or making a greater ass of yourself than those you are protesting against. No, far better to live your life as a totality . . . slowly and methodically with a sure knowledge of what you wish to accomplish. The kind of personal rebellion that will change the world is summed up by John Gardner in his concept of the "self-renewing man" "What is he? Who is he? Here is how Gardner describes him in the Carnegie Corporation Annual Report;

"The self-renewing man is versatile and adaptive. He is not trapped in techniques, procedures, or routines of the moment. He is not the victim of fixed habits and attitudes. He is not imprisoned by extreme specialization . . . In a rapidly changing world versatility is a priceless asset, and the self renewing man has not lost that vitally important attribute. He may be a specialist but he has also retained the capacity to function as a generalist. The self-renewing man is highly motivated and respects the sources of his own energy and motivation. He knows how important it is to believe in what he is doing. He knows how important it is to pursue the things about which he has a deep conviction. Enthusiasm for the task to be accomplished lifts him out of the ruts of habit and customary procedure. Drive and conviction give him the courage to risk failure. (One of the reasons mature persons stop learning is that they become less and less willing to risk failure) And not only does he respond to challenge, but he also sees the challenge where others fail to see it . . . For the self renewing man the development of his own potentialities and the process of self discovery never end. It is a sad but unarguable fact that most human beings go through life only partially aware of the full range of their abilities. In our own society we could do much more than we do now to encourage self development. We could, for example, drop the increasingly silly fiction that education is for youngsters and devise many more arrangements for lifelong learning . . . But the development of one's talent is only part, perhaps the easiest part, of self-development. The maximum "Know thyself" so ancient, so deceptively simple, so difficult to follow has gained in richness of meaning as we learn more about man's nature . . . as Josh Billings said "It is not only the most difficult thing to know one's self, but the most inconvenient." It is a life-long process . . . that brings us to the recognition that the ever renewing society will be a free society. It will understand that the only stability possible today is stability in motion. It will foster a climate in which the seedlings of new ideas can survive and the deadwood of obsolete ideas be hacked out. Above all it will recognize that its capacity for renewal depends on the individuals who make it up. It will foster innovative, versatile, and self-renewing men and women and give them room to breathe."

That's it, Margaret and Phil . . . that's Harrad . . . that's us! We hold the key to the future. The door is unlocked and open. Those who pass through are going into a new era, a new age. Not a Golden Age. My God . . . how dull that would be! No . . . rather an Age of Continuous Wonder . . . an Age of Creative Insecurity."

> *Love from all of us,*
> *Beth*

THE HARRAD/PREMAR SOLUTION

I hope you have enjoyed *The Harrad Experiment*. Over a lifetime, I have come to believe more strongly than anything else that all of us can learn to love each other and care for each other far more than we do now. I believe we can make a world in which people stop creating tragedies in their daily lives where no tragedies need exist.

Before the 21st century is over, possibly within your lifetime, I believe that religious leaders, educators, and government leaders[1] will unite in a shared belief that continuing education of the younger generation is the only way to provide a sense of national purpose for the United States—or, for any democratic nation.

This new approach to education will include a new sexual morality, which unlike most current Judeo-Christian teachings, moves *with* the grain of human sexual drives and not against it. Encouraged by their churches or synagogues, by parents and teachers, and by the media, young people will refrain from sexual intercourse until they are 17 years old. A young man's or woman's 17th birthday, coinciding with graduation from high school, would become a celebrated rite-of-passage, after which responsible sexual mating—with or without a marriage commitment—would become a natural part of life.

Prior to this, through their secondary schooling, young people would be socially indoctrinated to limit all sexual expression to kissing, fondling, genital play, as well as masturbation to climax for those who were too excited to forego orgasm. During their growing years—indeed from birth—young people would have had the opportunity not only to see men and women naked on beaches and in other areas where it is practical to be naked but also to watch, in movies and on television, people of all ages over 17 making love. By their 17th year they would be well-acquainted with the details of human loving and the sexual expression of it.

In essence, we will have grown up as a society and would no longer exclude young people from complete sexual knowledge. The only activities that would be censored from view would be child sex, violent and victimized sex, and explicit portraits of homosexual congress. (I will give the reason for censoring explicit depictions of "gay" sexuality later.)

The factor that would make this approach to human sexuality work would be a new approach to undergraduate education, which would be made available to all secondary-school graduates. I call it the Harrad/Premar Solution. This is the only sensible approach to education in the 21st century, and it would give American democracy a new sense of national purpose. By what name it is called is unimportant. You may have already guessed that *Harrad* is a contraction of the names *Harvard* and *Radcliffe,* and *Premar* is a shortening of *premarital.* Every person would have to graduate from high school to be eligible to vote,[2] and all high-school graduates would be guaranteed an additional four years of undergraduate education.

If you have just read *The Harrad Experiment* for the second time, you are probably in your middle forties, one of the "baby boomers" who grew up during the 1960s and settled down in the 1980s to become a "yuppie" or "dink" (double-income couple with no kids). When you first read *Harrad,* you may have thought it was a nice daydream and might appeal to the "flower children" but that it would never work in real life.

On the other hand, if you have just read *Harrad* for the first time, you are probably between the ages of 16 and 35 and were playing in a sandbox when *Harrad* was first published. As offspring of the "baby-boom" generation, you are known as the "baby-bust" generation because there are 6 percent fewer of you (quite a few million less) than there were of your fathers and mothers. This worries your parents, who are living much longer than their parents did, because your generation will be paying less to the Social Security fund to support them in their old age.

Between first publication in 1966 and 1978, when it went out of print, *Harrad* sold three million copies and was translated into most major languages, including Japanese and Korean. It was made into a movie that featured Don Johnson (later of *Miami Vice* fame). Because Johnson and his costar appeared frontally naked, the movie was rarely shown on network television or else the nude swimming pool sequence was omitted. In the final printing the cover still proclaimed that *Harrad* was the "Sex Manifesto of the Free Love Generation."

If you have just read *Harrad* for the first time, your reaction may vary all the way from great enthusiasm to a frightened, "I might like Harrad; but I don't think I'd dare go to a place like that" or "Harrad might be okay, if I could choose my own roommate." If you've been raised in a family where sexual discussion is still taboo, you may be a little shocked.

If you are a college sophomore, junior, or senior, you may be reacting, "So what's new? No one gets married today without screwing a bit beforehand, or even living together unmarried for awhile." You may be thinking that Bob Rimmer was ahead of his time in 1966 and helped pave the way for relaxed rules. The norm at most colleges and universities today is dormitories where men and women live together on the same floor, and in some schools the two sexes use the same toilets and showers. You may not live in the same room with a member of the opposite sex, but you can easily work out a sleeping arrangement. By your junior year, you may live off campus and share an apartment with a man or a woman, as the case may be.

The only ones who are still worrying may be your nervous parents, who pray that you are using birth-control pills and condoms so you won't get pregnant and/or AIDS.

Although *you* may have experienced sex with more than one person before you graduate from college, one thing hasn't changed. Despite the grim facts that almost 50 percent of all marriages end in divorce, that in the past 25 years—in order to retain 1966 family purchasing power—most women must be working wives, and that 50 percent of American males experience at least one adulterous relationship during their married life and nearly as many females take at least one extramarital fling—despite these realities, you still believe in the daydream of the rose-covered cottage occupied by a nuclear family (a husband, wife, and two children).

Maybe you'll be lucky and this will happen to you. Maybe you'll find the one and only person. You'll get married and never have sex with anyone else again. Maybe you'll have two kids and can afford to send them to college, at a cost of $100,000 each by the end of the century if they go to private schools. And maybe, Norman-Rockwell-style, they'll replicate your family life. You'll have grandchildren, and they'll join you for the holidays and celebrate your 50th anniversary of wedded bliss.

Some Background. Twenty-five years ago, if I had believed these things would happen I would never have written *Harrad* or many other novels exploring what I predicted would become alternate lifestyles by necessity.

The realities facing the 21st-century family were explored by *Newsweek* in the spring of 1990. The dream-style American family doesn't exist; maybe it never existed. As *Newsweek* pointed out, we still have fathers working while mothers keep house and take care of the children, but these are now a small minority. Most families today are dependent on working mothers and fathers, with day care for the kids or a latchkey. The divorce rate, still close to 50 percent of the marriage rate, is creating stepfamilies, which more often than not do not provide emotional or intellectual stability for children. We have single-parent families, in which the mother is the chief cook and bottle-washer, and we also have the horrendous problem of senior citizens whose children have no room for them in their high-rise apartments or condos, or can't afford to support them in independent housing.

These are only a portion of the "future shocks" that we are witnessing. Within the next fifty years the world's population may exceed nine billion. With four billion more on the planet than there are now, your lifestyle is going to change dramatically. In the United States we have a growing ethnic population that refuses to melt, an African American population that has never been absorbed into the mainstream, and an alarming total of 700,000 high-school dropouts annually. Fifty percent of the 17-year-olds who apply for jobs are unable to read at the ninth-grade level and are virtually unemployable in the skilled labor market.

America is becoming a new kind of class society. Ultimately, the undereducated will become completely powerless. If we don't change the educational process drastically, the skilled and better-educated will be swamped by taxes to save the poor, while those who actually own the United States (only about 5 percent of all Americans have any real financial equity in the capitalistic democratic system) will stand on the ramparts, wave the flag, and declare wars on poverty and drugs.

During the past twenty-five years top educators from John Dewey to Robert Hutchins and James Conant, along with presidential commissions from Truman to Reagan, have presented various proposals to solve our educational problems. They had one idea in common: If democracy is to survive and the U.S. is to maintain its high standard of living, we must, as the Carnegie Commission reported, "graduate a vast majority of students with achievement levels long thought possible only for the privileged few."

Unfortunately, despite thousands of community colleges that offer vocational education beyond high school, begun as a result of the Truman Commission Report on Higher Education (1948) or Terrel Bell's report, *A Nation at Risk* (1983), for the Reagan presidential commission, the nation's educators still haven't been able to translate the proposals into educational reality.

Since World War II we have "popularized education" so that today approximately 75 percent of all Americans graduate from high school and nearly 20 percent complete four years of college, but the *level* of education has dropped—indicated by declining SAT scores— and as many as twenty-three million Americans (many of them high-school graduates) are functionally illiterate.

In the 1990s we have a president and Congress who give lip-service to the problems of educating the next generation. But thus far both have failed to endow the education of present and future generations with a real sense of national purpose. Instead of getting to the root of the drug problem, which stems from a lack of education and a need to escape, even momentarily, from the grim reality of being a "have-not" in a society that extols having everything, like his predecessors, President Bush declares a billion-dollar war on drugs— his particular bugaboo. But this is a "war" that can only be won when a vast majority of people live fulfilling lives, when they aren't conned by the unreal worlds of "Dynasty," million-dollar-lottery jackpots, or dreams of becoming a superstar overnight.

A National Purpose. The basic problem facing the United States today is that we have no sense of national purpose. We are drifting into the future on a come-what-may basis. In late 1989 Mikhail Gorbachev yanked the seat out from under the Yankees. Our enemy, the "evil empire" with communism as its political and economic system, collapsed. During the past twenty-five years we have spent quite a few trillion dollars making the world safe for capitalistic democracy. Historically, controlled laissez faire capitalism has provided the best of all possible worlds for human beings. But an every-man-for-himself kind of greed doesn't provide a lasting sense of human purpose or even a continuing sense of well-being.

No one knows yet what glue will hold the U.S. together during the next century. Unless there is a crisis of frightening proportions, it won't be environmental problems. What pollutes and doesn't pollute is a subject of endless controversy. Jimmy Carter proved in the seventies that Americans refuse to accept a pessimism that affects their pocketbooks or constrains their lifestyles. Despite warnings and mounting evidence that Mideastern oil reserves are not infinite, we continue to believe that Americans are smarter and more creative than Asians or Europeans and that somehow they'll underwrite us forever by buying our Treasury bonds or our Rockefeller Centers.

With no sense of national purpose, we are on a "DDD" course—democracy drifting to disaster. Wars, hot or cold—unless we are attacked by nuclear missiles (increasingly unlikely)—will never again provide a sense of national purpose. There is only one sense of national purpose that can unite a democratic society. It's the belief that life is not an endlessly repeating circle. Whether it be true or not, we must have the notion of making progress toward a more individually fulfilling world—if not for ourselves, then for our children.

A national philosophy that would make such a belief possible is not so much that all men and women are created equal (genetically or environmentally, for one reason or another, we may not be) but that all people have an equal right—and the money to pay for it—to as complete an education as they can absorb. We must take America's historical commitment to a guaranteed education through the secondary level one step further.

We must devise a holistic concept of lifetime education that includes a new type of undergraduate education available to every citizen, followed by a financially guaranteed postgraduate education for those who qualify on merit. If every person who graduated from high school were guaranteed another four years of college which, in addition to vocational skills, would offer everyone a broad humanistic, historical, liberal perspective on his or her own life and "indoctrinate" them (I use the word benignly) into the joys of lifetime learning, we would have a new sense of national purpose that would inspire the world.

This essay is intended to point the way. Before I show how this approach is the real key to democratic survival, let me give you my perspective on our century.

A View of the 20th Century. During the affluent 1950s, the United States ruled the world technologically, but there was an underlying malaise. The nuclear family living in tiny "tacky Levittown" housing, made it possible for millions of GIs to buy their own homes. But "having it all" by the end of the 1950s wasn't producing happiness but rather a "lonely crowd," and the divorce rate was slowly rising.

Jack Kerouac hailed the new "beat generation." This was composed of "people who never yawn and say commonplace things, but burn, burn, burn like fabulous Roman candles, exploding like spiders across the stars and in the middle you see the blue center light pip and everybody goes 'Awwww!' " A few years after Kerouac wrote that, the "beats" would become hippies and flower children. By this time they had discovered that pot instead of booze, used by their parents to escape reality, was a new kind of turn-on. In the late 1960s, the only sense of national purpose was to "turn on" and "drop out."

Life magazine (then selling millions of copies each week) recognized the problem and called upon national leaders to enunciate national purpose for the United States. From its series of articles came many platitudes as well as a recognition that man "satisfied with goods" needed more from life than the "pursuit of happiness." But no thinker in the U.S. seemed able to propose a unifying concept for this country and/or for Western man. We had lost an overriding sense of mission. No one could answer the questions that every man and woman who has enough to eat eventually asks: "Why am I here? Where am I going? What is the purpose of my life?"

By contrast, the English Puritans who arrived in the New World in the 17th century and the "huddled masses" who arrived over the next two hundred years had much better defined purposes. Trusting in God, they were going to improve their own lives and make a better and more affluent world for their children. By the middle of the 19th century, hundreds of thousands of the new arrivals from Europe and China were being exploited by robber barons (newly created American "royalty" that began with the Astors, Vanderbilts, Goulds, and Morgans). First-generation Americans still believed they could make the world "safe for democracy," and in 1916-1917 we were eager to stop the Kaiser and the German Reich from again trying to rearrange the borders of Europe.

The sense of national purpose that motivated the country during World War I dissipated in the Jazz Age and was completely wiped out by ten years of Depression in the 1930s. But then, in 1941, when the Japanese attacked Pearl Harbor and we faced the grim necessity to rid the world of Hitler and his master-race henchmen, Americans were united once again around a common cause. However, it's worth remembering that in the middle thirties and the years prior to World War II, hundreds of thousands of Americans singing "Brother, Can You Spare a Dime?" were intrigued by Marx and Lenin. Many became so-called "fellow travelers," intent on convincing Americans that socialism and the *Communist Manifesto* provided the missing sense of purpose. Believers in socialism and communism haunted the government well into the Eisenhower presidency.

In the late 1960s, our political leaders tried to create a sense of national purpose around Vietnam. But the "domino" theory that the loss of Vietnam to communism would eventually trap us in a Third World War, didn't convince most Americans. If we couldn't save Hungary and Czechoslovakia from communism in the 1950s and 1968, the domino theory and President Johnson's Tonkin Gulf resolution didn't make much sense in 1964.

Fortunately, *The Harrad Experiment* was written prior to Vietnam, so I didn't have to deal with a growing antagonism among the younger generation, who were soon to be drafted into a war they didn't believe in. But most of their fathers, veterans of World War II, were under the delusion that they could turn a 15th-century agricultural society into an Asian democracy.

While I was a long way from being a hippie, like the young

people in the 1960s, I enjoyed the Beatles and wondered if "you'd love me when I was 64," and thought we were living "on a yellow submarine." In 1967, when the first Bantam Press edition of *Harrad* appeared, the younger generation hadn't turned their anger against the Vietnam War into a temporarily unifying "purpose" for part of the nation. They did believe that the "greening of America" was soon to occur. They were living their version of it in Haight Ashbury, San Francisco or in the East Village of New York. Or they were living in communes in New Mexico, where they called themselves "love children" or "gentle people." They extolled love, smoked pot, and believed as one male communard suggested: "All the girls are my wives, the guys are my brothers and all the babies are mine—it's true love!"

In the words of Mick Jagger, they were "all together" and tried to prove it at Woodstock where 400,000 gathered in 1969 seeking a sense of purpose that eluded them. In addition to smoking grass, they tried to find their true selves and a new kind of spiritual uplift with LSD, or else they sought "soul experiences" in communes like Drop City and Hog Farm, which offered "hog consciousness."

It was a mind-blowing world, where the true color was psychedelic. It was the Age of Aquarius, Marishi Mahesh Yogi, and Esalen at Big Sur, where the groundwork for the Human Potential movement was being laid. It was the age of the generation gap. You couldn't trust anyone over the age of 30. If you were under 30 and "with it," you adopted the mod look from Carnaby Street. Women flattened their breasts, and men grew their hair long and wore ankh symbols and love beads. Psychologists were proclaiming that sexual differences were disappearing and the world of unisex was just around the corner. It was also a time of student strikes against Vietnam, of the Black Power movement, and of a conviction that a free style of education developed by students themselves was superior to anything offered in college or university catalogues.

It was a time of awakening to the direction that the U.S. government was taking. We were suddenly spending billions of dollars annually on defense and to achieve military superiority. We were blithely interfering in other people's civil wars in the name of democracy, and napalming innocent victims. It was a time of growing realization that no one knew how to stop the military establishment, or if we ever achieved an agreement with the Soviet Union, how we would lower military spending and employ millions of Americans in peaceful and perhaps less profitable endeavors.

Few remembered President Eisenhower, the man who knew better than anyone else, who had said: "Every gun that is made, every warship launched, every rocket fired, signifies in the final sense a theft from those who hunger and are not fed, those who are cold and not clothed . . . this world in arms is spending the sweat of its laborers, the genius of its scientists and the hopes of its children."

The "feminine mystique" had been discovered, and it gave birth to the equal-rights movement, which was eventually sabotaged by conservative politicians. Dropping out, living communally, and giving up certain kinds of material goods (with the exception of fast automobiles and hi-fi equipment) were the messages. The designations "hot" and "cool" applied to books and television, as well as sexual relations. It was a world of "future shocks" and the realization that no one knew how to cope with the implications of our scientific breakthroughs, which continued unabated into the 1990s.

Those who tried to lead with new "trendy" ideas quickly discovered that the commercial business world could coopt their ideas so fast that they could become obsolete or "dated" before the originator even got off the ground. With million-dollar advertising campaigns, "living healthfully" became identified with breakfast cereals and even smoking certain kinds of cigarettes.

All the surface confusion produced billions of words of "interpretation"—mostly misinterpretation—while millions of Americans sat by their television sets for an average of more than ten hours a day and tried to ignore the real world by watching thousands of murders and acts of violence every week.

In the midst of assassinations and wars, astronauts landed on the moon in 1969, although thanks to the blurring effects of television viewing, some people believe it never really happened but was a television spectacular devised to keep people's minds off their troubles. We discovered lasers, DNA, and the possibilities of genetic manipulation, and computers moved from tubes to transistors, to silicon chips and bubble memories. Later, in the 1980s, we hadn't even begun to face the main problem of the computer age: whether the vast amount of information generated by computers and by television was producing an avalanche of facts and ideas no one could absorb. We were on the verge of an automated society, which would elimate most unskilled labor and create unemployment for millions of undereducated people.

Finally, the Vietnam War was "wound down" and eventually phased out. But before we could recover from the Watergate shock to our political idealisms, we discovered that Americans were consuming most of the world's energy and were dependent on the Arabs, some of whom didn't like us very much, for some very good reasons. Like it or not, by the middle seventies, the dream of American self-sufficiency was coming to an end. It was "Bye, Bye, Miss American Pie" in more ways than one.

During the late sixties and early seventies *Harrad* captured the imagination of millions of the younger generation. Hundreds of them wrote to "Harrad, Cambridge, Massachusetts" trying to apply for admission and many tried group marriages. But there *was* no Harrad, and without the deprogramming of Harrad-style human-values seminars, they were often floundering in their own ego conflicts.

After Vietnam, the drift toward disaster continued. Inflation, exacerbated by the rise in the price of oil, plunged the country into some long-needed soul-searching. For a few years, with the help of a grim President Carter, we almost had a sense of national purpose: We began to worry about energy shortages; we would stop wasting fuel; we could build smaller automobiles and return to the stick-shift, that consumed less gas per mile. Some became enthusiastic about nuclear power and some about the vast potential for solar energy. We began to believe that the Club of Rome prophecies might be true. Many realized that indeed we were exhausting the planet's natural resources. "Small is beautiful" became a slogan for those who wanted to return to the simpler ways of our forefathers. Ecology and Earth Days gave some of us a common bond.

But it didn't last long. We elected a new president who didn't think negatively. Supply-side economics became a new password to the future. Just let the rich get richer, and the poor will become less poor as excess money trickles down to them. For nearly eight years, the Reagan presidency seemed to work, but then we woke up to the fact that the national debt had increased to one and a half trillion dollars. We were importing far more than we were exporting, and our trade deficit was horrendous. But, never mind, the Japanese and West Germans were underwriting our Epicurean "I gotta be me . . . live today, tomorrow you die" philosophy. Once again, with credit cards expanding our purchasing power, we owed our soul to the company store. Why worry and why save? There might be more dollars; but every year the dollar would buy 5 to 6 percent less than it did the year before. As for national and international debt, why worry? Owners of the new company store were international bankers, but they couldn't afford to flush the toilet; they might go down the drain with us.

In the past twenty-five years, the only sense of purpose that some Americans have and that still motivates them in the Reagan/Bush era is expressed, to my way of thinking by Fritz Perls' lines, which he was happy to recite at Esalen (home of the Get-into-Yourself movement) while wearing a jumpsuit with nothing under it: "I do my thing and you do your thing. I'm not in this world to live up to your expectations and you're not in this world to live up to mine. You are you, and I am I, and if by chance we find each other it is beautiful. If not, it can't be helped."

In essence, that's the philosophy of the Donald Trumps, the Leona Helmsleys, the Ivan Boeskys, the Imelda and Ferdinand Marcoses, of S & L presidents, and of most politicians today. They and thousands more, including the corporate-takeover experts and the "insiders" trading on Wall Street became the mentors of millions of Americans. It was summed up by Michael Douglas, portraying a Wall Street banker, with the words: "Greed is good!" When we fail to win President Bush's billion-dollar war on drugs, we'll prove it once again. "Greed pays off."

During these years, the perversion of democracy and capitalism into a world of greed and conspicuous consumption—not all of it financed honestly—has thoroughly warped the so-called sexual revolution. We continue to commercialize and devalue human sexuality. Psychologists have told us that the big orgasm is equivalent to a sneeze. But millions of women continue to read the women's magazines searching for the "big O," the pot of gold at the end of the rainbow.

Within the last few decades we have almost eliminated censorship. At last we can read D. H. Lawrence, James Joyce, and even Henry Miller and the Marquis de Sade. The Supreme Court acknowledged that the human body was not obscene. Nudist magazines that first appeared in the 1940s no longer had to airbrush the genitals from photographs of naked men and women. What have we gotten in return? Adult bookstores, X-rated movies, the merger of violence and sex in R-rated movies, sick-sex magazines, and thousands of how-to-do-it sex books and motion pictures that more often than not have reduced the sex act to meaningless copulation between mental idiots.

Talking, while fucking—enjoying each other as thinking brains as I have described it in *Harrad* and many other novels—is not possible between programmed robots. Our sexual mentors try to teach us that the way to self-discovery is via multiple orgasms. And the brave new world of equal rights for women has been counterbalanced by a continuous, profit-oriented objectivization of the female, who now, in living color, could reveal not only her pubic hair to the male voyeur but her labia as well. In fact, one could peer so deeply into her tunnel of love that the male photographer and the viewer of his pictures could practically fall into the womb.

Beth Hillyer, posing for a *Cool Boy* photographer, would no longer have to shave her pubic hair; but the decision that Beth and her InSix friends would have to make in today's environment would be more difficult.

In the early 1980s, with the invention of the VCR millions of Americans, including a very large percentage of females who would never have ventured into the sleazy combat zones of major cities, could now watch in the privacy of their own home men and women copulating on their television screens. But in 95 percent of the X-rated movies, as I have pointed out in my *X-Rated Video Tape Guide,* there is very little caring sex or attempts to establish caring relationships. They do not portray sex as an act of mutual discovery or point the way for educators, churches, and synagogues to sacramentalize human sexuality; they do not portray the beauty of the human body and acts of fertility and love. Instead, we now have available 10,000 or more videotapes, produced since 1980, portraying a fairly simple type of human sex act. They are rented or purchased by a hundred million or more Americans. For the most part, all they offer is the mating of horny young female animals with ever-erect male studs, none of whom evince much interest in each other as thinking human beings.

Can we lift ourselves by the bootstraps and create a new kind of society where human sexuality and the total wonder of the human body and the human mind become the new religion—a humanistic religion, without the necessity of a god, because you and I and all the billions who could interact caringly with one another are the only god we need? I think we can, if we devise an entirely new approach to education.

Phase 1. This new approach could begin tomorrow with a federal program that would guarantee an additional four-year, work/study, undergraduate program for every high-school graduate. The additional four years of education would offer either complete vocational training or studies leading to a bachelor's degree—and ultimately (based on grades or testing) a possible additional four years of graduate studies. With such a program in place I believe the problems that have haunted other educational proposals would disappear.

In this educational environment, the function of elementary and secondary schools would be to educate all citizens to become competent in reading, writing, and mathematics, and to give them an overall view of human history, science, arts, and literature. Since computer learning would be part of the process, the only strictly vocational training in high school would be typing and computer literacy. Science would be taught in such a way as to give all students historical perspectives. It should be kept in mind that this approach to education would be equivalent to the present-day curriculum for college-bound students and would offer very few or no vocational subjects.

Young people today are getting a wide generalized education via television, and in their early teens many acquire some skills by working in supermarkets, fast-food franchises, nursing homes, restaurants, and other places during their high-school years. With the change in high-school education I have described, those who later pursue a strictly vocational undergraduate education, would have experienced a much broader general education that most high-school graduates receive today.

Upon graduation from high school, all students could apply for admission to an undergraduate living program in their area or in another part of the country and, depending on their high-school grades, could pursue an education leading to either a vocational degree or a bachelor's degree. Those who graduated in the higher percentiles could, if they wished, pursue an advanced degree in science, medicine, law, or some social science or humanities program, or professional education for teaching. In a sense these are also vocational degrees. Students would pay for their advanced degrees in a work/study program in their special interest, or, as future teachers, by guiding human-values seminars.

Those who did not graduate from high school would be disqualified to vote in local or federal elections. With few vocational skills, the inability to obtain skilled work, and potential disenfranchisement, they would have a real incentive to graduate from high school or remedy the problem in later life by further study.

No longer worrying about financial problems, students would obtain their undergraduate degrees from colleges and universities that operated on a thirteen-week work/study cycle and remained in session throughout the year. All students would be guaranteed a minimum wage, which would be adjusted for inflation. Assuming, as I write this, that the minimum wage would reach $5 an hour, each student would earn $200 a week in two work cycles, or a total of $5,200.

From these earnings, each student would receive a personal allowance of $20 a week, and the balance would be paid directly to his or her college or university to cover tuition, books, room and board. Assuming that a state university education, which costs much less than private colleges, averages between $5,000 and $10,000 a year, the deficit of $6,000 at the higher level between the student's earnings and the total annual cost would be subsidized by the federal government.

Obviously, at this level the cost of undergraduate education could be lowered, and the federal government would be responsible to keep the subsidy as small as possible. Assuming that at any time there would be approximately 20,000,000 Americans enrolled in a four-year undergraduate program, the federal subsidy would be about $150 billion annually. Federal and state educational subsidies are presently close to half of this amount, but we must also remember that welfare and unemployment benefits for this age group—and hopefully later—would be substantially reduced.

Also worthy of consideration is the fact that a fully educated citizenry is a better way to convince the world of the merits of democracy than the $300 billion we continue to budget in the 1990s for defense. The United States can give the entire world a "peace dividend" by committing itself to the complete education of future generations.

The economic effect of the doubling or even tripling of the number of people who receive an additional four years of education should intrigue economists. It is all on the up side and is a program on which liberal Democrats and Republicans could unite. If a four-year undergraduate education were available to all high-school graduates, it would sharply decrease the unemployment rate in future years, and by the first quarter of the 21st century, when millions of more Americans will be living into their seventies and eighties, it will provide a much more affluent and better-educated younger generation, who will be able to support them.

A completely educated body of citizens with a sense of its own past and of all human history can communicate better with one another at all levels. In addition, a holistic education would eliminate gaps among the professions of medicine, law, science, teaching, engineering, business, manufacturing, and trades, because, as undergraduate students, all members of the future work force would have been working or studying alongside one another, in everything from plumbing to auto mechanics, philosophy to acting, premed to painting and building construction, etc.

Ultimately a gradual leveling would occur. The huge gap that now exists in terms of income and prestige between "top" professionals and skilled tradesmen could disappear. The lawyer or the doctor who could not repair his or her automobile would quickly discover that the auto mechanic was as broadly educated outside his vocation as he or she was, because their undergraduate studies had offered all of them an integrated search for universal human values and taught them how to care for one another, no matter what their level of vocational expertise.

Back in the 19th century the idea of attending a university was not simply to obtain a degree in a particular subject but to experience and learn from the teacher/scholar interaction. There was an attempt to unify all human knowledge and to search for roots (the basic definition of the word *radical*). Today most college and university teachers are afraid to explore and question particular—often no longer valid—religious, economic, political, and sexual values (or lack of values) that govern our lives.

In a society committed to education and that truly believed in the joy of learning, young people could look forward to earning a living stipend and paying for their education by becoming a contributing part of the economic system as they entered the alternating thirteen-week work/study cycle. In the process they would no longer—as most undergraduate students do now—exist in a social vacuum for four years.

All students in this proposal for the 21st century would be required to take a weekly seminar in human values throughout their entire four years. The seminars would be run by graduate students and would expose them to a deconditioning process as they explored the world of ideas in fifty books each year. The annotated bibliography that follows this essay will give you some idea of how I would structure the human-values approach.

Up to this point I have given you a broad outline of Phase 1 of the Harrad/Premar Solution. In Phase 2, I'll detail how it could function along the lines of *The Harrad Experiment*.

Phase 2 would be entirely optional. If you can find a copy of *The Premar Experiments,*[3] it will give you much more background. I wrote this sequel to *Harrad* because thousands of people wrote me that the Harrad concept was too elitist.

The Premar Experiments, also written in journal form, describes the thirteen-week work/study cycle. Unlike Harrad students, Premars do not live in dormitories but in reconditioned low-income housing on the fringes of central cities, where they pursue their choice of undergraduate study in nearby colleges or universities. The living quarters are essentially a commune, with forty-eight students living in three-story tenement houses. Each house is run by a graduate student couple who are married. Known as Compars (communal parents), they would be four or five years older than the incoming freshman, and in a very real sense function as older siblings to the Premars. The forty-eight students living in the Premar housing stay together for their entire undergraduate years; they pursue either bachelor's or vocational degrees. They should be equally divided between men and women, and approximately one-fifth of the students should have African American, Native American, Hispanic, or Asian backgrounds. Rooming arrangements are similar to those of Harrad, except that the roommate exchange takes place every six months over a period of the first two years.

All students live alternately with four members of the other sex, one of whom will be from a minority background. Premars (or Phase 2 students as I refer to them in an update of the novel) cannot choose their own roommates until the beginning of their junior year. But if they wish they can drop out of Phase 2 and return to Phase 1 of the undergraduate program at any time. This would be a carefully considered option, since they could not return and if they left Premar they would continue their undergraduate years with a roommate of the same sex.

All students who were accepted into Phase 2 of the undergraduate program would provide blood and urine tests taken six months prior to their arrival, along with a physical examination, showing that they are free of the AIDS virus, venereal diseases, and drugs. (Keep in mind that when I originally wrote the Harrad and Premar proposals AIDS was nonexistent.) In addition, each student would agree in writing to confine sexual intimacies to other students within the group to which he or she is assigned and would be "monogamous" with each roommate in turn. Because of a strict and ongoing surveillance and frequent bloodtesting, the use of condoms by Phase 2 men would be optional. All women would either use birth-control pills, or, if the pill were not advisible, medically, they would be fitted for a diaphragm. While an abortion would be available, it would be cause for expulsion from Phase 2 and a return to Phase 1.

All Phase 2 students would agree that in spite of their possible attraction to a particular roommate, they would accept the no-choice roommate shift every six months in their first two years. It would also be understood that any Phase 2 students who wished to marry would drop out of both phases of the program. The reason that underlies this rule is that women in the 21st century should not have children until they are 21 or over. The use of hard drugs and excessive use of alcohol would likewise be cause for expulsion.

It would be understood by Phase 2 students that the sexual environment was designed to encourage happy, joyous, noncommitted premarital sex with each alternate roommate but that in each case foreplay to intercourse would be a mutually agreed-upon decision.

Obviously, in a total educational program of this kind, some students would be oriented toward their own sex. In Phase 1 this would occasion no problem since roommates would be of the same sex, and those with homosexual or lesbian orientations would find each other. Young people would grow up seeing loving heterosexual lovemaking on television and in films. While the basic thrust in human society is to encourage male and female mating, same-sex mating would carry no stigma. In all probability, in this new world of education young men and women who were sexually unsure of themselves would try the Phase 2 experiment. Flagrant, unstructured, multiple sexual contacts (either homo- or hetero-) in either phase would be cause for expulsion.

The logistics of grouping forty-eight students with two graduate students to run the weekly human-values seminar could be worked out easily in the present dormitory arrangements of many colleges. Obviously, student housing would have to be greatly expanded but with hundreds of army and navy installations no longer needed, they could be converted easily to student housing, and thus would take care of the "pork barrel" for many politicians.

The group of forty-eight students would give students a common identity. It is similiar to the house plans of some universities and would provide a much more normal coed environment for the four under-graduate years than now exists in sex-segregated sororities and frater-nities. The required human-values seminar would create a group inter-action and learning experience that is unavailable in most colleges and universities. Phase 2 students, with a healthy outlet for their sexual drives and a shared learning experience with a roommate of the opposite sex, would find a sense of purpose and the intellectual stimulation that do not exist in most academic environments today.

Delaying the entry of millions of young people into the employ-ment market and creating an entirely new work force of minimum-wage employees in the thirteen-week work/study cycle will solve some economic problems and create others. What to do with the million or so young people no longer needed in the armed forces would be resolved. All students on the work cycle would agree to job rotation and any kind of work to which they might be assigned. During the four years they would not only do much of the low-level, nonskilled "service sector" type of work but also under a carefully planned pro-gram they would gain experience in the business and industrial world in both the manufacturing and the advanced service sectors.

Many service businesses would be happy to relocate to university or college areas, where there would be a continual supply of minimum-wage workers. Citibank, with its headquarters in New York City and its worldwide credit operation in Sioux City, Iowa, is an example of what I am talking about.

At this point you may agree that, because of the growing costs of undergraduate education, the work/study proposal has some merit.

But you may be still dubious about Phase 2. When *The Harrad Experiment* was first published, I received many letters asking when I personally was planning to create a real-life undergraduate Harrad College. My answer was and is that all some progressive college has to do is offer the other-sex roommate program, along with the human-values seminar to an incoming freshman class. This would receive wide publicity, and the college would undoubtedly receive many applications from both sexes.

Thus far no educators have dared challenge openly what seems to be public morality. Surprisingly, in the past twenty-five years hundreds of parents and students have tried to locate Harrad in Cambridge, Massachusetts, and thousands of those who read the novel were enthusiastic about the concept.

What would happen if a Phase 1 and Phase 2 undergraduate program, as I have outlined, came into existence? My guess is that initially only about 10 percent of the students and/or their parents would risk or approve of the arrangement that alternated roommates of the other sex.

But that would produce several hundred thousand students annually who would try and "survive" the Phase 2 experiment. The interesting question is how this would affect their postmarital sexual lives and their sense of a life purpose and well-being. While no hard statistics are available, most young people, even those who have some premarital experiences, are not so promiscuous as some of the popular magazines would lead you to believe. My guess is that a majority of young people still marry the first and only person with whom they have a premarital sexual experience. The minority, who may or may not have had as many sexual experiences as the Harrad/Premar concept envisions, rarely experience day-to-day intimacy with a partner of the other sex in a socially permissive environment over a longer period of time—especially in an environment that allows them to communicate and share their experiences in an ongoing human-values seminar not only with uncommitted partners but also with other uncommitted couples as they become friends and lovers.

Young people who had experienced a Phase 2, four-year mental and emotional intimacy with four members of the other sex and continued to live with a person of their own choosing during their last two undergraduate years would presumably be better able to choose lifetime marriage partners. Whether they ultimately chose to marry one of the roommates they had lived with or delayed marriage until later, they would know how to choose marriage partners who would reinforce and confirm them as total human beings. In a very real sense, unlike most marriage partners today, Phase 2 graduates would be educated for each other and they would have a much better chance of making a primary pair-bonding that would last a lifetime.

These primary pair-bondings would not necessarily have to be monogamous. You will remember that at the conclusion of *The Harrad Experiment* each of the pairs, Harry and Beth, Sheila and Stanley, Jack and Valerie, were married to each other but also as a group. Later, in graduate school they are involved in a warm and loving, six-way, postmarital sexual exchange. In reality, they created a new style of family and remained closely involved as friends and lovers throughout their lives.

If you read my novel *Proposition 31,* at the end you will discover in some detail what happened to the InSix many years later; the Proposition 31 concept is actually a continuation of the kind of multiple, postmarital relationships that I originally proposed in *Harrad* and later in *Premar*. The premise is that if we give young people sound training in interpersonal relationships we can create new types of family structure *beyond monogamy*. With a Phase 2 background, up to three couples after they pass the age of thirty (hence the title Proposition 31) could merge their families and form family corporations where all members, including the children, were equal shareholders.

In many other novels I have proposed that we should legalize on an a priori basis other forms of interpersonal relationships such as bigamy, corporate marriage, and synergamy. As we approach the 21st century and the increasing financial problems of living independent single or monogamous lives, throughout a lifespan that is now close to 80 years, I'm sure there will be revived interest in creating small communal family groupings and new family structures that will give individuals the financial security and emotional strength that no longer exist in many nuclear American families.

Whether you agree that the Harrad/Premar premises carried to their logical conclusion would pave the way for stronger families, I'd like to argue that the roommate structure of Phase 2 is not so shocking as you might think. During question periods, after I have lectured to college audiences, inevitably some young woman will raise the question: "Do you mean that I'd have no choice? I enjoy music, books, and poetry. What if my roommate was a football jock who was studying to be a plumber?"

My answer with a chuckle is: "That is the best thing that could happen to you or him. In a Phase 2 environment you would quickly learn how to accept one another with more open minds. You both might even begin to think about a more creative world where sports and activities were coed and played for fun and not watched like big-league football or hockey to sublimate aggression."

Both *Harrad* and *Premar* have, in the past, been promoted by my publishers as extensions of computer-matched dating services. In actuality, attempts to match people of similar tastes—on the same "wavelength"—are never very successful. Living with an "opposite" can be not only a learning experience but it can also become a loving experience, if two people can laugh at themselves. Four years of undergraduate education integrated by the human-values seminar would ultimately create a common bond of understanding between you and a wide variety of people. Even more important, it would eliminte at a young age the adversary relationship between men and women.

You would learn how to maintain a loving relationship with many different kinds of people of the other sex. Lifetime friendships would ensue between people who had shared complete self-disclosure and mental and sexual intimacy. Keep in mind that Phase 2 would not be a sexual free-for-all. Roommates of the opposite sex wouldn't immediately jump into bed with a total stranger. Rather, over a period of weeks or months, a person would slowly discover the sheer wonder of divergences from and similarities with another person. You'd learn how to share your fears and hopes. Guided by the discussions in the human-values seminars, you'd gradually reveal and dare to become the kind of person you want to be, and your roommate would be responding in the same way.

In every sense, this 21st-century education would be a four-year adventure in self-discovery. Unlike typical undergraduate students today, a student would dare share himself or herself with many people as a total human being. Young people wouldn't experience the deep loneliness that many college counselors say is typical of the undergraduate experience.

Already, in our new, sexually open world we have to cope with a million teenage pregnancies annually and the social and financial cost of unwanted children, some of whom become future derelicts and criminals. We live in a world where a million or more divorces a year, involving more than six million children under the age of 17, has become a lifestyle. The nuclear family—husband and wife with two or more children—now represents only a third of the households in the United States; dwellings occupied by one person (or mothers on welfare) represent 30 percent of the seventy million households. We live in a world where single parenting has become a way of life for millions, and children try to find roots and security as they are shunted between high-rise apartments and condos or among a variety of slum dwellings. Many are among the homeless, either with one parent or as runaways.

We live in a world where various age groups no longer mingle, and millions of senior citizens move to a Sun Belt state, if they can afford it, to enjoy the mental comfort of their own peer group, as well as escape the cold climate. We live in a world where singles live with singles, a world where if singles wed they can't afford single-family housing and must continue to live in apartments, with no patch of earth of their own or for their children. We live in a world where if you are past 60 and haven't escaped to warmer climates, you may end up in a retirement center or a low-cost senior center from which in a few more years, you'll leave by the back door—so as not to disturb the tranquility of those still living—to a nursing home or the cemetery.

The Harrad/Premar solution is not a daydream. A financial guarantee to every young person of a complete education through their 21st year could prove as important as our historical funding of universal secondary education has been. Furthermore, there is proof that free education has supported democracy and capitalism that work better than any communist or socialist system. Combining a guaranteed Phase 1 undergraduate education with a Phase 2 for those who wish it, in a Harrad/Premar style of environment would give millions of young men and women a renewed vision. It would confirm the joys of their human sexuality, and let them discover the joys of loving and caring for one or more person of the other sex throughout a lifetime. It would open the door to many new styles of families.

It's up to you to dare to venture into a new world of human relationships and stop the drift to disaster that now prevails. Believe me, millions of Americans are ready now to climb to the next level of mental, sexual, emotional, and economic freedom, based on a deeper sharing of their lives with others.

Notes

1. I imagine the leadership among government personnel and politicians might be found within the framework of a new, liberal version of one of the present American political parties.

2. Nongraduates of high school could later take an equivalency test for voting eligibility.

3. This novel is currently out of print, but may be in libraries or second-hand bookstores. It sold a million copies in paperback (published in 1976 by New American Library), preceded in 1975 by a hardcover edition from Crown Publishers.

ANNOTATED BIBLIOGRAPHY

The annotated bibliography that appeared in the first edition of *The Harrad Experiment* contained fifty-six entries. It set at least one precedent. It was probably the first time a bibliography appeared in a novel. I suggested that any college or university could use the bibliography to run a human-values seminar. It is still my feeling that such a required seminar would integrate undergraduate learning in many ways.

In 1966, when *Harrad* was first published, very few colleges offered courses on marriage and the family. Today, many courses are available, with textbooks that not only cover all aspects of human sexuality in great detail but also explore the new sexual and family lifestyles that have become a way of life over the past twenty years. Many of these textbooks recommend *The Harrad Experiment* and *Proposition 31* as outside reading. When I was on the college lecture circuit in the 1970s I was surprised at how few men took these courses; marriage and the family was still the domain of women.

In 1978, before Bantam issued the 40th printing of *The Harrad Experiment* (after which it went out of print until 1990), I decided to revise the bibliography almost completely and confine it to fifty-two entries so that it would parallel the human-values reading program, which also underlies the thirteen-week work/study program described in *The Premar Experiments*. The idea, not fully developed in *Harrad*, but detailed in *Premar*, is that in addition to regular courses Harrad/Premar students would cover a book a week in discussions with seminar leaders, who would be graduate students.

If you have read the preceding essay, "The Harrad/Premar Solution," you will realize that I am proposing this as a practical 21st-century approach to educating the younger generation. You will also note that I have suggested that Phase 2, or living with a roommate of the opposite sex, is an option. The following bibliography is proposed for those who take this option. It should be understood that the following list is not cast in stone.

The idea of reading a book a week, in addition to required reading for courses, may seem like a formidable problem, but keep in mind that students, particularly in Phase 2, would be covering the same books with their roommates and would be meeting several times a week in the seminar. They would learn the art of skimming, plus the joy of absorbing ideas that are being explored by their peers at the same time.

Keep in mind that the seminar is in a very real sense a "deconditioning" process. Students would be guided throughout their undergraduate years in examining and reexamining values acquired from their teachers and parents during the first seventeen or so years of their lives. They would gradually build their own values—subject of course to continuous evaluation and possible modification—as the sine qua non of living a fully realized life.

During the past twenty-five years I have learned something about bibliographies. Some books have longevity, some don't! Less than twenty books have been retained from the original bibliography, and another ten or more have been deleted from the 1978 edition. Many of the books are concerned with every aspect of human sexuality, a prime concern of young people in a Harrad/Premar kind of environment. These same books will be of interest to people past their college years who may still be searching for answers. I have also included books that deal with every kind of problem facing us in the 1990s, and well into the 21st century.

If I were guiding a human-values seminar for teenagers (note that I haven't said "teaching," which implies indoctrination), I would concentrate on the books on human sexuality for the first month or so, including several on contraception which I have not listed, and then gradually broaden the subject matter. Thus, the numerical order in which I have listed the books might not be others' preference.

Harrad/Premar may be a few years down the road, but I firmly believe that a new style of education that embraces all Americans is inevitable. Capitalism and democracy are still viable ideas in a society prepared to toss out the shallow values of television that still inundate too much of our lives. You may not agree with me, but I think the only way to expand horizons is with the printed word. Turn off the tube a few hours a day and read . . . read . . . read. Harrad/ Premar students quickly discover that the key to living a full, self-actualized life is shared reading and the pursuit of knowledge with a loving friend.

1. Alex Comfort, *The Joys of Sex* and *More Joys* (New York: Crown, 1972 and 1974). Many Harrad/Premar students may have already discovered these volumes, but if they are used from the beginning of the human-values seminar they will give young people a common frame of reference.

2. Patricia Raley, *Making Love: How to Be Your Own Sex Therapist* (New York: Dial Press, 1976). It's a tossup whether this book or Comfort's should come first. Raley's book has photographs of loving couples, instead of the warm, erotic drawings which appear in Comfort's two books. Obviously, interest in both Raley and Comfort will continue for many months beyond the first two weeks.

3. Edwin J. Haeberle, *The Sex Atlas* (New York, Seabury Press, 1978). An illustrated guide. Every Harrad/Premar student will probably want to own a copy or at least share it with his or her roommate. It's an encyclopedic textbook covering *every* aspect of human sexuality with excellent text and hundreds of unique and lovely photographs.

4. Lennart Nillson, *Behold Man* (Boston: Little Brown, 1975). Sex without continuous awareness and amazement at the partner's inescapable biology lacks a sense of wonder, which is the best sexual turn-on.

5. Paul Kurtz, *Eupraxophy: Living Without Religion* (Buffalo: Prometheus Books, 1989). Most Harrad/Premar students will have had some previous religious education, or indoctrination. Since the human-values seminar is also a "deconditioning" or "deprogramming" experience, which often conflicts with established religious theologies

and moralities, it is important that students be exposed to the true meaning of secular humanism, and not the pejorative one often used in the popular press. *Eupraxophy* is a word coined by Dr. Kurtz, a professor of philosophy. It means "good conduct and wisdom in loving" without need for a supreme being. Kurtz is the author of *The Humanist Manifesto II,* which applies the Golden Rule in a wider context than Christianity has traditionally done.

6. A. S. Neill, *Summerhill: A Radical Approach to Child Rearing* (New York: Hart, 1960). When *Harrad* was first published, Neill's approach to childrearing had thousands of advocates. Whether or not it is viable by today's standards, it is a good book to examine a unique educational approach.

7. John W. Gardner, *Self-Renewal: The Individual and the Innovative Society* (New York: Norton, 1983). *Harrad* ends on an optimistic quote from Gardner's book, whose message is still viable as we approach the turn of the century.

8. Reay Tannahill, *Sex in History* (New York: Stein and Day, 1980). In the last printing of *Harrad,* Bernard Murstein's *Love, Sex and Marriage Through the Ages* was listed. A continuing goal during the four years of the human-values seminars is to give young people a wide historical perspective on every aspect of human affairs and relationships. Both of these books will provide a good learning experience.

9. Margaret Meade, *Coming of Age in Samoa* and *Sex and Temperament in Three Primitive Societies* (New York: New American Library, 1950). Although some of Meade's anthropological investigations have been challenged or discredited, all students should be aware of sexual life in less-repressed societies, where people were never exposed to the Judeo-Christian tradition or Sigmund Freud.

10. B. Z. Goldberg, *The Sacred Fire: The Story of Sex in Religion* (New York: Horace Liveright, 1932). An historical perspective on human sexuality that most people unfortunately are unaware of. Discovering the close tie between religion and fertility worship and exposure to the roots of all religious beliefs will encourage students

to consider new religious approaches to life, where the joy of sexual surrender becomes sacramental.

11. Kamala Devi, *The Eastern Way of Love: Tantric Sex and Erotic Mysticism* (New York: Simon and Schuster, 1977). Tantric sex and extended sexual intercourse are explored in many books, including *Male Continence* by John Humphrey Noyes, founder of the Oneida Community. This well-illustrated book, written by a loving woman, is the best introduction for young lovers.

12. Lester R. Brown, *State of the World 1990* (New York: Norton, 1990). Here's a change of pace from human sexuality. These annual reports from the Worldwatch Institute, "On Progress Towards a Sustainable Society," cover not only environmental problems but also the dangers of irresponsible (or religiously conditioned) procreation. If the population of the world doubles to 10 billion by the year 2030, the earth will become either a more communal place or a fiercely warring world.

13. Abraham Maslow, *The Farther Reaches of Human Nature* (New York: Viking, 1971). A complete collection of Maslow's basic writings, including his thoughts on peak experiences and Theory Z, the "play" approach to work and study that could transform education and the workplace if humans understood and accepted it.

14. Johan Huizinga, *Homo Ludens: A Study of the Play Element in Culture* (Boston: Beacon Press, 1950). The premise behind my novel *The Byrdwhistle Option* is that work can be transformed into play. Huizinga proves that when you are working, praying, studying, or even at war, essentially you are playing. Martin Buber called the book "one of the few informed works about the problems of man."

15. Richard Knight and Thomas Wright, *Sexual Symbols: A History of Phallic Worship* (New York: Julian Press, 1957). One more book showing how religious beliefs are interwoven with human sexuality.

16. Martin Buber, *I and Thou.* The emphasis on human sexuality in the first year of the human-values seminar and on sexual ecstasy

as a continuing part of human life is possible only if Buber's I-and-thou philosophy becomes a way of life.

17. Alan Watts, *Nature, Man and Woman* (New York: Pantheon, 1958). In addition to this book, which reflects the Harrad/Premar approach to human loving, Alan Watts left many joyous audiotapes that could be used in the human-values seminar.

18. David Cole Gordon, *Self-Love* (New York: Penguin Books, 1972). Exceptional insights into human sexuality and what occurs in the moment of orgasm with another person, or in one that is self-induced. A way of escaping momentarily from one's self, which Osho (Bhagwan Shree Rajneesh, see no. 26) proposes is also achievable through meditation, and which is also possible in Tantric, or extended sexual intercourse.

19. Bernhardt J. Hurwood, *The Joys of Oral Love* (New York: Carlyle Communications, 1975). Even with wide access to porn videotapes, which too often dehumanize human sexuality but at least make oral/genital sex a way of life, many young lovers still fear telling each other about their quite normal oral/genital desires. This delightful picture book, offered during the fifth month of the human-values seminar, will create discussion. Since by this time all Harrad/Premar students will probably be experiencing sex with their roommates, this open approach would help allay any doubts for both men and women.

20. Peter Webb, *The Erotic Arts* (Boston: New York Graphic Society, 1975). Eroticism, religion, and sexual wonder go hand in hand in this fascinating, illustrated historical survey.

21. Rollo May, *Man's Search for Himself* (New York: New American Library, 1967). Dr. May's books hold up well in the 1990s and make exciting reading as students search for answers to such questions as: Why am I here? What's it all about?

22. B. F. Skinner, *Beyond Freedom and Dignity* (New York: Bantam Books, 1972). Skinner, who conceived an educational utopia in *Walden II* (tried in reality and failed) will be familiar to Harrad/

Premars who take courses in psychology. But the premise of the human-values seminar is that many students in the undergraduate work/study program will pursue vocational studies that may not include the historical development of psychology. Skinner's controversial approaches will stimulate discussion.

23. Sydney Jourard, *The Transparent Self* (New York: Van Nostrand, 1964). The how-to-do-it book of self-disclosure. The ability to expose one's intimate feelings to another person is the essence of achieving Buber's I and thou.

24. Eliot Aronson, *The Social Animal* (San Francisco: William Freeman, 1976). Joyous reading on what makes you *you*. A valuable book to examine how people, unknown to themselves, are conditioned to behave.

25. Albert Ellis, *Humanistic Psychotherapy: The Rational Emotive Approach* (New York: Julian Press, 1973). The twelve irrational ideas, which Ellis suggests are at the root of all emotional problems, are examined by Harrad/Premar students, after which new self-knowledge can be incorporated into the day-to-day resolution of interpersonal problems and conflicts.

26. Bhagwan Shree Rajneesh. A year before he died on Jan. 20, 1990, Rajneesh changed his name to Osho, a Japanese word that reflected his communion with and love of men and women seeking enlightenment through meditation. In his lifetime Osho, who had close to a million followers, challenged all major religions, denounced nationalism, and proposed graduate studies where students would be "deprogrammed" from the religious and political beliefs acquired in their earlier years. Osho wrote, or dictated, 650 books before he departed his body. They are available from Chidvilas, P.O. Box 17550, Boulder, Colorado 80308.

His books, *The Zen Manifesto* (Rebel Publishing House in West Germany, 1989, for which I wrote an introduction) and *The Tantra Vision,* could introduce Harrad/Premar students to Osho's approach to meditation, along with his controversial life. I suggest that discussion groups deal with such questions as: If Jesus returned to earth in the 21st century, would he have any lasting effect on the world? Or, 100 years from now, about the time Jesus may be rediscovered, will millions of people be "dancing, laughing, and loving" and finding true enlightenment through meditation and the writings and video visions of Osho, a Zen master?

27. Ajit Mookerjee and Madhu Kharma, *The Tantric Way: Art, Science, Ritual* (Boston: New York Graphic Society, 1977). I'm sure that Osho would not have approved of using Tantric rituals to achieve *nirvana,* but an examination of them in this fascinating book will help Harrad/Premars understand Osho's more modern feeling that Tantra is but one way, as well as his belief that greater enlightenment can be achieved by the simple process of escaping oneself. He recommends meditation without drugs or any outside assistance.

28. Roger Lewin, *In the Age of Mankind* (Washington, D.C.: Smithsonian Books, 1988). A book that tries to answer the question of human origins. Learning who we are and how Homo sapiens evolved over the past 100,000 years makes our here-and-now existence and our ability to love and care for one another even more awesome.

29. Lester Milbrath, *Envisioning a Sustainable Society* (Albany, N.Y.: State University of New York Press, 1989). In covering topics from how to transform a dominator society to an inquiry on human values and social learning, Milbrath explores the biological, economic, scientific, environmental, and political problems we will face in the 21st century.

30. Ruth Leger Sivard, *World Military and Social Expenditures 1989, 1990, 1991* (World Priorities, Inc., Box 25140, Washington, D.C., 20007). This 60-page survey is published annually. It provides a social balance sheet of the annual costs for defense and war. Nearly $10 trillion were spent during the 1980s. It not only contrasts the costs of deterioration of the planet and human suffering in every part of the world but also proposes where the money (read, human time and labor) might have been spent to create a more fulfilling world for everyone. If my latest novel, "New Dawn, January 1, 2000," which proposes a destruction-of-all-weapons-now (DAWN) is published,

Harrad/Premar students will find it fascinating to wonder if this will ever happen.

31. Nick Douglas and Penny Slinger, *Sexual Secrets* (New York: Destiny Books, 1986). Every Harrad/Premar student will want to own his or her own copy of this paperback. Illustrated with line drawings by Slinger, it explores every aspect of Tantric sex in detail.

32. Johan Chang, *The Tao of Love and Sex* (New York: E. P. Dutton, 1977). This may be the best sex book ever written for men. Exploring the art of lovemaking perfected by the ancient Chinese, Chang shows how the male can enjoy extended intercourse for hours without ejaculating (or not at all) and thus presumably increase his longevity. The woman is encouraged to enjoy her own orgasms.

33. Wilhelm Reich, *The Sexual Revolution: Toward a Self-Regulating Character Structure* (New York: Farrar, Straus, and Giroux, 1974). Written long before "sex revolution" became part of the vocabulary of the 1960s, Reich's approaches to human sexuality will give the leaders of the human-values seminar the opportunity to contrast the theories of Herbert Marcuse and Sigmund Freud and to contrast both of them with the Harrad/Premar premise: we could be in better control of our sexual drives if we lived in a society that believed that satisfaction of sexual needs was just as vital to well-being as meeting hunger and thirst drives.

34. Renee Guyon, *Sexual Freedom* (New York: Knopf, 1950). A good book to provide historical perspective on where we were at the middle of the 20th century, as well as on the then-current limits to sexual freedom.

35. Maren Lockwood Caren, *Oneida, Utopian Community to Modern Corporation* (New York: Harper & Row, 1971). Harrad/Premar students can compare the communal aspects of their lifestyle with the most successful communal living experiment that ever occurred in the United States. It included sexual exchange between the married couples who lived in the commune, together with extended sexual intercourse and male continence as forms of birth control.

36. Alastair Heron, ed., *Toward a Quaker View of Sex* (Philadelphia: American Friends Service Committee). The first edition of this remarkable essay contains much of the Harrad/Premar philosophy and "conviction that love cannot be confined to a pattern." Unfortunately, in later editions the Quakers excised this quotation and an entire section that seemed to condone nonmonogamous, postmarital sex.

37. John Harris, *The Value of Life: An Introduction to Medical Ethics* (Boston: Routledge & Kegan Paul, 1985). A complete survey of most of the bioethical and moral problems facing human beings in the 21st century. This is a subject on which the human-values seminars will constantly seek valid answers for individuals and society during the four-year Harrad/Premar program.

38. June Singer, *Androgyny: Toward a New Theory of Sexuality* (New York: Doubleday, 1976). The potential of a religious or moral point of view based on androgyny, the theory that each of us has a blend of male and female characteristics.

39. Sol Gordon and Roger Libby, eds., *Sexuality, Today and Tomorrow: Contemporary Issues in Sexuality* (North Scituate, Mass.: Duxbury Press, 1976). This compilation of essays by outstanding psychologists and sociologists reflects the sixties' and seventies' interest in exploring all areas of marriage and the family, with a look into the future.

40. Roger Libby and Robert N. Whitehurst, eds., *Marriage and Its Alternatives: Exploring Intimate Relationships* (Glenview, Ill.: Scott Foresman, 1977). Essays on marriage and the family that give historical perspective but do not come to grips with the new-style families of the past 25 years. These depend on working wives or the "living together unmarried" lifestyle that mimics monogamous marriage.

41. Gordon Clanton and Lynn Smith, *Jealousy* (Englewood Cliffs, N.J.: Prentice-Hall, 1977). At some point in their first year of Harrad/Premar, students will have to deal with jealousy if they become too possessive of or enamoured with a current or past roommate. Clanton's and Smith's book not only dissects the nature of jealousy but also shows how to overcome it in sexual and other areas.

42. Kenneth Keniston, *All Our Children: The American Family Under Pressure* (New York: Harcourt, Brace, Jovanovich, 1977). A frightening look at the American family and our children that proves the necessity for and utility of a Harrad/Premar type of solution, as well as a nationally subsidized work/study undergraduate education for all young people.

43. Alan Harrington, *The Immortalist: An Approach to Engineering Man's Divinity* (New York: Avon Books, 1969). This book is an excellent jumping-off point to an underlying theme of Harrad/Premar. By helping students develop not a fear of death but a continuing sense of human contingency, they learn to savor each other and the joy of each moment and to not make tragedies of events in their lives where no tragedy need be.

44. Kenneth M. Roemer, *America as Utopia* (New York: Burt Franklin, 1981). A careful study of utopian thinking, particularly in the last half of the 19th century when experiments in new-style families, communes, and "free love" were rampant throughout the United States. Roemer is a well-known utopian scholar. His unique course, Building Your Own Utopias, uses, among other books, *The Harrad Experiment*. Students write a thesis, often in couple groupings, proposing their own utopian (but hopefully practical) solutions to social and interpersonal problems. A nice approach for human-values seminars. (For details and information on a guidebook, write Roemer in care of the University of Texas, Arlington, Tex. 76019).

45. Phil Donahue, *The Human Animal* (New York: Simon & Schuster, 1985). Although Donahue is a well-known TV personality, young people may not be aware that he is seriously concerned about the present and the future. In easy-to-read chapters, he tries to answer the questions: Who are we? Why do we behave as we do? How can we change? While he doesn't have all the answers, he raises most of the questions facing humans in the 21st century. It may be better to use this book earlier in the first year of the human-values seminar.

46. Joseph Heard and S. L. Cranston, *Reincarnation, The Phoenix Fire Mystery* (New York: Crown, 1977). Since most Harrad/Premar

students will come from Christian, Jewish, or agnostic backgrounds, the implications of reincarnation (a major tenet of Hindu thought), for moral living, here and now, are not appreciated. It will stimulate human-values discussion to explore reincarnation as distinguished from resurrection.

47. Robert Francoeur, *Biomedical Ethics, A Guide to Decision Making* (New York: John Wiley, 1983). Beautifully put together to get students involved in the ethical and moral dilemmas they will face in the 21st century, Francoeur's book exhibits a human-values approach in posing problems that already confront everyone daily.

48. John D'Emilio and Estelle B. Freedman, *Intimate Matters* (New York: Harper & Row, 1988). A history of sexuality in the Americas, this book will tie together and solidify the historical perspective students achieve in the first year of their human-values seminar.

49. Marquis de Sade, *Justine* and *Philosophy in the Bedroom* (New York, Grove Press, 1971) and *Juliette* (New York, Grove, 1968). By the end of their reading Harrad/Premar students are ready to examine pornography and determine whether a writer like de Sade, who devalues human sexuality, should be censored or whether a Harrad/Premar education would eventually create a saner sexual environment where human beings would grow up seeing each other naked as well as watch movies or television films of human beings making love erotically and tenderly, responsibly and caringly. Perhaps this would result in a female-oriented society, where male sadomasochistic domination of other males and of females has disappeared.

50. George Russell Weaver, *The Enrichment of Life* (Buffalo, N.Y.: Prometheus Books, 1986). Subtitled "Fourteen Keys That Reveal Some Secrets of Sports, Wealth, Sex, Mental Development, and the Enjoyment of Art and a Liberal Self-Education," this joyous book was written by a man in his eighties. It's a celebration of life that will become a way of life for Harrad/Premar students.

51. Richard Hagen, *The Bio-Sexual Factor* (New York: Doubleday, 1979). I am a man. You are a woman. Are your thoughts

and desires about sex different from mine? Are the differences due to cultural conditioning or biological realities? Do men have a greater need for sex or sexual variety than women? Near the end of their first Harrad/Premar year, roommates can argue, from their own experiences, the pros and cons laid out in this fascinating book.

52. John Carey, ed., *Eyewitness to History* (Cambridge, Mass.: Harvard University Press, 1987). This book cannot be skimmed in a week. Rather, all Harrad/Premars should own their own copy and read a couple of chapters a week. Carey has compiled several hundred selections from history, written by people who for the most part experienced the events first-hand. From a plague in Athens in 430 B.C. to the fall of President Ferdinand Marcos in the Philippines in 1964, it provides historical perspective on man's behavior and inhumanity to man.

Leaders of human-values seminars in Phase 1 or 2 should be trained to create an environment where undergraduate students not only discuss the issues and problems raised in the book-a-week program but also discover the fun of immersing themselves into the day-to-day problems of the world. In the U.S.—aided and abetted by the media—we prolong "growing up." In past centuries hundreds of thousands of young men and women in their teens or early twenties, have acquired the education, vision, or personal drive and ambition to excel at their chosen professions.

Assuming that the human-values seminar would be organized in small groups, the leaders should encourage students to skim the *Wall Street Journal,* whose three daily lead stories and editorials can be read in thirty minutes. Thus they will gain insights, for better or worse, into the problems of the world. They will learn that capitalistic democracies and free markets cannot *always* provide the greatest good for the greatest number of people. Students should also be encouraged to acquire the habit of watching the "MacNeil/Lehrer News Hour," which offers the only nightly in-depth survey of national and international problems on television.

In addition, public broadcasting stations, along with video-cassettes, offer a way to expand young people's horizons and wean them away from the shallow values of most network and cable television. Seminar leaders can expose young people to ballet, opera, classical music, and the 20th-century art form of filmmaking.

Young people who have grown up on MTV, slash-and-bash movies, and heavy-metal rock will discover the fun of watching the best films of the past and present, both American and foreign. In small groups they can discuss the realities of life as expressed by top screenwriters and filmmakers. Keep in mind that in Phase 2 of the Harrad/Premar experience young people, unlike most undergraduates today, would no longer spend much of their waking time trying to resolve their sexual drives one way or another. The human-values approach would expand most male horizons beyond baseball, football, and basketball, and build foundations for eventual marriages between people who have much more in common, which they could share with each other and their children.

Group leaders could also supplement the reading program by making students aware of what has become known as the alternative press. Thousands of magazines that offer different approaches and solutions to world problems circulate in United States. Some of them may be the cutting edge of the future.

The best source of periodicals with a dissenting point of view from the *Wall Street Journal, Time,* and *Newsweek* is the *Utne Reader*, a monthly magazine conceived by Eric Utne, 1624 Harmon Place, Minneapolis, Minn. 55403. *New Options Newsletter,* Mark Satin, ed., P.O. Box 19324, Washington, D.C. 20036, also explores alternative approaches to national and global problems in a provocative way. *Free Inquiry,* Box 5, Buffalo, N.Y. 14215, not only offers a stimulating, twenty-one paragraph Affirmation of Humanistic Thinking to expand one's horizons but also sponsors the Academy of Humanism, which includes such members as Isaac Asimov and Carl Sagan.

Finally, I'm in touch with many small groups such as Family Synergy, Delaware Synergy, Mensa S. (a group of people with high I.Q.s who discuss their interpersonal and sexual problems in a monthly bulletin), Polyfidelity Educational Group (which practices a kind of extended monogamy), The Truth Seekers, Interface, Esalen Institute, Elysium Institute, and others that are actually living or probing into 21st-century ways of living. If you are interested, drop me a note in care of Prometheus Books and I'll be happy to send you their addresses.

LOVING, LEARNING, LAUGHTER & LUDAMUS

The Autobiography of Robert H. Rimmer

During the late sixties and mid-seventies, when millions of young people were fascinated with the Harrad idea and with "corporate marriage," which I explored in detail in my novel *Proposition 31,* I was invited to speak at several hundred colleges, universities, and other institutions throughout the United States. Inevitably, during a question period after every lecture, I was asked details about my own life. For twenty-five years I grinned and answered: "Believe me, I write from experience. If I live long enough, perhaps I'll write my auto-biography, but right now if I went into detail it would disrupt other lives and my Doctor Jekyll existence."

If it hadn't been for Gale Research, I probably never would have attempted a mini-autobiography.* Thus far, they have published ten volumes in their *Contemporary Authors* series, with almost 200 auto-biographies of well-known authors, both American and foreign. My feeling is that if you get involved with a particular author's writings, it's a great learning experience to discover how he or she has, in one way or another, fictionalized his or her life or used his or her writings to amplify a search for meaning.

As I revise my autobiography in 1990, I have been married for forty-nine years to Erma . . . one wife for a lifetime. But in 1955,

---

*The account that follows is a condensed version of the original autobiography pub-lished by Gale Research, Inc., Detroit, Mich., in the *Contemporary Authors Autobiog-raphy Series,* Vol. 10, in 1989. The original has many photographs and a detailed explanation of why I believe that, as of 1990, I have been blacklisted by major American publishers. All have refused to read my latest novel, "New Dawn, January 1, 2000," completed in 1989. (I am grateful to Gale for permission to reprint my condensed autobiography.)

if she hadn't discovered that I was having an affair with "Elizabeth," and if she hadn't sobbed her anger to David, a doctor and the last of a breed of caring general practitioners, who told her that all men, including him, were led around by their cocks, I never would have met David's wife, Nancy—or finally discovered a woman whom I didn't want to play Pygmalion with. And if I hadn't met David and Nancy (whose names I have fictionalized and who are similar to one of the couples in *Proposition 31*), I never would have discovered just how anti-Semitic my father and mother were, nor way past midlife would I have found the focus for my first novel, *The Rebellion of Yale Marratt*.

I wrote *Yale Marratt* in my early forties, but it wasn't published until I was forty-seven. The reason why is the culmination of a kind of sexual odyssey which, combined with an early, loving oedipal rebellion, constitutes the main adventure of my life. Here, for the first time, I will try to show how my heroes and heroines are basically more daring extensions of my own life. I am sure that recreating oneself in fiction is a way of life for many novelists, but most of them refuse to admit it.

During the late 1960s and early 1970s, *Harrad* and *Proposition 31* became a part of the vocabulary of the so-called hippie generation. Most of the millions of *Harrad* readers had no idea that the author was long past thirty (and hence not to be trusted). But since these novels and later ones offered alternatives to monogamous marriage and "solutions" to the increasing divorce rate, they became recommended reading in college courses on marriage and the family. Many readers were sure that *Harrad* was instrumental in the sudden merger of men's and women's colleges, and the creation of dormitories where young people of both sexes lived together on the same floors. Maybe it also laid the groundwork for the young men and women living together unmarried.

Most critics were incensed. Bob Rimmer wasn't really a novelist but a preacher in disguise, who was writing thesis novels. For many critics, this approach to the novel is a literary no-no. Purists believe that the novel should reflect reality and the author should let you perceive his moral purpose, if any, subtly and by innuendo. But, like Edward Bellamy, Upton Sinclair, and Ayn Rand, I believed, and still do, that the novel can be a vehicle to show people how they can recreate their environments and live more self-fulfilling lives.

Assuming that you may not have read many, or any, of my thirteen novels, let me give you a little background. While I'm sure that my novels have interesting story lines that will keep you reading and wondering what comes next, with believable characters, there are no bad guys in any of them. The basic theme is that I believe we can devise saner approaches to premarital and postmarital interpersonal and sexual relationships, which could stabilize our new-style extended families. In *Proposition 31,* for example, I have proposed legal forms of bigamous marriage and what I have called "corporate marriage" of up to three couples, as well as created the framework for more enduring pair-bondings (monogamy), which could incorporate intimate satellite relationships.

In essence, I celebrate life based on the four L's: Loving, Learning, Laughter, and Ludamus (we and God are all playing together). These obviously incorporate the fifth L, George Bush's hated Liberal.

During our long courtship of each other's wives, David once told me good-humoredly, "Your problem, Bob, is that you haven't suffered enough. All great creative writers have suffered." Perhaps he was right, but I still don't agree with him. Fourteen years ago, Nancy died, and within two years, David had also disappeared from this life. Erma and I were desolate but we don't mourn them. We celebrate them and are fully aware that after living much of our married life in a kind of two-couple monogamy (for nearly twenty-five years), which I have philosophized about and fictionalized in *Proposition 31, Come Live My Life,* and *Thursday, My Love,* Erma and I learned how to love not just each other, but many people—including my domineering father and self-glorifying mother—whose paths crossed ours.

My Family and Childhood. On December 11, 1911, Francis Henry Rimmer, living in Dorchester, Mass., age twenty-five, married Blanche Rosealma Rochefort, seventeen, who had been schooled in a French convent in Spencer, Mass. Coming from a family who spoke only Canadian French at home, she could scarcely speak English, but she was very pretty and obviously a virgin. She could play any kind of music on the piano and sing along with it. Later, when Blanche took a part-time job at Kresge, where she would play sheet music for customers who wanted to hear a particular selection and also listen to her play, Frank spoke of her as "my million-dollar baby from the five-and-ten-cents store."

Frank was running an elevator at the age of twelve and his schooling ended at the sixth grade. Before he married Blanche, he had
discovered the International Correspondence School. With no parental
encouragement, but great determination—Ben Franklin and characters
in the Horatio Alger stories, which he insisted later that I read, were
his heroes—Frank studied to pass the ICS exams for postal clerk.
At ICS headquarters in Springfield, they were so impressed with his
diligence that they offered him a branch manager's job. Later Frank
sold vacuum cleaners door to door, then Victor typewriters. Five years
later, he was brokering printing jobs and quickly convinced his typewriter customers that he could get their stationery and business cards
printed more cheaply than they could. Somehow, he managed to
convince the First National Bank of Boston to loan him $5,000 (a
princely sum in those days). Although he had never run a printing
press and couldn't set type, he hired a plant manager and soon had
two platen presses.

Blanche, who admitted later that she slept in the office sitting
up most of the time, was his only secretary. She never bothered to
learn how to type. It was all she could do to answer the phone. Business
was booming. After I was born, Frank met George Duffy, who had
inherited $5,000 and convinced Frank to sell him 20 percent of the
stock of what was to become the Relief Printing Corporation.

I was born March 14, 1917, saving my Dad from the draft. By
the time I was three, I was Blanche's Little Lord Fauntleroy. Very
blonde, with brown eyes and a Dutch boy haircut, I was outfitted
with a cane and a beaver hat.

At five years old, I could read. In those days, there was little
other entertainment, for radio was rudimentary. I read fairy tales by
the hundreds—all of Grimm, Hans Christian Andersen, and the
expurgated Arabian Nights. By the time I was seven, I had discovered
Tom Swift and the Bobbsey Twins. Later, when I was about ten,
I also discovered Penrod, Tom Sawyer, and Huckleberry Finn, as
well as the Connecticut Yankee. Saturdays I often came home with
ten or more books from the public library. Neither FH, as I later
began to call my father, nor Blanche read much.

Today, having lived in the same house for forty-two years, I've
accumulated over 20,000 books. A kind of ongoing rebellion against
FH, perhaps, that has come full circle. Today, Erma reads very little,

and Rob, Jr., and Steve, my sons, do not have my Faustian need to know everything. Neither Blanche, FH, nor I were aware that the person I was to become and the books I would write were already being fertilized by three other aspects of my childhood.

First, Girls—Later, Women! Since I was five—for sixty-eight years—I've loved them all, the long and the short and the tall. But like Henry Higgins (Bernard Shaw's Pygmalion), I would eventually begin wondering, "Why can't women be like me?" Before I entered the first grade, most of my friends were girls. In the summer, in pup tents in the backyard and in hot attics, it was a happy, giggly game to touch and kiss each other's forbidden parts. In my childhood, I was perfectly familiar with the hairless female pudenda. But after I was seven, I never saw a girl/woman naked until I was seventeen. Like my peers, I spent many hours searching through *National Geographics* to see what women looked like. I probed the library for art books with a few reproductions of classical paintings where bulgy ladies out of mythology reigned supreme without clothes.

Next to girls, the driving force through all of my life has been a growing collection of hero/mentors. I began with Benjamin Franklin's autobiography and the "Bound to Rise" heroes of Horatio Alger. Basically, although I wasn't aware of it, all my mentors and heroes, including Tom Swift, were rebelling against individuals or a society that told them they couldn't realize their dreams. Despite the nay-sayers, they triumphed and finally became famous, or, if necessary—infamous.

Along with the rebellion, they seeded two other words in my dream vocabulary: *challenge* and *experiment*. Unlike the childhood heroes of later generations, my hero/mentors had focused rebellions— not against parents, but against entrenched power systems or outmoded ways of doing things. I have always been entranced by men and women who manage to defy the system, and yet make it work for them.

The third conditioning factor in my life was that in my youth FH never attended church, and Blanche, married to a Protestant and angry with her father's new Catholic wife, had abandoned her religion. Her family was sure that she'd go to hell and were, from then on, very circumspect with her. As a result, Sunday school was not a factor in my life. I was never indoctrinated in any church rituals and I never worried about God, Jesus, or the Devil.

In junior high school, it became obvious that I wasn't a man's man. In gym, I could never climb the swinging rope or balance on the parallel bars. None of the other kids wanted a physically uncoordinated kid on their softball or football team. On top of that, I was taking elocution lessons, arranged by FH. Although FH probably couldn't have specified his plans for me, he did want me to be famous. Later, when I was a junior in high school, FH was happy to pay for me to take a night course in public speaking with young men twice my age.

Although I was twelve years old when the stock market crashed in 1929 and grew up in the Depression of the 1930s, I was only dimly aware that the country was in dire straits. FH's printing business was so prosperous in 1924 that he bought a Phaeton Studebaker with disc wheels.

FH wasn't the only affluent one in the family. A few years later, I had a paper route which netted about $5 a week. Rarely a month went by when I wasn't paid at least $5 by various women's clubs and church groups to recite five or six monologues I had learned in elocution school. I had a repertoire that soon included fifty or more ten- to fifteen-minute recitations—complete with gestures and facial expressions. By 1988 standards, my purchasing power was equal to nearly $100 a week.

In addition, I had become assistant publisher of a mimeographed magazine called the *Boy's Pal.* Homer Jenks typed the stencils, and with me and another boy using a borrowed mimeograph machine, we produced the twenty-page 8½-by-11 magazine, collated it, stapled it, and sold a hundred or more copies of each issue at five cents a copy. It was no mean feat, since many sneering kids called it "the jockstrap magazine"—and in those days you could choose *Saturday Evening Post* for a nickel too.

We all wrote stories for the magazine. Now excelling in English, I fell in love with my English teacher, Dorothy Cole. She was only eight years older than I was. Look for me after school and I was erasing blackboards or doing any room clean-up chore for Dorothy, and waiting patiently until she was alone so I could call her by her first name and listen as she would suggest books that I should read. In class, she made novels like *Ivanhoe, Treasure Island, Great Expectations,* and Shakespeare's plays sound so exciting that I couldn't wait to read them, or act in them.

From six to sixteen, my interest in girls didn't diminish. My going-to-sleep dreams were always about lovely girls I had read about in novels. They all hugged and kissed me and adored me. In reality, I was a shy, pimply faced adolescent who blushed when girls my own age spoke to me. I was reduced to girlie magazines (*Playboy* hadn't appeared yet), which featured young women wearing abbreviated shorts, panties, and bathing suits. I had found my dream woman, Dorothy. I was aware, even then, that she was on the spot because everyone said that I was her fair-haired boy. She took me to local Shakespeare productions, called for me at home (to Blanche and FH's surprise, in her own car), and never protested when I was always underfoot. Perhaps, in a way, I was her dream man, too. I loved her, but with no sexual demands.

At sixteen, just before my final year in high school, I was a rebel without a cause. An exceptional student in English, fair in languages like Latin and French, mediocre in science, and dismal in math (compare Yale Marratt in the novel), I fell in love with "Gloria," a young girl who stayed with her aunt in Quincy during the summer. Very pretty and very sophisticated at fifteen, Gloria's home was in Brookline, some ten miles away. Somehow, blushing, I dared to ask her to go to the movies with me. Before the summer was over, I finally had once again seen and touched a naked girl/woman and held her pretty breasts in my hands, kissed her nipples and touched the lovely triangle of hair between her legs. I was delirious, totally in love all that summer. Since I practically lived in her aunt's house, Blanche and FH knew where I was. Of course, neither Gloria's aunt nor uncle knew what we were doing.

I was so much in love that I didn't care if I went to college or not. When you were kissing and hugging a girl every possible moment that you were with her, I was sure it was time to get married. It was now or never, especially since Gloria would go home to Brookline when summer was over.

I was spending much of my time conniving with my Italian friends, who all seemed to have cars, to drive to Brookline to see how the rich Brookline kids lived. I learned that Gloria's father made $18,000 a year (multiply 1934 dollars by ten), but I didn't discover until much later that FH made even more money from his 80-percent-owned printing company.

Even though I flunked two college boards, four exams given in those days in a modern language, English, science, and math, FH was determined that I was going to college. Harvard, of course. So, still mooning over Gloria and a mediocre graduate of Quincy High School in 1934, I was enrolled in a postgraduate course at Thayer Academy near Braintree. I was still too much in love to be intrigued by calculus, chemistry, or Virgil. Despite one more year of postsecondary education, I was no better college material than I had been in high school.

But neither I nor the deans of several colleges reckoned with FH, who proved that he could have made money selling refrigerators to Eskimos. FH contacted the dean of Bates College in Lewiston, Maine, and I was accepted on trial a week after classes had begun.

The reason I'm detailing my early life in this fashion is that if you read *Yale Marratt, The Harrad Experiment, The Premar Experiments,* or even my latest unpublished novel, "New Dawn, January 1, 2000," you will understand some of the motivating factors in the novels and how, much later, I transformed portions of my realities into fiction. Pat Marratt, for example is a fleshier, cigar-smoking version of FH. The conflict between Matt Godwin and his father in *The Immoral Reverend* has many similarities.

I was still in love with Gloria. Although we had finally consummated our incessant touching and made love without condoms— I had learned about *coitus interruptus*—I was dimly aware, and so was she, that, at sixteen and eighteen, we could never survive four years of separation. Assuming that I didn't have to make dates with her because we were going steady, I would occasionally arrive and discover that Gloria had gone out with some other boy.

College Days—and Nights. During the first six months at Bates, I slowly became aware that I was much more sexually sophisticated tham most of the guys I met. Very unusual for its time, Bates was a coed college. It was only twenty miles from Bowdoin, a kind of male monastery with six hundred guys who depended on special weekends when they could bring in female companionship. Thirty years later, when I wrote *The Harrad Experiement,* I contrasted a fraternity weekend with the saner sexual environment of Harrad. But Bates College was no Harrad. Young women went to class with you, but dating rituals soon set in. By the end of your freshman year, you were "going steady" or you were a social outcast.

Still a rebel without a cause, I detested the compulsory, presumably nonsectarian chapel assemblies which occurred every weekday morning at 8:30. As often as I could, I spent the half-hour that I was supposed to be in chapel in a local store called the Quality Shop, a few blocks away. I soon discovered a female rebel.

Bunny had widely spaced blue eyes and deep brown hair, and was as tall as I was. She was a fast learner, received straight A's in French and fairly good marks in other subjects. She could sing and play popular music on the piano. I was soon very much in love with her, but couldn't resist trying to remake her in my own image.

Was Bunny the inspiration for Cynthia in *Yale Marratt?* Not quite, but almost. Before we graduated in 1939, I was to all intents and purposes married to her. By the end of our sophomore year, we were making love regularly. Defying all Bates regulations, we sneaked away on weekends to nearby hotels and rooming houses or, in the Indian summers or early Maine springs, we snuggled together on a blanket alongside the Androscoggin River.

I was rooming with John Smith and Eddie Fishman, who were both on the dean's list. They were known in those days as "greasy grinds," instead of nerds. Womanless most of the time, they were amused by their romantic roommate. With their driving need to excel and learn everything, they became minor mentors in my life. Eddie was managing editor of the *Bates Student,* a weekly newspaper. Since there was no room for additional editorial help, I became advertising manager, persuading merchants in Lewiston to advertise their wares. After hours, the keys to the *Bates Student* office provided a convenient rendezvous for Bunny and me. Once a week, on Sunday night, we'd put the newspaper to bed.

One night, when there were not enough articles to fill the paper, I suggested to Eddie that we condense an article on premarital sex in American colleges that had appeared in *Cosmopolitan* magazine. A week later, when copies of the *Bates Student* trickled home to parents, all hell broke loose. The premarital sex that was detailed in *Cosmopolitan* didn't happen at Bates, but Eddie was forced to resign as managing editor.

By the end of our sophomore year, I convinced Bunny to major in English as I was doing. Before we graduated, we were, with a few exceptions, taking the same courses. Always studying together, with a small coterie of friends, we became somewhat notorious. Without being aware of it, I was playing Pygmalion to a willing Galatea, who turned her $2 weekly allowance over to me, and I was conning enough money out of FH to support my "wife."

I was spirited, but clumsy and unpredictable on the dance floor. She was a skilled bridge player, but playing cards bored me. She procrastinated endlessly when it came to writing theses and term papers, so I often wrote them for her, being careful to make her style different from mine. In my sophomore year, I took a year-long writing course, which Bunny did not take. I could imitate the style of well-known writers like Hemingway, Faulkner, and Thomas Wolfe, whose rebellion I admired.

Other literary rebels I discovered were Roman Rolland and his novel *Jean-Christophe,* George Bernard Shaw and *Pygmalion,* along with Bertrand Russell's famous *Companionate Marriage.* The authors were all rebels in various ways and delighted me. I was also reading everything I could find—and it wasn't much—on the vagaries of human sexuality.

Scarcely a month went by during these three years that Bunny and I didn't think our college days would come to a sudden end. She often had irregular monthly periods, and once, when she was a week overdue, we were sure that she was pregnant. We both hated condoms, and, although I knew about diaphragms, in the mid-1930s it was difficult enough to find a doctor who would fit a married woman with one, let alone a single girl.

Thus went my four years at Bates: in love, not having as much daily sexual contact as I might have wished (but more than most of the nineteen- and twenty-year-olds I knew), studying anything I wished. FH was happy enough that I was in college and had, to everyone's surprise, suddenly appeared on the dean's list, so he didn't interfere with my choice of courses. I also discovered a new hero/ mentor, Peter Bertocci, who had recently been hired to teach psychology and philosophy at Bates. I was so charmed by Peter's inquiring mind that, in my junior year, I decided I would take only minimum requirements for an English major and soon had, with Bunny, who protested at taking so much philosophy, a dual major in English plus psychology and philosophy. Before I graduated, Peter gave me a copy of the first of many books, *The Empirical Argument for God,* that he would write. He inscribed it to me: "With the sincere hope that your mind will continue to ask for reality and your actions continue to adjust to it."

Many years later, Peter Bertocci's human-values approach to teaching—he finally became full professor of philosophy at Boston University—would become a key element of the Harrad program. Peter and his wife became partial models for Phillip Tenhausen and his wife. *Harrad* ends with a quotation from Peter's book: "Extolling not a Golden Age, but an Age of Creative Insecurity," which Peter believed could be a common underlying philosophy for all of us.

On graduation day FH and Blanche met Bunny's mother and stepfather for the first time. They were all aware that Bunny and I were in love and wanted to be married quickly before I entered Harvard Business School. Bunny had been accepted for a buyer's training position at $18 a week at Jordan Marsh in Boston. I proposed my plan to FH for the first time.

In those days there were no married graduate students living on campus at Harvard Business School, and very few off campus. I told him if he would pay my tuition, and give me the cost of room and board at Harvard (equal to more than $18 a week), then together, Bunny and I could support an apartment in Harvard Square and get married. It wouldn't cost FH any more than he was already prepared to pay. In 1939, however, such ideas seemed outlandish. FH refused. He had nothing against Bunny and thought she should be happy to wait two years until I finished my education. The problem was that Bunny couldn't support herself in Boston on $18 a week. She would have to go home to Hartford, get a job, and live with her parents until I graduated. How could I explain to FH that I now needed a regular bed companion as well as a friend to save me from the Philistines at Harvard Business School. Before classes began in September, Bunny wrote me a good-bye note; two years was much too long to wait.

Without even having been married, I suddenly learned what divorce was like. Back home after four years, I had no friends, male or female. I was shipwrecked and totally shocked. A month later I met my Harvard roommate, Paul Williams, son of William Carlos

Williams, who was being hailed as one of America's best poets, although he made a living as a much-loved doctor in Rutherford, N.J.

The shock of losing Bunny was compounded by the first lecture from the nationally known dean Wallace Brett Donham, who had, with the help of a multimillionaire, George Baker, practically created Harvard Business School. Donham told us that we could now forget our easygoing college days. At HBS, unless you devoted seventy hours a week to classes and study, you were sure to flunk out. He assured us that 10 percent of the 1941 class would be gone after the first midyear exams. Paul had graduated from the Wharton School at the University of Pennsylvania, and unlike me, he had four years of undergraduate business training. Within a few weeks, I was sure that I should have been getting a masters in psychology or sociology from Harvard, which several of my Bates friends were doing.

My new roommate and I had some things in common. Paul, too, had lost the love of his life. Although Paul had no interest in becoming a writer like his father, because he had been raised in a literary household we were on a much closer intellectual level than we were with most of the first-year class, who were graduates of engineering and other business schools. If you read *The Rebellion of Yale Marratt,* you will get a fictionalized version of my two years in business school. Bunny was transformed into Cynthia, and FH is an interfering Pat Marratt.

Somehow, I survived the hard-driving, one-dimensional, "give it all you've got or you'll never succeed at business" philosophy of the Business School. At the same time, I continued my search for Galatea. I spent many hours in the co-op acquiring nonbusiness books to read as an escape from the boredom of solving endless mimeographed case problems and writing my solutions, which the professors insisted were too literary and not the kind of concise writing that top management required.

I also discovered a minor literary hero/mentor, Henry Miller, and after many discreet inquiries found a bookseller in Harvard Square who kept copies of *The Tropic of Cancer* and *The Tropic of Capricorn* (printed in Mexico) in a safe. When he had determined that I wasn't connected with the FBI or the Cambridge police, he told me the price, $25 per copy. It was exorbitant, but since I had no woman in my life, I had plenty of money to spend reading about sex.

Because my grades were good enough, during the final year at the Business School I was permitted to enroll in a special, one-year course that would teach us how to mobilize the United States into a full, wartime economy. The assumption was that those who completed their final year at HBS would end up in Washington, D.C., if war were declared, with an Army or Navy commission. With the wisdom we acquired at Harvard, we'd save England and bury Hitler. Another year would pass before the Japanese surprised us at Pearl Harbor. But even in a world at war, I was more concerned that I still hadn't found a woman with whom I could share a mental /sexual merger and the wide interest in literature, art, and music that I had acquired at Bates.

Erma, Dear Erma. In the fall of 1940, I met Erma. Blanche had mentioned that the family dentist in Boston had a new dental hygienist, Miss Richards. Since I was constantly looking for dates, why not ask her? Why not? I needed my teeth cleaned, and soon a very pretty blue-eyed brunette with firm breasts was leaning close to my face as she scaled my teeth, creating an aura of sexual intimacy. When she finished, I asked her point-blank, "How about a kiss?" There was no kiss, and no date. Dating clients was against the doctor's rules. But she warned me I must be sure to come back. I needed some new fillings, and missed appointments were charged. When I purposely missed the next appointment, I told the doctor it was because Miss Richards wouldn't have a date with me. He gave in.

Erma was a most affectionate and loving woman, who had recently been deserted by a former high school boyfriend. Not only didn't Erma reject me when we were finally naked on her parents' sofa, but she encouraged me. Even though I was sure that her father would soon stomp downstairs and put an end to me, we were frequently making love in her parents' living room.

At twenty, a year younger than I, Erma needed to be loved as much as I did. To my amazement, she seemed very willing to be molded into my ephemeral Galatea. I soon convinced her that while we were most certainly in tune sexually, if a long-lasting relationship were to develop, we must be able to communicate. The business world didn't matter, but I told Erma that she must read and acquire what Edward Hirsch would define as "cultural literacy" a quarter of a century later.

I was falling in love, and I was sure that I could re-create Erma, who was smarter than I was in the practical world, and make her more literary than all the women I had known with bachelor's degrees, including Bunny. I told her all she had to do was read—read and take a few courses, particularly in psychology. I had it made—a woman who loved me and was eager to learn all the things she had never been exposed to. Was I playing Svengali? Not quite. Time would prove that Erma had a mind of her own.

Before I graduated, after playing Russian roulette in the baby-making area for nearly a year, Erma and I set the wedding date, August 2, 1941. FH couldn't believe what was happening. A year and a half ago, I had been in love with Bunny. Since she couldn't wait two years, he agreed it was just as well I hadn't married her, but Erma Richards? A girl who worked for Dr. Tracy and cleaned teeth? What did I have in common with her?

Unknown to me, my always interfering father called Erma, interrupting her at work, and asked her point blank why she wanted to marry me. "Does Bob really love you? Did you know that he was madly in love with another girl just a year ago?" Obviously, FH was still trying to direct my life. In tears, Erma assured him that we were in love. If you read *Yale Marratt,* you'll find a similar story.

Erma and I were married. She soon discovered that, along with our wedding furniture, we had to make room for my close to a thousand books in our four-room apartment. I wasn't making much progress in sculpting my Galatea, but we were newlyweds who had many things to do, and we enjoyed sexmaking.

Erma continued to work as a dental hygienist for a couple of months, but then we bought a dog and were affluent enough for her to stay home. Not to read, but to cook and sew and decorate, at which she was very competent. In addition, for a few happy months, she was able to flit around Melrose in the handsome Ford convertible that FH gave me.

We had many Saturday-night parties with just-married friends and dating singles. Flirting with others in their twenties, aided and abetted by plenty of booze, was a way of life. The idea of playing strip poker was often bandied about, and not being adverse to seeing how women friends of Erma's looked in their birthday suits, I devised a variation on blackjack, which made it possible to play for several hours with a slow and tantalizing divestment of clothing. You'll find it described in *Yale Marratt*.

Within the first year of marriage, although Erma and I were monogamous, I managed to hug half a dozen of her friends after they had shed their last stitch and didn't know whether to run off or be embarrassed. But on December 7, 1941, our happy daydream began to end, like that of millions of other couples.

A Rebel in World War II. By late 1942, although I had quit Relief Printing and taken a job at the Fore River Shipyard division of Bethlehem Steel, hoping to be deferred because I was working in an essential industry, it was obvious that my number was up. To my shock, I quickly discovered that the months I had spent at HBS learning how to direct the war from a cushy job in Washington weren't about to be put to use.

I told Erma I still thought I might wangle a commission in the Finance Department of the Army, but two weeks later I was drafted as a private. I ended up at Fort Devens, headed for the infantry with a lot of nice kids who had never met a college graduate, let alone someone with a master's degree in business.

During four long winter months at finance school at Fort Benjamin Harrison, near Indianapolis, the Army finally decided I might prove of some value in the Finance Department. I quickly discovered that no one gave a damn about my "superior" education; survival in the Army (with plenty of infantry training) depended on strictly obeying orders and ass-kissing officers and noncommissioned officers, especially master sergeants. Rebellion was heresy. Since I was never able to obey orders, I was unable to get a weekend pass to leave the base.

When Erma, sure that I would be sent overseas, arrived in Indianapolis, I still couldn't get leave until a friend, wiser than I in the ways of the Army, offered to write me a pass so that I could leave the base and spend the night with Erma.

Finally I was shipped out of Fort Benjamin Harrison on a troop train destined for Shenango, Pa., a marshalling area for the European theater. At Shenango, when it looked as if I would soon be serving in bomb-blasted England and was prepared to bid a final, tearful good-bye to Erma, FH intervened. The change in my orders was the result of FH's phone call to his longtime friend, Congressman John McCormack. They laid the groundwork, and if I survived a finance school at Wake Forest University, I could apply to Officer Candidate School at Duke University. Three months later, I graduated from Wake Forest as a private first-class.

At Duke arduous infantry training was combined with endless hours learning advanced army finance. It made my first two years at HBS look like a tea party. Erma didn't come to Durham, N.C., until graduation day, which coincided with D-Day in Europe. During the entire four months at Duke, I was in continuous trouble, "gigged" for everything from insubordination to dust on coat hangers to inability to make up my bunk so the captain could bounce a quarter on it.

Every month I appeared before the flunk-out board, composed of seven or more officers who hurled questions while I sat at rigid attention and tried to figure out how to answer them. What I was reading, and had read throughout my life, was a source of great interest to them, especially since I informed them that I'd not only read Karl Marx, the *Daily Worker,* and magazines like the *New Republic,* but I had also read Hitler's *Mein Kampf,* as well as a current novel called *Out of the Night,* which was about a Communist spy. I told them that I thought "an officer and a gentleman" should know what both friends and enemies might be thinking. They weren't amused. By a miracle, and possibly because there may have been a notation on my records about the family friend in Washington, I survived.

When Erma arrived in Durham for graduation, we decided that the time had come to have a baby. Happily kissing condoms and diaphragm good-bye, we made up for lost time; she was soon pregnant. My first orders as a second lieutenant were to report back to Fort Benjamin Harrison, where I now had the opportunity to learn how real officers lived. Needless to say, in the Army, all men and women are *not* created equal. From Harrison, I was assigned to the Air Transport Command at Grenier Field in Manchester, N.H. While I was there, Erma had a miscarriage.

Suddenly, I received orders to go to Florida; from there, I was to proceed to Karachi, India. I looked at a map of the world in shock, noting that India was halfway around the world. I was assigned to the China/Burma/India theater, where the British, backed by the Americans, were determined to fight the Japanese all the way across the Chinese mainland if necessary. Everyone in the CBI theater was sure it would take at least another ten years to win the war this way. "The Golden Gate by '58" seemed an appropriate slogan.

Three weeks later Erma, pregnant once again, kissed me good-bye as I boarded a train for Miami. I'll never forget the sight of her standing on the deserted track, sobbing as the train pulled out. In my pocket were a dozen pictures I had taken of her naked and three months pregnant. Would we ever see each other again? Both of us doubted it. The United States was not only bogged down in Europe, but we were trying to defeat the Japanese island by island across the Pacific. It seemed in 1944 that World War II would never end.

Two weeks later, with stops in Algiers, Cairo, and Abadan, Iran, I was in Karachi, headed for Calcutta and ultimately an air force base in Shamshenagra, located in the upper Assam Valley, an area now called Bangladesh. India was a unique learning experience. I soon discovered that the Indians were great readers. In the major cities there were hundreds of bookstores, and there were all kinds of translations into Hindustani and other languages.

I became interested in Indian yoga and tantra—the wine, woman, and song approach to *nirvana* for those who did not want to pursue the ascetic yoga disciplines. I soon had a fully illustrated copy of the *Kama Sutra,* which in the 1940s and 1950s, along with James Joyce, Henry Miller, and D. H. Lawrence, would have put an American bookseller in jail if he dared to offer such a picturesque view of human sexuality.

Tantric sex offered the potential of extended sexual intercourse without ejaculation to achieve a blending of the *yang* and the *yin* as a path to *nirvana.* I also learned about tantric rituals in which sexual merger with a loved one wasn't necessarily monogamous. Joy in sex, tantric style, is discussed in the middle section of *Yale Marratt,* and it's one of the goals of a Harrad style of education I wrote about many years later. Subconsciously, although I didn't realize it until later, my Galatea and tantric sexual-merger daydreams were two sides of the same coin.

In August 1945, after receiving a telegram that my son Robert, Jr., was born on July 3, I was running a finance office in China, on a base with 3,000 men and an equal number of Chinese laborers. A few weeks later, the United States dropped the atomic bombs on

Hiroshima and Nagasaki, and suddenly it seemed that I might get home after all.

Then I was called back to Calcutta and given what presumably was a choice assignment but which entailed endless flying to strange destinations. When the Japanese surrendered, the U.S. Army quickly moved into occupied countries. More than a month had gone by since most American soldiers had been paid. My first flight was to Rangoon and then to Saigon and Singapore. In the latter, the Army had taken over the Raffles Hotel, where officers were living in high style.

Finally I received orders to return on a troopship with several thousand enlisted men and several hundred officers, whose cabins, twenty or so with triple-decker bunks, were topside. The only way to survive the three-week ocean crossing was to stay awake all night, try to sleep during the day, and thus avoid the snoring of your companions. Three weeks later, after steaming around India to Singapore and across the Pacific to Tacoma, Wash., I was on a four-day, cross-country train ride. Like a Jules Verne character, I could say that I had been around the world, but it took more than eighty days!

Blessed Civilian Life. On February 1, I stepped off the train in Boston, more than a little surprised to see Erma, FH, Blanche, and a contingent of Blanche's friends. It was Blanche's birthday, and I was her present. Since it was early Saturday evening when I arrived, she thought we should all go to a cocktail lounge and celebrate.

Hugging me after a year, Erma whispered, "What the hell could I do? They're your parents." I could see my son Bobby, who was now eight months old, and be with her later.

Erma had another surprise, which FH confirmed. He had bought us a house, putting $1,500 down on a six-room English bungalow and leaving only a $5,500 mortgage. I could pay him back in the coming years. The house was on a third of an acre, but only one house away from Blanche and FH's home. The trap was set and I fell into it—happily at first, I must admit.

Obviously, as soon as I was discharged from the Army, I was expected to go to work at Relief Printing Corporation, which had survived the war with no bigger problem than how to find employees to produce the business-card orders that had continued unabated. Even today, the Japanese and the Americans have one thing in common;

without business cards, their economies might grind to a halt.

Since I had a wife and a child to support and was no longer angry at FH for interfering in my previous love life, it seemed convenient to live near my parents on my new salary of $75 a week.

But I did have an old problem. Neither in the business world nor in my social life was I meeting anyone who was as fascinated with music, the arts, and literature as I was. Nor, spending my days as a salesman, was it easy to make contacts with anyone with equivalent interests. As a result, during the next ten years, I became like someone with a split personality—a kind of Dr. Jekyll and Mr. Hyde, who no longer bothered to play the Pygmalion game with Erma. She was proving to be a fun companion and wife in many other ways. As "Dr. Jekyll," I was a sober citizen and a hard-driving businessman, who soon proved that I could sell major accounts.

As a benign "Mr. Hyde," I was an enigma to my family and friends. As an antidote to the business world, I was reading novels and collecting anything that had been written about human sexuality, as well as more abstruse books in the areas of psychology, religion, and economics. I was omnivorously searching for answers to questions about life and death that I couldn't even formulate. I was also buying and listening to a wealth of music that was suddenly available on LP records, discovering chamber music, ballet, concertos, and symphonies, along with the world of art.

With business friends or people that Erma met through her women's clubs, I rarely revealed my true inclinations. With a few drinks of bourbon, I was one of the boys. But I told Erma that we were like two people on different trolley cars going in different directions but waving at each other as we passed. Still, in many areas, we were well mated. Erma soon proved her talents in our thirty-year-old bungalow, personally painting, wallpapering, laying cement walks, and expanding the house, as well as cooking gourmet dinners and taking care of Bobby. We had many goals in common, but little intellectual companionship.

In the late spring of 1946, a few months after I was discharged from the army, a friend whom I had known at Harvard came to Boston and phoned to see if I'd survived the war. In May, he and his wife Elizabeth came to see us, with their kids.

Libby, a brown-eyed brunette with almond-shaped eyes, coolly sexy, thought nothing of sitting on a sofa with her arms around her knees, well aware that she wore no panties and her nether parts were beckoning. She was a sharp contrast to Erma. Before she settled down with Bill, she had known quite a few boys and men intimately.

Arriving in our suburb, Libby couldn't believe her eyes. Here was a house filled with more books than some college professors owned, plus hundreds of records. Her husband read a bit and listened to some classical music but was an entirely different cup of tea from Bob Rimmer. I was charmed. Erma wasn't, but she liked Bill. During the weekend, I discovered that not only was Libby an omnivorous reader but she also wrote poetry, which her friends and family thought was great. Libby told me later that she loved Willy, as she called Bill's father, more than her husband, who was now a rising executive at a department store in Manhattan. During the weekend, I managed to take Libby alone on a fast auto tour of our area. We soon stopped for a torrential embrace, during which she told me that her marriage was falling apart and she was already having an affair.

The weekend ended with a few more discreet hugs from Libby and an invitation from Bill to spend a weekend near West Haven, Conn. Within a few hours after Erma and I arrived, we were all drinking gin, and Libby whispered that she really had to talk to me alone. How we were going to escape our spouses in such confined quarters was a mystery to me, but by nine o'clock, Bill and Erma had drunk so much that all they wanted to do was go to bed. Libby's hope that they might end up in bed together never materialized, but she and I went for a walk along the river. We were soon feverishly undressing each other. Despite the discomfort of bugs and sand, we nervously made love on a lonely inlet.

During the next two years, 1947 and 1948, I arranged sales trips to New York City about every six weeks, and Libby and I met. Did we feel guilty? A little, perhaps. We always ended shopping for presents to take home to our kids. I loved Libby, but I loved Erma too and never considered divorce. I kept wondering if we could ever match up Bill and Erma, who had a lot in common, but it never happened.

In the meantime, Erma was pregnant with our second child, Stephen King, who was born May 18, 1948. Long before I wrote *Yale Marratt,* it occurred to me that the solution to my dual life was not to create a Galatea but simply to enjoy two very different women.

Libby and I mailed books we were reading back and forth to each other. She wrote me five- to ten-page letters mailed to my office. I had never been privileged to enter any person's mind so completely. Libby was like a dammed-up river, bursting through the dikes of an unhappy marriage. She flooded me with a million words, seeking answers for herself and for me. At one point, I had four file drawers jampacked with every letter she wrote me, and I often thought if they were ever published, they would be among the most intimate revelations ever put down on paper by a woman, for Libby was a colorful writer.

Then, the bubble burst. Carelessly (or on purpose), Libby left a long letter she had been writing to me on her desk, and Bill read it. Within a week, a certified letter arrived at home. Erma opened the letter from Bill's lawyers. "Cease and desist seeing Elizabeth Jones," they wrote, or be sued for alienation of affection.

I thought it was silly, but, needless to say, Erma was hysterical. Did I want a divorce? No. I loved her and Steve and Bobby. I didn't believe in divorce. We might not be riding on the same trolley, but we had a lot of good things going for us. I simply needed a female friend in addition to a wife. I was intellectually lonesome.

Surprisingly, after a rocky month or two, Erma stopped asking for details of my extramarital love life. Six months later, I discovered why Erma had suddenly become so complacent. She had told David, the doctor she took Bobby and Steve to with various childhood ailments, about me. David had even been in our house and seen my large collection of books and told her, "My wife, Nancy, would go crazy if she saw these. She'd never leave. She reads all the time."

But poor Nancy, who read so much, was a recluse. In her childhood, she had had a severe attack of rheumatic fever, which damaged her heart. Although she had survived and even given birth to two very much wanted children, on her heart specialist's orders, she spent much of her time resting in bed and wondering if the next time she was out of breath, or her heart started fibrillating uncontrollably, it would be the last time. She was thirty-nine.

David and Nancy. With David, Nancy was a loving but limited sex partner. David couldn't understand how I could neglect such a pretty, healthy, and competent woman as Erma, but he told her she should accept male reality. Man had invented monogamy, not for himself but to keep women under control. If men, married or not, ever lost interest in the joy of loving and being loved by a woman, the world would come to an end. Erma was dubious, but ready to let him prove it.

Now, without me or Nancy being aware of it, Erma and David became lovers. It wasn't easy for a wandering husband and my wife, with four kids between them, to find a place to be alone. Erma didn't know Nancy, but she assured David that Bob would enjoy a woman with whom he could share all of his "damn books." The die was cast.

David convinced Nancy, who rarely went to social events, that she should attend a local hospital ball and he'd introduce her to a man who had enough books to keep her reading for two lifetimes.

Nancy was very pretty. Nearsighted with big, luminous brown eyes that you could drown in, she sighed when I asked her to dance, "I really shouldn't. My heart isn't very good." I told her that I wasn't a great dancer. "My heart is pounding too," I laughed. "We don't have to move fast. We could dance on a dime and just hug each other." And we did, most of the evening, to the exclusion of everyone else—including David and Erma.

Although we realized later that our spouses had been making love for several years, Nancy was under no pressure from me to have sex together. She knew about Libby, and much later, I told her the finale.

Arriving at the front door of the Relief building one morning at eight o'clock, I was shocked to see a woman smiling at me a few yards from the entrance. It was Libby. She had left Bill and her children, but not wholly because of me. "You knew our marriage was on the rocks from the beginning," she sighed. I reminded her, as I had many times before, that I didn't think divorce was the answer. I had known Bill at HBS for two years and I really liked him. I was sure that he loved Libby, but she shook her head.

"Bill is too possessive. He doesn't give a damn about my mind, but he wants my body exclusively," she said. Adamantly, she added, "If you don't want me, don't worry, I can take care of myself."

I saw her occasionally and kept trying to tell her to go home, but then she met a man who was evidently free to take off with her. Much later, she converted to Catholicism, lived with some Sisters of Charity, and occasionally served as housekeeper for a priest.

During the next twenty-five years, Erma, Bob, David, and Nancy became "the inseparables." This was no *Bob and Carol and Ted and Alice* scenario. We saw the film much later and shrugged at the silly ending. We weren't swingers. We never made love as a foursome. Our travels together eventually took us to Florida, the Caribbean, Europe, Africa, Greece, and Israel. We were often casually naked together and slept with each other's spouses, but we never made sexual comparisons to each other.

During the first year, we passed through occasional moments of jealousy, but it became increasingly clear that our love for each other was "in addition to and not instead of." Sexual and intellectual sharing became a natural way of life between the four of us, but we were careful never to reveal our sexual exchange to anyone.

We never merged households, but perhaps we would have, as I proposed in *Proposition 31,* had we all lived into our seventies. We maintained separate families in our attractive, middle-class homes. We loved our biological children as well as each other's kids, who then ranged from five to thirteen years of age. Many years later, as a foursome, we enjoyed the fun of being both biological as well as surrogate grandparents.

Parents and Friends: Love and Prejudice. Each of us grew emotionally and mentally in the unique marriage that I would later fictionalize (to Nancy's horror) and expand into alternate lifestyles in *Proposition 31, Thursday, My Love, Come Live My Life,* and *The Love Explosion.* Seeing Erma through David's eyes, I learned to appreciate her abilities to tackle almost any project that required mechanical and physical adeptness and to do it all by herself, if necessary.

Seeing Nancy through my eyes, David began to realize that her wide reading from childhood, her love of music—she introduced us all to the joys of opera—and the fact that she had me as a lover was making his wife a much more exciting woman.

Seeing David through mine and Erma's eyes, Nancy slowly became aware that David might not have a Park Avenue-style medical practice, but that he was one of the most caring medical practitioners around. He was a man who loved all of his patients, although many never paid him and tried to barter for his services. David blended his love for his family and ours with caring medicine and never-ending laugher. Whenever you find laughter in my novels, in scenes like that of the *meshuganah* ape in *The Harrad Experiment* or the party on Trotter Island in *That Girl from Boston,* David was the inspiration.

For me, it was a turning point in more ways than one. Two years after the four of us met, FH, now seventy years old, decided to become chairman of the board of Relief. When I was forty, he elected me president. My brother, Richard, at thirty-two, had finally joined the company. In twelve years, I had tripled the revenues of the company, which were now over $2 million annually. FH had given Richard and me each 14 percent of the outstanding stock.

Blanche was now wearing diamonds and mink and spending a month each year traveling with FH. But Blanche didn't ingratiate herself with her daughters-in-law, whom she never really liked. In fact, she often told her friends that the reason they lived so well was that "I gave them my dividends."

FH wasn't making me too happy either. When I told him that I had two boys to send to college, his answer involved a mixture of the following: "You're not doing too badly financially . . . if your Jewish doctor friend is making more money than you, that's your problem. I told you to use Relief as a steppingstone. Anyway, you don't have to worry, because someday you and Richard will own it all." He didn't add, "If you live long enough."

Nor did he or I realize that I was slowly moving a different kind of steppingstone into place. Thanks to Nancy and David, I not only discovered Jewish life and religion, but a sense of family and a caring, ethnic continuity that was a far cry from the warring relationship that Blanche and FH had with their families.

In the meantime, it was no longer a case of "some of our best friends are Jews." *All* of mine and Erma's friends were Jews. While it was impossible for me to convert to any religion—I was a humanist then without knowing the term—I not only read widely about Judaism, but I was also fascinated with the Israeli kibbutz. Long before Leo Rosen, and with no credentials, I was compiling a Yiddish dictionary. Beginning with *The Harrad Experiment* and culminating with *The Byrdwhistle Option,* many of my heroes were Jewish. In the bibliography of *Byrdwhistle* I extolled the contribution of Yiddish to the American language.

Continuing to live a life that now encompassed David and Nancy, Erma and I were soon under fire from Blanche and FH. They belonged to a popular local club which excluded Jews. FH's argument was that Jews did the same. Spending a week on the Cape with Nancy and David, I was shocked to discover that there was no room at the inn when they saw David.

But I was horrified when FH and Blanche refused to come to our house when David and Nancy (or any other Jews) were there. (Keep in mind that we lived next door!) FH believed that he wasn't prejudiced, because he did business with many Jews. "They have their ways and we have ours. They don't want you either." He was wrong. Even Orthodox Jews were delighted with my curiosity and wish to learn about their customs and rituals. After my first novels were published, I was invited to speak at many temples and synagogues— Orthodox, Conservative, and Reformed. Not a year went by when we weren't guests at Passover dinners.

Late-Blooming Writer. I was now writing. My anger at religious prejudice slowly combined into a larger-than-life hero, Yale Marratt. When the novel was finished, I knew it was much too long. Two years later, seventeen publishers had rejected the book. I finally decided I needed an agent and picked Scott Meredith, who today is a millionaire literary agent. For fifty dollars, he agreed to read the novel. He liked parts of it, but told me that I had committed the ultimate no-no. Women read all the novels, and I would never sell one extolling bigamy. As Nancy had told me, chuckling, when she read the finished manuscript, one of the women had to die. Since Cynthia was Jewish, she was the most likely one. My ego was rudely punctured. The original manuscript seemed unsalable. I was a prophet without an audience. But I wasn't about to rewrite *Yale Marratt.*

If I hadn't known David and enjoyed him almost as much as I did his wife, I probably never would have written *That Girl from Boston,* my next novel. Most of it takes place on an island in Boston Harbor called Peddocks. David's hobby was fishing for Boston flounder (the harbor wasn't as polluted then), and he was also the preferred doctor for all residents on the island, who, over many years, had built unheated and unelectrified houses on Peddocks. To support himself, David had wrestled his way through medical school, and I included a wrestling scene in the novel. *That Girl from Boston* pits upper-class Bostonians against the lower-class Irish.

Ultimately, *That Girl from Boston* sold a half-million copies. Before she died in an automobile accident, Jayne Mansfield wanted to star in a movie based on the novel. But in 1960, after I finished it, fifteen publishers and all of the major paperback publishers thought it was too sexy. They felt it would be the target of local religious groups who were trying to control the distribution of paperbacks with sexy covers and content.

Neil Doherty, an employee, asked if he could read my manuscripts. *That Girl from Boston* delighted him, but as a Catholic, *Yale Marratt* shocked him a bit, although he liked it. Later, he did an excellent editing job, introducing the bigamy trial at the beginning and then concluding the book with it. He wondered what would happen if we started a publishing business ouselves. All we needed was a little money. Neil knew how to edit and we knew how to get a book printed. One of the best printers in the country, Plimpton Press, was in nearby Norwood. A year later, I told Plimpton Press that Relief would guarantee the cost of printing 7,000 copies of *That Girl from Boston*.

We soon discovered that it wasn't going to be easy. The world wasn't ready for Challenge's belief that, in the words of an editorial on the dust jacket, "Writers should not only reflect their society, but they have the moral obligation to become the vanguards for a new and brighter world where the sexual relationship is no longer something hidden or depraved." On the cover was a picture of the heroine, Willa Starch, wearing a pair of abbreviated panties and walking out of Boston Harbor onto Peddock's Island. The *Boston Globe* refused the advertisement as "too salacious." Challenge Press's brazen invitation to enjoy sex with laughter made many reviewers and bookstores nervous.

Ultimately, Challenge's finances were in very poor shape, our books weren't being advertised and sold, and some promising ideas were aborted. My daydream of joining the ranks of Norman Mailer, Irwin Shaw, and James Jones, went down the drain.

Harrad and Success . . . and Mixed Success. Finally, in 1966, through a fluke I discovered Sherbourne Press in Los Angeles, which decided to publish a third novel I had written, which I had called "Experiment in Marriage." They named it *The Harrad Experiment*.

Sherbourne sold 10,000 mail-order copies of the book in a hardcover edition with a conservative jacket. The promoter and owner wasn't interested in bookstore distribution, and the book was rarely found in a bookstore. His audience was a mailing list of 200,000 sex-book buyers, which included the names of 6,000 doctors. I was assured that they were steady buyers, since they had never learned anything about sex in medical school.

I often wonder who bought the hardcover edition of *The Harrad Experiment*. It never appeared in any library that I could discover, and I never received any letters from readers. Most of them probably couldn't believe their eyes when they saw the introduction and the annotated bibliography.

The publisher insisted that 10,000 copies wasn't a bad sale for what he though was a first novel. He finally produced a second edition and sold 17,000 copies. Suddenly, I received a phone call telling me that *Harrad* had been sold to Bantam, who loved it. Bantam was the biggest paperback publisher in the United States. The advance was small—$10,000—but I shouldn't worry. Bantam was going to sell millions of copies in paperback.

In September 1967, Bantam released *Harrad* with a sexy cover and the slogan "The Sex Manifesto of the Free Love Generation." I saw the cover before publication and protested that the *Harrad* idea certainly wasn't "free love," but no one listened to the author. Across the country and in major colleges and university areas, Bantam was trying a new technique. They used billboards with a very sexy come-on to promote the book. Within a month, *Harrad* had sold 300,000 copies, and within the year, it was one of the top-selling paperbacks of 1967, with a million copies in print. Over three million copies were sold during the next twelve years.

I couldn't believe what was happening. Overnight, I was both famous and infamous. Letters were pouring in from all over the country and I was happily dictating answers to all of them at my company's office.

I had already written another novel, *The Zolotov Affair,* about a high-school chemistry professor who had learned the secret of alchemy and how to transmute lead into gold. Zolotov tries to use his discovery to save the world by threatening to destroy the world economies which are based on gold. Although Sherbourne wasn't excited about it, the press published it anyway because they were afraid of losing me. A year later, Bantam brought it out in paperback, but didn't push it. I was suddenly in the doghouse with both Sherbourne and Bantam.

In the meantime, on weekends, I was writing *Proposition 31,* the story of a two-couple marriage, justifying and exploring in another dimension our happy relationship with David and Nancy. The response to *Harrad* via thousands of letters that I was receiving proved that millions of perople were searching for answers to their marital and premarital problems, and that a *Harrad*-style undergraduate education, utopian though it might seem, might lay the foundation for what I called the "corporate marriage" of two to three couples. The novel takes place in California, and the title refers to a proposition that is put on the California ballot if enough voters agree in advance.

Writing the novel in 1967, I was only vaguely aware of the developing Human Potential movement. But then Abraham Maslow, whom I had first discovered through Betty Friedan's book *The Feminine Mystique,* phoned me. "I decided that I have to meet you," he chuckled. "The kids are all reading *Harrad* and driving me crazy." He taught at Brandeis and lived in Auburndale, about fifteen miles from Quincy. It was the beginning of a friendship that would last until his untimely death in Menlo Park, Calif. Abe was one more hero/mentor in my life, to whom I paid tribute in *The Byrdwhistle Option.*

I was now living in three separate worlds. One, in the prosaic business world where 99 percent of the people I encountered had never heard of Bob Rimmer, the writer. A second private world with Erma, David, and Nancy, where I could at least integrate what I was writing, and then the publishing world, where I was slowly learning my way around without an agent.

The subsequent publishing history of my novels contains elements of excitement and disappointment, as is usual with most authors. Suddenly, I was a hot literary property. In the next five years, I wrote one novel after the other, including *The Premar Experiments.* This was a sequel to *Harrad* that expanded the concept to include low-income and black students and introduced a thirteen-week work/study cycle.

It was followed by *Thursday, My Love,* proposing another style of two-couple relationship that I called "synergamy," to replace monogamy. Next came *Come Live My Life,* involving a very practical approach for monogamous couples to switch spouses and enjoy a two-week vacation with another wife or husband. I was able to negotiate a $100,000 guaranteed advance on each.

It would seem that I was on the fast track to becoming a millionaire writer, but during the late seventies a new "I gotta be me . . . I'll do it my way" philosophy was sweeping the country. The 1960s were over. Publishers were convinced I was a leftover hippie. New American Library agreed to publish my novel *Come Live My Life* in 1976 and *Love Me Tomorrow* in 1978—but only as original paperbacks, which meant there would be no reviews in the major media.

Most of the enthusiastic readers of my earlier novels never knew the later ones existed. Two years later NAL, which had published nine of my novels, let them all go out of print. The happy, multiple-sexual relationships that I proposed in these and other novels and which I believe could take place within the framework of lifetime monogamy were presumably too utopian for the Reagan-inspired generation, which still believes it can have it all and monogamy too.

Real Tragedy. Then suddenly, in 1975, writing and publishing were of no importance. It seemed as if a heart operation, performed at Mass General, would alleviate Nancy's problems and prolong her life—people with rheumatic heart disease rarely live beyond their early sixties and Nancy was nearly sixty. We were all afraid that she might die suddenly if her heart began to fibrillate out of control.

I had prolonged Nancy's life in *The Premar Experiments,* where I fictionalized her as Ellen.

Nancy's real-life valve implant was successful, but in the process, Nancy got an infection. After a terrible month, hooked to every possible piece of lifesaving equipment, unable to talk to us for weeks, she died. Our two-couple marriage was over. We were reduced to a potential ménage à trois, which didn't work. David thought that sharing one wife was an inequitable situation, though we remained good friends. A lonely man, missing the years the four of us had shared together, David died of a heart attack two years later.

It was 1976. I was nearing my sixtieth birthday. Suddenly, Erma and I were alone. Our son Bobby received an M.D. from Downstate University of New York. He was doing his residency in cardiology at Boston University and was married. Steve, despite my warnings not to get affiliated with the family business, was working for Relief, but his wife wanted him to quit and become a teacher with her. Blanche and FH were still traveling. Erma and I, still very two-couple oriented, had found no new friends.

We continued to travel, first to Guadeloupe with David, his daughter, and her family, where the volcano Soufriere had nearly exploded the year before. It was the subject of a documentary film by the famous German filmmaker Werner Herzog, and Gaudeloupe interested me as a setting for a novel. Two years later, because I wanted to experience a Caribbean island during Carnival, we went back to Guadeloupe with another couple, and I wrote "Soufriere, the Volcano." It was drastically rewritten by a new editor at NAL as a typical romance novel, a type which was then selling like hotcakes. It was published in 1980 as *The Love Explosion*, and although I protested, NAL insisted on retaining the annotated bibliography, which they thought was popular with my readers. It made no sense at all in the revised format. Today, I look upon "Soufriere, the Volcano" as an unpublished novel.

Suddenly, I became like a man without a country. While I was experiencing publishing disappointments, it became obvious, since no one in the Rimmer family except me would put a dime into Relief, that the potentially profitable company was in trouble. After long negotiations, I sold the company. The new owners assumed Relief's debt and guaranteed what amounted to a $200,000 payment divided between Richard and me over a period of ten years. I managed to exclude FH from the payoff. He was eight-five, and I assumed that he already had more than enough money. But when he discovered what I had done, he was so incensed that he revised his will, excluding me and my family.

It didn't matter. It was obvious that I would never become wealthy through inheritance. Over a period of twenty years, I had earned a million dollars writing. Combined with my income from Relief, it wasn't enough to make me a millionaire, but Erma and I had lived well and had a loving family with four grandchildren.

Recent Years. I probably never would have been published again, nor would I have continued to write, if I hadn't remembered another one of my hero/mentors, Paul Kurtz, of the philosophy department at the State University of New York. A dynamo of a man, he had been editor of *The Humanist* magazine and was a nationally known writer on humanism. I knew that among his many other endeavors, Paul had started a publishing company called Prometheus Books in

Buffalo, which published controversial nonfiction. Would he like to take a flyer with *The Byrdwhistle Option?* Paul was enthusiastic. We were both sure that after hardcover publication in 1982, it could be sold to a paperback publisher. But evidently my novels are still too controversial for paperback publishers, who prefer the tried-and-true formulas of Stephen King and Danielle Steele. (As I write, in 1990, my last three published novels have not appeared in paperback.)

By this time, Erma and I were slowly trying to put together a new lifestyle. After the death of both Nancy and David, we had joined the famous Unitarian Church in Quincy. I was fascinated by the emergence of Unitarian beliefs, deviating from the original Congregationalists and embracing some ideas from many religions. Unitarian/Universalists accept the philosophy that all paths lead to God. Their religious thinking includes an amalgam of ideas from agnosticism, theism, deism, and even atheism and humanism.

Intrigued with the fact that both humanism and U/Uism needed some kind of unifying philosophy that would attract the sixty million or more Americans who never go to church, I wrote *The Immoral Reverend,* and it was published by Prometheus in 1985. The basic thesis is that all religions (except the ancient Chinese and Hindu) have denigrated human sexuality in one way or another. My protagonist, Matt Godwin, a graduate of Harvard Divinity and Business Schools, proposes that sex itself should become a sacrament. This doctrine would be proclaimed from Beacon Street by the fictional president of the Unitarian Universalist society.

By this time, self-employed at the age of sixty-five, I decided to take a new tack. I wrote a nonfiction history of visual sex. The premise was that anything that could be written was no longer censorable (with the one exception of child pornography), but pictorial sex of the naked human body and of humans copulating (which had been drawn, painted, and sculpted for thousands of years, and in the last hundred had been photographed) was still forbidden.

I wrote this book, and in the process reviewed about twenty porno movies, which in 1979 had become the backbone of the videotape industry since regular filmmakers had not released any of their films. After several turndowns, Bruce Harris, editor and publisher of Crown Books, wrote me that Crown would be interested in publishing a book with reviews of adult films, since nothing like this existed on the market.

My shrugging, sometimes laughing interest in sexvids is explained in the first and second edition of *The X-Rated Videotape Guide* (1986). I have not only given, in about 250 words, a detailed review of the plot, the kinds of sex that appear, from normal to kinky and sadistic, but I keep suggesting that in a sane society, if children would grow up seeing human beings naturally naked and the media would show caring human lovemaking, it would make the portrayal of sick sex (and I include hundreds of other sexual come-ons besides adult films) boring and unnecessary. A sane society would laugh sick sex out of existence.

As an antidote to reviewing sexvids, in the process of writing *The Immoral Reverend,* I discovered another heroine/mentor, Anne Hutchinson, America's first feminist. Anne challenged John Winthrop, governor of the Massachusetts Bay Colony, in 1636, and lost. She was excommunicated from Massachusetts, and, in my opinion, through the machinations of Winthrop and Thomas Dudley was eventually scalped and murdered by a band of Indians at the age of fifty-three. In my novel, *The Resurrection of Anne Hutchinson* (1987), Anne arrives naked on my doorstep on a cold winter night. The novel includes the complete trials of Hutchinson.

Despite disappointments, I love to write, and keep on doing so. As Erma tells me, "What else would you do?" My ideas seem to be inexhaustible.

At seventy-three, after researching and studying the human brain for several years, I have completed a new novel I first called "The Oublion Project." It involves a drug that eliminates short-term memory and which is used by a German and an Arab doctor to artificially inseminate women. They are unaware that they are being used to create a new breed of humans (eugenically) who will, through a superior style of education, take over the world, and in the process, eliminate all production of lethal weapons. It's a fast-moving, highly controversial novel inspired by José Ortega y Gasset, who wrote a book in the 1930s called *The Revolt of the Masses.* Ortega suggests a coming takeover of the world by people with no historical sense, who will finally destroy it. I have retitled it "New Dawn, January 1, 2000."

Do I ever feel discouraged or angry? The answer is no. In truth, I have never been angry or hated anyone in my life. Nor do I blame my father or anyone else for the person I have become. If FH had not interefered with my life, I might have married someone else, and I might have been more successful. Or I might have divorced many times in my search for Galatea. My wife, my boys, and the people close to me long ago stopped reading what I write—even when it's published in book form. But rarely a week goes by that someone doesn't write me that one or more of my novels has literally changed their life for the better.

Although I discontinued putting extended bibliographies in my novels, afraid they might frighten readers who simply wanted to be entertained, the bibliographies that appeared first in *Harrad* and in all subsequent novels through *The Byrdwhistle Option* have inspired thousands of people to argue with me and to think! For that I am immensely grateful. I have apparently become a hero/mentor to hundreds of men and women who have gone out of their way to tell me so in writing.

There are always many aspects of a person missing in an autobiography—that's why biographers who dig up missing truths are so popular. Anyone interested in more details can find them in forty or fifty file drawers of correspondence—some of it preserved in *The Harrad Letters* and in *You and I . . . Searching for Tomorrow.* Thanks to Howard Gottlieb, who recognized this correspondence as a piece of mid-century Americana, it is preserved in the Mugar Library of Boston University.

As a futurist, I believe that the "I gotta be me" generation will finally wake up, and a new twist on the 1960s "love everybody" philosophy will prevail as the United States faces the inevitable. Millions of men and women throughout the world will slowly become aware, for multiple reasons, that we are not independent. We are all— billions of us—interdependent, and many of the approaches to marriage and the family and premarital and posmarital sex that I have proposed will be the only way to survive and live self-fulfilling lives. As I note in the dedication of *The Harrad Experiment,* my novels are for the men and women of the 21st century, who might find them quaint but will consider them germinal.

Finally, to end with a chuckle. When I told Bhagwan Shree Rajneesh before he died in January 1990, that I was writing my autobiography, he wrote me: "Now is not the right time. Your autobiography should end with *sannyas.* Why let the world renounce you. Why not you renounce it? When a man dies it is ordinary. But when a man renounces, his consciousness reaches to the heights that are possible. *Sannyas* is not a religion. It is simply a rejoicing in life and a rejoicing in death. My whole concept is that from the cradle to the grave life should be a dance."

Let's go dancing!